RACHEL

TEN: A DARK & DIRTY SINNERS' MC SERIES

SERENA AKEROYD

DEDICATION

To Nanna,
    May you be rocking to 'My Sweet Lord' as I type this.
    I love you,
    Jemima Puddleduck <3

PLEASE READ

Darling Reader,

I don't often speak of my process, mostly because I don't have one. But with the Sinners, it's been one hell of a ride and I've been blessed to have a wonderful content editing and proofreading duo that have made this possible.

From all the loose ends that were caught, from all the fact checking and typo catching and the Britishisms that were snagged up, my team have helped me bring this to you today.

They made sacrifices for this book and my gratitude goes to them. Anne, babe, I couldn't have done this without your eagle eyes and your support. That you got through this when you were sick is a testament to just how fucking awesome you are. Norma, thank you for always being so kind when I come crawling into your DMs asking for miracles. You are a diamond. <3

So here it is, darlings.

139,000 words of my blood, sweat, and tears.

Of a story that some might say is too long but I say is perfect. Not because I'm an asshole, but because everything is there for a reason.

That's not hubris. That's me being shifty AF in a universe where a small detail is the start of a new story. Nudge nudge.

I wanted you to know that to celebrate REX hitting 500 reviews, there were some bonus scenes.

Here's Bear's letter to Rachel:

https://dl.bookfunnel.com/j7bjf5218i

Here's a Posse group chat regarding a baby shower that might amuse you: https://www.facebook.com/groups/serenaakeroyd steaandspoilersroom/posts/64501696989890048/

And the second RACHEL hits 500 reviews, you should know there'll be another bonus scene dropping in my groups so be sure to join them for that and for giveaways too!

Divas: www.facebook.com/groups/SerenaAkeroydsDivas

Spoilers: www.facebook.com/groups/SerenaAkeroydsTeaAnd SpoilersRoom

I'd also like you to know that I took liberties with the political timelines for the mayoral election.

Trigger warnings as always… GRAPHIC violence in this one, lovelies, and references to assisted suicide, rape, as well as sexual assault and domestic abuse.

So, my darlings, you've reached this far and I thank you for that.

The Last Bachelor has fallen. Now it's time for him to claim his First Lady.

This might be the end of this Chapter's series, but it's also the beginning…

Much love, and happy reading,

Serena

xoxo

Triggers:

- References to rape,

- References to assisted suicide,
- References to domestic abuse,
- References to sexual assault,
- Graphic violence

PLAYLIST

If you'd like to hear a curated soundtrack, with songs that are
featured in the book, as well as songs that inspired it, then here's the
link:

https://open.spotify.com/playlist/6rSOgmKNhPs92ADFepkaI6?si=
afd55831ob184526

ONE

REX

SEMISONIC- CLOSING TIME

"D-Dad, I need help. T-There are Triads here and they won't leave until they've spoken with you."

The second I hung up the phone, after promising Wynter I'd be there ASAP, Rachel snapped, "I'm coming with you."

"You can't come with me. I need you to sort things out with Nyx and Harlow."

She blinked at me. "You can't be serious. This is our daughter! A daughter who has Triads demanding to speak with you in her fucking living room, Rex. Only God knows what's happening—"

"Nothing's happening. Nothing until I get there." I clucked my tongue. "You can't think I left her unprotected."

She licked her lips. "If they're in her apartment then whoever you chose to protect her is fucking useless."

"They'll keep her safe."

I felt sure the Disciples were good for that.

Blade was supposed to be a fucking genius—he'd have to be a goddamn dipshit to screw me over.

Crouching down in front of her, I stared into her eyes and vowed, "She'll be safe. I'm not nervous."

She swallowed. "Why aren't you nervous? Are you crazy?"

"No." I reached for her hand. "She'll be okay, Rachel. I will burn LA to the ground if they hurt even a single fucking hair on her head."

Because she was born to reign at my side, she sucked in a shaky breath that was soaked in her relief. "Okay, good. I should still come—"

"You're needed here," I disagreed.

Her mouth quivered. "I've never... She's... She needs me too."

"She needs *me* right now," I told her gently. "I'll fix this but I can't focus on her if my mind is stuck on what's happening here. I need you to get Nyx out of jail and to save his ass from himself."

I stared down at her phone where there was a picture of Dead To Me's calling card.

The assassin was making a name for herself with that goddamn setup of hers—black and pink balloons attached to a gift bag with 'Sucks To Be You' embossed onto it.

Reaching for her cell, I asked, "Why would your old college roommate receive this?"

"You know what it means?"

"I do. You don't?"

"No. I'm guessing it's not a gift?"

"It means he has a hit out on him. Lodestar can help call the shooter off, though."

"A hit?!" Another blink. "Lodestar? She's behind this?"

"No. She's friends with the woman who sent it."

Rachel's lips pursed. "You know more than you're telling me."

I wasn't about to argue with her, so I just peered down at my phone and started trying to find a flight out tonight for Burbank.

"I need to get to the airport," I said as I bought a ticket, settling on LAX when the next non-stop Burbank flight was leaving in the morning.

"Do you think the Triads will use her for a ransom?"

"I don't think so."

"Then what's their game?"

"Connections."

She frowned. "You don't know that."

"Just a guess."

For their sakes, I'd better fucking be right.

I knew Wynter's prick of an adoptive father was in over his head with them, but that didn't mean they wouldn't try to use her as leverage now that I was on the scene.

My presence—oh, the fucking irony—had probably made the family more interesting to the Triads.

I didn't say any of that though.

There was no use in speculating. I just needed to get my ass back there.

She cupped my cheek, somehow drawing me back to her, and I was reminded of where we were. What we'd been on the brink of doing.

I stared up at her, her semi-naked self, that pooch on her abdomen that told me her body was busy making another one of our kids, and I felt myself fall for her again.

Over and fucking over.

It was my curse and my gift—to constantly and consistently fall in love with this woman.

"I love you, Rex," she whispered, her mouth twisting at the end of the sentence in a way that, I knew, was a warning she was about to burst into tears.

"I love you too, Rachel," I replied calmly, trying to exude it so that she wouldn't just hear the words, but feel it.

Both her pregnancies had been during times of high stress now, so if I could make this one easier on her, I'd move fucking mountains to make sure that happened.

"You'll come back, won't you?" she rasped.

"I'm not going to die—"

"I don't mean that," she blurted the words over mine. "I mean you won't stay there for the next few months? I-I know she needs you but we need you too. Can't you bring her home with you?"

I stared at her. "You need me?"

Of the millions of things she could have said, that was the last thing I'd anticipated.

Her bottom lip trembled. "I-I do."

She'd never needed me before. I felt as if most of the previous two decades had been spent with her tolerating me, but I saw the need in her eyes—a deep kind of yearning that needed no words to be conveyed—felt it in how she clasped me to her. Knew it from how her shoulders hunched and she crouched against the bed as if life were crippling her.

I was her man.

It was my duty to protect her from that shit so I nodded. "I'll bring her home."

It was a promise I had no right to make, but one that I made all the same.

Wynter had already been talking about moving here for college. After what was going down as a result of her adoptive dad's behavior, I didn't see why she'd turn her nose up at the idea of moving sooner.

Of course, nothing was ever simple with the Laker women. I'd beg, steal, and borrow to get her to come back home with me though. Rachel didn't need to know that.

I speared upright, pressed my mouth to her forehead, then murmured, "Let me grab a change of clothes and we'll go to your room so you can get changed too. Would you ask Lily to pack my things up and take them back to West Orange?"

She frowned. "I'll do that."

"You'll be busy with whatever Nyx has gotten himself wrapped up in," I said grimly.

"Murder," she muttered, her gaze dropping to the level of my chin.

I blew out a breath. "Fuck."

"Yeah."

"Whatever it takes to get him out, Rachel, do it."

"I will. Let's keep it under wraps for the moment, though. Nyx said something about the cops not reading him his Miranda rights until they were back at the station."

That had me arching a brow. "That's an oversight."

"It's definitely not as big of a problem as *CSI* makes out," she drawled. "But mostly, I'm more interested in the fact he said they smacked him around."

"That's a hell of a fuck up. Was he resisting arrest?"

"This was in the precinct. I'll get more details later."

"Don't tell Giulia."

"She deserves to know," was Rachel's immediate answer.

"I don't dispute that, but let's see what magic you can reap, huh? If you can get him out on small details like those, then there's no need to worry her at all."

I could tell she didn't approve, but that she also saw the benefit to what I was saying.

"She'd be difficult at the station," I pointed out, which hit the nail on the head.

Rachel shuddered. "Difficult isn't the word. Okay, go and get a change of clothes. I'll text Lily and ask her to pack your things up and take them back home with her."

With another nod, I strode over to the wardrobe where I'd unpacked last night, and as I grabbed a Henley, some jeans, my boots, a sweatshirt, and my coat, I felt her glance on me as she fastened her dress back up from where she'd pulled the two halves aside to bare her belly to my covetous gaze.

"Ask," I said gruffly as I turned back to her. "Don't just bottle up whatever's on your mind."

"Where's your cut?"

"With Wynter. She wanted to make sure I was coming back to her." Her eyes rounded. "Oh."

"We get along well," was all I said.

"Seems like it." Her brow furrowed as she stared down at the ground. I wasn't sure what to expect from her next, but I didn't prod, just tucked her hand in mine and dragged her back down the hall toward the elevator because we needed to get shit moving.

When we were in her room, she finally said, "I'm glad you've built a relationship with her, Rex, and I'm so sorry that I'm the reason why you weren't there to watch her grow up. You must really hate me—"

My hands were cupping her cheeks before she could finish that sentence. I rested my forehead on hers, and I spoke the words against her lips so she could feel my breath.

"You have nothing to be sorry for. What was done to you was not your choice. You are not the reason things didn't work out with Wynter. You survived, Rachel, and that's all I could have asked of you. That you somehow worked out how to wake up day after day and to keep on with your life.

"Wynter—I wish we'd been able to raise her, don't get me wrong. But it's never too late to have a relationship. For us to be close. We weren't there at the start, but life lasts for a hell of a long time, and we can be there for her now, can't we?"

Her lips trembled. "She'll hate me for not coming with you."

"I'll explain." I pressed my thumb against her quivering mouth, needing to stop that tremor. "I'm good at explaining, and she'll understand.

"Nyx can *not* be in jail, Rachel. I need you to get him out of there, do you hear me?"

Shivering, she nodded.

"If it means you have to pull all the favors you have, if it means you have to break the law, you do it. Agreed?"

"Agreed," she said on a whisper.

"However, you do not put yourself in danger or in harm's way, Rachel. Understand?"

"I understand."

"Good."

Her lips parted as she stared up at me. Nothing about Rachel was easy to decipher, but at that moment, her eyes darkened with emotions that might as well have spelled out letters for me to read.

L. O. V. E.

W. A. N. T.

N. E. E. D.

They were feelings I hadn't seen in her expression for years. Not running simultaneously, at any rate. Want and need were one thing, but love, deeply entwined among them, was another.

Seeing them here, *now*, imbued me with a strength I didn't know I possessed.

I cupped her chin and, mouth hovering over hers, whispered, "I won't kiss you goodbye."

"You left your cut with Wynter and are leaving me with the promise of a kiss?"

Grinning slightly, I nodded and traced my fingers over the soft line of her jaw. "We both have things to do, and if I kiss you, we aren't going anywhere."

"You're right." She sighed. "I hate that you're right."

I pressed a kiss to her forehead. "It happens sometimes."

TWO

RACHEL

Watching him drive off in a cab as Emile took me to the precinct where Nyx was being held was a special kind of hell.

I didn't want him to leave without me.

I wanted to go with him.

I wasn't overly maternal, but every single motherly instinct inside me was screaming at me to go with him, to let Nyx stew in a cell for a couple days—it wouldn't kill him.

Not like a bunch of Triads could kill our defenseless, underaged daughter.

Nausea and I were no strangers thanks to this pregnancy, but the need to puke had me opening a window to the cold night air and letting the stench of gas slip inside the backseat of the car.

I sucked it in because the last thing I needed was to vomit.

If I could get Nyx out tonight, maybe I could hop on a flight tomorrow to join Rex and Wynter in LA...

Maybe. I had to try.

We got stuck in traffic around ten minutes in, and because thinking about Wynter trapped with the Triads was a vicious kind of torture, I decided to distract myself.

Instead of replying to Hunter via text, I hit the connect button, hoping he'd answer so he could further distract me.

Thank fuck he did.

"Hey, Rach!"

As always, he sounded super zen.

I'd only seen him be anything less than chilled that day when he'd killed Marcus, Rory's husband.

It was a sad twist of fate that while our friendship had survived the years, every time I thought of Hunter, I inevitably thought of him that day.

I had a feeling that Aurora felt the same way about him, and that was why she'd put up so many roadblocks that he could have lived in Australia, never mind in the desert, for how much space separated them.

"Hunter, what's with the photo you sent me?"

"Weird, right?" He chuckled. "I think it's actually a death threat."

"You do?" I asked cautiously, not wanting to alarm him but needing to scope out the situation. "What have you done to deserve a death threat?"

"Recently, you mean?"

I sniffed. "Well, yes."

"I've done a lot of shitty things over the years," he pointed out.

"I know. I was there for a few," I drawled, which made him chuckle.

His guilt had long since died a death; something I'd helped perpetuate. In the aftermath of Marcus' attack, of Wynter's birth, of my attempt to get back on track with my studies, Hunter had been my stalwart strength.

"This is very true," he agreed. "Still, I don't think I've done anything to deserve death by assassin. That's usually above my pay grade."

His wording had me tensing. "What is your pay grade?"

"Do you really want to know?" he asked smugly.

"If it's pertinent to whoever wants you dead, then yes," I retorted with a huff.

"Add a couple of zeroes to whatever your top paying client pays you and that's about right."

I narrowed my eyes at that. "The fuck?"

"Do you want into my pants now?"

"This isn't funny, Hunter!"

"I think it's hilarious."

"You would," I sniped. "This is serious. Someone's threatened your life."

"Gah, someone's always doing that; this is just the first time it's been gift wrapped. I've heard rumors about an assassin who does this, of course, but I've never seen it before. Wonder who she gets to send the gifts—"

"Why? Do you want to use them for the next party you host?"

He chuckled. "You know I don't host parties. What's got your panties in a bunch, anyway? Rory told me you were full steam ahead with the FAST gala. My donation is in the charity accounts, by the way."

I pulled a face at that. "Thank you, Hunter."

He hummed. "Very welcome, very welcome."

He was far too generous, and for someone who made a point of scalping everyone in her vicinity for cash for her charities, that was really saying something.

"I wish you'd come to one of the fundraisers though—"

"We've discussed this."

We had.

"I don't see the point of fundraisers. Someone pays forty grand for a plate, right? But a lot of that money goes to waste on renting the hall, on the food, on the entertainment—"

"We get subsidized rates and we also get a lot of things donated—"

"I don't care. I just think it's dumb. But you did have a nice lot in one of the auctions. I bought it over the phone."

"Meaning you had someone come to the party that you disapprove of?"

"I did."

"Who?"

"That's for me to know, not you."

I rolled my eyes though I had to admit to being amused. Hunter, even in the most stressful of circumstances, had a habit of making me smile. He was just that kind of guy.

As I pondered the question of whether he and Link would get along well, I retorted, "Let's get back to the matter at hand."

"You mean the death threat?" He hummed. "Yes, very intriguing."

"Not intriguing," I grumbled. "What are you going to do?"

"Not sure," was his candid retort. "I mean, ordinarily I'd go to my people, but I sometimes contract out without their knowledge, and if this is to do with that then I'm screwed on two fronts."

"Do you make a habit of contracting out to other people?"

"No. Just the Valentini family."

"Should have known that without asking."

"You really should." He tsked. "You're slipping."

"Pregnancy makes me forgetful," I discounted.

"It might make you forgetful, but it doesn't make you stupid."

"That's harsh, isn't it?"

He chuckled. "Should I say sorry?"

"Yes," I sniped.

"Sorry, Rach," he declared at his most penitent.

But, with Hunter, that wasn't saying much.

"Does Rory know you help the Valentinis?"

"Nope. Only Custanzu."

A couple of things that had happened over the last six weeks suddenly made sense.

"Is that why you shoved Lodestar onto them?"

Because he didn't want to be working with Rory up close and personal?

"Sure is. My people were starting to get suspicious."

Hmm.

"Could they have sent you the death threat?"

A snort escaped him. "No."

"Well, you're not as clever as you think, Hunter, because not only did someone send you that pretty package in the mail, they sent it somewhere that actually got delivered to you—"

"Shit, you're right," he groused. "I need to move, don't I?"

"You don't. That's the last goddamn thing you need to do. You move and you'll get hit."

"Damn. This is an inconvenience," he complained. "I have a routine, you know? I go for—"

"I don't need to know if you still have a coffee and a Danish every morning after you go for a run," I grumbled. "Rex told me that he knows someone who could, potentially, call the shooter off."

"And you rang me first and not them?!"

"I wanted to check in with you first."

"Ah, you wanted to know I wasn't dead yet."

My lips twitched. "That too." I stared at the road ahead, saw some of the traffic had begun clearing up, and felt my nerves start to twist into being again.

Tonight had been a clusterfuck.

Sucking in a breath, I muttered, "It's been a busy night."

"I bet," he said somewhat sympathetically. "I'd really appreciate—"

"You don't have to ask. The hacker you shoved onto Custanzu is the one who knows the assassin anyway, so..."

"Lodestar knows Dead To Me?"

"Dead To Me?"

"That's the assassin's name. To be honest, I thought she was an urban legend. I didn't realize there was a sniper batshit enough to go around giving her victims gift baskets, but you live and learn."

Despite the situation, I smiled. "Seems like she has style."

"I can't disagree. I'll get in touch with Lodestar. Leave it with me."

"You sure? Will you call me to tell me you're not dead?"

I heard the grin in his voice. "It'll take more than a sniper's bullet to kill me, Rach. But if she comes at me with a flamethrower or a pitchfork then know that I love you?"

As always, he shoved humor at me, and though my lips twisted of their own accord into a smile, it didn't diminish the fact that his words *hurt.*

"I love you too. Please, Hunter, stay safe."

"I will," he told me, his tone more serious now. "I promise."

He cut the call, leaving me staring at the slowly moving traffic for a handful of seconds.

One thing about being a defense attorney that sucked was that if life were a game of chess, you were shoved into the match halfway through and, somehow, had to protect your client's moves all while making your own.

Well aware that I was going to have to maneuver around Nyx's very sticky past, it took me too long to text Lodestar:

Rachel: *A man called Hunter is going to call you tonight. I think you know him, because he knows you, but if you don't, then remember, he's a friend of mine. Anything you do for him, I'll remember, and I ALWAYS pay back my favors.*

When I didn't receive a reply, when the two ticks didn't even turn blue to inform me that she'd read the message, I had to accept that she could be busy working or even might be sleeping—anything was possible with Lodestar.

By the time we arrived at the precinct, I'd managed to shove aside the last couple hours' worth of stress and tension and settled into the mask I wore at all times—Rachel Laker.

Not Rach.

Rachel Laker.

Two names.

Not the one.

People sneered my name. They spat it. They grimaced when they heard it. That was the reputation I'd crafted; one I'd built and forged in the fire that was life in this criminal underbelly in which I'd subsisted for so long.

Rachel Laker didn't lose.

She might have to negotiate, but she did. Not. Lose.

Giulia would have her Old Man back in her bed—tonight. No later.

With that resolve fixed firmly in place, I climbed out of the car once it pulled up to the curb, told Emile to wait for my call, then stared up at the building.

Sucking in a sharp breath at the bitter cold, I firmed my jaw and climbed the steps.

My mask slipped, however, when the first face I saw in the precinct wasn't a cop, but a Five Pointer.

Irish Mob.

An O'Donnelly.

THREE

RACHEL

Aidan O'Donnelly Sr. had a distinct reputation in certain circles—the ones in which I ran.

Some said he was insane. Some said his wickedness was all the worse because he *was* sane. Some said the life had turned him, and with as many wars as he'd been involved in, I had to think that was the likelier option.

No one was born evil.

I'd met enough scum in my years to know that.

A dash of child abuse here, some neglect there, and over a person's adolescence, any potential was driven out for good.

It wasn't the first time I'd met O'Donnelly Sr.—we often crossed paths at fundraisers—but whenever I had the misfortune of coming across him, I always hoped it would be the last.

Especially now, when he was looking straight at me with the gravitas of a king in a throne room, I recognized that we might as well have been in the Palais de Versailles and not a shitty police precinct in East Harlem.

The man had to have a million warrants out for his arrest, yet here he was, calm as you like, and that aura of calm put me on edge.

When he smiled at me from a face that was as handsome now as it had been when he was younger, it was like spiders crawled up and down my spine.

I knew what that smile was—*a summons.*

Veering away from the front desk, I strode over to O'Donnelly.

He watched me, not in a creepy way, but hawkishly. Taking the measure of me.

Not appreciating being summoned, I wasn't obvious about it, but I straightened my shoulders and lengthened my spine as I finally came to a halt in front of him.

"Mr. O'Donnelly, what a surprise to see you here." I raised my arm to check my watch. "And at such a late hour."

"This is the city that never sleeps, Ms. Laker," was his simple retort. "Bedtime is for children and those innocent fools who think their country isn't forged on corruption."

Well, that got heavy *fast.*

"You don't strike me as a man who lets *things* disturb a good night's sleep."

"Maybe once, but not now." His brow furrowed as he looked up at me. "Thirty years ago, if you walked in here, you'd have been laughed out of the precinct. Instead, I've been hearing grumbles from the cops ever since your man, Nyx, made a call to you." His lips twisted into a smile. "They're terrified of you."

This was a monster who knew how to inspire terror in people. *Real* terror. True terror.

"They're terrified of the paperwork I cause," I corrected stiffly. "Nothing more, nothing less."

"The paperwork and the potential of losing their job."

"If 'my man' *has* been beaten during his arrest, I can guarantee they'll be hauled into an IA inquiry tomorrow morning," I agreed, my tone saccharine-sweet.

He winked at me as he patted the seat at his side. It was a grim moss-green Formica that likely hadn't been updated since the seventies. "I've read all about you, Rachel Laker. Most formidable. Very impressive."

"I'm surprised you haven't tried to approach me as a client," I retorted coolly, "if everyone speaks so highly of me. Unless, is that what this is? A job interview?"

His smile deepened. "In a sense. Just not for you."

I arched a brow as I took a seat at his side, staring onto the miserable precinct in this miserable part of the city. Poverty and despair went hand in hand in these parts—I'd know. I'd spent most of my childhood in areas like these.

That whole 'evil being cultivated' belief was something I included myself in.

Had I been raised by my mother my whole life, undoubtedly I'd be behind bars now as well, but Axel had come along, so had the Sinners and Rex.

Ironically, they were my saviors even as some of the Sinners' brethren had been the catalyst for my downfall.

"The job interview isn't for me..." I mused, nose crinkling when a hooker strode past me, rubbing at her wrists where cuffs had recently been biting into the flesh. She stank of cheap perfume, sweat, and vomit. Great combo. "So I suppose it's for Nyx?"

"You'd be surprised how gossip spreads."

"What kind of gossip?"

"About a man seeking the righteous ends of people who don't deserve their next breath. About a man who's been castrated by the women in his family, who urged a promise out of him that someone of his leanings can't avoid forever—"

Anger spiraled inside me. "No one 'castrated' Nyx."

"Why's he here then?" came the soft taunt. "If he wasn't castrated, if that promise was freely given, why are we sitting here today? One slither of temptation and he falls."

"You're mixing your theology, Mr. O'Donnelly. Shouldn't the women be the ones proffering temptation and not his salvation?

Aren't they a man's downfall seeing as he has no free will of his own?" I mocked, because his misogynistic BS stank to high heaven.

"I'm not against playing the role of the serpent from time to time." His smile drifted. "He's safe from the law."

I scoffed, "Of course he is. I'm his attorney."

"I like a woman with confidence. Shame all my boys are taken or I'd have tried to set you up with one of them."

Eyes flaring wide, I choked out, "I beg your pardon?"

"This was a test, Rachel Laker," he said, ignoring my question. "A test Nyx failed. Now, I don't judge him. If anything, I respect a man with his principles, and I have an offer for him."

"An offer that hinges on his freedom is no 'offer' at all."

"I'd like to see you in court," he mused. "Unfortunately, I have a distaste for legal proceedings.

"Liberty can be bought with incompetence and ignorance, Rachel Laker. With such a skilled legal representative on his side, I doubt he'd spend a full night here anyway, but your talents won't be necessary—"

"Good, because I intend on making sure he gets home to his pregnant partner. *Tonight.*"

"Very few people interrupt me, Rachel Laker."

It amused me that he was using my full name, much as I did when I was in these situations.

"That's because I'm not afraid of you, Mr. O'Donnelly."

"No?" He quirked a brow at me. "Why aren't you?"

"I've dealt with worse men than you and survived."

He stared at me, his eyes seeming to slice into me. That quirked brow of his softened, and his mouth tightened. "I'm very sorry to hear that, Rachel Laker."

Funny how those were the most honest and earnest words he'd uttered since we'd started talking.

"I appreciate that," I said blandly, turning away from him to stare over the precinct.

"One thing I've learned, it's a woman who pays for the sins of men... not their sons." His jaw clenched. "Rape is so unimaginative a punishment but clever, so clever. When those men learn the truth, they'll trigger a war for their woman. One they might not start for their sons."

"Rape shouldn't be a catalyst," I argued.

"It is if you have the right man at your side."

His intoned words had me tensing. *And* changing the subject. "Nyx isn't one of the good guys. He's inherently flawed, but his guilt eats into him like a cancer.

"If he doesn't get himself killed first, then his shame will do the job. He's already rotting away in a jail cell, but it's of his own making. Locking him up is just cruel."

"I know how he feels," O'Donnelly murmured.

"I highly doubt—" I broke off before I could finish the sentence. I thought about what I knew about the man, and I shut my mouth.

It was well known that his wife had been gang-raped by Aryans. Kidnapped and abused simply for being Magdalena *O'Donnelly.*

I thought about how glad I'd always been that my suffering was private. That I'd never had to bare the gruesome details to the cops. That I'd never had to sit in front of a jury who'd decided that I deserved to be raped because I'd worn a low-cut top.

Pity didn't fill me.

Respect did.

It took a strong woman to withstand that. To go about society, to face the whispers, to know that everyone in the room was aware you'd survived hell and had come back to tell the tale.

He wasn't wrong about rape being a catalyst—hadn't it been for him?

"Cat got your tongue?"

I heard the taunt. I didn't ignore it. Instead, I dipped my chin. "You're the reason your wife was kidnapped."

His cocky expression was knocked askew. "You're the only person brave enough to tell me that in at least a decade."

"Telling the truth is a brave thing to do," I said on purpose. "What's your deal with Nyx?"

He stared at me. "I have names and I don't need a conscience or 'promises' getting in the way."

"Names that," I hesitated, "need *deleting*?"

"Yes."

"He can find names of his own."

"These are important men. Men of consequence."

"And you can't easily pay someone to do this for you?" I mocked. "You had to involve someone who's going to be a father?"

A hiss escaped him at my judgmental tone. "I'm a father myself, Rachel Laker. I know the weight of the burden that's about to rest on his shoulders. I also know that freedom isn't as cut and dry as you think.

"You said it yourself—he's already in a cell. I didn't have to put him in one to incarcerate him."

An ache surged to being in my temple.

He was being cagey, and it was starting to piss me off.

"So you're doing this out of the kindness of your heart?"

"Many would say I don't have a heart."

Me included.

"I see you agree."

"I'm sure he can find *names* himself," I argued.

"Not and pay off a debt to me."

"A debt you accrued on your own behalf," I retorted.

"That's the best kind of debt." He smiled at me, but it was wooden, and I knew my frankness had hit home.

Oddly enough, I wasn't proud of that feat. Kicking an old man where it hurt wasn't how I got my rocks off.

"What's the end game, Mr. O'Donnelly?"

"Deletions."

"So this *isn't* for Nyx's sake?"

"In a sense. Murder is murder. But these men don't deserve that fate. They deserve a righteous end."

Mind racing, I asked, "An eye for an eye?"

Slowly, he nodded. "It's the only way to achieve rightful vengeance."

And if that wasn't a fucked-up logic, I didn't know what was.

"Does it have to be Nyx?"

He studied me a second. "What does that mean?"

"Does he have to be the one in charge of deleting?"

"You want it to be a group effort instead?" he mocked.

I shrugged. "Maybe."

But I was thinking of Harlow.

Harlow who O'Donnelly hadn't even mentioned yet.

I just knew he'd been arrested too.

The older man monitored my expression—or the lack thereof. "What are you planning behind those icy eyes, Rachel Laker?"

"Nothing," I countered. "No plans—"

"Don't lie to a man who can see through bullshit better than a cowboy."

"The only time you've seen a cow is when you've gone to a farm to dispose of... something."

"You've got the wrong animal. Pigs are good for that kind of disposal. Not cows. But I see where you're going with this. A righteous kill is what I want, Rachel Laker. Nothing less will serve me."

He clearly didn't know Harlow's story.

"You're the reason Nyx's arrest has been unorthodox?" I queried, wondering how much power O'Donnelly had in this precinct.

Without conferring with the front desk, I was still blind as to what was happening here.

"The cops were there on my say, they arrested him on an irrelevant charge, and my boys handled the body then arranged for the poor woman to get home.

"That means your man will be home tonight without needing to drop a dime on a lawyer such as yourself. My name can move mountains, Rachel Laker." He got to his feet. "You should remember that."

"Is that a threat?"

He turned to face me and did the damnedest thing—he reached down for my hand and pressed his lips to my knuckles.

Beneath my fingers, I could feel the slightest of tremors in his digits.

Just the slightest.

"Threats are the only kind of language I know. But I'm speaking to someone who's fluent in them too."

"What did they charge him with?"

"Excessive speeding and reckless driving." He winked at me. "Pleasure doing business with you, Rachel Laker."

"You could have stopped the rape from happening." If my tone was bleak, well, how couldn't it be considering my past?

"Innocent blood gets shed every day," he said, but for the first time, a sorrowful cast shaded his features. It wasn't enough. "He'll never be able to hurt another victim. I take comfort in that."

That might have comforted him, but what good was that for the poor woman who'd been attacked tonight? Who was probably trying to scour her body to get clean? Who was worried about STDs and pregnancy in a nation that blamed the rape victim and not the rapist for her attack?

"May we never meet again, Aidan O'Donnelly Sr."

"That's a promise I can keep. The places where you run aren't my idea of a good time. That being said, I did hear about that gala of yours tonight. Expect a nice donation from Acuig Corp."

With that, he strode out of the precinct, leaving me wondering how many loopholes I'd left wide open in that deal I'd just struck with the devil.

FOUR

REX

"It can't really be as simple as that," I rasped once Rachel had finished recounting the events at the precinct.

The video call picked up on exactly how tired she was, and I felt that in my fucking bones.

I'd wanted to spend the night in a bed beside her. Not on a fucking red-eye back to LA.

"Apparently it is." She shrugged. "An eye for an eye is what he wants, and Nyx is clearly the only man O'Donnelly knows with the inclination to deliver *lex talionis* to his door."

"Nyx and Harlow are back in West Orange?"

"They are. No one's the wiser for where they've spent most of their night as far as I know."

I reached up and ran the edge of my thumb along my bottom lip as I pondered why the fuck O'Donnelly Sr. had just pulled a stunt like that.

We were fucking allies.

Allies didn't tangle with the goddamn VP of my MC and get the fucker locked up.

Senior was reckless—everyone knew that. He was also certifiable, but he'd gone too far tonight.

"What happened?" I demanded grimly, finding myself annoyed by this fucking situation but mostly pissed she'd had to deal with him on her own.

"Nyx found a woman being raped."

I sighed, stopped rubbing my mouth and started rubbing my eyes instead—it had been a fucker of a night. Worst thing being that it wasn't over yet.

Still on the road to Burbank, I had another twenty minutes before I made it to Wynter's apartment.

I'd left my hog back at LAX and was using a rideshare again. This shit was bad for my rep but I'd gone this route, one, because I was exhausted and this endless day didn't need to end with me crashing. Two, because I needed to speak with Rachel without a mouthful of bugs and I wanted to see her as we talked. Three, because I didn't have the time to waste on releasing my bike from the secure parking lot.

The second I'd gotten another rideshare after I'd armed myself, I'd contacted Rachel and she'd started giving me the lowdown.

"Nyx was too late to stop the rape?"

"He was," she confirmed, her tone as cool as ice water.

Sometimes, I was jealous of how she compartmentalized because I sure as hell wasn't as good at it as she was.

Casting the driver a look, I saw he was still wearing earbuds even though it was illegal.

Seemed like small fry in comparison to tonight's events.

Grateful for the privacy, I asked, "He killed him?"

"Of course he did. It's Nyx. According to the laws of the land, however, no murder happened, neither did any sexual assault. That poor woman." That was the first time her voice broke.

My hands itched to pull her close, to comfort her. Fucking Triads. "What *did* happen?"

"A reckless driving charge and an excessive speeding fine for Nyx. Harlow was arrested for loitering."

The corruption involved in this bullshit was insane.

"Did Nyx know he was walking into a trap?"

"I think so," she mused. "His hog and Harlow's cage were impounded so Emile drove us home. On the ride back, he was pretty quiet. If he didn't think it was a trap before he went to Harlem, he has to now."

"You didn't bring up O'Donnelly with him?"

"No. I didn't feel like starting a riot in my town car," she said dryly.

"You certain there are no repercussions from what went down?"

She derided, "I'd be impressed if it weren't terrifying. Even with the pitiful charges, O'Donnelly made sure that his arrest was bungled from the start.

"No Miranda rights were read to either of them, and Nyx was beaten as he was taken to his cell—" About to ask if he was okay, she raised a hand to stall me. I wanted to reach through the video call and snag her fingers in mine, but as good as technology was, it wasn't that goddamn good. "He's okay. It was minor, just enough for me to raise hell about his treatment and get his release processed faster. By the end of it, Harlow was the one in more trouble."

"What about the victim?"

"O'Donnelly said he had her taken home."

"And the body?"

"His men dealt with that too."

"So, what you're telling me is that no crime happened last night?"

"Not according to the law. Even if a kid playing dress-up as a cop could have done a better job than Nyx's arresting officer last night, he'd still be safe."

"So O'Donnelly was throwing his weight around?"

"He was."

"And your magic skills weren't required?"

"No."

"It seemed like O'Donnelly wanted to talk with you."

She studied me a second then slowly dipped her head. "I think you're right."

"You sound surprised."

"I have no affiliation with the MC. You're my client—"

"You're family," I countered gruffly as my ride headed down another stretch of lonely highway. "Family is the only kind of language a man like O'Donnelly knows how to talk."

"I doubt he'd agree with you there."

Her smile had me frowning. "What's with the smile?"

"He was more charming than I'd anticipated."

"Charming?" I hissed under my breath. "The hell? The man's worse than a fucking snake."

"I think that gives common snakes a bad name," she retorted. "I'm not saying I liked the man. In fact, I think what he did to that woman was horrendous. He knew who the rapist was, knew where he'd strike, but he let it happen because he wanted to ensnare Nyx. Regardless, I'm only saying that he has a way about him."

I rolled my eyes. "Understatement, much?"

She laughed. "Are you jealous of a, what? Seventy-year-old man?"

"No," I groused.

"I swear it's a good thing I think you're pretty or that possessive side of your nature would piss me the hell off."

"Let you flirt with Valentini last night, didn't I?"

Temper flashed in her eyes. "Flirt? I handed him a ridiculously overpriced purse."

"And danced with a bunch of other bastards who had their hands all over you."

"What do you want to do, Rex? Lock me up in the clubhouse and keep me in a glass case that only you have the key to?" she sniped.

"I would if I fucking could," I replied grimly. "Everyone wants their fucking hands on you—"

"You're the only one who can change that."

The purr in her voice would have stopped a lesser man in his tracks.

"No brand until you know what it represents," was my stony retort.

"I've known what it represents for a fucking lifetime, Rex. Did you know Axel never gave my mom one? Not even after she gave birth to Rain."

I grimaced. "I knew that."

"You did?" She shrugged. "I don't blame him. I wouldn't have branded her either. Vicious tramp that she was, she didn't deserve it. Still, you try being the charity case surrounded by a bunch of kids who *belonged* to the MC."

"You weren't a charity case," I argued.

"I felt like it sometimes."

"I made you feel as if you were?"

"No. But I know that you had to do a hell of a lot of defending to protect me from people who should have considered me family."

"You've always been family."

"To you, maybe. To the current council, I'm learning it's the same. But the rest of those motherfuckers you call brothers? No. They'll only accept me if I'm branded. Why the hell are you fighting this, Rex?"

Riled up, I shot her a glower. "Wanted you branded when you were fourteen goddamn years old, Rachel. Don't tell me that I'm fighting this when you're the one who's spent the two decades since fucking with that."

"You wanted to brand me when I was a kid?"

"Yeah. You're mine. Always have been. Always will be."

She rubbed her temple. "I don't understand you."

"You don't have to. You just need to know that I've spent most of my life working toward us being together. If I find myself surprised that suddenly you want the same thing after fighting it for so fucking long—"

"Ever heard of that saying, 'Never look a gift horse in the mouth?'"

"Yeah, ever heard of the saying, 'Don't pull a tiger by its tail?'" I immediately retorted. "The second you're branded, Rachel, that's the second I'm not letting you go anywhere. It's the second you're stuck fast to my side. It's the second that I beat the fuck outta any man who looks at you, never mind goddamn touches you. It's the second that you don't become just my Old Lady; it's when you become *the* First fuckin' Lady.

"That's when you rule the place like my mom did. When you take over shit you have no interest in taking over. When we stand side by goddamn side and make sure that the bunch of outlaws and fuck-wits we call family stay with us instead of rotting away in a grave or in a jail cell.

"It's the moment you stop giving a fuck about flying all over the country to fight fancy lawsuits in California for serial killers who are tied to the mob, and it's the moment you stop fighting what we have and start accepting that you. Are. *Mine.*

"You ain't just taking ink, Rachel. You're taking me. You're taking the club. You're taking every-fucking-thing.

"I'm not being a pussy by not branding you. I'm giving you time. Not an out. Just time. You were always gonna be the only woman who got my brand. I've waited this long. I can wait some more for you to figure out what's coming your way."

"You're a fucking asshole; do you know that?" she spat, and I had to grin at her outrage. I doubted she'd see it in the meager light but I didn't give a fuck if she did.

This, I'd take.

This was Rachel.

My fucking wildfire.

"I do know that," I crooned. "You're the one who fucking loves me. What does that say about you?"

She let loose a shriek that was pure exasperation wrapped up in frustration and snarled, "Tell me when you get Wynter out of there."

"I will."

"Don't you dare fucking die, Rex, do you goddamn hear me?"

She cut the call without waiting for an answer and I didn't try to call her back. Not only because I was a few minutes away from Wynter's place according to the rideshare app, but because she needed a breather to think.

It was the first time she noticed she had a very long leash around her pretty neck, and because I wasn't a prick, I never tugged on it.

I only had today because she'd insisted.

I was *not* like my dad.

I never fucking would be either.

When we reached Wynter's building, I asked the driver to ride around the block, trying to scope out if there were any Triads sitting in black sedans surveilling the place. I didn't mind walking into a trap for my daughter, but I wanted to know about it first.

My cell buzzed.

"That you in the rideshare?"

I recognized Ryder's voice. Goddamn Disciple had an attitude problem worse than Nyx. And the fucker just had to be the one to see me in a cage. Typical.

"That's me."

"The fuck you think this is? A carousel ride at Disney?"

"Checking shit out."

"More like you were checking out that we were watching. We were. Now go and get your fucking daughter."

"I will now I know you'll gut the fuckers if they shoot me first."

"Got enough BS to be dealing with of my own right now. This ain't my battle, but if those bastards don't fight fair, I'll make sure they pay for screwing you over."

"Appreciate that."

I narrowed my eyes at nothing in particular but told the driver to pull up outside the building.

I cut the call then left the car.

My ride here had been in two stages.

The first vehicle had taken me to a gas station over in Westmont. That was where I'd bought the gun I'd tucked away at the small of my back. The second car had brought me here.

Once the rideshare merged into traffic, I retrieved the weapon, palming it, and immediately felt better for having its cool weight in my grasp.

I stared up at the building, noticed that only one floor had any lights on, and I strode over to the entrance and began the walk up to her apartment.

There was no one waiting to sabotage me on the stairs, but that didn't make me let down my guard any.

A single knock to the door heralded a hub of activity that froze as someone called out, "Come in."

Wynter had never let me inside because, I figured, it was a shithole and she knew I'd say as much—then would try to convince her to let me help her move out of the damn place—and my guess wasn't wrong.

The door opened to reveal a neat and clean room; I had to give her that. But it was small and crowded with just a sofa bed as the main feature.

There were watermarks on the fucking walls, the smatterings of mildew and black mold around the tiny windows, and a musty smell in here that I did *not* want my daughter breathing in.

There were also three fucking Triads sitting on her bed.

I tightened my lips at the sight. "Where is she?"

"In the bathroom."

One of the men got to his feet and raised his hands. "We meant her no harm. We have left her in there since she agreed to make the call. You can ask her yourself."

I squinted at him, took in the expensive suit, the slick haircut, and reared back to knock on the bathroom door.

"Stay in there, honey, but tell me if you're okay. Did they hurt you?"

"They didn't," Wynter called out, her voice shaken, her fear evident.

Despite her assurance, rage filled me.

"The fuck are you doing here?" I snarled, turning on the prick with a glower.

"My name is Charles Xiang."

My top lip curled. "Pleasure to meet you."

"You are the leader of the Satan's Sinners' MC. The one they say has deadly hands."

I didn't roll my eyes at the rep, just jerked up my chin and corrected, "Prez."

Charles conceded that with a nod. "Her father, Jeremy Kinnock, owes a substantial debt to one of my Mahjong gambling rooms.

"He offered her to me as payment, however I'm not an animal. Mr. Kinnock did not seem to realize that was the case until I taught him otherwise." A silken gleam that was about as threatening as a knife to the belly speared through Charles' eyes. "I have no desire to take on an underaged girl as a repayment of debt.

"When I learned you were her biological father, I knew I wouldn't be out of pocket for long."

"How did you learn that?"

His smile was cold. "We have our ways."

That had better not have anything to fucking do with the Disciples. If they'd run their mouths... God help them.

"How much?"

"Ninety thousand."

"I'm going to reach for my phone," I warned him.

He uttered something in Mandarin that had the men sitting on Wynter's sofa settling back. "Thank you for the warning."

"I have no intention of getting shot or stabbed today." I arched a brow at him. "You accept bank transfers?"

"I do." Charles smiled. "But I don't want money."

They never fucking did.

"You want a favor?"

He nodded. "Do you understand the ranking of the Triads, Mr..."

"Rex," I interrupted. "Just Rex. And to a certain degree. What you let outsiders know, at any rate."

"A wise man knows his enemy."

"I'm no enemy to the Triads, and they're no enemy to me. We don't cross paths that often."

"You crossed it with me and you didn't even know it," he pointed out.

I hated that he was right.

"If I'd known Jeremy Kinnock was drowning in debt, I'd have given him a better place to die."

"Venice Beach?" Charles mocked.

"Somewhere picturesque like that, sure." We shared a look. "What do you want?"

"I enjoy a similar rank to your own. I am the Dragon Head of this area."

"I've met the Dragon Head of New York City," I told him.

"I know. You have, therefore, met the Chairman. Very few people know he holds both roles."

This was the first I was hearing about any rank called a 'Chairman.'

"What *is* the Chairman?"

"You are the President who oversees multiple chapters, are you not?"

"I am."

"The Chairman is like you. He sits above all Dragon Heads in the USA. It is a wise man who courts his favor. Especially when his son has been kidnapped."

My brow furrowed. "I had nothing to do with that."

"I did not say that you did. But I know you have certain people in your acquaintance who might be able to help the Chairman with his current dilemma." He bowed his head. "I have no wish for your money. I have no wish for your daughter. But I will kill her and you if you do not accept this gesture of goodwill and extend me the courtesy of utilizing the hacker known as Lodestar to find the boy."

Word had spread that Star was with the Sinners? I wasn't sure she'd appreciate that.

Hell, I didn't know if *I* appreciated that.

"Sounds like a fuck-ton of *bad* will to me," I mocked.

Charles merely smiled. "Information is painless."

"The people I know..." I purposely didn't use Star's tag. "...won't have the answers immediately."

Although, knowing Star, maybe she did and she just hadn't said anything.

"Of this I'm aware," he said, his tone uncomfortably *reasonable.* "So long as we have them before the boy is killed, I'll consider our debt satisfied."

"What do you get out of it? You want me to put in a mention that you're the guy who found the Chairman's son?"

"I do not have to curry favor with the Chairman. I am a father. Much as you are. Would you wish to share his pain?"

"No," I said grimly, but I wasn't buying what he was selling. "Selflessness isn't a part of our world."

"Do you understand what a tithe is?"

"I'm not an idiot." Understanding flickered through me. "He was skinning you all alive to pay the ransom?"

"For far more than the paltry ninety thousand Kinnock owes me." Charles dipped his chin. "Make the call."

I narrowed my eyes. "What did you do with him?" I'd noticed he hadn't said much about the location or the status of the bastard who thought *my* daughter was a commodity he could trade.

"He and his wife are somewhere safe."

From his lack of expression, I knew that was as much of a reassurance as I'd get. Not that I gave a fuck about Kinnock, but Ally was another matter entirely.

Knowing that Xiang was leveraging their safety too, I made the call to Lodestar. When less than a minute later it was severed, I knew she had her phone switched off. Annoyed, I called Maverick who, thank fuck, answered.

"Rex? What's up? Is it true you were wearing a tuxedo last night? Lily told Link and he told me but I don't fucking believe—"

"Maverick, I'll tell you fairy tales later. I need your help."

Charles watched as I gave Maverick the lowdown.

"Lodestar's better suited for that shit than I am," Mav said uneasily.

"She ain't answering her phone."

"No, she came home late. Been sleeping upstairs ever since."

"Can you go and wake her?" I told him the consequences of failure and, grunting, he promised:

"I will. I'll be in touch soon. Does this Xiang dude want his prints on the situation?"

I caught the other man's eye for confirmation he wanted nothing to do with the 'rescue,' but he shook his head.

"No. Anonymity is the key."

"Anonymity and Lodestar don't go hand in hand," Mav warned with a snort. "Leave it with me."

As he disconnected the line, I told Charles, "Keep my daughter out of this."

"Now that I have your compliance, I will. But I'll be watching you all." Charles shot me a smile as he clicked his fingers at his men who immediately started to walk toward the front door. As he followed, on the doorstep, he murmured, "I would have thought a man as wealthy as you would have provided better accommodation for his daughter."

He didn't wait for an answer.

It was a damn good thing he didn't, seeing as I wanted his face to meet my fists.

Annoyed, I watched the fuckers head down the hall to the staircase, then I moved toward the bathroom door. Knocking on it, I called out, "It's okay, Wynter. They're gone."

In less than two seconds, she was out of there, the door whirling open as she hurled herself at me.

Her sobs broke me, but the way she clung to me gave me hope for a deeper relationship in the future, all while I knew that it hinged on Lodestar managing the unthinkable—finding a kidnapping victim so that Wynter's mom didn't die a brutal death at the hands of the Triads.

And so that my kid didn't blame me for something that wasn't technically my fault.

But I'd been the one to give her to the Kinnocks...

The original sin was mine.

TEXT CHAT

Rex: *Can you do me a favor?*

Rachel: *Favor? Fuck favors, Rex. How's Wynter? What's going on with her?*

Rex: *She's okay. I figure that's all we can ask for right now. She's sleeping in the connecting room at my hotel.*

Rachel: *Keep an eye on her. She might have nightmares.*

Rex: *I will, sweetheart. The door's open. She left it like that, not me.*

Rachel: *I should be there.*

Rex: *No, things are too dangerous here.*

Rachel: *Is that why you need me to do you a favor?*

Rex: *No. I need you to overnight that safety deposit key to me.*

Rachel: *Really? You're going to deal with that now?*

Rex: *Yes. It's a waiting game. Might as well kill two birds with one stone.*

Rachel: *You okay?*

Rex: *No, but it's not like I have a choice.*

Rachel: *I could fly over, Rex.*

Rex: *Thank you, sweetheart, but it's fine. I prefer you to be home rather than here.*

Rachel: *I'm not your little girl, Rex. She's in the room next to you.*

Rex: *There's an active threat against ONE of my girls. You think I can handle having both of them and my unborn child at risk?*

Rachel: *I'm at risk in Jersey.*

Rex: *Don't say shit like that. Your contacts make you untouchable. You're safe there. I need you safe. I need you on the ground. I need you running point for me.*

Rex: *I trust my brothers with my life, but with Wynter's? No. I only trust you with that.*

Rachel: *Okay.*

Rex: *Okay?*

Rachel: *Yes. I'll get the key in the mailbox before the end of day.*

Rex: *Thank you. Hey, I love you, Rachel.*

Rachel: *I love you too. Even if I want to strangle you sometimes.*

FIVE

RACHEL

"Okay, so I know it's really bad of me to tell you this, and it's like eavesdropping but not—"

I rubbed my forehead where a headache had stopped brewing and had decided to take up permanent residence inside my skull. "What is it, Lily?"

"When I was packing Rex's things up last night—by the way, how do men pack so light? It's a miracle—"

"Lily, stay on track, please? I have a killer migraine."

She clucked her tongue. "Guess you can't have any of the good meds."

"No, Giulia's already shared the joys of children's acetaminophen with me," I grumbled. "What do you need from me?"

"I put Rex's things in the kitchen, but I couldn't resist bringing this to you." She pushed a box at me. A small box. A *jewelry* box. "It's what you think it is," she whispered.

I blinked at her. "You found this with Rex's belongings?"

Her head bobbed up and down. "With his socks. I wish he and Link had gone to the same school of laundry folding. It's a good thing we have maids—"

"Lily!" I half-barked. "Please, honey. Migraine, remember?"

"Sorry," she said with a wince. "I'm just excited. Open it!"

"You haven't?"

"I peeped," she admitted. "The second I saw the solitaire, I knew what it was and didn't open it anymore. I shouldn't have looked in the first place but I was super curious."

"Rex was going to propose last night," I rasped, trying to reconcile that with what had actually happened.

She released a soft snort. "Looks like it. I mean, he's not seeing anyone else, is he?"

No. He wasn't.

So what was all that bullcrap about brands?

I palmed the box, brain whirring with what this might mean.

"Old Ladies don't have to be wives, do they?" Lily asked quietly.

"No. They don't."

Apparently, my confusion was obvious because she asked, "Has he asked to brand you?"

"The opposite."

"I'm not sure what the opposite of that is."

"He says I can't talk about it until I'm ready to accept what it entails."

Her lips twitched. "I think Rex believes his own press sometimes."

"Gee, ya think?" I mocked, but I was smiling too. "He gets all wrapped up in his role that he doesn't see the forest for the trees."

"Where did he go last night?"

"LA."

"Why?"

I hedged, "Business."

"Club business?"

"Personal business." I fudged the truth. "It's to do with Bear's will."

Her eyes widened. "Oh. Sorry for asking."

"It's okay. I didn't tell you anything that I wouldn't tell the club."

"Maybe you shouldn't? I know there are a lot of mutterings going on right now."

I reared back at that, which did nothing for my head. "Mutterings?"

"Men bitching about where he is. Asking when he's coming back. Link says Nyx is keeping things under control but he doesn't have Rex's finesse."

"Nyx and finesse are alien concepts. He's a sledgehammer to the skull, not just a fist."

"Rex is a knife to the heart," she agreed. "So maybe don't mention anything? I know people are on edge about Bear too."

"What about him?"

"His funeral. They want to put him to rest. Bear was popular."

"You don't need to tell me, Lily," I drawled then immediately regretted it when her cheeks flushed.

"Sorry, I forgot my place."

"Your place? This isn't a Dickens novel. I'm sorry I'm in a pissy mood. I just didn't need to—" I sighed.

The ring.

These so-called mutterings at the club.

It was too much.

Much too much.

"I get it. Sorry," she repeated with another wince. "I got caught up on all the gossip with Tiff this morning and I wanted to keep you in the loop."

Her words resonated deeply with me because, to her, I was the First Lady, even if Rex hadn't branded me yet.

"Thank you, Lily," I said rawly.

Her smile was genuine. "Apparently, Kendra left in the middle of the night."

"That cat got kicked out?"

"Tiff doesn't know, but Kendra's motel room's empty." She shrugged. "Unless Giulia killed her and buried the body with all her worldly possessions, of course. I don't think she could manage that with the size of her bump right now though. So I'm thinking she just took off. Maybe being puked on was the final straw?"

I couldn't stop myself from grinning at that, and Lily and I shared our amusement in a show of female solidarity.

I'd learned over the years that some clubwhores weren't all bad. Then, you got one like Kendra who epitomized every ounce of scum in the world.

It made it even harder to accept that that same woman was Rex's half-sister. Bear's daughter.

Not that I could tell Lily that.

Not that I could tell *anyone* that.

It was Rex's secret to share, if he ever wanted to.

Even as I was wondering how the hell Bear had let his daughter become a clubwhore, Lily was saying, "Anyway, those ideas I was talking about last night?"

"Ugh, we just finished one fundraiser. I need a break before I contemplate the next one." When her face fell, I rubbed my brow tiredly. Killing enthusiasm like that was a foolish move on my part. Myopic too. "How about this... You create a game plan, bring it to me so I can check it over, and we work from there?"

"Sounds great," she declared, beaming a megawatt smile at me. "I'll liaise with your events organizer. You don't have to do a thing!"

She proceeded to go off on a tangent about the charities and the parties, and why fresh flowers as table settings were a poor environmental choice...

By the time she stopped talking, my head was banging and I was relieved when, full steam ahead, she retreated from my office and left me in peace.

Not that I got to enjoy it for long.

Shortly after, Nyx stormed in, demanding, "Can we talk, Rach?"

This was the last conversation I needed to be having.

Sighing, I eyed the bruising on his jaw. "Sure. We should get our stories straight about last night anyway. You worked on that with Harlow?"

Nyx grunted. "Yeah."

"You picked up the cage and your bike from the pound?"

"I did."

"Who went with you?"

He stomped forward and took a seat where Lily had just been perched. Unlike her, he seemed to fill up the space with his size—his glower alone was bigger than Texas.

I arched a brow at him. "You'd think you'd spent the night in jail from that expression of yours."

That didn't lighten him up any as he snapped, "We got a rideshare to the city, okay?"

I tried not to laugh.

First Rex, now Nyx?

Clearly not a happy bunny—and that I was unsure if it was about needing to take a rideshare to cover their tracks or about last night's situation was a testament to how bewildering his priorities were—Nyx ground out, "I killed that fucker, Rachel. More than that, I was found standing over the goddamn body and Harlow was discovered watching me do it. Why the fuck aren't I being sent up?"

"Is that a complaint I hear?"

"No, it's a demand to know what the hell's going on."

I tapped my nails against the desk and murmured, "Funny how you're the one demanding to know what's going on when, from my side of the table, you need to be answering *my* questions."

"What do you want to know?"

"How about you tell me why I had an impromptu meeting with Aidan O'Donnelly Sr. last night, huh?"

"O'Donnelly Sr.?" Nyx's eyes rounded. "The Five Pointer?"

"*The* Five Pointer," I retorted, putting the stress on the appropriate word in that label.

"I knew I'd come to his attention," he muttered, scratching his stubbled chin. "But I don't get why he approached me this way."

That latter part was mumbled mostly under his breath.

Unluckily for him, I had great hearing.

"You sound confused."

"I am."

"Not angry, is what I meant," I rasped.

He shrugged. "Home, ain't I?"

I gritted my teeth. "What's going on, Nyx?"

"Around Christmas, I started getting some calls, a couple texts." He heaved a sigh. "It was always from *Unknown Sender* or *Unknown* so I never put much weight behind it. Then, one day, I got a picture of a bag of bones with a text: 'To incinerate or not to incinerate, that is the question.'"

"A bag of bones?"

He hummed. "Kevin."

Aghast, I demanded, "O'Donnelly Sr. was behind the theft of the body from the morgue?"

"Apparently. He said he took my problems away, and I was curious about what I was being fed. I didn't see any harm in meeting up with him."

Now he was calm, he was starting to piss me off.

When I thought about how he'd fucked up my evening, how Rex had been able to use him as an excuse to keep me on the East Coast, I could have throttled him.

"You didn't see any harm in meeting up with a stranger?" I seethed after he just stared back at me and didn't run for the hills. "A stranger who turned out to be the head of the Irish Mob? A stranger who, in fact, trapped you into getting arrested just so he could show you how much control he has over precincts and over measly things like homicide cases?"

"Yeah."

"Fuck, Nyx. I know you're a man of few words, but that's beyond a joke. According to him, he's got a list of perverts who need to die.

"He already knew about the promises you made to your family. He thinks they castrated you when they forced you to make that promise."

His scowl was immediate. "How the hell did that get back to him?"

"We have a bunch of men who cluck harder than hens in a coop, Nyx. Half the criminal underworld probably knows about your 'castration.'"

That had him snorting. "Castrating—"

"Giulia told me she thinks you're not coping well," I butted in before he could be dismissive.

"I ain't."

"Reassuring." I exhaled. "The fact you went there, period, tells me there's something going on with you that you aren't telling me."

"Temptation..." He grunted. "The temptation *was* strong, but I went there with good intentions."

I scowled at him. "Nothing about last night came from the angle of good intentions."

"*Unknown*, well, O'Donnelly talked a good game, but I wanted to..." He rubbed his eyes. "You know, before, Mav used to find me my kills. It worked out fine. I got to appease the beast, a fucker died, everything was good.

"But Mav ain't the same Mav. Every moment he's on the computer, it's shitty for his health. The MC needs him for more than just me getting my rocks off. This way, I figured, I'd have a new source for when Harlow and I go off on a hunt together."

"You did this to spare Maverick?"

He hunched his shoulders. "Do you know what Mav used to do for me?"

"No. I mean, I can imagine," I said uneasily.

"He used to verify each case. That meant scouring their computers for proof. Maverick's done more for me than even Rex has. It's no wonder his brain's fucked up. I probably didn't help."

"That isn't how CTE works."

His gaze remained fixed on my desk. "Who knows how brains really work. They can't cure him. They can't make him better. They can just make him find a base level and stick to that."

There were many things he could have said that wouldn't have soothed my temper, but his genuine guilt worked a miracle on his behalf.

These men were so fucking sensitive.

"He got blown up and shot at, Nyx. Then the clubhouse fell on his head." My hands flopped onto the desk. "I mean, that's why he's like this. The other stuff, it was bad, not going to say it wasn't. But that was more emotional, I'd guess?"

"Maybe that was why he kept his ass glued to a wheelchair for all that fucking time." He pinched the bridge of his nose. "Any-fucking-way, I thought I found an alternative."

"You did," I grumbled. "That's exactly what O'Donnelly wants. He'll provide you with the names and now, he's tied you in so you can't say no."

Nyx shrugged. "Don't need to say no. Harlow's gotta learn somehow."

My brow puckered. "You don't mind being exploited?"

"It was a power play. I knew that when I got on my bike to head into the city." He stared at me. "O'Donnelly *told* me that he could guarantee I wouldn't spend a night in jail. Looks like he means it when he doles out promises."

"You trust him?"

"We talked a few times. Texted a lot. He was always cagey, but he told me that someone in his family was molested." Nyx's jaw clenched. "I believe him."

I thought about the man I'd met last night and, slowly, nodded. "I can see that. He wanted righteous kills. Nothing less would suit. He's old school."

"Eye for an eye?"

"Yes."

"From the outside looking in, I know what he did seems fucked up. But from the inside, I wouldn't have believed him if he hadn't made it happen.

"Rach, I killed a man. Sure, I got arrested for it, and the police were clearly sent to that location to find me. But I'm free—"

"You weren't arrested for murder, Nyx. If you'd listened at the time you'd know that."

"Didn't think I needed to. Knew you'd get me out."

Of all the lazy...

"You were arrested for reckless driving and excessive speeding, Nyx."

"That's fucking power."

"Don't you dare sound impressed," I hissed.

He just smirked at me.

I narrowed my eyes back at him. "Rex isn't happy about any of this."

"No. Didn't think he would be. Doesn't like being outmaneuvered. You gonna tell Giulia about last night?"

"That's what concerns you?"

"She's my only concern," he said, and it was so effortlessly uttered that my pique of before faded.

Goddamn these Sinners and their devotion.

Despite my softening, I still had to call him out on his BS. "If she was, then you wouldn't want to go on the prowl, would you?"

"I would," he disregarded. "If her happiness hinges on my sanity, then my sanity is on the fritz." He reached up and rubbed his temple. "I can fucking feel it, Rachel. I don't want... Giulia should have a man worthy of her. I can never be that but the least I can fucking do is stay sane."

Concerned, I rasped, "This isn't the way forward, Nyx." Sanity couldn't be found in butchering pedophiles, for God's sake.

"It is." His tone was desperate. "It's always kept me steady. It's only once I went cold turkey that shit got bad."

Sighing, his desperation getting to me like little else could, I informed him, "I told Rex, and that's it."

"Why? Thought you and Giulia were friends now."

I blinked at his reasoning.

It was, dear God, *sound.*

Was I really friends with the raving lunatic that was Giulia Fontaine?

I didn't realize I'd zoned out until Nyx clicked his fingers in front of my face. The second he did, I jerked back then blurted out, "We are."

He snorted. "She gets you like that."

"Like what?"

"Like heroin."

"I'm not addicted to her," I drawled.

"I am," he said glumly. "Treated a lot of women like shit over the years, I know that. Know I was a jerk and that I deserved an ass-whooping, but I figure I'm being paid back with an ornery bitch for an Old Lady."

"She'd give you that ass-whooping you deserve if she heard you call her an ornery bitch."

"Naw, she's proud of it." His grin was sheepish. "Damn thing is, I love her for it. She won't take my bullshit without doling me some back. Needed a woman like her, you know? Someone to go head-to-head with me. Someone who wasn't afraid of me."

I pondered my next words, unsure if I should even utter them, but Giulia wasn't the kind of woman who cried and that she had, for this man, put me on edge.

"She isn't afraid of you," I agreed, the words falling from my lips slowly. "But of losing you? That scares her."

"She isn't going to lose me."

"I told her that."

His brows rose. "*You* told her that?"

"I did. When she was crying because Kendra said you'd been sleeping together."

I watched as his hands tightened around the armrests on his chair. "I'll deal with it."

"I'll deal with *you* if you cheat on her," I warned, but satisfaction filled me at *how* Kendra would be dealt with if she dared show her sorry fucking face at the compound again.

Something gleamed in his eyes, and it took me a moment to understand what it was—*appreciation*.

"I hear your warning and will be mindful of it," he said, his words beyond formal for a man who probably hadn't read a book since before he'd stopped bothering to worry about graduation.

"Good."

"I don't wanna scare her with what happened last night, Rachel. That's a different kind of fear. I won't have her thinking she's gonna lose me to a jail cell, either, because she ain't, is she?"

"I'm not going to say anything," I said easily. "And no, she isn't going to lose you because you're going nowhere. Not that I had any hand in that. It was all O'Donnelly Sr.'s handiwork. You've gotten entangled with the wrong man, Nyx."

"We're already entangled with him. We're allies," he pointed out.

"Then why did he approach this differently? Why lead you into a trap, get you arrested, then free you all in the same night?"

"Because he's a twisted fucker."

"He wanted leverage, and being allies isn't enough." I pursed my lips. "I know Harlow wants in on this hunting business of yours, and I think O'Donnelly Sr. will accept him as a willing tribute."

"So long as the fuckers die by someone who's earned the right to take their lives," Nyx drawled, a soft satisfaction lacing the words.

It rammed home what Giulia had told me back at the beginning of the year—Nyx's need wasn't dormant. It was there, beneath the surface, just waiting to burst free.

Like it had last night.

You'd never know that he'd killed a man.

You'd never tell that he had more blood on his hands.

I rubbed my forehead. "You need to make sure Harlow doesn't tell Giulia if that's a concern for you."

"That's dealt with. He won't say anything. He's not exactly fitting in, and what he did was stupid, so he knows he's lucky I'm not throwing him out."

"Why the hell *was* he there?"

"Wanted to hunt too."

If that wasn't disturbing, I didn't know what was.

"Wonder how this is going to work."

"What do you mean?" I asked.

"Is he gonna send names via snail mail? Is he going to give us cut off dates?"

'Cut off' being the appropriate words, I figured.

"I don't know."

"Guess we'll find out."

"I'm sure we will, but don't think it'll be easy. He's got you tied to him now," I warned.

Nyx shrugged. "I'm not afraid. This isn't business, Rachel. This is a different kind of vendetta.

"Even after everything that happened to you, I don't think you understand it. Rex might if you told him what you went through."

"I've shared that part of my past—"

"Then he'll get it."

Annoyed, I sniped, "So the victim wouldn't get it but a victim's loved one would?"

"Yeah. You endured it. It's your right to process that however *you* need to. But a loved one ain't got no horse in that race. We just sit by that person's side, try to make shit better, regretting that we weren't good enough to have kept them safe.

"We know that we're the reason victims were hurt. We know that we let them down—"

"That's ridiculous," I countered. "It wasn't your fault that Kevin hurt your sisters, Nyx."

A darkness overset his eyes. A flatness that would have disturbed a lesser woman. "One time, I told my father that Kevin was a creeper. Didn't say what he did. Didn't go into details. Just wanted to know what his reaction would be. Guess what it was?"

"Can't imagine it was anything good if you were the one who ended up blowing Kevin's head off, Nyx."

He nodded. "You'd be right. I got the beating, not Kevin. I should have made him listen—"

"You were a kid. That wasn't on you. Just like it wasn't on Rex that his uncle did that to me. Just like it's not on Giulia that her dad hurt me." I braced myself and, deciding to keep Rex out of it, confessed, "I overheard you talking with Bear at Carly's wake, Nyx. I, more than anyone, know you tried."

He jolted in shock at my admission, but his expression remained as frigid as ever. "Too little, too late."

Goddammit.

"You're all so busy taking the blame that you don't see that we don't need you to. That we're not *asking* you to. We want acceptance, kindness, understanding, not for you to avenge us.

"Not all of us want to look to the past. Some of us try to focus on the future because while the past can't be unwritten, that doesn't mean we have to lead our lives by it as if it were the gospel truth.

"I've let what happened to me define me for too long. I didn't even realize that was the case, Nyx. I thought I was..." I sighed. "I've attained all my career goals. After Grizzly and Dog raped me —" He had no idea how difficult that was to say out loud to him. "I determined that I'd never be in that position again. Never allow my station in the MC to dictate what other people might believe of me.

"I became a lawyer. I got power. I got riches. I made myself respectable, Nyx. I was so focused on never being *that* again that I didn't realize what I was missing out on—my friends. My family. Rex. My daughter." I blew out a breath. "Maybe that doesn't mean much to you because I'm not Carly or Indy and I'm not Giulia, but I wish you'd hear me on their behalf.

"You are *enough*, Nyx. Just as you are. You don't need to do anything else other than be their brother, their friend, their lover. That's all they need from you."

His jaw was clenched so hard that I was surprised his teeth didn't fall out. "So many Old Ladies have been—"

"Over forty percent of women in the US have encountered sexual violence, Nyx. Ninety-eight percent of rapists walk free without any accountability or consequences. America's a dangerous place for women. The council's just unfortunate that their Old Ladies are stacked against the odds."

My stats didn't ease him any. If anything, dammit, they made him more troubled.

"Some days, I think I'm gonna lose my mind," he rasped.

"What's sanity look like, Nyx? You going around the country killing people who belong in jail?"

His head bowed. "Waste of taxpayer money."

"That's why you do it, huh?" I mocked, amused despite myself. "Nyx, go and hang out with Giulia before that baby of yours pops out and causes me more trouble down the line."

"Can't cause all that much trouble as a baby," he groused.

"With parents like his, I wouldn't put it past him. Indy and Giulia will never hear from me what happened. Rex won't say a word. Last night was either a lucky break or something you let define you. It's your choice which road you take."

When he stalked off, the pressure in the room lightened as if there'd been a storm that broke the stuffy heat in here.

Reaching for the ring box Lily had given me, I twirled it between my thumb and pointer finger before I went to the kitchen to gather Rex's things.

As I took them upstairs to my room, what I hoped would become *our* room, I tucked the ring box back in his socks where Lily had found it then shook my head, accepting that I already knew which path Nyx would take.

Some men couldn't help themselves.

Some men were born to exist in the darkness.

SIX

REX

A whoop sounded from behind me, and I grinned as Wynter half clung to me and half pumped her arms in the air as we slowly made our way toward San Bernardino.

Though I was well aware that I was on a short leash with the Triads, especially with Wynter on the back of my bike, my time in California wasn't endless.

Wynter needed me, but Rachel was pregnant, and that kid needed me too. Not just because I had no idea how Rachel would deal with being pregnant this time, but because danger followed us around like shit on our shoes.

Ideally, Wynter'd move east to be with us, but I wasn't sure what she wanted.

Since the other night, she'd said painfully little, and only when I told her I needed to go on a short road trip, and asked would she like to come with, had she brightened up any.

When the key had arrived, I'd put this off but I had to go home eventually, and that meant I needed to get this off my back.

So, here we were.

On the road to meet a woman I never wanted to meet.

On the road to meet a woman my father had created a child with; a child who consistently wreaked havoc on my home.

This morning, when I'd asked Rachel for the subdivision and the woman's name via text, she'd tried to call me, but I hadn't answered. This was a chore I needed to complete—one final task from my father.

As I pulled onto Maria's street, it dawned on me why Dad had waited until his death to tell me about Kendra: I'd have shunned him and he knew it.

He'd done the unthinkable.

An allegiance I'd have protected with bloodshed, I was shoving aside because he'd broken it.

Anything he asked of me, I'd done—something I thought I'd proven with how he'd met his end—but once the bequests in his will were finalized, that was it.

It was over.

The house was small but respectable.

At some point, I thought an old Christmas tree had been planted in the front yard because it was taller than the one-story house, and on the veranda, there was a rocking chair. The siding was painted, and the roof was well maintained as was the garden.

Kendra's mother took pride in her home.

When we pulled up outside it and Wynter had stopped her whooping, the arms she'd slid around my waist for more support during the tighter bends to reach the house squeezed me.

"King, are you okay?"

I wanted her to call me 'Dad' again.

I knew that was bad. But I did. I couldn't help what I wanted. One day...

"I've been better, sweetheart."

"She might be nice," she offered.

"I'm sure she is." I cut her a look. "Doesn't take away from what she represents."

Wynter hummed. "Not her fault. It's your dad's fault. Or, at least, it takes two to tango, you know?"

"I know that more than most, but it does take two and she must have known he was married because everyone knew about Bear and Rene. They were the Sandy and Danny of goddamn West Orange."

She was quiet a second then, astonished, demanded, "Is that a *Grease* reference?"

"Ask Rachel about that summer when she watched it twice a day every day."

"Wow. Big fan?"

"Ironically enough, no. But that doesn't mean she's forgotten all the lyrics to 'Summer Nights.'"

My dry response had her chuckling. "Seems like someone else would know the lyrics too." When she nudged me in the side, I hid a smile.

"It's a little like water torture. Sticks with you after a while."

She snorted. "I'll ask her if you sang along with her."

"Why does that sound like a threat?"

"Because it is?" she rejoindered in a singsong voice.

I smirked at nothing, bewildered that she'd managed to make me smile on today of all days.

Deciding that I had to get this over with, I asked her, "You okay to get off the bike?"

She tutted. "I got my bike legs ages ago."

"It isn't like sea legs."

"It is," she argued, huffing as she climbed off and I kept the hog steady.

After, when I was standing on the sidewalk, I stared at the house again and released a rough exhalation.

She tugged on my hand. "Come on, King. You need to pull this off like a Band-Aid."

I cast her a look and rubbed at my eyes. "You shouldn't be here for this. I should have left you back at the hotel."

"Left me there thinking about Mom and the mess Dad has made of everything?" She sniffed. "I'd prefer to be here. Helping you."

I tugged back at her grip on my hand. "You're a good kid, Wynter."

Amusement lit up her eyes. "Not always."

"Oh, really?"

She grinned. "Really. But that's a tale for another time."

"Maybe a tale for never if you don't want me to have nightmares for the rest of my life."

"Big, mean guy like you having nightmares about me? I doubt it."

"You'd be surprised," I retorted, staring back at that fucking house.

Kendra's goddamn mom had better be in, that was all I was saying.

"What do you mean?"

I pursed my lips. "Seen shit, done shit that'd give most people nightmares."

I thought about the time Giulia had set fire to a pedophile in one of our Coshocton warehouses. His screams should have haunted my sleep for years. Not even that night, my skin still stinking of smoke, had I not slept like a baby.

"Only thing that gives me nightmares are you and your mother."

"Well, that's not very kind, is it?"

A bark of laughter escaped me. "No. It's supposed to be a plea not to terrify the living shit out of me."

"You mean to tell me you're okay walking into an apartment with three enemies and that won't scare you, but *I* will?"

"It's only the things that matter that can trigger fear. Fear of loss. Fear of failure. Fear of not being good enough. I'm not scared of the Triads. Not for myself. For you, sure. I *was* terrified. I wanted you out of there."

Her eyes were rounded but I saw the quiver in her lips and knew she was on the brink of tears.

Not that I could blame her.

The past week would have overwhelmed anyone—never mind a teenager.

Hauling my arm over her shoulder, I muttered, "I didn't mean to upset you."

"I know you didn't. I just... I never looked at it that way. I was raised—" She inhaled. "It might seem dumb to say this after what happened, but honestly, it was a normal childhood.

"BBQs in the summer and fireworks on July 4th. Pumpkins on the porch at the end of September and an inflatable Santa climbing the chimney on the first of December. Regular, *boring*.

"Nothing about your life is regular or boring. It's scary. But you weren't the one who brought those men into my apartment. Dad did. It's just tough to make sense of."

"It is," I agreed, settling my eyes on her, needing her to know that I wasn't running away from this conversation.

"Why do you stay in this world, King?"

"Because it's all I know. It isn't what you know, and while I tried to shelter you from it, Kinnock brought it to your door anyway. That's the problem with this part of society, honey. The darkness is always there, hovering, just waiting to overtake the light."

"You control the darkness?"

I pulled a face. "No one can control that. They might think they do, but that's hubris talking. Nah, I don't try to. I maintain a firm hold on *my* patch and that's it. I work hard to keep my men safe and in one piece and not in a prison cell. That's what I *can* control.

"I want the best for my people, Wynter. Always have. It's a dirty world, but we don't wear blinders. Most folk might think what happened to you is something that'd only happen in a movie. But it's not, is it?

"You're real, honey. You're from the side of society that has pumpkins on the porch and an inflatable Santa climbing your chimney at Christmas," I quoted. "Well, your—" I couldn't call him father. Not for the fucking life of me. "—Kinnock made shit worse.

"Our connection is why the Triads were at your place. I'm not innocent in this but I *am* in a position where I can make this better. That's why I prefer to have some control rather than to live in blindness."

"I can understand that," she whispered, her eyes still big.

I tugged her deeper into my side, hugged her, and mumbled, "You've got nothing to be afraid of, honey. I'll never let anything happen to you again."

"You'll have to go home at some point."

"I will, but I'll make arrangements."

I was still hoping she'd come with me, but I didn't want to pressure her.

I knew how teenagers worked. Pressure would do the opposite of what I wanted—it'd just push her away, not draw her closer. I'd made a promise to Rachel that I'd bring her back with me, but it might be one promise I wouldn't be able to keep.

I wasn't about to destroy the budding relationship we had with Wynter over this. She'd just have to have more guards than POTUS himself if I left her here.

"If I wanted to stay with you and Rachel, would that be okay?"

Containing my relief wasn't easy, not when her words almost made me sag with it.

Trying to sound as normal as possible, I murmured, "It'd be more than okay. You can do whatever you want to. You have options."

Peering up at me, she whispered, "I heard them talking. They didn't know that I can speak Mandarin."

I frowned. "You speak Mandarin?"

She shrugged. "Yeah."

Yeah.

Like that wasn't one of the most difficult of languages to learn.

"I also speak Russian," she chimed in, pride brimming from her.

Hell, I got it. I was proud as fuck too.

"You aiming for the UN?"

"Maybe. Not like your generation has managed the situation well."

I grinned at the burn but couldn't deny it. "Nah, we fucked it up for real." My smile died, though, as I asked, "What did the Triads say?"

"That Dad had given me to them." She stared up at me, the innocence in her gaze slightly tarnished now. "How do you give a person to someone?"

I wanted to tell her that I'd kill him for that. Wanted her to know that I would make him pay for making that offer, but how did I do that? How did I tell her that both her so-called fathers were monsters?

Gritting my teeth, I settled on, "You know in my MC, there's a lot of shit we do that's wrong. I won't try to hide that from you, even if I suggest you don't go looking into things. But we leave the skin trade alone—"

"The skin trade? He wanted me to..." She sucked in a breath. "He was going to...?"

"That was his intention. Some Triad groups are into that, not all of them though. We're lucky that Charles Xiang isn't or the other night could have ended a lot differently."

Wynter gulped. "How could Dad do that to me?"

Because he's a worthless piece of shit?

I didn't say that though.

I thought that was probably the fucking moment where I grew up for real.

Not bad-mouthing a man who deserved it to spare her feelings was about as self-sacrificing as could be.

It hurt; fuck, it did. But I managed to choke out, "Desperate men do desperate things."

She shook her head so hard that her hair whipped from side to side. "You'd never do that."

"No," I concurred. "I wouldn't."

"*Can* I then? Come and stay with you and Rachel, I mean?"

"I think your—" I heaved an aggrieved sigh. "I'm gonna end up calling Rach your mom, okay? You need to forgive me for that. I don't mean any slight against Ally, but it's a tough habit to break."

"It's okay," she whispered.

It wasn't, but she had to know if it slipped out, I wasn't being disrespectful to her adoptive mother.

Her adoptive dad could go for a really long walk off a very short pier for all I fucking cared.

"I was gonna say, Rach and I are together now."

I thought about the ring I'd intended on giving her last night. A part of me wondered if Lily had given Rachel the ring box or if she was safekeeping it for me. It was only when I'd left JFK that I'd remembered the fucking thing, and a quick call to the hotel assured me that everything had been cleared out.

"You're *together* together?"

I heard her excitement and had to smile. "We are."

"Why didn't you tell me sooner?"

"Because you passed out asleep the second I got you to my hotel and you've been quiet—" Read *moody*. "—ever since." I pressed my lips to her temple. "Let's see how the next few days go. You'll always have a place with Rachel and me. Always."

"You mean that?"

"I do."

She squeezed my waist. "Thank you."

"You don't have to thank me. I'm your dad, Wynter. We might not have a regular relationship, but all the best things in life are irregular anyway."

My kid grinned up at me. "That makes no sense."

"And you sounded just like Rachel," I teased which, surprise surprise, only made her grin widen.

I'd kill to keep that smile pinned on her face.

Maybe, in the coming days, that's exactly what I'd do...

It wouldn't be the first time I'd killed someone I was supposed to protect for my women.

Jeremy Kinnock, did he but know it, had a death sentence hanging over his head.

He'd sealed his fucking fate by offering *my* daughter as a bargaining chip.

Maybe not tomorrow, maybe not even next week, but one day, his death would be at my hand.

SEVEN

REX

Maria's initial reaction to the sight of me was fear.

Eyes gaping as wide as her mouth, tension making her as brittle as an overcooked wishbone, she shivered in front of me, whispering, "Grizzly?"

Wynter tugged on my hand when I didn't reply. "No, his name's Rex."

Rubbing her temple, Maria gasped, "Rex? Bear's... boy?"

If, with a night's stubble and a fresh haircut, I still looked like Grizzly, it was no fucking wonder Rachel thought I was him after a nightmare.

I was, it seemed, cursed with their looks.

And cursed was the right word considering her goddamn reaction.

"Yes. I'm Bear's son."

She whispered stiffly, "He isn't here."

Confused, I retorted, "I know he isn't. He's fucking dead."

"Rex!" Wynter grumbled. "That was uncalled for."

Maria shook her head. "No! Bear's not dead."

Seeing her disbelief, her grief, I swallowed down my bitterness and told her, "He is. He's..." I blew out a breath. "He died. On Christmas Day."

"He was here last year—"

He fucking was, was he?

"A lot can change in a year. I guess you don't talk with Kendra all that much anymore, do you?"

She tensed even more. "No. Kendra's a wild card, but I guess you'd know that seeing as she's spent most of her adult life with the Sinners."

I dipped my chin. "I do know that. I just don't understand how my father could have let his daughter whore herself out."

Sorrow had Maria's shoulders slumping. "He didn't know at first. Then, after, it was too late. Kendra's stubborn. She said she liked that way of life..."

"Dad would have stopped her if he'd cared."

Her breath hitched. "Kendra was a source of great shame to your father."

"Go figure seeing as I only found out about her after his death." I tried to contain my anger by retorting, "I only found out about *you* too. Seems you kept in touch with him after Mom passed away if he visited last year?"

It was ironic that her cheeks burned then, when Kendra's had stopped years earlier. Her mother retained an innocence that the daughter had long since lost.

"We were friends, Rex. I-I understand that you probably hate me, but I appreciate you coming here to tell me about his passing."

"Because you did it so kindly," Wynter muttered under her breath at me.

I refused to feel guilty.

"You knew he was with my mom," I rattled off, unable to hold the words back. "You knew and you still shacked up with him anyway."

"I had nowhere else to go and he helped me, Rex." Her mouth wobbled. "It wasn't like you think—"

"Somehow you made a baby, and unless the birds and the bees changed over the last couple decades, I know my train of thought is correct."

She made to close the door on me, and while that pissed me off, in her shoes, I'd have done the same. On the brink of turning around, leaving her the hell alone, Wynter tugged on my arm and said, "You inherited something from Bear. Rex can't go until he gives it to you."

Maria whispered, "I don't need anything from him."

My top lip curved into a sneer, but only Wynter's presence kept me from releasing my toxic bitterness out into the world.

My kid had one piece of shit for a father already. I didn't need to add to her woes.

It was hard, so fucking hard, but as pleasantly as I was able, I informed her, "Bear wanted you to have it."

I didn't wait around, just reached into my jeans pocket and pulled out the key Rachel had sent to me.

Shoving it at her, I said, "Whatever went on between you, it was enough for him to remember you in his will."

Unable to stay there much longer, I dragged Wynter away and tugged her along to the bike.

"I'm not like my daughter."

The words had me freezing in place.

"You can condemn me for falling in love with a married man, but I wasn't a home wrecker. The home was already wrecked, and he wasn't the one left raising a daughter on his own and with a broken heart too."

And with that, she closed the door.

"That question on the tip of your tongue... I think you were too much of a jerk for her to answer it for you."

I cast Wynter a glance, saw her disapproval, and asked the one question my kid always said 'yes' to: "Are you hungry?"

TEXT CHAT

Rachel: *How did it go? And before you bitch, I'm through with emailing. This is faster.*

Rex: *Whatever. It went about as bad as could be expected.*

Rachel: *Shit, really?*

Rex: *Really. I blew my top, and Wynter was there to see it. She doesn't hate me though. So there's that.*

Rachel: *I don't think kids work that way, do they? One and done?*

Rex: *Fuck if I know. I'm feeling pretty much one and done with MY dad.*

Rachel: *That's different.*

Rex: *From where I'm sitting, it isn't.*

Rachel: *She didn't ask to leave the hotel? Or ask to go back to her apartment?*

Rex: *No.*

Rachel: *That's something, right?*

Rex: *Not really. Would you stay in the dump where you were held prisoner for eight hours?*

Rachel: *No. But I don't think that's why she's there. You make her feel safe.*

Rex: *I do that to the Laker women.*

Rachel: *Lol. Tooting your horn springs to mind.*

Rex: *If I have a horn, the only person I want to TOOT it is you.*

Rachel: *Bahahahaha. You know I don't do that yet lol. You might not want my mouth anywhere near your horn. I could suck at it.*

Rex: *Key word there is YET.*

Rex: *And you could never suck at it. (I'm proud of how I'm refraining from teasing you about your choice of phrasing there.)*

Rachel: *:P*

Rex: *Minx.*

Rex: *You're a chronic overachiever.*

Rachel: *Maybe. I'll watch porn and try to figure out how to do it before you get back.*

Rex: *Are you trying to make this worse on me?*

Rachel: *LOL.*

Rex: *I'm gonna change the subject now because I can't call you and jack off to the sound of your voice when our daughter is watching a documentary ten feet away from me.*

Rachel: *The sacrifice of being a parent...*

Rex: *The sacrifice is fucking real, let me tell you.*

Rex: *ANYWAY, she wants to come back with me.*

Rachel: *That's GREAT news!*

Rex: *Maybe. I want to bring her home, but I can't see it happening. :/*

Rachel: *Why not?*

Rex: *Ally. She talked about her over dinner. They're close. I think leaving will be harder than Wynter expects.*

Rex: *I don't want to pressure her.*

Rachel: *I think that's the right move. Are you staying there, then?*

Rex: *No. I'm coming home.*

Rachel: *Thank God.*

Rachel: *I need to know she's safe, Rex, but I don't think I can do this pregnancy thing on my own.*

Rex: *You won't have to, baby. I swear, I'll make it right. I'll keep her safe. You have my word on that.*

Rachel: *Thank you. <3 I feel selfish but I, just, it's rough.*

Rex: *You're not selfish. It's traumatic for you. You're holding up like a dream, but you need your man at your back. I'm honored to be that guy. And hey, I WANT to be there.*

Rachel: *Did I tell you today that I love you?*

Rex: *Lol. Not yet. Love you too, sweetheart.*

Rachel: *<3*

Rex: *Just FYI, I told Wynter we'd be living together when I came back to West Orange.*

Rachel: *We've been living together for months.*

Rex: *You know what I mean. Are you going to have a problem with that?*

Rachel: *Which part of 'Where the fuck is my brand?' aren't you computing?*

Rex: *I'm glad we're on the same page.*

Rachel: *You're fucking annoying, do you know that?*

Rex: *It's good that you figure this out now rather than in forty years' time.*

Rachel: *We'll be dead then.*

Rex: *Not if I have my way.*

Rachel: *Does the Grim Reaper listen to you?*

Rex: *If he's called Cruz, he does.*

Rachel: *Note to self: live a good life so you don't get visited by Cruz.*

Rex: *Indy probably likes being visited by him. Lol.*

Rachel: *Yes, I learned that today.*

Rex: *How was the group meeting?*

Rachel: *Fine.*

Rachel: *Okay, that was a lie. It was DIFFICULT.*

Rachel: *Hearing about all the things everyone has gone through isn't easy.*

Rachel: *Nyx said something to me the other day. He was all up in arms about how so many of the MC's women have been abused, and I gave him the statistics to prove that we weren't alone.*

Rex: *Bet that cheered him up.*

Rachel: *Not really. That wasn't my intention.*

Rex: *I know what your endgame was, but I stopped trying to get him off that path a long time ago, Rach. Best wasting your energies elsewhere.*

Rachel: *Easier said than done when O'Donnelly Sr. is breathing down your VP's neck. I leveraged Harlow for Nyx. He better not make me regret that.*

Rex: *Harlow, if he knew, would be all in. You haven't told him yet?*

Rachel: *Nothing to tell. Nyx has agreed to keep a moratorium on this until you get back. When will that be?*

Rex: *I'm not sure. When Wynter's family's safe, I guess.*

Rachel: *Any news from Lodestar?*

Rex: *Could you hit her up for some updates?*

Rachel: *She's been quiet.*

Rex: *Unlike her.*

Rachel: *Yes. Maverick's positive so I don't think it'll be long.*

Rex: *That's what he told me. He's better at bullshitting than you think.*

Rachel: *That you believe he's capable of lying to me is hilarious.*

Rex: *You're a defense attorney. Not a lie detector.*

Rachel: *Need to be both in this job.*

Rachel: *I'll catch up with Lodestar, see if she can work some magic.*

Rex: *Thanks, babe.*

Rachel: *My pleasure.*

Rachel: *You said that Wynter wants to come back with you.*

Rex: *I did.*

Rachel: *If you CAN keep her safe, and she's torn... then maybe bring up school?*

Rex: *You're going to be the responsible parent, aren't you?*

Rachel: *Lol, I'm the one who paid attention in class and didn't consider every day a vacation. You're such a lucky bastard that you still got straight As anyway.*

Rex: *Luck is a fool's construct.*

Rachel: *Says you.*

Rex: *:P*

Rachel: *You told me you pay for her education. Is it a charter school?*

Rex: *Yes.*

Rachel: *Finding a school that lines up both curriculums at this late stage might be hard. I think if you tell her that, then she won't feel bad about staying with Ally.*

Rex: *I'm confused. Don't you want her to come back with me? I thought you did.*

Rachel: *I want her to be here if she's ready for that. If, right now, she thinks staying with her mom is the best thing then that's her decision. If she decides to come with you to New Jersey, that's her choice too. I want her to have options and I don't want her to feel bad for deciding to pick them over us.*

Rex: *So self-sacrificing.*

Rachel: *We going to get into an argument? Because if we are, then I've got better things to be doing with my time. You're pissy about meeting with Maria, I get it. I won't let you take it out on me.*

Rex: *Sorry.*

Rachel: *So you should be.*

Rex: *When's your next OB/GYN appointment?*

Rachel: *Two weeks.*

Rex: *I want to be there.*

Rachel: *Then you know what you have to do.*

Rex: *If she refuses to stay, I won't make her.*

Rachel: *I'm not asking you to. Jesus. I'm giving you an out for HER. Not you. She can come and visit during summer vacation.*

Rex: *When's the baby due?*

Rachel: *End of August/early September.*

Rex: *God, our lives are going to change, aren't they?*

Rachel: *They are.*

Rex: *How are you holding up?*

Rachel: *Better than before.*

Rex: *I'm glad.*

Rachel: *You can say it.*

Rachel: *I know you're relieved.*

Rex: *Of course I am. For your sake and the baby's.*

Rachel: *I need to tell Rain that I'm pregnant. Have you told Wynter yet?*

Rex: *No. Want to do it together?*

Rachel: *I'm concerned she'll be jealous that I want to keep this baby when I didn't want to keep her.*

Rex: *You said it yourself, Rach. She's a logical kid, and she knows the circumstances of her birth and this baby's are different. Throw reason at her, and she'll understand.*

Rachel: *Teenagers are highly emotional. Hormonal. I don't want to make things worse.*

Rex: *You won't. She wants to know us. Your being pregnant won't change that.*

Rachel: *She already knows you.*

Rex: *She knows parts of me. She hasn't seen me at the MC.*

Rachel: *Do you want her to see that side of you?*

Rex: *I can't push off my responsibilities forever. There'll come a day where she sees my true colors. I'd prefer to control how and when she's exposed to it.*

Rachel: *Do you think she'll be frightened?*

Rex: *I think she's frightened now. I think she's seeing me as the good guy in comparison to Kinnock, and I'm not above capitalizing on that.*

Rachel: *I can't blame you. It's weird how both of us want to impress her, isn't it? I was at the gala the other night, thinking about that last conversation we had about work, and I thought to myself THIS is what I need to show her.*

Rex: *I think it's a case of us trying to prove that we didn't waste our lives. We gave her up for adoption for a reason. Those reasons are justifiable now. We didn't piss those years away against the wall.*

Rachel: *No. We didn't. Rex?*

Rex: *Yes, babe?*

Rachel: *I miss you.*

Rex: *Miss you too. I swear I won't be long.*

Rachel: *If she elects to stay down there, how will you keep her safe?*

Rex: *Arrange for them to live in a gated subdivision. Have some allies watch over her more. Private guards, shit like that.*

Rachel: *That enough?*

Rex: *Don't see why not.*

Rachel: *Doesn't seem like it to me. Unless...*

Rachel: *You're going to deal with Jeremy Kinnock, aren't you?*

Rex: *Do you want to know?*

Rachel: *I think if there's ever a time to forget your morals, it's with that piece of shit.*

Rex: *She won't like me for it.*

Rachel: *Use your imagination.*

Rex: *Consider it done.*

Rachel: *If only you were always this amenable.*

Rex: *Lol, you wouldn't love me so much if I were easy.*

EIGHT

RACHEL

"Rachel?"

I frowned at Link. "You're looking at me like the Ghost of Christmas Past just showed up on your doorstep."

He grimaced. "Please tell me you're not here for Lily."

"No, I spoke to her earlier when I was here with the Posse." My nose crinkled as I realized he was looking sweaty. "Ew, Link. Why did you answer the door if you were otherwise engaged?"

"Because you kept your finger on the goddamn buzzer and I dismissed the staff for the day."

Lips curving, I retorted, "Those are words I never thought you'd say. 'I dismissed the staff for the day.'"

"Same here," he grumbled.

"You can carry on dining on Lily if you want. I'm here for Lodestar."

He made a sign of the cross on his chest. "There is a God. She's in her room."

He loped off without waiting for me to reply, and I grinned as I closed the door behind me. Every time I'd visited this place, Lodestar had been in the kitchen, but I knew she had a room on the second floor somewhere. How hard could it be to find her?

I got my answer twenty minutes later when I found that there was a separate wing at the back of the house that I'd yet to explore. When I heard girlish giggles, I thought I might be in the right place.

I'd yet to meet Katina, Lodestar's foster daughter and Alessa's baby sister, but I'd definitely heard her.

"Lodestar?" I called out at the top of a landing. "It's Rachel. Can I come and speak with you?"

A door opened at the end of the hall and a little girl smiled at me. "She said you can."

When she skipped over to me, then tumbled into a few forward flips, I blinked as, blowing her curls off her face, she held out her hand and introduced herself. "I'm Katina. Who are you?"

"I'm Rachel Laker."

"I know you." She beamed a smile at me. "You're Rain's sister."

"I am." I frowned. "You know Rain?"

She grinned at me. "Cyan has a massive crush on him. When I say massive, I mean it's the size of America."

Amused, I asked, "That big, huh?"

"Maybe even bigger," was her serious retort. "She didn't want to leave him behind when her mom made them move to Ohio, but I think it's romantic."

"You do?"

Her head bobbed up and down, those golden curls dancing with the movement. "It will make it so much sweeter when they come together again."

The words were oddly adult, as if she'd seen a movie she shouldn't have watched and memorized the lines. Seeing as her foster mom was Lodestar, that wouldn't come as a complete surprise.

With my hand tucked in her clammy one, she tugged me down the hall, chattering about how Cyan thought Rain had the nicest hair, giving me way too much information on the reasons why a pre-teen girl would consider Rain to be boyfriend material.

Grimacing, I was relieved when Lodestar barked, "Kat, are you running your mouth again? What will Cyan do when she finds out everyone in the MC knows she's got a crush on Rain and it's all because of you?"

Kat's cheeks flushed. "She won't know it's me."

"She will if I tell her," Lodestar grumbled, her face hidden behind a screen.

I took in the layout of the space and had to wonder why she preferred to work downstairs. Not only was it much bigger, but she had more than one computer in here.

"You wouldn't dare tell Cyan!" Kat shrieked.

"I would. Especially as you haven't cleaned up your room even though this is the fourth time I've asked you."

"If I clean it now, can we renegotiate the terms?"

My lips twitched.

"We can renegotiate the terms," Lodestar agreed. "If you can convince me that you've put one-hundred-percent effort into the job."

"What if I put in ninety-eight-percent effort?"

"I'll know." Her face loomed over a screen and the glow cast the gauntness in her cheeks and eyes into stark relief. "Remember, I know everything."

"You don't," Kat cried.

"I do." She smirked. "I know who your Rain is."

A horrified gasp escaped the little girl. "You don't!"

"I do. Haven't we established this already?"

"One-hundred-percent effort and you won't tell anyone?"

"I won't say a word."

Kat didn't hang around. She got the hell out of there and raced off to, I assumed, her own room.

When I turned back to face Lodestar, I saw she was watching me.

"We all have our own style of parenting."

"I see." I half-smiled. "Yours is definitely unique."

"What can I say? I'm creative."

"'Renegotiate the terms?' How did you keep a straight face when she said that?"

"It is a mouthful for her, isn't it?" She laughed. "But it's the only way to get her to do anything."

"Rain used to be like that. Had to lock him into a contract."

Lodestar arched a brow. "I forget that you had more than a hand in raising him."

"Axel died when he was still young."

"Your mom?"

I hesitated. "She's not been around for a long time."

"Want me to find her?"

"No. I doubt she's alive," I dismissed as I walked into the chaotic tangle that was several computer desks, each with a screen atop it.

The very air was stuffy from all the processors running, and there was a TV blaring something in a language I couldn't understand behind her. That oddly ozone-esque scent in the air reminded me of a lab.

In fact, with how Lodestar's hair was all over the place, she might as well have been a mad scientist.

"Irish Gaelic," she informed me when she saw where my attention had drifted. "I like to keep abreast of the news."

"In Ireland?" I asked dubiously.

"In Ireland," she confirmed.

"I didn't even know they had TV channels in Gaelic."

"That's because you're American. You expect everyone to speak English."

"Hardly," I argued.

"Why do you think she's dead?"

I leaped with her into the conversational direction she was taking. "Because she was a bitch. It was a wonder she survived as long as she did."

"Who do you think killed her?"

"Why do you care?"

"Says a lot about her if you don't care who killed her."

"It does."

"You think Rex did it?"

My mouth tightened. "Why would you ask that?"

"Seemed obvious."

I heaved a sigh. "I don't want to know if he did."

"Why? Would you blame him?"

"No, I might thank him. She left me in a lot of shitty situations, but I don't think she deserved to die for it. If he did kill her, then there's a reason for that, and I really don't want to know that either."

"Wouldn't have thought you were the kind of person who buried her head in the sand."

"After that first group session, you really don't think I'm an ostrich in a suit?"

Her lips twitched. "I guess."

"You should have come to today's meeting."

"Why?"

"It would help you."

"I don't need help."

"I doubt that. Everyone needs help from time to time."

She just grunted.

"I'm surprised you went at all."

"Was curious. Heard a lot about you. Know a lot more about what you're capable of." A gleam snapped through her gaze at that. "Wanted to see what made you tick."

"So, it was a fact-finding mission?" I queried, oddly disappointed.

"Maybe. Maybe I didn't want to be alone either."

I tilted my head to the side. "Is something wrong?"

"Nothing's right," she mocked, her attention drifting to her screen.

Unsure of how to answer that, I hovered in place until I blurted:

"I feel better, for what it's worth. I'm not saying I'm a different person," I added hastily, "but it feels less like a knot of heartburn and more like something I could vomit out."

Her gaze darted to mine. "That's better?"

Her suspicious tone made me smile. "It's better. Heartburn you have to wait out. Vomit, once it's in the toilet bowl, that's usually it."

"You've never had stomach flu, have you?"

I snorted. "I've had that and morning sickness. Trust me, heartburn can be so bad that it makes you vomit anyway."

She sniffed. "Why are you here, Rachel?"

"Did Hunter Lachlan call you?" I queried, not for the first time wondering how the pair knew each other.

When she shook her head, I grunted under my breath in annoyance.

If you want something done properly, do it your-fucking-self.

Still, I had priorities so I dealt with the real reason I was here first: "Rex wants an update on the location of the Chairman's boy."

"You're his messenger?"

"When required. It's urgent. My..." I paused. "My daughter's safety hinges on it."

"First time you called her that?"

"To someone who wasn't Rex, yes."

"You know, the MC has an abundance of rape survivors and shitty mothers—"

I tensed, prepared for the incoming insult.

Only, it didn't come.

"Amazing how you've dealt with both but you knew giving your kid up would be the better choice for her."

"Rex had more of a say in it than I did."

"I looked into you," she mused. "You were suicidal and self-harming *and* they were scared you'd kill her—"

"I don't want to talk about this. If you're trying to distract me, it isn't working."

Lodestar shrugged. "I'm a cunt, but I'm not that big of a cunt."

My lips twitched. "Good to know. Any updates?"

"Yes."

"What's the problem then?"

"No problem. I'll be passing the appropriate details to the Valentinis tomorrow."

"Why tomorrow? And why the Valentinis?"

"I'm still going through all the information, and because the Triads will investigate this. Let's not come under their radar, hmm?"

"All the information?"

"What?"

"You said 'all the information.' What information?"

"Do you really want to know?"

"I think I should, don't you?" I questioned.

Lodestar hitched a shoulder. "I already knew where the Triad boy was being held—"

Eyes flaring wide, I stormed over to her, demanding, "And you didn't tell the cops?"

"Well, no, Rachel," she sniped. "It's almost like ninety-five percent of the things I do are illegal."

I growled, "You could have told me. A kid's been in captivity while you dick around—"

"Do not mistake my lack of anticipated action for inactivity," she snarled, her jaw clenching as she glowered at me. "The reason I knew his location was because of a laptop the Valentinis sent me. That laptop contained a lot of information. I wasn't about to throw them the info and have them hold it against the Triad kid."

"The Valentinis aren't like that. Luciu is honorable."

"Oh, *Luciu* is honorable, is he?"

I frowned at her mocking retort. "He's a client."

"Thought the MC was your only client."

"That's none of your business."

"I'll bet it's Rex's."

"He knows."

She hummed. "If you say so."

"I do," I grated out. "Why are you waiting until tomorrow to tell the Valentinis about the boy?"

"Are you not listening or just being stupid? The laptop I was given housed enough data to keep an FBI department busy for the next three years."

"What kind of data in particular?"

She pursed her lips. "Why?"

"I want to know," I demanded. Rex called me the Queen of Loopholes, and well, I could scent someone with similar talents better than a bloodhound. "What did you find out? Blackmail material?"

Her eyes narrowed into slits. "You're good."

"Who?"

She shrugged. "A lot of prominent people."

"How did the Valentinis get that laptop? And why was the boy's location on there?"

"The people behind the Triad boy's kidnapping—it's a ring. The Valentinis broke into the ringleader's apartment. The Don appears to have a grudge against him. I can't blame him with the photos I found on the laptop."

"What do you mean?"

"His girlfriend's in a lot of compromising positions on there."

Anxiety prickled down my spine. "What kind of compromising positions?"

Our eyes met. "You can imagine."

I swallowed. "He forced her?"

"She was drugged."

Sick to my stomach, I staggered over to the nearest desk and slumped in the chair. "The ringleader's dead?"

"From what I've been told, he is. I think Luciu was behind his death. Bastard deserved it."

"You can't tell Luciu about those photos."

"Why not? That he has the laptop at all tells me he at least suspects his woman was abused. Plus, he's my boss, isn't he? At least, in this he is."

"It'll..." I hesitated. "It'll ruin everything for them. You don't need to confirm or deny that she was hurt."

"Not all men fear broken women, Rachel."

Something in her tone was like salt in an open wound. Which was ironic considering she'd defended Rex at the group meeting.

"Rex isn't the one who's scared."

"No?"

"No," I ground out, outrage flooding me. I welcomed it though. It was better than wanting to vomit. "He was there... I was the one who pulled away. Luciu is—" I thought about what I'd seen of them at the gala, how he'd bid on that ugly purse. "He's in love with her."

"He'll still love her after he finds out."

"Why risk it?"

"You can't play with people's lives—"

Anger had me jumping to my feet. "Talk about the pot calling the kettle black, Lodestar. All you fucking do is play with people's lives. Leave—" An ache exploded behind my eyes as a thought literally struck me. "Wait, the kidnapper drugged her and took photos?" More nausea hit me as I realized what that meant. These bastards never did shit like that just the one time. "There are more on there, aren't there? Not just Luciu's woman."

"There are," she confirmed, no dissembling.

In fact, her candor had me rearing back in reaction.

"That's the blackmail material, isn't it?"

My stomach wasn't just churning now. I darted over to the nearest trash can and I hurled. The breakfast I'd been proud to keep down, the lunch I hadn't forgotten, all of it went in the trash.

Panting in the aftermath, tired and feeling ancient, I wiped my mouth as I whispered, "You were going to blackmail the women in the photos."

She arched a brow and, without a shade of guilt, told me, "Only *some* of them."

My mouth wobbled. "How could you do that? They're like us—"

"Some of them are; some of them aren't," she bit off.

"What's that supposed to mean?" I spat.

"It means that not everyone was a seventeen-year-old babysitter,

Rachel," she snapped. "It means that some of them are important people who would serve us well to have in our pocket.

"I'm a survivor. I survived a lot of shit, and I will *never* be imprisoned again. But this is about more than just me. I have a lot of people to protect. This isn't about a bunch of women sitting in a prayer circle discussing what men have done to us. This is bigger than any of us.

"The Sparrows are dying, but for every one of those pieces of shit that dies, there's someone willing to jump into the vacuum. Don't be naive about that.

"When Steel brought Donavan Lancaster back from Cambodia, I knew what I was faced with—I have thousands of women to bring home. Thousands of women like *me*. Like Alessa. Like Amara. Like Tatána and Sarah, God help their souls.

"Women like Jennifer MacNeill have their own men who'll keep them safe, but what about the nobodies in Asia who are stolen from their beds to marry Chinese men whose idiotic government effectively legalized the culling of baby girls once upon a time?

"What about the Eastern Europeans and the Middle Eastern women who are commodities for the Sparrows? And make no mistake, those parts of the world still have Sparrows. They're just going by a different name.

"No, Rachel, if it means blackmailing some politician's wife or some businesswoman with what I have here, I'll do it because this is who I am.

"You don't have to like it. You don't have to approve. You have to accept that I've sacrificed a lot to be where I am, and I'll sacrifice a hell of a lot more to make sure that people *pay*," she growled, "for thinking that women are commodities. For daring to believe that no one is watching, that no one is listening.

"They will drown in their arrogance, and I will watch them choke and I will bring fucking Flamin' Hot Cheetos to watch the show because this will end with me.

"I will see to it, and no one, no *fucking* one, not you or Rex, not the NYPD or the Feds or fucking Interpol is going to stop me." She slammed her fist against the desk, making the monitor jump. "Do you hear me?"

"I think the whole house did," was all I said, placing the trash can on the closest table to me. Stepping over to her, I rested a hand on her desk and rasped, "You might freak the fuck out of the Sinners because they're blinded to what you can do, they just know you're too clever for your own good, but you don't scare me.

"You're slating the Sparrows for using women as commodities. What the hell are *you* doing? Just using them in a friendly game of checkers?

"I want a list of names, and it had better be goddamn thorough, Lodestar. I want every single one. I *will* read through that list and *I* will be the one who ascertains the files you can keep. Not you.

"You're not God, and to be frank, after that speech, I know you'll throw us all to hell, yourself included, if it's the difference between success or failure.

"If they're underage, they're automatically excluded. You will delete those photos. As for the rest, I'll be the one deciding."

"What the fuck makes you think I'll listen to you?"

I leaned into her, unafraid of the psychopath staring back at me because I'd been tangling with worse motherfuckers than her for two decades. "I'll have Katina thrown into a foster home faster than you can fucking curse me and your ass in jail for child endangerment and kidnapping."

She sneered at me. "She's Alessa's next of kin—"

"I know. She won't be in a home for long, but you won't be around to know, will you?" I straightened up. "I have no desire to separate Katina from her family, but she's the only person you seem to give a damn about."

"Threatening her was a bad move," she hissed, hatred flaring in her eyes.

"Threatening to burn down my house while we're all in it was a bad move on *your* part. I think this is what we consider a stalemate.

"Your fight is a just one, Lodestar, and I'll back you all the way to the goddamn Supreme Court if I have to, but you will not hurt my family. You will not bring the attention of 'important people' on my family, and you sure as fuck will not sacrifice them for this cause. Do *you* fucking hear *me*?"

With distaste in her eyes, she turned her focus back to the screen. "I'll have the list of names to you by tonight."

"Good." My jaw tensed. "Rex told me you know someone called Dead To Me."

She frowned. "I do."

"I want to speak with her."

"Anything else, your fucking majesty?" she ground out.

"No, that's it. Remember, Lodestar, this is a balancing act. I help you; you help me."

"Saying you'll take my kid away from me doesn't sound very balanced to me."

"I have resources. I'll use them to help you."

"What resources could *you* possibly have?"

"An underworld of fuckers, capable of things worse than you, on my cellphone. Each of them owing me a favor for getting them off of heinous crimes. My rolodex, as it were, is yours..."

Our eyes met, measured with our mutual anger, cold reason clashing with bitter resolve.

I wasn't a woman who believed she was better than anyone else, but I knew what I was capable of.

For the first time, I knew I'd met my match. But so, I recognized, did Lodestar.

"I'll have Dead To Me call you."

I dipped my chin, grabbed the trash can with vomit in it, and murmured, "Thank you."

TEXT CHAT

Charles Xiang: *Your help was most appreciated.*

Rex: *The boy is safe?*

Charles Xiang: *He is.*

Rex: *You've released the Kinnocks?*

Charles Xiang: *Yes.*

Rex: *Well? Where are they?*

Charles Xiang: *As of right now, Trinity Cross Hospital.*

Charles Xiang: *The Chairman was most grateful.*

Rex: *Glad to hear it. Lose this number, yeah?*

Charles Xiang: *Only a foolish man cuts ties with potential allies.*

Rex: *You threatened my daughter.*

Charles Xiang: *I threatened her worthless parents.*

Rex: *Who told you I was related to Wynter?*

Charles Xiang: *Our children attend the same school.*

Rex: *Jesus. Loose lips.*

Charles Xiang: *Indeed. I meant it when I said I'd never hurt her. There are many of my brotherhood who might have, but I am not of their ilk.*

Charles Xiang: *Believe me when I say this: we could be of help to each other in the future.*

Rex: *I won't lose your number.*

Charles Xiang: *Good.*

Rex: *Just leave my fucking family alone.*

Charles Xiang: *You have my word.*

Rex: *Is that worth much?*

Charles Xiang: *How much is yours worth?*

Rex: *Guess we're both going to find out, aren't we?*

Charles Xiang: *Indeed.*

NINE

REX

"Thank you for coming with me, King."

With how I'd spent the second half of last year, I was no stranger to hospitals.

That didn't mean I was eager to return to one, especially when Jeremy Kinnock was the patient.

Still, Wynter needed me, so here I was.

"You don't have to thank me," was all I said, my voice gruff.

I meant it. No thanks were necessary. But neither was I about to break out in welcoming grins when I clapped eyes on the fucker who thought he could offer up *my* daughter as collateral for his debts.

With the Chairman's kid back home, the Kinnocks had returned to their humdrum lives with little fanfare.

Ally was no worse for wear, but after a call with her mom, Wynter had told me that Jeremy's injuries were bad.

A smile danced on my lips at the thought.

I'd left him with a couple broken bones and bruises, but the Triads were particularly adept at gifting invisible injuries.

The fucker would be pissing out of a tube for the next six months.

Almost whistling under my breath with glee at the thought, I strode into the hospital room with her and came across a wan Ally who was trying to sleep in one of the uncomfortable chairs that were the same the world over.

I could have told her that there was *no* comfortable way to catch some Zs on those torture devices, but I didn't waste my breath.

Wynter's fingers tightened on mine before she tugged hers free. I let her go, feeling...

Fuck.

It was stupid.

But I felt the crack appear between us, the genesis of a chasm as she wandered over to Kinnock's bedside.

As predicted, he wasn't overly bruised. What was there lingered from when I'd beaten him, but he *was* pissing in a bag and he had casts on all four of his limbs.

I hoped the Triads had done some serious damage to his system— the fucker deserved it.

Shoving my hands into my pockets, I watched as Wynter's bottom lip trembled. She moved around the foot of the bed and placed her lips gently on Kinnock's cheek.

A soft breath gusted from him, but he didn't wake up.

I collected his chart and peered at it. When I couldn't make out half the shit I was reading, I took some photos and sent them to Stone for analysis.

Ally's eyes popped open at the sound of my camera clicking, but she saw Wynter first. "Wynter, baby," she rasped.

Her hands were outstretched for her, and Wynter dashed around the bed, dropped to her knees, and slipped her arms around Ally with an immediacy that made me feel the chasm widen some more.

At that moment, I might as well not have been there.

I knew what Rachel would say—these were her parents. They'd been there for her since she was little. I, on the other hand, was still a stranger. It was the first time I felt that way though. As if I were intruding in her life.

It sucked.

Shit, it more than sucked. It fucking *hurt*.

Annoyed by my stupid emotions, I backed out of the room. My beliefs were rammed home when she didn't look up at me once as I retreated to the waiting area.

For a couple minutes, I didn't do much else other than pace.

Then, when I decided I'd sound like a real fucking wimp if I bleated to Rachel about how I felt pushed out, I chose to be proactive.

Maybe I was jumping ahead of myself, but in my gut, I knew what was gonna happen.

I'd been hopeful, and had thought Rach was being negative, but in actuality, she was a realist.

Wynter wouldn't be coming back with me.

Not within the next week or so anyway.

That meant I had shit to do and not a lot of time to do it.

I had to find them a secure address, and I needed to make sure the Triads were genuine when they claimed they no longer held any interest in the Kinnocks.

I didn't have to worry about Kinnock and gambling, not with the fucker laid up, so that was something.

The urge to snatch her away, to drag her back with me was strong, but I couldn't.

Whatever time she gave me and Rach was a blessing, a gift. She could remove herself from our lives so easily. She owed us nothing. So I had to take it carefully.

Fuck, I hated that.

I was the President of the goddamn Satan's Sinners' MC. I didn't do shit carefully. I had the power to handle situations with a jack-hammer, not a scalpel.

My cell buzzed before my temper could explode.

Spying Stone's name on the Caller ID, I picked it up and told her by way of a greeting, "You could have just texted me."

"Who did that chart belong to?"

"Acquaintance of mine."

She grunted. "You shouldn't have taken photos of it."

"Shouldn't do a lot of shit. What did it have to say?"

"The guy has cirrhosis of the liver. Combined with that beating, he's gone on the list for a liver transplant."

My brows rose. "Cirrhosis of the liver's from drinking, right?"

"Yeah. That's the most common trigger."

From what Wynter had told me, that didn't come as much of a surprise. It wasn't a big stretch to think that Kinnock was into booze *and* drugs if the guy came back from nights out with a temper fierce enough that he beat on Ally.

Not that Wynter had told me *that*.

The Disciples had when they'd confirmed that the cops had been called in for domestic violence at their place.

I didn't give a damn about Kinnock's liver. In fact, I'd do everything I fucking could, including bribing Lodestar, to get him shoved down to the bottom of the list of organ transplants every fucking time he surged up on it, to make sure that he never left his hospital bed. If he was stuck in here, it wasn't like he could get drunk or high or go and gamble at the mahjong clubs.

"You gonna tell me who the patient is to you? I mean, the chart tells me it's Jeremy Kinnock, but who the hell is he and why are you sending me his chart?"

"No."

"Wasn't the school QB a Kinnock?" When I didn't answer, she grumbled, "Fucker."

"That's me."

"It sure is. When are you coming home, jackass?"

"I'll be back soon. That's all that matters. Was there anything else on the chart?"

"Some internal bleeding from the beating. He was intubated until yesterday after a procedure."

"He's pissing into a bag."

"Yeah. He'll be doing that for a while. There's damage to the penile tissue too."

I smirked at nothing. As a guy, I should be wincing in commiseration. Instead, I felt nothing more than satisfaction.

I liked how Xiang worked. Maybe we *could* get along well together.

"Good to know."

"It is?" She snorted. "Not for him, the sorry fucker."

"Nothing 'sorry' about him." In more ways than goddamn one. "I'll speak to you later, Stone."

"You'd better. You've had us all worried. Take care, Rex. See you soon, I hope."

She didn't let me reply, just ended the call.

One side of me was glad about what I'd just learned. The other side knew that Wynter's bleeding heart was gonna be broken.

And I wasn't wrong.

Later that afternoon, she came out of Kinnock's room on legs that seemed to be unsteady.

Elbows on my knees, I'd spent most of the day crouched over my cell, trying to find her a suitable place to live that was close to school, so when she sunk into the seat beside me, I didn't have the opportunity to hug her.

I didn't consider myself a hugger.

But fuck, Wynter opened up a side of me that not even Rachel had breached.

I was her dad.

I wanted to fucking hug her.

Seeing the devastation etched into her expression, I heaved a sigh when I knew she'd learned that her dad had fucked up his liver.

It almost made me feel bad for what I was going to do to Kinnock, but not bad enough.

She could forgive him.

I wouldn't.

"You okay?" I asked gruffly, watching that quivering mouth that made her whole head shake as she tried not to cry.

She sniffled. "Been better."

"Want to talk about it?"

Her gaze collided with mine, and for some reason, that was when she let go.

Massive tears burst free and it set off a quake in her system that made her whole body shudder with the ferocity of her grief. She didn't argue when I jostled her into sitting on my lap and didn't complain when I wrapped my arms around her waist and hauled her close.

Wynter just buried her face in my neck and wept for the man who didn't deserve her tears.

As for me?

One day, she'd lose me too. One day, she'd cry. One day, I vowed to be worthy of those tears she shed on my behalf.

TEXT CHAT

Aurora: *He's getting out!!*

Rachel: *What? Who is? You don't mean your great-uncle, do you?*

Aurora: *I do! Currau's coming home!*

Rachel: *The hell?*

Aurora: *I just got the news. Thank fuck! He's dying, Rach. He's fucking dying, and they're letting him out to die, but that's okay. That's better than him being in that shithole at the end.*

Rachel: *Yeah. It really is. This is great news!*

Rachel: *TTYL? I got an appointment.*

Aurora: *Sure, me too. Just needed to tell you.*

Rachel: *I get it. So pleased for you, sweetheart. Know you've been fighting this for a long time.*

Aurora: *xo*

TEN

REX

"You were born and raised in West Orange, Kinnock. What about your childhood made you think you could ignore the warning of a Sinner?"

Kinnock's eyelashes fluttered as if he were still unconscious, but I knew that was bullshit.

I'd been leaning against the wall, watching the man who my daughter had gifted her loyalty to, stare up at the ceiling.

I'd been so fucking quiet that he hadn't even known I was there.

Most of the nurses didn't know I was here either.

I'd crept into the bathroom and had stayed there until it was the early hours, just waiting for this moment.

"You can pretend with Ally and Wynter that you're sleeping, but I'm not as inclined to believe you," I drawled, boots clipping against the linoleum as I moved over to the bed. "You can't face them, and you're being a dick about it. That you just tensed up told me your ears are working fine."

Not stopping until I was looming over him, I watched his eyes pop open to glower into mine.

Irritation masked his fear.

Poorly.

"What the fuck are you doing in here?" he ground out, his voice raspy from misuse. "If you even think about touching me, I'll press the alert button!"

"With which set of broken fingers, huh?" I mocked, smirking at the warning which was when my hand snapped out and I pressed my thumb to his eye.

The lid darted down then widened as he tensed and froze in place when my hand didn't move. Against the pad of my thumb, his eyeball was wet. The eyelashes were crispy.

"W-What are you doing?" he whispered, preternaturally still, and not just because he sensed there was a predator in the room with him.

Kinnock was unable to defend himself seeing as the Triads had shown their displeasure by breaking a bone in each of his limbs.

That they'd left a mark at all was sign of their displeasure with the man.

I wasn't sure I believed Xiang when he claimed he wasn't in the skin trade, but I could be grateful he preferred to deal in favors rather than underage girls.

"What does it feel like I'm doing, Kinnock?" I breathed, looming over him as my thumb slowly pushed into the socket. He began choking, his head starting to whip from side to side, the heart rate monitor on his chest beginning to surge.

I ignored it all.

My thumb was inexorable.

Down, down, down, I pressed.

Soft flesh conceded to my force as I growled, "You think I'd let you get away with trying to *sell* my daughter?"

"I-It wasn't like that," he croaked, his forehead butting forward to try to dislodge my hold.

It didn't work.

A soft scream escaped him just as his heart monitors went wild.

I immediately pulled back, watching him pant and strain to

collect his breath, his head tilting down as if he could shield his eye from me.

"You do anything to endanger my daughter again, Kinnock, I'll scoop out your eyeball with a teaspoon and force-feed it to you," I hissed in his ear, just in time to back away as a nurse came bustling in.

I shot her a winsome smile. "He got overexcited when I told him last night's scores... I'll get out of your hair though," I said before she could chide me.

And I made my exit.

Kinnock had better heed my warning or he'd spend the little time he had remaining blind.

EMAIL EXCHANGE

From: K1ngS1nn3r1@gmail.com
To: Rach3lLadyLiberty@gmail.com

Subject: Wynter

You knew this would happen, didn't you? All that bullshit about giving her an out if she needed it... You knew she'd pick them.
K

From: Rach3lLadyLiberty@gmail.com
To: K1ngS1nn3r1@gmail.com

Subject: Re. Wynter

She's staying?
R

From: K1ngS1nn3r1@gmail.com

To: Rach3lLadyLiberty@gmail.com

Subject: Re. Wynter

*She is. Kinnock got worked over by the Triads. When
the doctors were treating him, they found he has
cirrhosis of the liver. The bastard needs a liver
transplant.*
She wants to stay here until he gets a liver.
She wants to stay even though he tried to sell her.
Fuck.
*Anyway, my plans have changed. I'm on my way
back. I'll go through Coshocton and spend the
night at Storm's.*
I love you, Rachel.
I love our kids.
*Somehow, you're the only people who can piss me off
more than anyone else fucking can.*
K

From: Rach3lLadyLiberty@gmail.com
To: K1ngS1nn3r1@gmail.com

Subject: Re. Wynter

*Don't be too harsh on her. He's her dad, King. I under-
stand why you're mad, and I also understand why
you didn't call me because you knew I'd tell you
that and you didn't want to hear it, but it's the
truth.*
*As much as I'd like to cut off his balls, to Wynter, he's
the man who put her to bed as a kid and read her
bedtime stories.*
He's her dad.

Our role isn't the same as theirs.

Jeremy doesn't deserve her. Maybe, in time, she'll realize that. Maybe she won't. It's one of those life lessons, honey, that we shouldn't have to learn but do.

She's got a good heart—that's something we should be thankful for.

I'm guessing you found them a safer place to live?

Ride safe on the road and call me when you get to Storm's.

I love you.

This isn't the end of your relationship, King.

Have faith.

<3

ELEVEN

REX

When I pulled up outside Storm's place, he greeted me with a twelve-gauge.

"Rex? Where the fuck have you been, you dipshit?"

Not sure that I blamed him for his anger, considering the circumstances.

Storm and I were close. Closer than fucking close, in fact. I hadn't talked to him since Dad died though. Hadn't mentioned shit to him about where I was, hadn't said dick period.

I watched him study me and had to grimace.

I knew he'd probably have been able to forgive me if I'd looked like a pile of shit, but I was mostly clean-shaven—was getting into the habit because I knew I was gonna spend the rest of my life making sure I in no way looked like Grizzly—and I even had a tan from the California sun.

Was I surprised when he stormed out of the front entrance and before I had the chance to greet him, he punched me in the shoulder? Nah. I *was* surprised that he hit me hard enough to shove me on my fucking ass.

As I went flying, he loomed over me, snarling, "Well? Where the fuck have you been?"

I didn't bother standing. If anything, I didn't have the energy. The ride from Cali had taken its toll, sure, but leaving Wynter behind in that den of soul-sucking fuckers had drained me more than anything else had.

I'd left a piece of me back there, just as I'd left a piece of me in Jersey, and it didn't feel right.

I didn't feel whole.

I was tired of feeling like that as well. I'd spent most of my adulthood knowing I'd lost a piece of me, and it shouldn't be that way now.

Uncaring that I was lying in the snow, I stared up at him, watching him watch me. Maybe he'd kick me, maybe he'd smack me around some, but at that moment, I didn't particularly give a fuck.

Maybe I even wanted that.

Storm was part one of my coming home.

I knew that for part three—when I went back to the MC—I'd be in for a doozy of a greeting as well.

Only part two wouldn't suck donkey balls.

Disappointingly, Storm didn't beat on me further, just sighed then plunked his ass in the snow beside me.

Not only that, but he joined me by lying back on the frozen grass and staring up at the miserable sky.

It was a shitty day, in a shitty week, in a shitty fucking month.

The only thing that had gone right was Rach and me, but the world was so much fucking bigger than us. If it wasn't, everything'd be right in it, but nope, we were just two small cogs in a bigger fucking machine.

I wasn't sure why the first thing I said was, "Kendra's my half-sister," but damn, it felt good to get that off my chest.

There was Wynter to discuss, Rachel too, but Kendra was a mutual sore spot between Storm and me, and this confession felt like a load off.

Unfortunately for me, Storm didn't leap to his feet and start screaming and shouting about Dad being an adulterous fuckwit. Neither did he defend him.

He stayed silent.

Fucking silent.

"You knew?" I rumbled after a few seconds, head rocking to the side. A part of me hoped he'd say he didn't know dick, but he just released a long exhalation.

"Found out a few years back."

Like he'd shot a lone bullet into the sky, one that had all the birds in the vicinity darting into flight, my brain raced. Each bird a memory. Each memory revolving around the many times I'd grumbled about throwing the bitch out.

"That why you never let me toss her out?" I groused.

"Well, it wasn't because I was in fucking love with her."

"I thought that was why." I'd been half-certain at one point he had deep and real feelings for the bitch.

"I know. It was easier to let you think that."

I rolled my head to stare at him. "I can't believe it."

"Trust me, Bear didn't believe it either—"

"Why did he confide in you and not me?"

"Because I asked him if he'd ever cheated on your mom, and I wanted to know how he made it right."

"Christ," I said with a hiss. "I-I guess I thought he was faithful, which is crazy—"

"Why is it crazy?"

"The point is moot considering he *did* cheat on Mom."

"No. It isn't inevitable that people will cheat. You think Nyx is gonna cheat on Giulia?"

"No, she'd chop his dick off. He ain't as insane as everyone thinks he is."

He snorted. "Link wouldn't cheat on Lily, Sin on Tiff, Mav on Alessa, Steel on Stone... They're in it." He emphasized the word 'it.'

"Never seen a man more all-in than you, Storm. But you fucked it up." I still wasn't sure how he'd done that when he was obsessed with Keira, but fuck it up he had.

"I did," he agreed grimly.

"Anyway, I thought he'd have wrapped that shit up at least. Christ." I grunted under my breath as I rubbed my eyes with the butts of my hands. "That why you always steered me away from her? Not that I liked her toxic cunt. She was always mooning after you, anyway. Those fucking cow eyes were a turn off.

"Plus, I've always been more discerning than most of you bastards." My dick was one and done for Rach, after all.

I'd never been more grateful for that than right this goddamn second.

"You never fucked her? Ever?"

"No. Can't say I picked up on a vibe or anything, just always hated the bitch. Thank God, huh? Man, that'd be fucked up. Even for the Sinners."

"True dat."

"Storm?"

"Yeah?"

"Why did you do that? Why did you fuck it up with Keira?"

His mouth tightened. "Didn't mean to."

"Just fell on Kendra? X marks the fucking spot?"

"No. I didn't fuck around as much as everyone thinks. It happened, often enough that I'm goddamn ashamed, but it was never me just getting off for the sake of getting off. I was always high.

"Don't forget, I wasn't using all the time. Most of my marriage didn't pass by in a fucking blur."

"No. Because I used to throw your ass in the Fridge," I reminded him.

He pulled a face. "Thanks?"

My laugh was short. "Trust me, I hated doing that as much as you hated me for it. Wasn't about to let you ruin your life though."

"I appreciate that, brother," he rasped, meaning it less in the MC way and more fraternally.

I knew that because I rumbled, "I wish you hadn't messed shit up with Keira."

"Me too."

"I don't even know why you fucked them. You had blinders on ever since you met her anyway. Never seen a dipshit more head over heels than you."

"I used to think I was fucking Keira," he managed to choke out.

I stilled. "You kidding me?"

But, fuck, there was a bizarre kind of logic to that, wasn't there? Storm was as insane for Keira as I was for Rachel.

Christ, I breathed Rachel, and Storm was the same. My security efforts could be considered moderate in comparison to his. I just had her driver guarding her. Storm had someone tailing Keira at all times. And I meant at *all* times too.

"No. Wish I were," he said gruffly, making me realize how hard this had been to tell me.

"That's messed up." Beyond messed up.

"I know."

"Jesus."

We shared a look. A single fucking look. It was loaded with his discomfort, *his shame*, and I knew.

I knew what he wasn't saying, what he couldn't verbalize. Knew what he *wouldn't* say because this shit 'didn't happen' to men.

Men weren't raped.

My hands tightened into fists.

That bitch. That goddamn bitch.

My blood. My fucking blood. She'd done this to Storm. *She'd raped him.*

I'd hated her before—hell, hatred was too small a word to encompass the feelings that woman triggered in me—but now, I could have slipped my hands around her neck and choked her to fucking death.

She'd raped my brother.

The man who wasn't my blood but might as well have been. I felt more for him than I ever would for that cunt with whom I shared DNA.

Silence fell between us, and I let it because I wanted so goddamn badly to jump on my hog and hunt that cunt down.

My fists tightened as I fought the urge. I was exhausted—that was one of the reasons I'd stopped here. I wanted to catch up with my brother, a fellow Prez, but also, I needed a break.

I didn't have the energy to play Whack-a-Mole with my half-sister.

Not yet anyway.

"You remember when your mom had that miscarriage?"

Surprised at the change of topic, I hissed out a breath. "Yeah. I remember. She froze us all out."

Christ, that year had been hell.

One of the worst in my childhood.

The MC life might have been crazy, but my family was happy. Always had been. Mom and Dad had been tighter than tight until she'd gotten pregnant and had lost the kid.

We'd almost lost Mom too.

She'd gone so far in on herself that I didn't know if we'd ever get her back.

She'd lie in bed most days, either staring at nothing or watching endless amounts of daytime TV. I knew more about *Days of our Lives* because of her than I wanted to.

Back then, I'd given a damn about school and homework, so I'd go in there, sit on the floor next to her bed, and study.

To this day, I didn't know if she'd ever even noticed my presence.

"About eleven months into that, your dad got a girlfriend. Got her a place in town—"

"Holy shit," I rasped. "How do you know this?"

"We only ever talked about cheating that once. Second your mom was back to herself, he got rid of her. Paid her to leave. Kendra came back because she said she was the daughter of a clubwhore. She didn't tell him until after Rene died."

"Christ."

"Yeah."

"How old were you when you found out?"

"Twenty-seven?" I could tell it was a guess from his tone. "It was a few months after Keira gave birth."

"When Keira left you again?"

He sighed. "Yeah."

"Why did she keep leaving you?"

"Because she had sense?"

"Bullshit."

"Because life wasn't as pretty as she thought it would be," he said simply.

"What happened? Why did she come back?"

"I don't know. She just came back like she usually did."

Yeah, Keira was like a yo-yo.

I'd say it was weird how Storm and his wife were around each other, but who the fuck was I to judge? Rachel and I had never fallen out of love and yet we'd spent the last two decades apart. It wasn't as if we were going to win an episode of *The Newlywed Game.*

Still, this wasn't about Rach and me. Wasn't about him and Keira. It was about Dad.

My cheating fucker of a father.

I thought about the man I'd believed Dad to be, and I wondered out loud, "Did he know his girlfriend was pregnant?"

"No. He found out when Kendra gave him a birth certificate. I think she knew no good would come of that news being brought into the light while his Old Lady was around. At least, I think so. Never spoken to her about it."

"He believed her?"

"I think Kendra's mom was a good woman."

He was right. More to myself, I mumbled, "Christ, irony."

"Yeah. She bred a viper."

"Probably Dad's intervention. His DNA probably made her a cunt."

When he snorted, I rolled upward, resting my arms on my knees to stare over at his house. "Dad's kid or not, she deserved to be kicked out of the club for what she did to Keira."

"I know she did."

"Then why didn't you let me? Why, when Link raised the subject, did you come to me and tell me not to?"

"I was looking out for future Rex. I knew when you found out, it would mess with your head if you'd kicked her out."

"Maybe," I said slowly.

Did I really give more of a fuck about some bitch who just happened to share blood with me over the family I'd been raised with?

No.

"Being my half-sister don't give her a free pass to be a cruel bitch, Storm."

"You can say that now," he rumbled. "But you might not have done before."

Was he right?

Why did I feel like there was a parallel here with Wynter and her family?

"Why didn't you just fucking tell me?"

"Because Bear asked me not to."

Anger rippled through me. "Do you know what I don't understand about you?"

"What?"

"How someone so fucking honorable can get himself into so much shit with his wife."

"I wish I had an answer to that."

"Me too," I snapped. "Rachel read me Dad's will. It wasn't official because he had a lot of bequests but..." I blew out a breath to try to calm myself down. "He left you something."

"What?"

"Don't know. Rachel does, but she wouldn't say."

"We've been waiting on the funeral for you."

I rocked my head. "Had to get away."

I could feel his disapproval as he muttered, "Couldn't have left a message?"

"Checked in with Rachel from time to time." Understatement.

"She never said anything."

I scraped a hand over my jaw. "Talked to her as the club's lawyer." *Lies*, but I didn't want to discuss us just yet.

"Where you been?"

"Does it matter?"

"You're lucky I didn't beat your ass."

"Instead, we're gonna freeze it off, huh?"

"Yeah," he retorted as he joined me in sitting up and staring over at his house.

His phone buzzed, and I watched as he pulled it out of his pocket to check the notification.

Jump: *Want me to stop this before it starts?*

My brows rose at the sight of the picture on his screen. Keira was kissing some guy.

"You still having her followed?" Was I altogether surprised about that? Nope.

"What the fuck do you think? 'Course I am."

"Poor goddamn Cyan," I mumbled. "Let me guess, you got her being tailed as well.

"Where the fuck did you go wrong, Storm? Jesus. It's not like you even 'see' other women. Just... Please tell me you weren't like Dad. Please tell me you used a condom."

"Of course. I always use a condom."

Something in his tone had me frowning at him. "Even with Keira?"

"Especially with Keira."

"Huh." I waited a beat. "Why?"

"Because I don't want to risk her getting pregnant again."

Though sympathy filled me, I remarked, "She ain't gonna die in childbirth, Storm."

"How do you know that?" he rumbled. "The U.S. maternal mortality rate is the worst of any developed nation."

"You always wanted a big family," I pointed out.

"Want her alive more."

"What if she'd wanted another kid?"

"She did. We argued about it. A lot."

"You won, obviously."

"She froze me out for six months," he said wryly. "That was painful."

"Did you cheat on her then?"

"No. Didn't need to get high for that one."

"I wish I got what went down in your brain."

"Me too." He hesitated a second then admitted, "What you feel for Rachel... is it love?"

I found it more difficult than I should to admit, "Yeah." Not because it was hard to say, hard to share, but because this feeling inside of me was deeper than love.

Calling it that was diminishing its power.

But what word existed to encompass the great welter of feelings I had for my future First Lady?

"What I feel for Keira borders on an obsession. I know it's crazy, but that's how it is. I spent half her pregnancy terrified I'd resent the hell out of Cyan. I never wanted to share Keira. Ever. A second kid..." His words drifted off for a while. "I don't know how I'd cope."

"Your mom did a real number on you, Storm." I shook my head, resenting his mother more than I resented Kinnock at that moment. Which was really saying fucking something. "Not sure why that surprises me, but it's true. Love don't work that way. It's generous; it isn't selfish."

"If you say so," he rasped.

"I've seen how you are with Cyan, man. Jesus, you're one of the best dads I've ever known."

His shoulders hunched. "Thanks."

"Believe me or don't, it's the truth. You should have more kids.

You got too much love in you; that's your problem. Anyway, I ain't gonna convince you so what are you going to do about that guy?"

"Nothing."

His attention shifted onto the screen, and I could see his despair rattling around with his anger.

Still, he stunned me by typing:

Storm: *Leave it. Just make sure if things get deeper, and she tries to stop it, that you're there to help out.*

Jump: *Seriously?*

"Seriously?" I sputtered.

The moron cut me a look. "She deserves to find happiness."

Storm: *Seriously. Just make sure she gets out safe. She won't spend the night.*

Jump: *Gotcha. Your funeral.*

"Your honor code is messed up," I snarled, furious on his and Keira's behalf at the dumbfuck move he was making.

"We know that already," he said tightly.

"Did you guys talk about dating?"

"I told her I was proud she dumped my ass, and she told me that we'd never be together." He shot me a look. "Which part of that was supposed to give me hope?"

I pursed my lips. "What if she's supposed to find happiness with you?"

"She'll never find that with me. I'm toxic for her. I'm just lucky she's letting me stay here for the time being."

Exasperation filled me. "Martyrs don't get the girl."

"I want what's best for her."

"Dipshit," I grumbled. "Never understood why you treat her the way you do."

He frowned. "What the hell's that supposed to mean?"

"It means you treat her like she's a kid." We'd argued about this so many times throughout their marriage that I was starting to feel like a broken goddamn record. "I told you to keep it traditional, not fucking paternal. Bet you ain't never told her dick about her old man and the games he's pulled over the years, have you?"

"I had it under control."

"I'm sure," was my dry retort. "Just so you know, I'll only let you pull this martyr shit for so long before I snap. Even if you ain't high, I'm not above hurling you in the Fridge to make you drag your head out of your ass." Before he could reply, I demanded, "Anyway, how's Cyan doing?"

"Better now I'm here."

"Maybe Keira will take you back because of her?"

"She shouldn't."

I growled and punched him in the shoulder, much as he'd done to me. "Maybe she doesn't want you to just passively accept her fucking other guys, Storm. Maybe she wants you to grovel, huh? Maybe she wants you to get in her face and tell her that she's yours and that you're hers?"

"I'm not good for her."

"So? Is Nyx good for Giulia?" was my rejoinder. "The fucker needs to kill people to find inner peace, Storm. Jesus. How he's gone clean for so fucking long I don't know. He's gonna blow at some point. That sound healthy?"

Not that Nyx was still 'clean.' Not when he'd just murdered a rapist, but I'd promised to hold my tongue about that.

Nyx didn't need that shit getting out. Not even to Storm.

When he just stared at me, I grunted, "Sometimes shit doesn't have to be healthy to be right." At his silence, I grumbled, "I need coffee."

"How long you been riding?"

"Eighteen hours."

"Jesus. What the hell were you doing down on the West Coast?"

"It doesn't matter." I couldn't deal with telling him about Wynter yet. "How are things going here?"

"Better. We bought a diner, a local motel, and a garage. We're looking into buying a factory as well. They fabricate auto parts."

I arched a brow. "You're working fast."

"Most of the plan to legitimize the Sinners in West Orange was my idea," he said dryly. "Just repeating what we did. Why fix what ain't broken?"

"The brothers accepting you?"

"Yeah. Few rumbles from a guy who's pissed I didn't make him VP—"

"He a problem?"

"No. Don't think so."

"What about the Sinners we ran off? Any issues there?"

"No. It's a good chapter. There were just a few bad eggs. It's very family-oriented."

My brows rose. "Really?"

"Yeah. All of my council are family men. I'd say nearly eighty percent of the remaining brothers have kids and Old Ladies."

"Jesus. So, the Ohio Chapter is like the Sinners' version of The Waltons?"

He smirked at that. "Yeah, you keep on thinking that, John Boy."

I shoved him in the arm then fell quiet as the cold sank even further into our bones.

"Storm?" I asked after a few minutes.

"Yeah?"

"Dad... I—"

"I miss him too."

I cleared my throat, but it didn't do much for my voice as I choked out, "He woke up before he died."

"Seriously? What did he say?"

For all that I was furious with him, tears burned my eyes as I rasped, "He asked me to help him get to Mom."

He knew what I was saying because he muttered, "Don't tell anyone else."

"I won't."

He grabbed my shoulder and whispered, "He was waiting to be with her."

"I know."

Like two jackasses, we sat in the dark, on the frozen ground, hunched over, both of us trying not to cry as we mourned the man who'd been our father.

As we mourned the mom we'd lost too young.

And prayed that, if there really was a God, he delivered Bear into Rene's arms.

Even if I was pissed at my dad, even if Storm's revelations gave me some answers I didn't like, that was all I could ever really hope for—that they truly *were* together again.

TWELVE

REX

LATER THAT NIGHT

"Hockey star's miraculous escape from his abductors—Liam Donnghal's exclusive interview with TVGE tonight at eleven!"

Switching off the news, I flicked onto the next channel.

"Liam Donnghal's harrowing imprisonment at the hands of a notorious kidnapping ring—"

The next channel was running with the same headline.

"Interpol has confirmed that the gang who kidnapped hockey megastar, Liam Donnghal, is also behind hundreds of high-profile abductions over the past fifteen years!"

"This is getting fucking boring," I mumbled under my breath as my phone rang.

Reaching for it, seeing Wynter's Caller ID, I pulled a face and answered it.

"King?"

I heard her hesitance. "Hi, Wynter."

"Did you make it to your friend Storm's?"

"I did."

"You were supposed to call me," she complained.

"Storm and I got into a fight. The prick nearly tackled me off my bike the minute I rode up. It's been non-stop ever since."

It had as well. I'd told him about Wynter, and he'd smacked me in the gut. He'd said he wasn't raped, that he'd asked for it, and I'd had to stop myself from smacking *him*.

Then, I'd had it out with Keira. Tried to make her pull her head out of her ass.

And people thought being the Prez was fucking easy.

"What?! He tackled you off your bike?"

Lips twitching at her outrage, I said, "He was mad at me."

"Why?"

"Because I didn't tell anyone where I've been since Dad's death."

"You just let them think you were gone?"

"I'm an adult, Wynter. I don't answer to many people."

"That's bullshit—"

"I'm a bad influence if you're swearing."

"Yeah, damn straight you are. You totally answer to people. You answer to me, don't you?" Her voice spiked with fear, which immediately made me feel guilty. "Just like I do to you. You wouldn't go away and not tell me, right?"

"No, I wouldn't."

"And Rachel—you wouldn't with her either?"

"That's where you're wrong, kid. I did."

She gasped. "That's terrible."

"I'm terrible sometimes," I muttered lightly, getting to my feet and staring out onto the row of suburban houses where Storm had made himself a home.

At least, half a home.

He'd moved to Coshocton to evade police interest but also to fill in the empty space at the head of the council here. As Prez, he was the only man I really trusted in this chapter, and after the last fucker, I'd needed him to keep a tight hold on the men.

While he stayed under this roof, Keira was dating other guys, Storm was beating himself up for shit that had happened to him that wasn't his fault, and I was left wondering which letter Rachel would be sending to him after a year had passed...

My father was hoping they'd get back together, but after seeing them tonight, I didn't have a clue if that was possible.

Throw in the fact that I'd learned my brother had been raped, *by my half-sister,* and it had been a hell of a day.

When I'd pinned him down on the subject later on, needing to make sure I'd understood, he'd rasped, "It was my fault."

"How is it your fault? Did you ever consent?" I'd grated out at him.

His mouth had tightened. "No."

No.

Just a single, simple word. The most destructive of any language.

"King?"

I released a sigh as she broke into my thoughts. "What?"

I couldn't tell her where my mind had drifted. It wasn't something I could share, but just knowing that the reason Storm's marriage had broken up was because he'd been sexually assaulted, *repeatedly,* made me want to kill every single bunny who'd taken advantage of his addiction to try to get themselves an Old Man.

"You're mad at me."

Realizing she was misreading my silence, I denied, "I'm not mad at you. I guess I was looking forward to you coming to New Jersey. That's all. I get why you want to stay there now though."

I didn't.

But I did.

It was annoying to understand both sides of things.

"I'm sorry," she whispered.

"You don't have to be sorry. I'm just tired. It was a long journey. I'll always pick up the phone, Wynter."

"Even if you don't want to?"

"Even if I don't want to. But I don't think that's gonna happen with you. I'll always want to pick up the phone."

I heard her swallow. "And you'll always tell me where you are?"

"I will if you ask."

She released a breath. "Thank you."

"You don't have to thank me."

"I-I didn't choose him over you."

My spare hand curled into a fist. "I know you didn't. And you don't have to excuse yourself. They're your family."

"He's in the hospital, King. I couldn't leave them when he's like this."

"I understand," I told her, my tone brighter. "You did what you thought was right."

"I did." She sighed. "Mom's okay. She just won't stop crying."

No, I'd just bet she wouldn't.

Her monster of a husband had tried to sell their kid to pay off his debts.

"She'll calm down eventually. It's only been a few days since Xiang freed them both."

A hiss sounded down the line, "This is *his* fault."

"Do you know what displacement is?"

It was a testament to my shitty state of mind that I said anything at all. That I even bothered trying to open up her mind to reality.

"In physics?"

I should have just kept my fucking mouth shut, but now I'd started, I couldn't stop myself. "No. Psychology."

"I-I guess."

"Charles Xiang offers a service. His patrons are responsible for their own behavior. You can't blame a fast-food joint for making their clients fat, can you?"

"No," she mumbled.

I just hummed, aware I'd made my point without losing my temper and without her losing hers. After the way shit had gone down recently, I'd take that as a fucking win.

"They really hurt him," she argued.

"He owed them a lot of money."

"Would you have done that to someone who owed you money?"

She sounded breathless as she asked the question. Like she'd blurted it out and wished she could take it back. As if she were dreading my answer because she knew what I was about to say.

"Perhaps."

"Perhaps?" she shrieked.

"If someone offered me their daughter in lieu of their debts, you can bet your—" I cleared my throat. "You can bet I'd make them repent for making that offer."

She was quiet a moment, then she muttered, "I spoke with Rachel today."

I arched a brow at that. "You did?"

"It was the first time without you there."

"How did she do?"

"Do you remember at school, the first time you go on stage in front of everyone, and it's like you've forgotten how to speak?"

I blinked. "I didn't take theater class. I didn't play an instrument either."

"Well, you can figure it out, surely?"

"She was nervous?"

"She stared at me like she didn't remember that you're supposed to imagine judges are naked when you're performing."

I grimaced. "We need to work on that, don't we?"

"I'd like to," she said, her voice small. "I don't want her to always be so on edge around me."

"She wants you to like her. It makes things awkward." I cleared my throat. "Did you talk about anything?"

"She wanted to make sure the Triads didn't hurt me." The drop in her voice might not have been noticeable by anyone else, but I heard it. "That was important to her. After, we spoke about the weather."

My lips almost twitched. "The weather?"

"Yes. It was like talking to a British person."

"How many British people do you speak with?"

"There are a couple in my class, actually," she sniped.

"And they talk about the weather?"

"When they're nervous."

I rubbed the bridge of my nose. "The Triads *didn't* touch you, did they?"

"I already had this awkward conversation once today, King. I don't need it twice. You know they didn't. They left me in the bathroom." A soft breath escaped her. "I know I'm lucky."

She was.

It was on the tip of my tongue to prod her on the subject. To demand how she could forgive Kinnock, but like she knew what I was about to say, she muttered, "I'd better go. Mom's calling me."

Somehow, I didn't believe her.

"How is Ally?" I asked before she could end the call. "You said she's crying?"

"She's okay. Tell me when you get home?"

"I will. Is the new place okay?"

"Yes. Thank you for sorting that out before you left."

I didn't even smile. "You're welcome. Wynter... I..."

It was only a lifetime of dealing with her mother that had stopped me from dragging her kicking and screaming back to Jersey with me.

The Laker women were a special breed.

They weren't greenhouse flowers that needed careful cultivation. They were wild blooms with thorns that would strike and wound. Jersey-bred Venus flytraps that could and would bite.

I wasn't afraid of bleeding. I had plenty of scars. But I was pretty fucking sure that if I'd pushed Rachel, she'd have done something neither of us could repair. I wasn't sure what. With her connections, I'd probably have ended up with my ass in jail. Either that or dead.

Wynter would just cut me out of her life.

The prospect was worse than I could imagine. Worse than any scar her mother could etch into my flesh.

"What, King?" she prompted at my silence.

"Rach and I... We'll always be there. When you're ready." *To come home.*

She sucked in a breath. "I-I know that."

"You do?"

"Yes." She swallowed, but she didn't take the conversation any further. "Night, King." She blew out a breath and, on a rush, said, "I miss you."

The next thing I heard was dead air.

A smile curved my lips this time, however.

"She misses me."

My grin lasted me through brushing my teeth—which was fucking awkward—and when I laid my head on the pillow, it was still there.

I'd gone to LA with nothing.

No one.

I was going back to Jersey with a woman and two kids.

Not a bad deal.

THIRTEEN

RACHEL

"Rachel Laker speaking."

"This isn't the first time I've heard your name. Rumor has it you could get Hitler off of war crimes."

Warily, I asked, "Who is this?"

The last couple days had been crazy.

On a personal and professional front.

Currau Valentini was free, Aurora had announced her resignation as DA, Hunter was still in danger, Wynter had decided not to return to Jersey, Rex was pissed, Lily had tried to pitch me another date for a fundraiser in the summer and I'd agreed, Acuig Corp, O'Donnelly's company, had deposited a million dollars in FAST, and that was just the start of the madness.

I wasn't in the mood for games.

"Lodestar requested I speak with you. You know me as Dead To Me. I'm sure you'll understand if I don't introduce myself further."

"Hitler couldn't pay me enough to defend him."

"Good to know you have morals."

"Not many. But some."

"I'm the same. I choose my morals though. Who's to tell me what's right and wrong? It's down to me to make those decisions."

"Is this your way of justifying sending a 'present' to one of my best friends?"

She paused. "Hunter Lachlan is one of your best friends?"

"He is."

"Interesting."

"Why is that?"

"Do you know who he is?"

"As well as anyone *can* know a friend."

"Do you know who his family is?"

My brow furrowed. "The Lachlans? I think I met an uncle once. Why?"

"Did you know that Lachlan is his middle name?"

"I didn't. Why would I know that? We attended college together, and he only went by Lachlan."

"Lachlan is his mother's last name. His father's is De Laurentiis."

"Like the chef?"

Dead To Me chuckled. "More like the mobster."

Praying that she was telling me Hunter was related to a famous TV personality, I rasped, "Hunter makes great gnocchi."

"I'm sure he does. His crimes aren't in the kitchen."

"Hunter's a good man."

He went for a Danish and a coffee every morning after a run, had a collection of Marvel comics that would make a twelve-year-old weep in envy, and thought the best move to make when a hitman came a-calling was to *leave* his house.

That wasn't the repertoire of a hardened criminal—I'd be the one who'd know.

"Not to some he isn't."

"He is to me." My nails dug into my palms when I clenched my fist. "He's a good man," I repeated.

"Good and evil are like right and wrong. They're subjective."

"I'm sure they are. Why did you send him that 'gift' in the mail?"

"Were you aware that I have a 100% success rate? It's why I'm so popular with my clients."

"I'll bet," I whispered. What I *was* aware of was that she hadn't answered my question. "What can I do to make this go away? To change your mind about the transaction going forward?"

What the fuck have you done, Hunter?

"The money was transferred into my account the night he received the gift bag, Rachel. The transaction is underway."

"I'll pay you more."

"I'm not trying to up my price. I have a reputation to protect."

"I know you do. I'm Lodestar's friend. Hunter's *my* friend. Please —" I swallowed, realizing that I was sweating and on the brink of tears all at the same time. "Please, I'm not against begging."

A soft whistle sounded in my ear. "The great Rachel Laker is begging *me* for mercy."

I swallowed. "Do I know you?"

"It's possible. We may have crossed paths inadvertently."

A shudder whispered through me.

"I was the defense council for someone who hurt a family member?"

She hummed. "It's okay though. I never liked him."

"Who?"

"Now that would be telling, wouldn't it?"

"I guess it would." Nervously, I said, "Hunter's a good man."

"You said that before. I just told you he's a De Laurentiis, Rachel. Have you never heard of the Camorra? In your line of work and with your client list?"

"He's a desk jockey," I argued. "He works behind the scenes."

"That's where you can cause the most chaos," she dismissed. "Look at our mutual friend. Lodestar gets into more trouble behind one of her computers than she does with an assault weapon."

"Hunter *isn't* Camorra." I knew I sounded desperate but... No. Just, *no.* Hunter was my Golden Retriever buddy. He wasn't a made man.

"Have you ever asked him what he does?"

"I just know he works with computers."

"He does. For the Camorra," she said like I was a moron.

"I managed to figure that one out," I ground out, then immediately regretted it. "Why does your client want him dead?"

"Do you think I ask for a profile of sins before I shoot someone? This isn't a dating site, Rachel. I'm mostly interested in whether they're trying to entrap me or if they're good for the fee."

"*I'm* good for the fee. You can charge whatever you want—I'll pay it."

"You don't think I hear that all the time?"

Anger exploded through me. "Why did you take this call if you were only going to toy with me?"

"Initially, I didn't realize you were fond of Lachlan, and when Lodestar told me your name, I couldn't resist."

"I've read up on you," I muttered. "I know that, normally, you make the kill much sooner than you have with him. Why's he special?"

"Because he's Camorra. Because he's onto me. Because he hasn't left his house since he received my present, and his property doesn't have windows—"

"It doesn't have windows?" I half-shrieked.

"Never been?"

"No. We're not like that." I knew how odd that sounded and mumbled, "He hasn't been to my home either. We have each other's back, but distance doesn't matter."

"If you say so. No, he doesn't have any windows. They're all internal, looking onto an inner courtyard. He's quite intelligent."

Was it just me or did she sound impressed?

"He's more than 'quite,'" I defended.

Hunter could ram heads with Aurora and I without any difficulty at all.

Too few people in my life had that capacity. Rex, Maverick, and Lodestar being the only other ones I knew.

"It would seem so. But, you're in luck. I have need of an attorney and you need to know who my client is so you can save Lachlan's hide. I'm willing to make a deal."

"What kind of deal?"

"What happened to 'I'll do anyfink for my best fwend,'" she mocked in a babyish voice that made me flush with irritation.

"I will. Within reason. Are you Hitler? As we've already established, I won't defend him."

"Don't worry. I shaved off my toothbrush mustache a long time ago. My crimes are many and varied but nothing you're not used to."

"How do I know you won't kill him?"

"That's the fun part. You don't." I heard her smile. "That's part of the price you'll be paying for his safety."

"Why do you need a lawyer? I refuse to work with people whose identity I don't know."

"The moment that becomes an issue, I'll share those details with you. But as it stands, we need to build up some trust."

"How do we do that?"

"By you taking on a little task for me. What ties do you have with the State Department?"

I rubbed my temple. "A few, but I can make more connections if need be."

"A man called Eamonn Keegan has allegedly been released from jail. I'd like to know if that's true or not."

Blinking, I repeated, "Eamonn Keegan, okay, I'll find out. What prison's he in?"

"One in the UK."

Blowing out a breath at her impudence in thinking I had contacts across the damn pond, I merely told her, "I'll find out what I can."

"I already know if the rumors are true or false. Impressing me is how you keep your precious friend safe. Do you understand?"

I gritted my teeth. "I understand."

"Good."

She ended the call, and it was a good thing because if she hadn't, I might have thrown my cell at the wall.

"I actually think I've met a woman more goddamn infuriating than Lodestar," I hissed at no one as I slammed my palm against the desk.

"Talking to yourself is a sign of madness."

"It's also the only way to get any sense." I modulated my tone so Rain wouldn't know how stressed I was.

Me: *Hunter, I just spoke with Dead To Me. There's a price tag on her not shooting you. I'll pay it but stay underground, do you hear me?*

Hunter: *How much is it? I don't need you to pay on my behalf, Rach.*

Me: *It's information. I'll be in touch if I can't get the answers she wants.*

Hunter: *What are you talking about?*

Me: *She wants me to dig around my contacts at the State Department.*

Hunter: *What the hell for?*

Me: *Don't know yet. I'll keep you in the loop, just don't get killed before then. TTYL.*

Casting him a glance as I set my phone down, I tried not to appear surprised—easier said than done when he was looking...

God, he was a man.

I could feel my mouth wanting to crumple at the sight of him.

Axel would have been so fucking proud.

As for me, I felt numb.

"Rach, are you gonna cry?"

His tone was teasing, but there was a plea in it too.

We didn't do tears.

I rolled my eyes. "Why? What have you done to break my heart?"

He shot me a sheepish grin. "Hit 99th percentile in trig?"

"The way into any sister's good books." I shared his grin. "You doing okay?"

"You mean since you saw me in the kitchen this morning?" he teased.

"Yes, since then, dick," I grumbled. "It's not often you visit me in my office."

He hitched a shoulder. "I guess."

Ambling deeper into the room, he stuck to the sides, edging around them and picking up ornaments on the console tables here and there.

As I watched him dawdle, I tried not to think that I didn't have time for this. There'd come a moment where he'd stop consulting with me—hell, he'd pretty much been autonomous since he'd hit sixteen. But when he left for the army, I knew that was it. He'd never ask me for anything unless it was legal advice.

That was the price of maturing—a baby brother didn't need his older sister anymore.

Yikes, that hurt.

Pushing Hunter's problems aside for the moment, I asked, "Everything okay?"

He cast me a look. "Harlow told me he was arrested the other day."

Shit.

"He told you that?"

What the fuck had he said?

Nyx, I internally screeched. *Can you do nothing fucking right?*

"He did. Said he got pulled over for speeding in Manhattan."

What the hell?

Why had he said that when he'd been charged with loitering?

Aware my brother was trying to lead me, I waited for him to speak, not eager to fill a silence that I wasn't sure how to maneuver around anyway.

"I just wanted to know if there's anything I can do to help."

My brow puckered. "For a speeding ticket?"

"Well, you don't get arrested for those usually," he drawled. "I assumed, you know what with you being a lawyer, you'd have figured that out by now?"

"Since when were you such a jackass?"

He grinned. "I picked it up from my big sis."

"He told you he got arrested?"

"Shouldn't you know? Seeing as you're the club lawyer?"

"You sure you want to be a soldier and not an attorney?" His cheeks flushed. "What? Didn't you think I'd figured that out?"

He grunted. "Don't want to talk about it."

"Tough. When were you going to tell me? The day you enlisted?" I wafted a hand at him as I leaned back in my chair, preferring it now that he was in the hot seat and not me. "Did you think I didn't notice you pumping up?"

Another grunt. "It's important to me, Rach."

"It was important to Axel," I said carefully. "That's not the same thing."

"He'd have wanted me to do this."

"With the uncertainty in the geopolitical sphere, I'm not sure if he'd have the same opinion now as he did back then."

"It'd matter to him. You know he wished he'd gone into the Forces."

"And I'm sure Mom would have liked me to walk in her footsteps and become a fucking stripper, Rain. That doesn't mean I went to an audition at the local titty bar."

His eyes flared with temper. "Don't talk about her like that!"

My mouth tightened. "You didn't know her. I did."

"She wasn't a stripper."

"No, strippers have 401Ks and are studying in college. Mom just sucked dick to put a roof over my head. What they want for us, isn't what we have to do.

"If you want to be a soldier, go and be a fucking soldier. That's fine with me. You go and get your ass blown up if it's what you want to do. But I don't think it is. I think you're doing it out of some messed up ideal because your dad gave you war stories about your grandfather."

"This is why I didn't want to talk about it with you, dammit. I knew that's what you'd say. You think I don't want to serve my country?"

"There are ways and means of serving it," I sniped back. "With your brains, you're too fucking smart to just enlist. Get your ass to West Point. Become an officer—"

"There's nothing wrong with going in from the ground up, but that's why I wanted to be an Eagle Scout. I'll start at a higher rank and pay grade."

"Look, anyone who dedicates their lives to that is a fucking hero, but you won't be going in as a fucking lieutenant, Rain. Eagle Scout or not. And not everyone is general material like you."

He folded his arms across his chest. "I'm not general material."

"Your report card says otherwise. But, like I said, if that's what you want to do, then good for you, Rain. As for Harlow, I'm not sure why you're interested. Have you spoken more than ten words to the man?"

"He's been staying with us, Rachel." He shook his head. "Of course I speak to him."

"Enough to become friendly?"

"Yeah."

"Why are you worried?"

"Because you don't get arrested for a speeding ticket," he snapped. "Aren't you fucking listening?"

"He's a client. I don't discuss a client's personal legal status with family."

"Is this because of the army thing?"

"No," I groused. "It's because of attorney-client privilege." Dissatisfied with our conversation, I told him, "Harlow's a grown man. You don't have to worry about him."

"Like you don't worry about Rex and Nyx and the rest?"

"That's different. I was raised with them. They're..." I inhaled. "... family."

He arched a brow at that. "Are they?"

"Yes. They are," I said firmly. "Speaking of which, our family is going to start growing." At his frown, I explained, "I'm pregnant."

That had him blinking at me. "What? How? Immaculate conception?"

Feeling my cheeks tinge pink, I grated out, "The regular way."

"Who's the dad? Man, Rex is gonna be angry. You know he pisses on you like you're a fire hydrant—"

I scowled. "He does not."

He snorted. "Yeah, he does. Any dude looks at you, he's practically growling. Jesus, who's the unfortunate sperm donor?"

"I know we agreed that you're a pain in the ass but I think we can throw in 'disrespectful' pain in the ass too. They won't like that in the military," I crowed. "No talking back, no sniping, not without having to peel ten goddamn tons of potatoes as a punishment."

"That was in Granddad's time."

"I'm sure there are plenty other miserable tasks out there. Like cleaning up the shower stalls with a toothbrush." I smirked at him, pleased when he shuffled on his heels. Rain didn't like the idea of that. Ha. "Rex is the father, Rain."

"I repeat, by immaculate conception? I mean, he's been away for months."

"He's been away since Christmas Day," I retorted. "And I'm about to enter my second trimester—"

His eyes bugged. "You've been pregnant all that time and didn't tell me?"

"I didn't find out until recently. I just thought I was sick." I raised a hand and gnawed on a corner of my nail. The gel didn't budge, but God, I wished it would. "I'm not. So there's that."

Rain blinked at me then staggered over to the chair in front of my desk. Hunkering down, he muttered, "How are you feeling?"

"I'm not in the best shape. I don't eat enough—"

"Didn't need a doctor to tell you that. I could have told you," he pshawed.

"Jackass," I grumbled. "Underweight, anemic, low blood pressure. I'm working on it."

"Does Rex know?"

"About the anemia or the pregnancy?"

"The pregnancy." The 'duh' went unspoken.

"He does."

"What was his reaction?"

"He was…" I thought about the night of the gala, and a soft smile curved my lips. Sure, everything had gone to hell after, but the way he'd touched me left me in no doubt. "He's happy."

"Good, or I'd have had to beat the shit out of him."

I snorted. "You don't have to sacrifice yourself for my honor, Rain."

"Rite of passage. Dad's not around to do it, but I sure as fuck am. If he doesn't treat you right, Rachel, you tell me and I'll fix it."

I'd have laughed, but I knew he meant it. Even if the idea of Rain pitting himself against Rex was slightly ludicrous in my mind, I didn't prick his pride. Not when he was saying that out of love for me.

"I love you, Rain."

"Love you too. I mean it, Rachel," he warned with a frown.

"I know you do. Thank you. But I don't think you need to worry."

"You sure? Something's kept you two dipshits apart all these years. It has to be something he did. You're too rational—"

"It wasn't him, Rain," I interrupted softly then, and when he just made a scoffing sound, I shook my head. "It wasn't. It was me."

"Can't be. You love him! Why would you put roadblocks between you?"

"How do you know that I love him?"

"You said it yourself, sis. I got a brain. And a pair of eyes. Anyone with both could see that. Even Lever, and let's face it, he ain't the sharpest tool in the shed."

"There's no point in denying it, I suppose."

"No. No point at all," he drawled. Then his expression darkened. "Have you been in a relationship all this time and you just didn't tell me?"

"No," I grumbled. "That would be more palatable. I've just been focused on my career, that's all."

"Maybe I should have asked if you're okay with having the baby..."

I nodded. "I am."

"You sure?"

"Yes."

"Positive?"

I clucked my tongue. "Positive."

He pursed his lips. "I don't see you going into 'momma mode' any time soon. It's not like you're the most maternal person."

"Hey, I raised you, didn't I?"

Rain shot me a sheepish grin. "You did. Did a fine job of it, too, if I say so myself."

"You'd better because no one else would," I teased, grinning back at him as he snorted. My tone grew more serious as I reasoned, "I don't know what's going to happen between Rex and me..."

I thought about the ring Lily had given me. Thought about the fact that Rex was insisting I wasn't ready for his brand. Two such contrasting acts. Would I ever understand that man?

"You mean he's not going to move in permanently?"

"He is," I said slowly.

Although, now Wynter wasn't coming, would that change things?

"Aren't you supposed to be the genius here?"

I flipped him the bird. "It's not as easy as that."

"Isn't it?"

"No. And maybe we're going to be non-traditional—"

When he started laughing, I just glowered at him. When the laughter freakin' continued, him howling like he was losing his mind, I ground out, "Rain! For God's sake. What's so funny?"

"You!" he said, choking on his laughter. "You?! Not traditional? Rachel, oh my God—"

Off he went again.

Starting to get pissed in earnest, I hurled an eraser at him. When he caught it, I hissed under my breath.

I'd never been good at sports, but Rain excelled at everything he'd signed up for.

Sickening—that's what it was.

"I'm not that traditional," I growled. "I'm thirty-five and I'm not married and I don't have one point nine kids. I hardly ever cook—"

"I never said you were Wilma Flintstone. Rach, you live in a house in New Jersey despite the fact that most of your work is in Manhattan. You have several bedrooms that are calling out to be filled, and the backyard is made for a swing set. You work from home and your work/life balance is atrocious because you're addicted to it. The second you and Rex get together permanently, I totally expect you to start cooking and wearing those slippers that shine the floor while you walk across the house."

I squinted at him. "Do you even know me?"

He grinned. "That last part might be made up, but a brother can hope, can't he? If you do buy those slippers, I want to take a photo. I'm putting it on IG for posterity."

"You're not supposed to be mean to pregnant ladies."

"I'm a feminist," he countered.

"So, what? You can be mean to me?"

"Exactly."

"If you were on public transport, would you give up your seat for a pregnant woman?"

"Of course."

"Just checking," I groused.

He smirked, but as he looked at me, it slowly died. "I know you and Mom didn't get along, Rach, and..." He sighed. "I know we don't see eye to eye on her memory, but I know for a fact you'll be a thousand times better than she was because you raised me and I was lucky enough to have you in my life. Any kid who calls you 'Mom' is damn lucky too."

Cheeks burning and, I'd admit, my eyes watering, I murmured, "Thanks, Rain."

"You didn't have to come back here full time. We could have moved to Manhattan like I said. Hell, you didn't even have to raise me. You could have shoved me in a home. Thank you for not doing that."

I shot him a shaky smile. "You don't have to thank me for that. It wasn't always easy, but I don't have a single regret."

"It must have been rough, back in the early days, after Dad passed?" he asked gruffly.

"It was. The MC helped."

"I don't remember that."

"You were too young. It was a different place back then. Rex's mom was still alive." I pursed my lips. "Have you ever been to a party at the clubhouse?"

"Will I get in trouble if I say yes?"

"If you weren't eighteen, yes," I mocked.

"Okay, then I have."

My nose crinkled. "I knew it! Last fall?" He gave me a sheepish nod. "You swore blind you didn't go."

He shrugged. "Sneaked in. It's not that hard to cross over our yard into theirs."

"Well, back then, it wasn't all sex on the pool table and oral in the hallway," I grumbled. "It used to be PG-rated."

"Is that why you don't go there anymore?"

"Not exactly. It's one of the reasons, I guess, but I've not been comfortable there for a long time."

"Why?"

I shot him a bright smile. "I didn't fit in before when it had more of a family atmosphere. I sure as hell don't fit in now. I wasn't like you, Rain. I didn't just gel with everyone I met.

"That charm of yours is one of the reasons I'm damn sure you could be a general. Hell, you'd probably save our asses from a nuclear threat if you ever earned four stars."

"I'm not that charming."

"I think the fact that you somehow bounce off of a cluster of women without them hating on you *or* each other says it all. I've seen your gaggle of geese hovering around you at the country club. I didn't think the management liked you fraternizing with the clients."

"They don't." He shot me a smug smile. "Rules were made to be broken."

"Spoken like a true soldier," I mocked, not even laughing when his smirk morphed into a scowl.

I knew he was trying to annoy me, and it worked when he said, "Guess that means you'll have to move onto the compound."

I snorted. "No, I won't be reigning over the clubhouse."

"He's the Prez, Rach." He cocked a brow at me. "Being his woman means more than just popping out his kids. You do know that, right?"

I wanted to laugh off his words. His confidence. But... damn. He was right. Rex had said it himself.

Wresting control from the clubwhores and doling out chores then enforcing them, keeping the brothers in line around the kids, making sure that the clubhouse was spic and span, not letting them bully the Prospects too badly, refereeing the Old Ladies—such domestic issues, and that wasn't me at all.

That, I realized, was why Rex wasn't branding me.

A ring was one thing—it tied me to him. A brand another—it tied me to the club.

One, I was more than ready for.

But both?

I wasn't so sure.

FOURTEEN

REX

I didn't drive straight to the clubhouse.

I should have.

But there was plenty of shit I should've done, and plenty of shit I wanted to do instead.

Duty had been my guiding hand for too many years. Right now, I wanted to see my woman, so that was what I was gonna fucking do.

Only her SUV was in the driveway when I arrived, and a part of me hoped she was alone in there. It had been a helluva long time since Christmas, and the night of the gala felt like a lifetime away as well. I wanted to see more of her. Those new curves of hers—I wanted to sample them, *taste* them.

I wanted to look at her and know this was fucking happening. No more looking back, no more distance even though we were living next door to each other.

Just us.

Simple.

Our kid wasn't here, and I'd had to leave her behind when that was the exact opposite of what we wanted; but, one day, when

Wynter realized what her dad was, she'd come home. It was only right that when that happened, her mom and I were a solid front—*staunch*. Unwavering in the face of any shit that was hurled our way.

As I rode home, that was what had made me put mile after mile between Wynter and me.

The knowledge that things were on the right track with Rach and I, but we weren't set in stone yet.

Not until my ring was on her fucking finger.

Like a pussywhipped fool, I'd had my hair cut.

After I filled up the gas that last time, I'd hunted down a barbershop and had gotten the whole nine yards. My chin was smoother than a Georgia peach and my hair was back to being neat. Well, before the journey had wrecked it, but I swiped my hands over it, wanting to make sure she saw *me* when she let me in.

Not that fucker Grizzly.

Me.

Maria's reaction to me when she'd opened her front door would stick with me until the day I died.

Before I headed toward the house, and knowing that Lodestar or Maverick might have seen me ride in through her gates, I shot Mav a text.

Me: *I'm back.*

Maverick: *Saw.*

Me: *All good? No fallout from the kidnapping?*

Maverick: *Not on us.*

Me: *Good. Don't disturb us.*

Maverick: *Wasn't gonna.*

Maverick: *You finally stopped pussyfooting around her, huh?*

Me: *Fuck off.*

Maverick: *:P*

Maverick: *See you on Monday.*

I grinned.

Freedom came with tethers.

It was Thursday. Mav was silently telling me I had until Monday to enjoy myself but that was when I had to go back to the old grind.

Fucking brothers—gave me more shit than the IRS.

I was still smiling as I jumped onto the porch though, and when I tried the handle, found it was locked, I had my confirmation that Rachel was alone.

Grateful, I knocked on the door and heard her yell, "On my way!"

She dragged it open a second later, a polite smile fixed on her face. She'd give that to a judge or the mailman. It was innocuous.

Throwaway.

But when she saw me, that smile wobbled, her eyes turned glassy, and before I had time to reach out and grab her, she was there. In my goddamn arms. Where she was supposed to fucking be.

She started sobbing. I wasn't used to that from her, but pregnancy worked on a woman's hormones so I didn't expect any less. If Giulia could cry when she was carrying her kid, then my woman sure as hell would too.

I held her through the storm, kept her steady, and enjoyed the freedom that came with having her in my arms.

A couple minutes later, she sniffled, "I'm sorry for getting snot all over your cut." Her fingers brushed the leather. "She gave it back to you?"

"She did." I'd wanted her to keep it. A token, as it were, for her to have a reason to come here, to save face if need be. "And you don't have to apologize for snot. I'm sure it'll wash off."

Her lips curved. "It's seventy-five percent tears."

"Good to know," I said lightly, reaching up to cup her chin. "You look tired."

"I am." She sighed, tipped her face into my hold, and whispered, "I missed you. Don't care that you weren't gone for long this time. I missed you. I don't want to have to miss you again."

It was phrased as a command, and I smirked at her. "Next time I go anywhere, you gonna come with me?"

Her nose crinkled. "You just want me on the back of your bike."

"Ideally," I teased.

Her fingers drifted to my lips, and I felt her shape the curve of my smile. "Before you left, you promised me a kiss..."

"Come and get it," I rumbled.

Slowly, delicately, she leaned up and pressed her mouth to mine. The acceptance inherent in that one move made me shudder. I groaned, unable to stop myself, and immediately opened up to her.

Her tongue slipped against mine, gently, at first, and because I was so used to drifting from zero to a hundred in less than three seconds with her, this felt good.

Different. Right.

She drank from my lips, and I let her. A part of me wanted to make a claim that hadn't been staked in too fucking long, but another part of me just wanted to let her have me.

Any way she wanted me, she could have me.

Her hands slipped into my hair, the tips of her fingers streaking down over the silken smooth lines that had just been cut into it, and as she did, I felt the pressure of her stomach against me. Her belly, in the time I'd been gone, was a lot more solid than it had been before.

I felt it.

Our kid.

I reached for her waist, hauling her into me, holding her tight. My fingers shaped her lean curves, one hand dropping to her ass where I palmed the sweet flesh. She was still slender, but there was more meat there, and I fucking loved that. Palming the other cheek too, I kneaded the sleek muscles as I drove my tongue into her mouth, needing more, needing *everything*.

The slower, gentler pace shifted up a gear, and we groaned into each other's mouths as I pushed us forward a couple steps, just so that I could slam the door behind us.

When she permitted that of me, I twisted us around the second I kicked the door closed and I pinned her to it, reaching up to grab her forearms and to hold them above her head.

My dick grinding into her belly, I nipped at her bottom lip before I whispered, "You're mine, Rachel."

The sweetest, softest smile graced me.

A smile that was the girl I'd always known.

My girl.

"You're mine, King."

Sighing, I let our lips lock once more. I tasted her. Savored her. Explored her. I had the freedom of time, something I never had where she was concerned. I had the liberty of touching her and caressing her at my own leisurely pace.

She wanted this.

She wanted me, and fuck, I *craved* her. This was so much more than want or need for me. I was addicted. She was my drug of choice and I'd gone far too long without a hit.

I pulled back again and traced my tongue along the hard line of her jaw. Moving lower, I nipped my way down her throat, finding the spot that I knew always got her hot. It was a few inches higher than the join between neck and shoulder, and the second I suckled there, tongue palpating against the flesh, she moaned, rasping, "King, God, King."

I shuddered at the words; she'd uttered my version of 'Open, Sesame.'

Reaching down, I started to drag her skirt up her legs, higher and higher, letting my fingers curve toward the backs of her thighs so that I could draw every nerve ending she possessed to life.

A shaky moan whispered from her lips, and when her skirt was tucked between us, I made her jump by snatching her legs out from under her and locking them around my hips.

"Jerk!" she squeaked, her fingers digging into my shoulders for balance.

I let loose a laugh, feeling the joy of teasing her exploding through me, and I used the new, better angle to get even closer to her.

This time, when I pressed kisses to her jaw, I moved higher, sucking down on her earlobe, blowing on it gently as I whispered in her ear, "There was too much distance between us, Rachel." I tutted. "That was a situation that needed rectifying immediately."

Her laughter was part-snort part-groan when I started to nibble along the curve of her ear. Her nails dragged through my hair, and I felt the scrape of them, the prickle against the tender flesh of my scalp as they made a mark.

I rocked my hips, dragging my still-clothed dick along the crotch of her panties. At this angle, her belly was even more prominent, and our kid was a more solid presence. Knowing how she felt about pregnancy, I didn't say anything, because I wasn't a fucking moron, but God, it lit me up to know her body was protecting the life we'd made together.

Unable to stop myself, I brushed my lips against hers. Slowly, *appreciatively.* Fuck, the knowledge wrecked me in the best possible way.

Cock as hard as nails, I rasped, "Rach?"

"King?" she whispered.

"I want to come home."

Her swallow was audible.

She gave me a nod.

It was awkward because of the positions we were in, but I made it work. It kinda reminded me of the early days when we were both nervous—her because it was new to her, me because I didn't want to hurt her and fuck things up with the only woman who was ever going to be mine. That was a hell of a lot of pressure on a kid.

Smiling to myself at the thought, I made sure I dragged my knuckles down her covered pussy as I lowered my zipper. My dick made shit easy on me by popping out of the fly because I was going commando, and I dragged the crotch of her panties away.

When bare flesh met bare flesh, we both sighed.

Then, I rocked my hips again, letting the glans nudge her clit, letting it get drenched in her juices which were reassuringly plentiful, letting it tease her until she was whimpering.

But the best part?

That her eyes were on mine.

She saw me.

I saw her.

There was nothing between us.

Nothing.

"King," she whispered.

"Rachel," I replied.

"I love you."

"I love you too."

She pressed our mouths together and united us that way as I let the tip of my dick find the notch of her slit.

And I came home.

The only home I'd ever wanted.

She let loose a soft moan and I swallowed it as I slowly began to thrust into her.

As hungry as I was for her, I didn't need this to go fast.

I needed this to be slow.

I needed her to know I wanted everything with her.

Slow, fast, hungry, sated.

Forever.

I drowned in her kiss, lost myself to it, to her, and gradually, I felt the inner quiver of her muscles give that dance that was so familiar.

Nothing about my woman was easy to read apart from her pussy.

I knew when it wanted slow, knew when she craved fast.

So I gave it to her.

At her pace, at her speed.

When her moans turned to whimpers, her quivery breaths became heady gasps, I increased my pace.

Her nails dug into my scalp again and, smiling against her lips, I gave her what she silently begged for.

Filling her full, she clamped down around me, and gravity was my friend as I drank from her mouth. Tasting and teasing, nipping and playing, making love to her there like I was making love to her body.

Giving her romance, showing my love.

Gifting her with the pleasure she would have forever because she was mine forever.

No more suffering, no more pain.

No more hurt.

Only love.

Only pleasure.

Only us.

FIFTEEN

RACHEL

When he walked us through the house, up the stairs, and toward my bedroom, the orgasm continued winging a blazing path through me.

His dick was still hard and buried in my pussy. Something which made the walk somehow both more pleasurable and more painful.

Little bursts of ecstasy kept exploding into being, and I just rested my head on his shoulder, grateful because that hadn't been the homecoming I'd imagined, but it was somehow all the better for it.

I was hungry for him, but he'd gifted me that reconnection I hadn't even known I needed.

Hell, I hadn't even known he'd be back this early! I should probably have chided him for riding so fast; it couldn't have been safe, but I was so happy to have him back that I couldn't argue with him yet.

On a soft exhalation, I rubbed my forehead against his throat. It was free from stubble. Like silk. His hair felt that way too. Cut again, even though he'd only been to the barber prior to the gala.

I sighed as I rubbed my fingers down the soft satin at his nape. It felt good against the tips.

"I should be annoyed at how easy it is to fool my brain, but I'm just relieved," I mumbled.

A soft laugh escaped him. "You mean the mastermind that can befuddle every DA in the nation is convinced by a haircut and a shave?"

I hummed.

"We shouldn't run before we walk."

"I know," I said softly. "You're going to spend the night, aren't you?"

"I intend to live here, Rachel," he drawled, ignoring my sudden tension to tease, "We've had a two-decade-long courtship; I think we're ready for this next step."

My arms clung to him. "Good."

"Good?" He barked out a laugh. "Why do you never say what I think you'll say?"

I shrugged. "To keep you on your toes."

"It works," he quipped. "When you tensed up on me, I thought you were going to say you didn't want me to move in."

"I want to give this a chance."

"Me too. So why the tension?"

"I thought you were going to go back to the clubhouse tonight. Now that Wynter's staying in California..."

He shook his head. "You didn't want that? Me to return to the clubhouse?"

"I didn't," I agreed. "But I thought there might be a possibility you'd want me to move there."

"Hell, no! You, in the clubhouse? Jesus Christ, you'd lose your mind."

I released a relieved breath. *He wasn't wrong about me losing my damn mind there.*

"Why didn't you just say that you didn't want me to return to the clubhouse? Why didn't you tell me that you didn't want to live there either?"

"Well, it would have been out of context."

"This isn't a courtroom, Rach. If you want something, or if you don't, you need to verbalize it. Just like I do. Agreed?"

I nodded.

He heaved a sigh. "Say it, Rach. A nod isn't enough."

I clucked my tongue. "Yes..." Then, lips twitching, I taunted, "Daddy."

He laughed, a great booming chuckle of a sound that made me grin wider. Pulling back to peer at him, to soak in the sight of his amusement, his *joy*, I could feel my eyes sparkling as he looked into them.

"That's not my kink, sugar."

"No?" I arched a brow. "The way you're going, I'm starting to think it is."

Rex snorted. "The only people I wanna 'daddy' are Wynter and Junior."

"Well, if that's the case, leave the patronizing by the front door, huh?" I stuck my tongue in my cheek. "I know I've fucked up the last two decades, and I know I could have dealt with things a lot better—"

"Hey, that isn't why I'm being overcautious," he chided. "I think you've dealt with things remarkably. Babe, the only thing you're not overachieving in is your personal life. Well, you fixed that. I'm here, ain't I?"

My throat suddenly felt thick. "You are."

"I am." The corner of his mouth quirked up in a half grin. "Nowhere else I wanna be than here, home with you. I just want to set things off on the right foot. So if I *am* patronizing, I really don't mean to be."

"Don't worry, I'll call you out on it," I told him sweetly. "And if you start mansplaining, expect to be womansplained to in turn."

He snickered. "Can't wait."

Lips curving, I merely said, "Now, driver, are we staying in the hall or are you taking me to bed?"

"You got a draft up your ass?"

My nose crinkled at the bridge. "You're as indelicate as ever."

"And you love it," he teased, but he finally walked us into my bedroom.

He took a second to peer around the space, all mint and duck egg blue. "I like my new digs."

Trying not to smile, I murmured, "Relieved everything isn't fuchsia?"

"Very."

We headed over to the bed, and he took a seat at the edge and flopped back, meaning that I was straddling him now.

"You make a good taxi service."

"If I get fired from the MC, I know what to do."

"Nah, I'm not sharing you."

"You're rich. I'll be your Emile. Although, I don't do cages unless strictly necessary so I'd have to take you into the city on my bike."

"You're out of a job already. Do you know how much work I get done in the back of that car?"

"Really?" He arched a brow at me, seeming supremely, well, *everything*. Confident, comfortable, happy, settled, all of those things in one as he looked up at me. "I remember when you used to get car sick riding on the bus home from school."

"God, I remember that. Thank goodness I don't get that way anymore." Placing my hands against his chest, I said, "It's good to have you home." My pussy clamped down around him at that which made him groan.

He lifted his arm so that he could rest the back of his head on it, murmuring, "It's even better to be here. Fuck, I'm tired." He yawned. "That journey was a killer."

"You can't have taken many breaks to rest."

"Is that disapproval I hear?"

"It is. I need you to be safe."

He grumbled, "I was safe. I wanted to be back here. Plus, my mind was racing and it kept me aware on the roads."

"Didn't help that the situation with Wynter is still up in the air," was all I said.

Rex sighed. "No. She made her choice though."

She had. But we both knew it was the wrong one.

"You worried?"

"Very."

I bit my lip. "I'm due to talk to her in a couple hours—"

"She wanted me to text her when I got back."

"Wait and we'll do a video chat?"

He grinned. "I'd like that. I also like that my girls have been talking while I've been riding home."

I pulled a face. "It wasn't the best talk. I-I kind of froze up on her."

"She might have mentioned it."

"That bad?"

"You need to lighten up around her."

"It's easier said than done." I wiggled my shoulders. "It's so simple with Rain. Why can't it be with her?"

"Because you're overthinking everything." He smoothed his hand down my arm, only stopping to tangle our fingers together. "Anything I need to know?"

When I saw Rex and Wynter talking, there was an ease, a familiarity, that we didn't have yet. I figured that was because of me. Because I was cold by nature.

Things weren't exactly strained between us, but they were definitely not as comfortable as Wynter was with him.

I wished I could tell him otherwise.

Still, she'd been open. I didn't think she knew how to be any other way.

"There seems to be no lasting effects from the situation with the Triads," I said carefully.

"They didn't hurt her," he said flatly.

"No, and she told me she knew you'd come."

"Of course I was going to come," he snapped, his brow puckering.

I shrugged. "From what I could infer, I don't think she'd have had the same faith in Kinnock."

His nostrils flared—his outrage clear. "Then why the fuck is she staying there for him?"

"Because she's loyal," I told him, though I'd admit it gnawed at me too.

I knew Rex had blinders on about her because he thought this situation had tainted her, but he'd been sheltered. Considering his world was dark and gritty, that sounded crazy, but he was Bear's son —the heir to the Sinners. Money was no object, and he had more power in his pinkie than most could imagine. He'd also had parents who adored him and who'd go to war for him.

I didn't have that. I knew what it felt like to have a gnawing ache in my belly because Mom preferred to spend her wages on cigarettes and booze than on crackers and peanut butter.

I knew what it felt like to have to barricade my bedroom door with a dresser before I went to bed at night because one of her boyfriends might stagger into the wrong room when he went to take a piss.

No, Wynter was still a protected soul. She was still open. Still trusting.

I'd kill to keep her like that.

Wiggling off him, I twisted onto my back to stare up at the ceiling like he did. Only difference was, I knew he'd have carried on lying there, cock out, with no embarrassment. I grabbed a throw and covered us both with it before I pressed my face into his arm.

"They don't deserve her loyalty," he muttered, his tone grim as he picked up the conversation where it had left off, and he rolled his head to stare down at me.

"They raised her well, Rex," I countered. "People have flaws and faults. She's a polite girl. Has good morals. She's studious and forward-thinking. That didn't have anything to do with her genes. I didn't imbue a love of books into her in the womb.

"The Kinnocks might have lost their way over the last couple of years, but that doesn't negate her whole childhood."

His tension told me he did *not* like my defending them, but hell, I wasn't blind. Neither was he. He was just pouting.

I patted his chest. "She'll come, Rex."

"I want her here," he rasped.

"I know." I sucked in a breath and admitted something that shocked me, "I want her here too."

"You do? You're not just saying that for me?"

"I'm not just saying that for you." I didn't take offense because it also surprised me. "I want to get to know her. Do you..."

"Do I, what?" he peppered when my voice grew quiet.

"Do you think she'll react badly to the baby?"

He shrugged. "I think she'll be jealous. She was of Rain. I told her that you gave up everything to be here for him."

"Hardly everything," I chided.

"Mostly everything, then," he grumbled, rolling his eyes. "I could see that she was questioning why you could do that for him and not for her."

I blew out a breath. "She's within her rights to think that."

And therein lay the crux of the issue.

She wasn't as guarded with Rex as she was with me because I was her mother.

Mothers were supposed to be maternal.

They were supposed to fight for their kids.

They were the momma bears.

I hadn't fought for her.

I'd given her away.

Fathers didn't have the same expectations as mothers.

Unfair but what about this situation was fair?

"Wynter's entitled to feel whatever she feels, but that doesn't mean I'm going to let her take it out on you. There'll be a period of adjustment for us all when we get her here. But we're not going anywhere this time."

Playing with my bottom lip, I mumbled, "No."

He grunted his satisfaction. "We missed the first seventeen years, but we'll make up for it with whatever we have left on this godforsaken planet."

I snorted. "Cheerful."

He pressed a kiss to the crown of my head. "I try."

"You gonna get some sleep?"

"Yeah." He breathed out a sigh. "Just a couple hours."

I hummed. "I'll nap with you."

"You don't need to go back to work?"

I did, actually. But the only thing I *really* needed was to be here. With him.

"I need a nap more."

He tightened his arm around me. "I don't want to sleep without you again, Rach. Had enough of that to last me a lifetime."

I knew how he felt.

I just prayed my subconscious played ball.

SIXTEEN

RACHEL

The usual dreams woke me up.

The feel of their hands on my skin was repulsive. Vomit-inducing. But this time, when they touched me, I didn't just endure.

I fought back.

That night, I'd pleaded.

I'd begged for them to stop.

I'd tried to fight, but they'd held me down, and because they were so much stronger than me—Grizzly, in particular—they'd overpowered me easily.

Tonight, they didn't.

They still touched me. *It* still happened.

But I managed to hit them.

The girl back then had been weak.

The woman today wasn't.

She knew how to defend herself.

She was stronger now.

It wasn't perfect, but it was a start.

It meant that when I woke up, I didn't claw at my skin like I often found myself doing after I slept with Rex.

I was mad.

I wasn't scared.

How could I be when I came out fighting?

I could feel the adrenaline buzzing through my system as if I'd taken a direct dose of epinephrine to the heart.

"Rachel!"

My name being barked out in a gruff undertone had my eyes popping open.

Rex was staring down at me.

His haircut as fresh as before. His jaw shadowed with the onset of stubble, but not prickly.

Rex.

King.

Mine.

I let the thought process ripple through me.

Not Grizzly.

King.

Mine.

I realized my knuckles were aching, and, sleepily, I took note of how he had his hand curled around my fist.

The move might have felt like he was caging me, but I knew from the lightness of the clasp that he was merely stopping me from attacking him.

I blinked at him, aware that he was grinning at me.

"You punched me," he said proudly.

"I did?" I blurted out.

He nodded.

"I'm so sorry."

His grin deepened. "Don't be."

"I don't usually do that?"

I thought I knew the answer, but he'd seen this side of me more than I ever had.

"No. You tend to—" He heaved a sigh, his grin dying. "You tend to wipe at your face, scrub at your arms. Sometimes, you even scratch them. If you hit me, you slap. It's less of an attack and more desperate."

I grimaced because I *knew* the difference.

Desperate was the word for my attempts to escape.

The girl had hit out.

The woman had fought.

It was the difference between sun and moonlight.

I released a soft breath and told him something I'd never disclosed to anyone before. "They came on my face. That's why I wipe at my cheeks. I can still remember doing that. It was sticky and it was in my hair. I wanted to pour boiling water all over me to clean it off." My skin crawled at the memory. "I settled for alcohol wipes."

After, I'd still felt dirty.

Some days, on the bad ones, a new makeup product could feel like that. I never used highlighter serum for that reason alone.

At my admission, Rex froze.

I wasn't an idiot. I knew why.

Not because of what I'd revealed, but because of the act of sharing.

Giving him a truth he didn't want, but knowing he'd bear the burden as much as I did—it was my leap of faith. A sign of trust.

"The fuckers," he said softly, his tone belying the fury in his eyes.

"Yes," I agreed. "They pulled my hair and they dragged my body about like I was a rag doll." I sucked in a breath, closing my eyes and tucking my face into his throat. "You okay with me telling you this?"

I already knew the answer, but now that I'd told him a disgusting fact about that night, he could have changed his mind.

"I want to know whatever you want to tell me."

It was what I wanted to hear, but...

"You can push me sometimes, Rex," I said. "I won't break."

"They pushed you—"

"No. They forced me. There's a difference. You pushing me isn't the same.

"We all need a little shepherding sometimes. Don't I guide you onto certain paths that you wouldn't ordinarily take with the MC?"

His nod, when it came, was slow. As if he were measuring his response.

"I think, before, you read me well. You sensed what I could take and what I couldn't—"

"It wasn't easy," he rasped. "I had to go against a lot of my natural inclinations."

"You did that because you love me, though."

It wasn't a question.

"I-I need something different now." I exhaled. "You, but the real you. And I need to be me. The real me."

He lay in silence at my side, but I felt his tension. "Who is the real you, Rach?"

I tilted my head so that my nose was burrowed in his throat. God, he smelled so good. Like aftershave and us.

I didn't recognize the aftershave, but it was minty and fresh and clean. From the barbers?

Smiling at the thought of him coming to me straight after a haircut and shave, I found it easier to be brave when I told him, "I'm your girl. I'm just... a little battered around the edges."

"You've always been my girl," he said staunchly.

"Maybe to you," I countered. "But not to me. I fought it. You made me... I believed that love made me weak, and I didn't think I could afford that, but now I know that I can't afford to be without you so my priorities have to change."

"Is that a bad thing?"

"No, quite the contrary." I cleared my throat twice. Once from nerves, the second time because when I tried to talk, I couldn't get the words out. Eventually, I croaked, "They spit roasted me. They laughed too. It was a weird kind of cackle. I can still hear it. I'd have known they were high from that alone. I-It lasted thirty minutes. Thirty minutes of pain and misery and suffering. Of them taking something I didn't give them, yes, but of them ramming home how this wasn't my place. How everyone would believe them over me. They didn't just rape my body; they raped my mind."

"I'd have believed you," he whispered.

"M-Mom was pulling stunts again. Don't forget Axel was shocked when Rain finally did show up because it was her third time of claiming to be pregnant to keep him in line."

"It wasn't about your mom, Rachel," he argued quietly. "I never judged you for what *she* did. You're mine. You've always been mine. I know you would never have—" He sighed. "You have to understand that I've always known you're different around me.

"I'm not just talking about sexually, or about how we love each other, I'm talking physically. You let me in. You have since those days in the crawl space.

"Before Carly died, you were closed up. After, you were locked in your shell and nothing would drag you out.

"You were inexperienced back when you were raped. I worked hard to make you responsive, and even then, you only were because it was me. I might have been a teenaged jackass, Rach, but I was aware of that much." He pressed a kiss to my temple. "I'd always have believed you. Always.

"You can think that's me saying this now, that there's no way of knowing if I would have or not, but I know you, Rachel. I always have." His hand moved to cup the ball of my shoulder. He dragged it up and down the length of my arm. "You can tell me everything; you can tell me nothing. This is a safe space, baby girl."

I released a shaky breath through my nose. My eyes prickled with tears, but I wasn't sad or upset. Mostly, I was just tired. Tired of the constraints of the past. I didn't want them to control me anymore. They were a burden I carried and I was weary of their weight.

"In my dreams, they always rape me and I always struggle but it's the struggles of a girl. I-I was small and they were strong. They used their size against me and they controlled me like I was a marionette."

"You took self-defense classes in college, didn't you?"

"I did. If anyone tried to hurt me again, I could stop an attacker now." I swallowed. "I could stop *them* now."

"Good." Such a simple answer, but it packed as much of a punch as my own fist flying into his gut would. The thought had me wincing. Because I *had* hit him. Somewhere. "Did I hurt you when I punched you? I'm sorry if I did."

"No. Winded me and made me jump but I'll take that over the screams."

I'd often woken up with a hoarse voice from shouting and screeching in my sleep. Sometimes, I even woke myself up screaming.

"I must be a nightmare to be around," I said with a wince.

"It's a nightmare to be without you," he corrected, and suddenly, his fingers were stroking down over my hair, soothing me.

I bit my lip as I sank even further into his hold.

Trusting him not to bruise the fragile parts of my nature, trusting him to face my fire with his own.

I'd always thought Rex had the knack for politics.

I just didn't realize that knack made him perfect for me.

"What are you thinking?" he rumbled after a couple of quiet moments.

"That I..." I licked my lips. "I believe you."

His hand stilled. "About what?"

"You wouldn't have thought I was lying."

Rex jolted at that, then he shifted up and away, twisting over me so that he was looking down at me.

"Say that to me when your eyes are on mine."

His voice was a growl.

Guttural.

Demanding.

I shot him a small smile—all I was capable of at that moment—

and whispered, "I trust that you would have believed me about being raped."

His nostrils flared then his mouth was back on mine.

Not rough, not soft.

A signature on a verbal contract.

My favorite kind of kiss.

SEVENTEEN

REX

"You look tired."

Rachel, for the first time since the video call with Wynter had begun, relaxed. She released a short laugh as she elbowed me in the side and, to Wynter, not me, said, "He greeted me that way too. I swear I fell for his charm."

Wynter shot her a sheepish grin, but deep in her eyes, I saw the tiny flickers of a flame stirring to life.

A flame that spoke of curiosity, of happiness.

A glimpse at the real Rachel triggered both.

Her desire to know her birth mother hadn't abated despite my departure.

I'd figured that would be the case, but it was nice to know I was right.

"I *am* tired," Wynter retorted.

"Aren't you getting enough sleep?"

"Evidently," Rachel sniped. "Otherwise she wouldn't be tired, would she, Captain Obvious?"

I squinted at her. "I'm asking questions without asking questions.

Thought you'd be able to read between the lines considering your career choice."

"You wouldn't last two minutes in court. You'd already have ten objections for leading the witness."

"I'm the witness in this scenario?" Wynter joked.

"Most definitely."

I looked down my nose at her. "So, why aren't you sleeping then?"

"Things are up in the air."

"Understandable." Rachel sniffed. "Ignore Rex. When he was younger, I used to joke that he'd be able to sleep through a bomb blast."

"What changed?"

"Nothing," I said with a grin. "I could still sleep through a bomb blast."

"He's got a dark and dirty conscience," Rachel teased.

"It's always been dark and dirty," I mocked. "Stop messing with my rep."

"*Always?*" Wynter chuckled. "Wow, you must have been a nightmare as a kid."

"He was."

"Now who's being charming?" I grumbled.

Rach smirked. "I didn't sell myself as the charmer here."

"Neither did I."

"You just don't know you're making a sales pitch," she argued.

"You two are different when you're together, aren't you?"

Wynter's comment broke apart a glance that, unbeknown to either of us, went on for a good minute.

Within those sixty seconds, all I fucking knew was that the sparkles of glee in Rach's eyes were back. I felt each one like they were a piece of shrapnel piercing my flesh.

The pain was sweet.

Delicious.

"We like each other," Rachel said primly, her gaze darting to our daughter. "I just forgot that for a while."

"I didn't," I said smugly.

Wynter reached for her drink and took a deep sip. It was a coffee cup from the place she worked at.

My brow furrowed at the sight. "Are you still working at the coffee shop?"

"Of course."

"You don't have to worry about rent anymore. Why do you need a job?"

Wynter huffed. "To earn money to buy things."

"No, is that really what currency is for?" I mocked. "I know what money does, Wynter. I just want to know why you have to earn it now that I'm covering all your expenses."

Rachel elbowed me in the side. "If she wants a job, there's no harm in that."

"No harm? She's not sleeping, her father's in the hospital, she has band and chess club and theater and she's in AP History and Math. When the hell does she have time for a job as a waitress?"

Rachel frowned. "You're in AP Math? Rain is too."

Though she looked curious at the mention of Rain, Wynter just shrugged. "I like numbers."

"Rex was the same," Rach said with a smile. "He wasn't in AP Math though."

"I wasn't in many classes," I mocked.

"You skipped school?" Wynter demanded, aghast.

"I did. Many times. They didn't teach me anything I didn't know."

Rachel's nose crinkled. "He sounds bigheaded, but unfortunately, he's being honest. He was reading Plutarch when I was still salivating over Tolkien."

Wynter's eyes rounded. "Plutarch?"

Rachel reached for the mug of herbal tea she'd brewed before the start of this call. It smelled like lawn, but when I'd told her that, she'd blamed my kid for the no-caffeine rule and, wisely, I'd shut my mouth.

Both of us looked normal from the waist up, but she wore no

pants, and I wore a pair of boxer briefs that I'd been ecstatic to find in a drawer in our room.

What the kid couldn't see, wouldn't hurt her.

"He used to read it in Ancient Greek." Rachel took a deep sip. "Didn't you?"

"I used to," I agreed, folding my arms across my chest. "Little rusty now. But stop trying to change the subject, Rachel."

She huffed. "If Wynter wants to run herself ragged, that's her choice."

"I'm not running myself ragged," Wynter argued. "I can cope."

"You know what the dictionary definition of 'cope' is?" I answered before she could speak, "To deal effectively with something difficult."

"You've out-argued yourself," Rachel pointed out. "'Effectively' is the key word there."

"No, 'deal with' and 'difficult' are," I argued.

"You bicker a lot. I didn't see that before."

Rachel's tone was dismissive. "We don't bicker."

"It's how we roll," I disagreed, unfolding my arm from across my chest and slinging it over her shoulder. "Anyway, Rach was on her best behavior. I bring out the wild side in her."

Wynter grinned. "This is the wild side?"

"Rachel's ability to rebel was stunted at birth," I teased.

She elbowed me in the side again. "It was not. We weren't all princes to an MC legacy. Even at fifteen you could get away with murder."

I winked. "I wasn't an overachiever like you."

She sniffed but ignored me to ask, "How's your father, Wynter?"

I controlled my expression by the grace of God.

"He's not doing too well," was our daughter's careful response.

So the fucker was still breathing.

What a shame *that* was.

Grunting under my breath at the thought, I watched as Rachel asked the right questions, smoothing over my lack of interest in Jeremy Kinnock's mental and physical health.

It was an interesting shift—I'd been playing this part for her since we'd started holding these video calls but she'd picked up the mantel now that we were together again.

It made me wonder what else would change now that we were together.

Knowing how damn smart she was, I didn't worry, but I *was* curious.

"Are you mad at me for staying?"

The question, uttered hesitantly, had me tuning back into the conversation.

For a moment, I thought Wynter was asking me, but she wasn't.

"I understand why you stayed," was Rachel's careful response.

"That isn't an answer."

"She's a lawyer." I attempted to shield Rach. "Evasive answers are in her blood."

Wynter smirked, but Rachel's hand grabbed mine. I thought her nails were going to burrow through the back of my hand, but though her grip was tight, her voice wasn't:

"If you feel your place is there, then who are we to argue with that?"

"So, you believe I have the right to choose?" Wynter asked carefully.

"Yes." Rachel paused. "Even if it's the wrong choice." I didn't know why, but once she'd uttered those words, she reached up and rubbed at her temple. "I guess I need to start practicing what I preach."

"What? Why?" Wynter queried, her brow furrowed with concern.

"My brother wants to enlist. I got into an argument with him over it." She pulled a face. "I was trying to convince him that enlisting was his dad's, my stepfather's, dream."

"Was it?"

She grimaced. "Yes. But I can't have one rule for Rain and one rule for you. You're pretty much the same age. Rain's closer to graduating, but that doesn't mean anything. You're both almost adults."

"My mom doesn't have the same opinion as you."

Rachel cast me a glance. "How did Ally react to your presence in LA?"

"Mostly, she ignored me, but I stayed out of her way."

"Before the thing, you know, with the, um, the Triads—" Wynter cleared her throat. "She wasn't happy about you being here. She called me every night to plead with me not to talk to you."

I tensed but managed to hold my tongue.

Fuck, I was almost proud of myself for accomplishing that feat.

Rather than comment, I just grunted.

"You didn't listen?"

"No. Rex... King, he showed me a side of himself that let me believe he was capable of everything Mom said, but I still wanted to get to know him anyway."

Rachel blinked. "Why? I can't imagine Ally's tales were pleasant."

"They weren't," Wynter confirmed the worst. "But it's hard to associate the man with a small militia under his command with the same guy who practically force-fed me every time we met up."

Rachel smiled. "He's like that. Gets under your skin."

"Like a parasite. Great!"

She peeped a grin at me. "You have your ways about you, Rex. Laker girls are particularly susceptible to them."

My nose crinkled but Wynter's gleeful laugh took away any embarrassment on my behalf.

"What else did you like about Rex?" Rachel asked, her hand tightening around mine, this time in a silent warning to shut up. Something she compounded with a swift glare.

Wynter's cheeks were hot as she said, "He talks about things adults don't share with kids. At least, not in my family. He was open and honest, and when Mom was telling me he was a bad man and that I should do my best to cut him out, all I knew was that..."

"What, honey?"

She stared down at her lap. "Mom said that Dad was a good man, but he isn't. Is he?"

"No."

I definitely deserved a reward for keeping *that* answer short and sweet.

"No," she agreed. "He was going to use me to pay off his debts. He's beaten Mom; he's cheated. King told me that you were it for him. Have you cheated on Rachel?"

"No."

Rach squeezed my hand.

"Have you cheated on King, Rachel?"

"No."

"Would you ever beat her?"

"Of course I wouldn't," I grumbled. "And before you ask, I'd sell *myself* before I'd sell you."

"And, Rachel, is that the man you know? Those words aren't BS, I mean, are they?"

"No, they're not. On the outside, he's this rough Sinner who'll kill and steal and trade in things that he should be locked up for. But he's the best kind of man, Wynter. He always was."

Wynter nodded. "I knew all that before everything went down. I- I went with my gut, I guess."

I squeezed Rach's hand and said, "Wynter, we need to talk to you about something."

Rachel shot me a look then, seeming to realize what was going on, blanched.

"You do?" Wynter asked, her tone wary as she clearly spotted Rachel's reaction to my comment.

"One of the—" I hesitated. "We..."

Rachel cleared her throat. "We're having a baby, Wynter."

Her mouth worked, then her gaze drifted between us. "Are you happy about that?"

Rachel sniffled. "I'm very happy. I'm... I'm scared, but I'm happy."

"Why are you scared?"

"I don't like hospitals or doctors, and just going to the appointments is rough." She sucked in a breath. "I don't like my body, I don't like being sick, and it's all really difficult, but I'm... I'm stronger now." She stared at Wynter, and I could see her silently pleading with our daughter for her to understand. "I'm, we, you... I just—"

"Is this why you're getting back together?" Wynter asked cautiously before Rachel could stutter through the dictionary.

"No. I found out before Christmas, but I didn't tell Rex until the night of the gala."

Wynter winced. "Oh. I'm sorry. I ruined that—"

"You have *nothing* to be sorry for. I'm just so glad you're safe." Rachel's mouth trembled. "I don't want you to hate me for this."

I'd stayed quiet until now, but I couldn't hold back from saying, "Wynter won't hate you, will you?"

She licked her lips. "You still want to talk to me, don't you?"

Rachel sniffled again, but this time it warranted me getting up and grabbing the box of tissues so she could blow her nose. That required some awkward shuffling so Wynter didn't have to see her dad's junk. I really should just have put my jeans on.

"Of course I do," Rachel whispered. "I want nothing more than that. It's my fault you don't want to talk to me as much as you do with Rex because I know I'm so awkward, but I promise I'm trying."

Wynter shot me a pleading look, and hiding a smile as she waggled her hands, silently telling me to do something to fix this, I hauled Rachel into my side. "Rach is crying more than usual." After spending a single afternoon with her, I already knew that to be a fact.

"I don't do tears," she said with a haughtiness that was spoiled by a hiccup.

Wynter hunched her shoulders. "If you don't want to stop talking to me, then I'm happy for you." A notification sounded on her phone, and I could tell she wasn't sorry to say, "I need to go."

I sighed. "You don't."

"No, I do. I need to visit Dad."

Gnawing the inside of her cheek, Rach blurted out, "We can do this again when you have a moment. I-I really hope you want to."

Wynter's smile was genuinely relieved. "I'd love that," she said earnestly.

"Wynter?" I asked, buoyed by her reply.

"Yeah?"

"Why, if your dad is someone you'd consider to be a bad man, are you staying down there to be with him?"

Her gaze collided with mine. "Because everyone deserves a chance."

Before I could argue that her giving me a chance wasn't the same as her sticking around her toxic fucker of a father, she gave us a quick wave and ended the video call.

I got to my feet the moment the screen went black and I strolled over to the jeans I'd dumped on the floor.

"I'm gonna be about twenty minutes," I ground out, any joy at Wynter's acceptance of the baby diminishing after she compared me to that bastard.

Rach didn't reply, but I could feel her eyes on me.

Just like I knew they were still on me when I stormed out of the house and went to the pile of logs she had out there.

This was clearly one of Rain's chores because the stack was nice and high but that didn't mean I couldn't get in on this.

I had to do something to burn off the sudden surge of my temper.

I hefted the ax in my hand, plunked down a log on the stand, then sent the blade flying.

Over and over I chopped the wood, until ten minutes had passed and I was throwing my shirt off and tossing it onto the ground.

Burning off the negative energy felt good because there was no way I was about to start an argument with Rach, not on my first day back.

We *did* bicker. That was fine. But arguing wasn't something I wanted. That had been our common ground over the last twenty years. It was our fail-safe. I didn't want that anymore.

A wolf whistle sounded behind me, and though I was still riled up, my lips quirked at the corners.

I gave her a couple back flexes to tease her, and she mumbled, "Good Lord."

That definitely smoothed over my bad mood.

Turning to stare at her over my shoulder, I demanded, "Enjoying the show?"

She grinned at me. "Definitely."

"You got dressed," I groused.

"So did you. Plus you left the house to have a hissy fit."

I sniffed. "I don't do hissy fits. I have—"

"Temper breakdowns?"

Quickly rolling my eyes, I derided, "That's just a synonym."

"A *manly* synonym, when really what I should have called it was a temper tantrum," she teased. Her hand settled on the small of my back where sweat had beaded. She surprised me by not grunting in disgust but by twirling her fingers there. "You can't get mad at her for giving him the chance she gave you."

I grumbled, "I deserved the chance. He doesn't."

"She didn't know that."

"She knows how bad Kinnock is."

"She's got a lot of good memories too. They outweigh the bad, I reckon. They must. Otherwise, I don't think she'd even be trying." She tilted her head and rested it against my arm. "She's a good kid, Rex."

"Too good. She'll get hurt."

She placed her other hand on my belly as she patted me there. "We all get hurt, baby. At least she has us to keep her from the worst hurts."

I sucked in a breath. "She has private bodyguards watching over her."

"I'm sure she does but I wasn't just talking physically." She kissed my shoulder. "At least she knows about the baby now. That's something. Anyway, come inside. It's cold out here and we have enough wood cut for the next year at least."

I snorted. "Hardly."

"This is the outer stockpile. Rain's got a whole bunch stored in the garage. He's like you, works out his tension on innocent dead trees."

She backed off to let me lodge the ax in the log on the ground, and I turned to face her after I grabbed my shirt.

"Did you work out when you were in LA?" she queried, her eyes all over me.

I grinned at the heat in that stare. "What else did I have to do with my time?"

I didn't let her speak, just put those extra muscles to good use and hauled her over my shoulder.

TEXT CHAT

O'Donnelly: *Francis Merriweather, Mikhail Korolev. Decisions, decisions.*

Nyx: *When?*

O'Donnelly: *Not who?*

Nyx: *Don't care. If they touch kids, they need to die. When?*

O'Donnelly: *I'll be in contact.*

O'Donnelly: *Rachel Laker was most impressive.*

Nyx: *Leave her the fuck out of this. This is between you and me.*

O'Donnelly: *Protective of her... Interesting.*

Nyx: *Not interesting. She's my Prez's Old Lady. Leave her the fuck alone.*

O'Donnelly: *Calm down, Nyx. I'm a faithful husband.*

Nyx: *So how is it Finn O'Grady exists?*

EIGHTEEN

REX

"Rex!" Rach shrieked out a laugh as the kitchen counter hit the back of her legs.

Grinning at her, I stacked my hands on either side of her hips and murmured, "You shrieked?"

"Nyx and Giulia will be back soon. I don't want them to see me naked in the kitchen."

I arched a brow at her. "If Maverick hasn't told them to steer clear of this place until Monday, his mouth'll be meeting my fist the next time I see him."

She snorted. "Have you kicked Rain and Harlow out as well? This is a YMCA for Sinners now, don't you know?"

My brow furrowed. "He's staying here?" Then, before she could answer, I held up a hand. "You're on the kitchen counter, Rachel, and the only thing I'm intending to eat off of this marble, sweetheart, is you. I don't want to be thinking about business yet. That's for Monday."

"You've put off thoughts of the MC for a while now...," she mused.

"It can wait some more." I narrowed my gaze upon her. "Eighteen fucking years they've had my complete dedication. Shit's going to change because I'm not about to let them come between us again."

Her cheeks flushed even as a hint of surprise peeped into her gaze. "You mean that?"

"I do."

Her chin dipped, the move surprisingly coy. I reached up and slipped my hand along that burnished cheek, murmuring, "This is going to happen, Rach."

"I'm glad," she said, her eyes meeting mine.

"No more putting business between us. No more closing each other out. Agreed?"

"Agreed."

"I come home here every night."

She swallowed as if she were nervous, then just as I got ready to argue with her, she said, tone as clear as day, "Home. Yes."

I smirked at her and, with my free hand, cupped her knee, then started to smooth it along the inner curve of her thigh.

"Technically, this is my home," I mocked as I drifted my fingertips over her yoga pant covered pussy.

She squirmed against the marble, but her legs parted, and if that wasn't an invitation for more, I didn't know what was.

"My baby mama needs to eat," I told her teasingly, knowing she'd hate me calling her that—the crinkle at the bridge of her nose confirmed that suspicion. "But I need some sugar first and then I'll make you a sandwich."

She licked her lips at my words then whimpered when I bowed my head and pressed an open-mouthed kiss to her throat. I traced small pecks over the arch of her collarbone toward her breasts.

My hands dropped to the hem of her sweatshirt—technically, it was *mine*—and as I started to draw it higher along her abdomen, I came across the thick swell of her stomach.

My kid.

Fuck.

In a rush to see more, I pulled back and drew the rest of the sweatshirt over her head, only taking care as her hair got tangled up at the end.

"You look good in my clothes," I teased as I peered down at her nakedness, thanking Christ she wasn't wearing a bra. "But you look better like this."

Her smile was shy. "Good to know."

I traced a finger along her collarbone, muttering, "Still the most beautiful fucking thing I've ever seen in my goddamn life."

If my voice got thicker toward the latter half of that statement, then so be it.

I let that finger trail down to her nipple, and I watched it pucker beneath my touch. Stepping closer to her, my mouth mimicked the trail of my finger and I pressed a kiss to her collarbone, then slowly moved toward her tits.

Teasing one nipple with my breath, I brushed it with the tip of my tongue, not stopping until the crinkled flesh had become as tightly furled as a fresh rosebud. Only then did I continue my journey.

She angled herself backward, resting her weight on her hands. I let my lips glance over the hard roundness of her stomach because that was another minefield to battle but it could wait for tomorrow.

I let my tongue sweep along the band around her waist instead of spreading kisses over her bump like I wanted, then I murmured, "Lift your hips."

She put her heels to the edge of the counter and shimmied into a bridge so that I could drag the waistband down over her ass and to her thighs. I swept them off all the way a couple seconds later.

"No panties," I said thickly, eyes tangling with hers.

"Not today," she retorted with a smirk which told me not to get my hopes up every time I saw her wearing these torture devices.

I tutted. "From now on?"

"Sometimes," was all she'd concede.

Humming in approval, I moved my fingers to her thighs, shaped her knees with my fingertips, then slowly drew them apart.

Pressing my mouth to her navel, I moved down to her pussy, and then, I was where I wanted to be.

She scented of soap. She scented of Rach. *She scented of my girl.*

I growled as I let my tongue drift between her parted folds, flicking it against her clit before delving deeper. I grabbed one leg and angled it high on the counter, resting her foot on the marble so I could move in closer.

A hand drifted through my hair, her nails digging in deep as she released a guttural groan when I sucked on her clit before I thrust my tongue into her, tasting her essence. Tasting that sugar that was all fucking mine.

Groaning, I buried my face in her cunt, savoring something she rarely gifted me.

My nose rubbed against her clit as I sank into her, going as deep as I could, eating her out like the starving man I was.

She creamed against me beautifully, her groans and cries serenading me like a concert violinist.

She made better music than Mozart or Metallica.

Grunting as I fucked her with my tongue, I moved higher and suckled her clit. My hands longed to shape her belly, but her words to Wynter rang like a death knell in my head.

Instead, I pulled back to let a finger thrust into her. She immediately clutched at it. My other hand went to the one thigh that was still hanging limply against the counter, and I angled that high, too, so that she was spread out and open for me on the marble.

With a groan, I dove even deeper, wanting her to go wild, to be as free as I was when we were together and I let myself go.

I sucked on one of her labia then moved higher to nibble on her clit. She squeaked at that, which made me smirk, and I gave it some love by shaping it with my tongue tip.

As I feasted on her, she started to ride my face, hips rocking with an erratic rhythm that shattered my soul because this was how I remembered her.

I wanted this.

All of this.

All of her.

For-fucking-ever.

With a shriek, she came.

It was loud and raucous and everything I could ever want.

Her nails dug into my skull, her hands tugged at my hair, and she squeezed my head, greedy as she savored her orgasm.

As she came down, I continued to suck on her clit, gently though, just keeping her primed, letting her know this was round one.

Only when she soughed out a sob did I pull back.

Only then did I unfasten my zipper even though my dick had to have the tines imprinted on it from how fucking hard it had been pushing against the fly.

She watched me with dazed eyes as I freed my cock, and then as I pulled it out, she blew my fucking mind by reaching down and spreading her pussy lips apart.

My brains scrambled, a hunger for more hitting me—I wanted this.

I never wanted it to end.

I wanted her always.

I stepped closer, stepped home, and carefully shuffled her to the edge of the counter.

"Did you know this would be the perfect height for me to fuck you on?" I rumbled, letting my lips ghost over hers.

A snicker of laughter escaped her, making me grin. "No, King," she retorted, her voice hoarse. "I didn't imagine that when I was picking out counters."

"Shame on you." I shook my head then winked at her before I started a kiss that had her arms coming to clasp my neck.

She wriggled against me, all her nakedness rubbing up against mine, and she kissed me back.

She fucking kissed me back, as hungry as me. As desperate.

I lost it then.

Lost my soul to her because I'd given her my heart a lifetime ago.

As she drew from me, I drew from her, and together, our tongues fucked as I reached between us and thrust my dick into her so that all of us became whole.

I released a guttural grunt just as her high whimper drifted from her as I filled her to the max.

Her legs shuffled. I felt one angle itself, her heel back on the counter as she tilted herself into me so that I could go even deeper.

With a groan, I slid in that extra inch. "I love you, Rachel."

She mewled, "Love you too, King."

I wanted those words tattooed on me.

Indy wouldn't call me a pussy if I asked her to do that, would she?

Nipping Rachel's bottom lip, I pulled back and rumbled, "You ready, princess?"

She sighed, pecked my mouth, nodded.

Slowly at first, I retreated, hissing as my cock abandoned the cosseting silk of her cunt.

Her nails buried themselves into my shoulders as I slowly pushed back in.

Slowly, she hissed.

Slowly, I grunted.

It went on like that a couple times.

I lived and died by that adverb—slowly.

This wasn't the first desperate time.

This was the beginning of forever.

I wanted it to be good.

Hissing when my cock was left out in the cold, she proceeded to light up my life—her heels were suddenly burrowed in my ass and she was snapping, "King, if you won't fuck me, I'll fuck myself."

Grinning at her, feeling the beads of sweat at my temple, the hammer of my heart, I silently told her to have at it.

And she did.

Sitting half upright, she ground into me, moving around so that she could ride me, and hell if that didn't feel like heaven.

As she wriggled and writhed, her cunt called me home, and when she was screaming with frustration, unable to give herself the pounding she so desperately needed, I curved my arms around her then, rounding my back, did as she demanded.

I fucked her.

Hard, raw.

I gave myself unto her.

All of me.

And I was gifted all of her back as she fucked me in return.

It was a mutual pounding as we tore pleasure from each other's bodies, and she was screaming as she came, her pussy muscles doing the salsa around my shaft as it demanded I drench it in my cum.

I kissed her as I let her cunt milk me, only stopping when my brain was bleached from the bomb blast that was an orgasm with my woman.

She fell back against the counter as if her muscles had turned to goo, and I followed her.

How long we stayed that way, my face burrowed in her tits, her legs loosely holding my hips, I had no idea.

I only moved because I heard the sound of footsteps on the front stoop, then the door clamored as it was opened and slammed shut.

I felt her panic, but I soothed her by smoothing my hand down her arm and hollering, "Rain, if you don't want to see my naked ass then you'll keep yours outta the kitchen."

"Rex!" Rachel snarled in my ear, making me smirk.

"I prefer it when you call me King," I teased.

"Aw, man, you're fucking in the kitchen?" Rain whined.

A snort sounded, and a low voice muttered, "Had to happen eventually."

My brow furrowed at that, but Rachel said on a whisper, "Harlow. They've been hanging out."

"Kitchen's are supposed to be hygienic," Rain complained.

"I'll bleach the fuckin' counter afterward," I retorted. "And when you get your own woman, I'll remind you of this conversation, huh?"

I heard a grunt, then the stomping of feet as both men took the wisest course of action—they made a retreat.

"He's never going to let me live that down," Rachel groused, her cheeks bright pink.

"It's something he's gonna have to get used to."

She rolled her eyes, but the slightest smile curved her lips.

It had been a long fucking time, too fucking long since I'd seen that, but I knew what it meant even if she didn't.

Rachel was happy.

I'd spend the rest of my fucking life making sure she went to sleep and started the day with that smile.

And that was more of a vow than anything I could make to her in a church.

NINETEEN

RACHEL

"I'm ready."

I peered at him. "For what?"

We were watching one of my shows on TV, a blanket curled around us both, naked as the day we were born.

Last week, if you'd told me before *90 Day Fiancé* started that I'd be watching it from Rex's lap, I'd have laughed hysterically.

Not only because Rex hated this shit, but because I didn't think I'd be comfortable enough to sit like this with him.

Comfort levels changed after sex.

I'd forgotten about that.

Post-sex had always been borderline traumatic. Memories and horrible reminders that I wasn't the same woman as I was before had always plagued me.

But after two nights of nightmares that didn't end with me screaming and yelling at Rex, of going to sleep with baby's butt-soft cheeks nuzzling up against mine, slowly, I was starting to associate sex with good times.

Nice intimate moments that weren't life changing for the most part, but were for me.

I'd woken up with Rex's hand between my thighs and while he'd been asleep so I couldn't chide him for it, neither had I yelled down the house because my brain had accepted that his touch was reality.

Theirs was a memory.

It was a two-decade-long process, and I didn't know what was making it happen now, but I was fucking grateful.

So fucking grateful.

Especially because, right at this moment, my freezing feet were tucked under his large paw despite the fact that my body felt like it was roasting as it was snuggled up against his.

Everything about Rex was hot.

Everything.

He was like a living, breathing hot water bottle.

"For Dad's letter."

I blinked, jumbling his words together so that they made sense to me.

"You're ready to read the letter Bear left you?" I translated.

He grimaced. "As ready as I'll ever be."

"Now?" I whined. "When we're all comfortable and *90 Day Fiancé* is about to start?"

His lips quirked into a grin. "You can press pause, Rach. It's not like this is a new episode or anything."

I pouted but said, "You did this on purpose so I'd have to streak across the room."

"Hey, I need cheering up," he defended, but I noticed there was a definite gleam in his eye that told me I'd caught him red-handed

Huffing, I clambered off his lap. "Give me the blanket."

"But I'm comfortable."

It had been so long since Rex had been playful with me that it took me a good thirty seconds to calm myself down and not get mad.

Huffing again, I held out my hand, watching that sparkle in his eye all the while as I tapped my foot, well aware that it made my tits jiggle.

He hefted up, dragged the blanket away, and handed it to me. As cool as you please in his delicious nakedness. "Spoilsport."

"Bet your ass I am," I said with a sniff as I wrapped the blanket under my arms and knotted it between my breasts.

Walking over to the door, I did my best not to break my self-imposed role, until I opened said door. Then, I twisted around, unfastened the knot, flashed him, before I darted out into the hall.

My grin broke free as I heard him howl with laughter, and cheeks red hot, probably above *and* below, I dashed down the stairs and headed toward my office.

Even from the hall, I could hear his cackling and it filled me with warmth. I needed it too. This letter, whatever it contained, was going to break the mood for sure.

But that was a part of being together, I guessed.

Being there for the rough and the smooth, while getting each other to the other side.

I'd stored the letter in my desk drawer, and grabbing it, I realized I'd left my phone in here when I'd gone to open the door to Rex the other day because the screen flashed with a notification.

God, small wonder it had been quiet—my phone was in here and in 'do not disturb' mode because I'd just gotten off a call when Rex had showed up.

"I didn't even miss work," I mused under my breath as I tugged it off the charger and scanned my notifications.

There were a lot from Parker.

Parker: *Are you dead?*

Parker: *You'd better be dead if you're ignoring this many of my calls.*

Parker: *SOS! Omg, where the fuck are you?*

Parker: *I had to call the clubhouse. I hope you're happy now. I know you're alive, and I know Rex is with you. I demand a full recounting by way of apology. Do you hear me?*

My lips twitched at that, but I didn't bother replying because I knew she'd make me pay on Monday so I might as well maintain radio silence before then.

Plus, if I'd answered, we'd have gotten into a conversation, and that would have just delayed the inevitable—handing over the damn letter to Rex.

Heaving a sigh, I forced my mind off work.

Especially when I saw a couple emails from the ins I had at the State Department.

I got to my feet.

Went to the door.

Hunter's grin flashed before me as if he were standing there.

Huffing, I twisted back and headed to my desk.

I pulled up the emails, scanned the contents.

Each one was goddamn different.

Eamonn Keegan died in 1997.

Eamonn Keegan was released from prison in January.

Eamonn Keegan is listed as a prisoner of HM Prison Wormwood Scrubs.

I scrubbed my forehead at each one, wondering whether any of them, or none of them, were correct.

Because I was at a loss, I forwarded all three to Hunter and sent him a text.

Me: *I'm going to bed, so I won't see this until the morning, but I need information on a guy called Eamonn Keegan. He's who Dead To Me wants info about. I'm not sure if this is a trap, I'm not even sure what the fuck is going on when I get three completely different responses from my people in the State Department, but I don't need to tell you how important it is that I give her the right answer.*

Me: *Love you, Hunt.*

Me: *Be a good boy and get me what I need.*

When I saw the arrows turn blue, indicating that he'd read the message, I turned my phone over and dashed out of the room.

That was Monday's problem.

Okay, who was I kidding?

Tomorrow's.

Returning to the bedroom, I found Rex staring at the wall, his laughter long since gone. I was glad I'd given him that, especially as the letter in my hand felt like it weighed a ton.

I figured that was emotional weight because the envelope was as light as a feather.

Rex's gaze landed on me as I closed the door, and wandering over to him, I grabbed another blanket from the bottom of the bed, sat myself on his lap again, then covered us both with the new blanket because I didn't want to take off the one I was wearing.

When I was seated, I handed him the letter, only he shook his head. "Read it to me?"

Cringing, I asked, "Are you going to shoot the messenger again?"

He shot me a rueful smile. "No shooting."

"Good."

He slipped his arms around my waist and tugged me close.

Sucking in a breath, I opened the envelope and pulled out the letter. Tucked between the folds was a credit card. At least, it appeared to be a credit card. Upon further inspection, I realized that it was a room key card.

Frowning, I passed it to Rex before I started to read the letter out loud:

Son,

I've tried to write this letter a couple times and no matter what I do, I can't seem to get my thoughts down right.

It's hard because as I write this, I know when you read it, I'll be dead.

That's a fucked-up way to approach this, and it's harder than I'd like to admit.

So, first things first—why am I leaving you this letter?

Because I think my death will be untimely, unexpected, and there won't be a chance to give you a proper goodbye.

That breaks my fucking heart, son. I love you, but there's the rub—I love you too much to get you involved in this preemptively. If I die, I die. There ain't nothing I can do about that, and if my business is still unfinished, then I'm hoping you'll be there to end shit for me.

Okay, so let me deal with this in a logical order.

By now, I figure you've learned that I was weak, and I'm pretty sure that you hate me. Or, at least, a part of you hates me. I'm hoping that by the time we next meet, you'll have forgiven me.

Your mom did.

I need you to know that.

I told her everything, aside from Kendra's existence because even I didn't know about that until after Rene had died.

Learning who Kendra was broke me. She told me the day after the funeral, and I didn't react well. You'd be ashamed of me, and to be fair, I'm ashamed of myself. I ran from that problem, ran from everything, and dove headfirst into someone else's troubles.

I was a good father to you, King, but Kendra wasn't so lucky. She's I don't really know what she is. She's nothing like her mother, nothing like me. She finds joy in bringing others pain, and that kind of bitterness never ends well.

I'm pretty certain that I'll get to see her again before I see you, and I hope that's the truth. I can make my peace with her then, but for you, King, I hope you live a long and fulfilling life.

You need to get your ass back with Rachel, son. Make right whatever you did wrong because, fuck, she's perfect for you. Your mom realized it a long time before I did, and Rene was always the smartest one out of the pair of us.

I'm also hoping that before you're both old and fucking gray, you'll wife her and brand her. I'd like to think of the Sinners being reigned over by the pair of you. You'll take it from a bunch of ragtag outlaws into something better. Something more.

With you two, the sky really is the limit.

Whether you forgive me or not for Kendra, I want you to know that I love you. I want you to know that I'm proud of you, that I've always been proud of you. I want you to know that I have faith in you and that there was never a day where I wasn't grateful to have you as my son.

I wanted Rach to give you this letter after I died because I knew you'd have questions. Maybe I should have given you the opportunity to ask them <u>before</u> I died, but truth is, I couldn't have dealt with that.

Kendra is the embodiment of my weakness. I'll always be ashamed that I let your mother down. Kendra doesn't deserve that, but I don't feel like she's my flesh and blood. I believe her mother, don't get me wrong. Maria's a good girl. But Kendra, there's no link there. No connection.

I left her no bequest. That's wrong of me, and it's even worse for me to say that I ask you to give her one. Maybe you could help set her up somewhere, get her a house, do something to make her stop whoring herself out. I don't know if she'd even want that. The MC means something to her so maybe she'll refuse, but try?

I include a copy of a key card to a motel room in the next town over—Hanover. I've been living out of there since I left. It's my base. I own the place, well, you do now, so go visit it. There might be something in there you find useful.

The world is a lot more complicated than I ever realized. Your mother's death helped me uncover a crazy web that I didn't share with you because I figured you'd think grief had turned my head—some proof's in that room.

Please, forgive me my failings, and know that I never set out to hurt you. I know you'll hate me, and I say goodbye to you deeply regretting the mistakes I made.

When you're living them, it's like looking through fog—no

way out. I know you'll have been there, and I also know you're a better man than me.

You always made me proud, and I know that'll continue once I'm gone.

I love you, son.

Your loving father

I wasn't sure how I didn't break off to cry when he spoke about Rex and me, but I fell back on my role as Ice Queen to get me through. Only pausing in that when Rex burrowed into me, his face smushing up against my throat to hide from the world.

I couldn't blame him.

Bear had a habit of yanking the rug from under our feet.

"Wonder what's in that motel room," was the first thing he said after a good ten minutes of silence.

Neither of us mentioned that I could feel the slick moisture from tears against my skin.

I was just as wrecked.

Having received one myself, I knew these beyond-the-grave missives were tough to handle.

"Want to go tomorrow?"

He was quiet a second. "Okay."

He hit play, which made me jump because the sound from my show blared on, but I didn't say anything, just squeezed him tight and held him close as I tried not to think about whatever Pandora's box Bear had in his motel room.

RACHEL

It was a pleasant, run of the mill motel.

Nothing special, but nothing shady either.

Rex's hog stood out amid the family sedans, which meant Bear's would have too.

It was an odd choice for a biker.

"Why didn't he just rent somewhere? Why buy this place?" Rex muttered as he flipped the card between his fingers and headed over to the room number listed on the back of it.

"Housekeeping's included, I guess."

His nose crinkled. "If there's proof in that room, how likely is it that he let maids in, do you think?"

"True." I shrugged. "I don't know. Your father was a mystery to me most days. Did you know he's the one who..." I cleared my throat then, under my breath, whispered, "...offed Luke Lancaster?"

His brows lifted. "Giulia—"

"She told me earlier this year. Said that Bear asked her to keep it quiet."

"The fuck? Why?"

"I don't know. He'd come into town to change his will."

"What were the additions?"

"Storm's bequests. He wrote his letter to you too. Added a couple of donations to some charities as well."

"Which charities?"

"I don't remember the names. They're all in his will. As executor, you'll need to make the transfers."

He nodded his understanding, but I could tell he was as bewildered as me.

When we made it to the room, he opened the door, and both of us peered in.

I whistled under my breath.

Rex didn't utter a word as he stepped into the wilderness in here.

"No way he used this as a base because there was housekeeping," I mumbled, closing the door behind me as I tried to avoid the tangled network of string that filled the room.

It was like a spider's web.

Those strands of string were everywhere, crossing through the center of the room, pieces of paper, photos, post-it notes, pegged here and there. On the back wall, there were pictures with names on them. Names I recognized.

Just looking around the room made me exhausted, and I headed over to the bed and plunked my ass down to stare at the space all while my gaze kept flicking over to Rex.

He was taking this better than I was, that much was evident.

As clear-headed as I knew Bear had been the last time I'd seen him before the blast, the Gordian knot that was this room had me wondering if he'd been losing it.

Rex was reading, scanning, studying, however.

He did that for over an hour, long enough for me to not just sit down on the bed, but to lie flat out and cover myself with a blanket because this room was frigid.

I didn't lie down only because I was cold and tired, but because there were Venn diagrams above the bed. One in particular drew my attention more than anything else.

It didn't consist of just two intersecting circles, but five so the end shape was almost like a star.

FBI, SCOTUS, NYPD, LAPD, Homeland Security.

Then, inside the interlocking circles, there were names. Some underlined, some, very few in the grand scheme of things, with question marks.

I sucked in a shuddery breath at the sight of DONAVAN LANCASTER which was underlined several times and surrounded by dollar signs. 'Money man' was jotted down too.

If he'd gotten that right, as well as the other names I recognized from the recent glut of exposés that had been in the news because of Savannah Daniels, I felt as if those that were unknown to me were guaranteed to be Sparrows too.

If I unpicked that piece of paper from the ceiling, I could hand that over to Lodestar, and she could make sure that every single man and woman detailed on there was sent to hell.

But the information overload didn't stop there.

There was a simpler Venn diagram.

Three circles this time.

New World Sparrows, Old World Sparrows, Eastern Sparrows.

More names inside each interlocking circle.

Three in bold, where Bear had written over the names a couple times, in the main circles. Then, other names, names I recognized. Some were royalty, there was a general or two that Bear had doodled a flag beside to denote their nationality, a couple prime ministers/presidents in East Europe and Asia, and several cardinals were listed as well.

'ACTIVE GROUPS IN THE US WHO ARE ENEMIES OF THE NWS/OWS/ES' was the next sheet I read.

This one consisted of just a list:

- **Five Points** (Irish Mob. Watch out for that fucker O'Donnelly Sr.)

- **Camorra** (West Coast/Sicilian ties. Camorra head has under-the-radar familial links to LVPD Chief.)
- **LVPD** (Camorra ties. Las Vegas is unfriendly to Sparrow activity.)
- **Bratva** (Moscow holds no interest in Sparrow activity. KGB under orders to kill any Sparrow who approaches them.)
- **New York Triads** (Chairman is not a friend of any Sparrow body. Not even Eastern Sparrows which has a wide net over Asia.)

There were other lists, one of the groups Bear believed were enemies of the international bodies of Sparrows.

As I read that one, my heart pretty much froze in my chest. Because bold as brass, in Bear's scrawl, was the name I'd been hunting info on.

- **ECD** (Eamonn Keegan is the leader and he's a twisted cunt. That last bomb in London he got sent up for wasn't even for the ECD cause but was because it was a meeting between NWS, OWS, and ES. Killed sixty-five Sparrows. High-ranking ones too. I'd like to shake that bastard's hand. Sister was murdered by an underling. ECD will only be strong once Keegan's free and can take the reins again.)

"Lodestar and Maverick need to see this room."

I blinked at Rex's bland statement, my mind jerking from Bear's notes on Eamonn Keegan. I didn't disagree though. Just...

"You sure Maverick is well enough for this?"

"He'll be pissed if he isn't included."

"He will," I concurred, but that wasn't exactly an answer to my question.

"This place is…" Rex exhaled. "If I didn't know better, I'd say he was nuts."

From the state of this room, it was easy to imagine that Bear was definitely off his rocker, and yet, the contents of the web each strand of string uncovered spoke of an intellect similar to that of his son's.

Rex was beyond smart. Crazy smart. Seemed like I had proof it was in the blood.

When I didn't speak, only sat up at the side of the bed and found some other info dump for me to tumble into, Rex picked up his cellphone and made the calls.

Within forty minutes, Lodestar and Maverick were sharing the space with us.

Things had been strained between Star and me since our last argument, but when she took a seat beside me, I had no choice other than to raise an arm and curve it around her shoulders.

Which was when she wept.

This brave headcase wept.

<u>We had answers.</u>

We had names.

We weren't in the dark anymore.

This, I realized, was the first time Lodestar had felt the light in years, and it was granted to her by a man she'd never even met.

I blew out a breath as my own eyes burned. This wasn't my cause, wasn't my fight, yet Bear had died because of it.

Lodestar was subsisting for it.

Was this the end, though? I asked myself as I stared around the space. *Or,* I thought fearfully, *merely the beginning?*

I guessed only time would tell.

TWENTY-ONE

REX

Sunday didn't end how I hoped it would, and Monday's start wasn't great either.

Waking up with Rach put a smile on my face, at least, but after she went to her office to prepare for a morning in court in Manhattan, and I had to head to the clubhouse, my good mood had already waned.

It seemed ridiculous to ride my bike down the hill to the compound, when it was less than a five-minute walk, so I determined that I'd keep my hog parked up there and would return home on foot.

The Prospect manning the gates greeted me with wide eyes, and the few men clustered around the garage area—a new space that was set to the side, away from the clubhouse itself and nearer to the road —watched me ride up with bug eyes too.

Like a game of Telephone with teenage girls messing around at a sleepover, the message somehow had been passed from one side of the compound to the other.

By the time I was parking and nudging my kickstand into place, Nyx had stepped out too, with Link, Sin, and Steel rubbing shoulders alongside him.

Nyx greeted me with a clap to the back, Link in a bear hug. Sin dragged me into one too and Steel punched me in the gut.

"Fucker. Don't you dare leave for so long without telling us where the fuck you've gone, you hear me?"

"Yeah, Mom," I mocked, rubbing my stomach with a scowl until he pulled me into a half-hug.

"It's BS about you wearing a tux, ain't it, Rex?" Sin demanded.

Ignoring him and the question, I shoved him aside and found Maverick was watching us, leaning against the doorway, and I nodded at him before I caught sight of the many, many faces behind him.

I'd wanted to catch up with the council first, wanted to tell them about what we'd uncovered in Dad's room yesterday, but that clearly wasn't to be.

For all that I could see my men were relieved I was here, there was a lot of malcontent in their expressions too.

Deciding that I was better off nipping that in the bud, I told Nyx, "Get everyone here for general church."

Whispers sounded, spreading amid the crowd like VD in a whorehouse.

General church, AKA 'Mass,' was rarely called in the Sinners.

I wasn't like Dad. I led the place democratically in a sense, but I used my council more than he had. That meant Mass was a rare occurrence because, to be frank, I didn't see the point in getting the opinions from a bunch of dumb fucks.

I'd go to war for my brothers, would kill for them, but rely on their smarts?

Nope.

Because being gawked at for twenty minutes wasn't my idea of fun, I headed to my office. It was warm in here, a fire burning in the hearth, and I noticed that a laptop was running on my desk too—Nyx had clearly been making use of this space.

Another Prez might have been pissed, but I wasn't most men.

Nyx had held the fort down for me, the least he could enjoy was the spoils of a comfortable office.

Rubbing my temple as I collapsed in the desk chair, already wishing this were over, I glanced at the computer screen. I saw he had a bunch of spreadsheets open, but they weren't for Sinners' business.

My lips twitched as he strode in, slamming his laptop lid down with a force that couldn't be good for it.

"Rachel told me you were looking for your own place. Didn't think I'd live to see the day."

He grunted. "Had to happen at some point."

"Not hygienic to have a baby roaming around the clubhouse," Sin pointed out as he settled himself in one of the chairs around the conference table at the other end of the room.

In fact...

Was that conference table different than the one I'd picked out? Not that I'd seen it in person. But I'd have sworn the one I selected was a deep mahogany, not a brassy oak.

"Nyx's never worried about hygiene before," I remarked, my gaze drifting over the wood as I tried to figure out if I was losing it or if it wasn't the same table as what I'd selected online.

"Wasn't liplocked with Giulia before." Link cackled. "You should have heard her whining when the brothers hazed Harlow."

"What did they do?" I wasn't altogether interested, but there had to be a reason Harlow was living at Rachel's and not at the clubhouse.

She'd said it herself—her place was turning into the YMCA for my men, and I was about to nip that in the bud.

That place was ours.

"Set fire to dog shit on the front stoop," Nyx rumbled.

I winced. "Jesus. Our new fucking stoop?"

"Apparently you and Giulia are likeminded. That was her first thought," Sin said with a grin as he steepled his fingers together. His gaze was watchful. "You okay, Rex?"

"Been better." I scratched my chin then my eyes bugged. "What the fuck is that?"

Link followed the direction of my pointer finger. He smirked. "Posse."

"Like that says it all?"

I strode over to the side table where there was some JD and a couple glasses waiting for me to crack the bottle open. What offended me was the goddamn pink tapered candle in a stand. Upon my approach, I realized it stank of flowers.

Picking it up as if it were the aforementioned dog shit, I threw it at Nyx. "Get rid of it."

Nyx stormed over to the door and threw the candlestick out into the hall. All of us ignored the subsequent yelp as, clearly, it collided with someone.

"What's going on, Rex?" Sin queried.

"Why'd you think something's going on?"

"You look stressed as fuck?" Link countered, rocking back in his seat and resting his ankle on his knee.

My jaw worked before I admitted, "Dad left me a letter with the key to this place he was staying. Visited there yesterday."

Link arched a brow. "Packing up his stuff can't have been fun. You should have called us in. We'd have helped."

I knew he meant that.

Fuck, I had the best family.

"Thanks, bro, but his stuff wasn't what he left behind."

"What do you mean?"

"Bear went in deep," Maverick rasped, his voice low and husky as he settled in a chair too. "Don't even know how he found out half the shit he did."

"What did he leave behind?" Nyx demanded, folding his arms across his chest and wincing as he did so.

Rachel told me the beating he'd gotten during his arrest hadn't been terrible, but that wince told me he'd fractured a rib at least.

"I'm not even sure how to describe it," I admitted. "I've never seen anything fucking like it in my life."

"Think 3D murder board for anything and everything related to the Sparrows," Maverick explained.

"You saw it?"

At Link's query, Maverick nodded. "Rex called Star and me in."

"Why?" Nyx asked. "Why not all of us?"

"We're the ones running point on most things Sparrow-related," Mav excused. "Plus, it was... It was intense."

Understatement.

I cast Mav a look. "We already knew Dad had been investigating the Sparrows, but this shows he went in far deeper than we realized. He had photos and news reports and all kinds of shit that he'd tied to Sparrow activity. Names we know from Amara were there... I don't have a clue how he found out all this stuff."

"He dedicated the remaining years of his life to the hunt," Maverick drawled, cracking his knuckles. "Every year spent without Rene did not go to waste."

As mad as I was with my father, the words resonated.

I sucked in a breath, nodded, then muttered, "You guys handled Inked?"

"Cruz did that," Sin mocked.

"Good. Good."

When no one asked me why I'd murdered a brother, I had proof of their trust in me.

Staring at the laptop, I asked, "Nyx, you don't need help financing a place, do you?"

He squinted at me. "Got plenty of money."

"What was with the spreadsheets?"

"Kids cost a lot."

Rolling my eyes, I said, "You can afford a kid and a house."

"I know I can."

"Then," I repeated, "what was with the spreadsheets?"

"Wanna buy a plot of land from you."

"Where?"

"On the compound. Near the Fridge."

Link snorted. "So you and Giulia can hear our enemies cry at night? That your idea of a serenade?"

Nyx just shot him a glare.

That he didn't argue or deny it had me shaking my head.

"You don't need to buy land from me. Pick out a plot and you can have it."

"You sure?"

Mav elbowed Nyx. "Told you he'd say that."

Nyx wasn't the most emotional of men, but even with his face downturned, I still saw his Adam's apple bob. "You did. Thanks, Rex."

"No need to thank me. Same goes for all of you. You want land, we got plenty of it. Only problem is you'll need to use Sinners for construction, so don't all land grab at once."

Steel scratched his chin. "I'd be game for living on the compound. We can wait until Nyx's place is done though."

I shrugged. "Fine. Got plenty of it. You know we own most of this hill."

"You gonna be living with Rach?" Steel questioned.

"Yeah. You got a problem with that?" I grumbled.

He smirked. "Only that you didn't move in sooner."

Link cleared his throat. "She told us what she went through, Rex."

I eyed him. "I know."

"We learned you have a kid too—"

"Don't start," I sniped at Nyx, glowering at him as he glowered at me. "Wynter was... I didn't need to talk about her. I didn't need you guys to know."

"Why the fuck not? We're your goddamn brothers."

"Yeah, you are, but I didn't talk about her with her mother, never mind with you." I tightened my jaw. "I was hoping she'd come back with me, that you'd get to meet her, but that wasn't to be. Yet. I'm hoping she'll come to the city for college. Maybe then you'll get to meet her."

Link rubbed his hands together. "Baby Rachel. Betcha she looks just like her."

"Yeah? Fifty says she's all Rex," Sin jeered.

Nyx sniffed. "I got a hundred that says she looks like Rene."

I shook my head at them but had to hide a smile.

All the while they were bitching, each of them dropped a snippet of info about what the last couple months had been like. When Kendra's name kept cropping up, I knew I was backed into a corner.

"Got news about Kendra."

Nyx turned to frown at me. "What about the bitch?"

"Dad..." I pursed my lips, unsure of how to even start this conversation. Because I was still in my feelings over the situation, I blurted it out.

I was almost relieved to see they were as stunned as I'd been.

Nyx's mouth gaped, Link had eyes rounder than a silver dollar, Steel had dropped his deck of fucking cards, and Sin looked as if he'd shit a brick. Even Mav was surprised, and that took a lot.

In the background, I heard the roar of engines, the screech of brakes, and when silence fell outside, I knew most, if not all, of the men were here.

"We should head on out," I mumbled.

Nyx scrubbed a hand over his face. "That toxic cunt is your half-sister?"

"She is."

"Jesus," Link rumbled, his fingers tugging on his rosary as if that'd give us divine assistance in making sense of the nonsensical.

Steel frowned. "When?"

"You remember when Mom had that miscarriage? Then."

"Not like Bear to give up," Sin remarked.

"No, it wasn't. But she was..." For a second, I stumbled over my words before I realized I didn't have to.

I wasn't about to excuse what my old man had done.

My woman had been more of a wreck, for nearly twenty fucking years, but that hadn't changed anything for me.

"He fucked up."

"Now we're paying for that mistake," Nyx said grimly.

I dipped my chin. "She's on a short leash."

"Why?"

I turned to Link. "If all the recent BS wasn't enough... Storm told me some shit about what happened with her." My mouth tightened. "Not my story to tell, but let's just say he didn't sleep with her out of choice."

Sin's eyes bugged. "You're saying she raped him?"

"Storm wasn't comfortable phrasing it that way but I am."

"Then why the fuck don't we get rid of her?" Nyx demanded.

My hands balled into fists at my sides.

I owed the woman no loyalty, but Dad's letter ran on repeat in my head.

Maybe you could help set her up somewhere, get her a house, do something to make her stop whoring herself out. I don't know if she'd even want that. The MC means something to her so maybe she'll refuse, but try?

"We'll discuss this later," I said gruffly, uncertain of what to say or fucking do.

Dad's request went to war with what I knew about the woman.

Getting to my feet, my council's words in my head of the recent malcontent in the club—something I'd seen for myself—at a loss over how to handle the Kendra situation when instinct told me to shove her out on her ass quicker than she could count to ten, I strode out the door and over to the bar.

Five times bigger than the last one, it fit every single brother. There were still remnants of the pink Rach had told me about that were a leftover of a Posse punishment, but it was scuffed around the edges.

A quick glance and a rough head count keyed me into the fact that every brother was here.

There were a lot of relieved faces, some pissed ones, some gloomy ones.

I didn't catch anyone's eye, just headed over to the pool table and leaned against it. Around me, my council lined up at my side. I didn't need their support, but fuck, it felt good to have it.

In California, I'd been kinda naked. It had felt freeing not to have the weight of the MC on my shoulders, but it had also been weird not to have these dipshits at my back.

I scratched my chin as a low murmur set up around the room, one that had Nyx roaring, "Shut your motherfucking traps."

My lips curved when there was immediate silence.

On the ride to Jersey, I'd had nothing else to do but think about what to say when my brothers were in front of me, so I pieced all of that together.

"A long time ago, a wise man once told me that the Sinners were more than just a Motorcycle Club—they were family. Families celebrate each other's wins; they mourn each other's losses. That man, as I'm sure you can figure out, was my father.

"Bear meant something to all of us. You either served under him or knew to respect him as the Sinners' OG Prez. You feared him or you steered clear of him. Whichever, Bear was Bear. He was a great man. Not perfect. Made plenty of mistakes, and he died for them.

"A death in the family makes you think about life. Makes you think about where shit went wrong, where it went right. I've had a lot of time on my hands to think about the Sinners, and I've realized that my biggest concern is losing any one of you to jail or to the undertaker.

"In some ways, we're turning legit, but those legit fronts are ways to launder cash from our main sources of income. We're one-percenters, there's no breaking free of that, nor do I want to. Federal law ain't my law, and it ain't your law neither.

"Over the next couple years, I've decided that we're going to increase our numbers. Now, that'll mean your cut's going to change to account for this expansion, but with the way we've diversified, I doubt you'll see much difference.

"The reason I want to do this is because as brothers get older, as Old Ladies are branded and kids are born, I want those family men to shuffle out of the line of danger.

"Those at high risk will get danger pay. Their cuts will be better. But if there's one thing I've learned over the years, it's that my father said the Sinners were a family but he didn't adjust shit to encompass that."

There were a couple of murmurs at that, but as I looked around the room, I saw some pleased expressions as well as some angry ones.

"Unfortunately for you, what I say, goes. The only right you have is to leave, and you know full well that leaving the Sinners ain't easy. If you don't like the sound of what I'm planning for the MC, then you can bitch about it among yourselves, and you can speak about it with one of my councilors.

"But truth is, brothers, I don't give a fuck about your opinions on this. I give a fuck about your kids. Your women. I give a fuck about the next generation, because *they* are what count. You don't like it, then you shoulda wrapped it up.

"We've been living like we're in a frat house for too long, and that's about to change. You've had years of that, and to be sure, some of that's gonna go down still, but there are gonna be more family occasions. Because the next gen is *everything*. It always was; I was just late in seeing that.

"In my defense, I took over the role of Prez too early. Dad shouldn't have passed down the mantel to me for at least a decade, but he did. I made choices that were a young man's, and now, I'm older. *Wiser*—"

"What if we don't want to take pay cuts? What if we want to take part in runs?"

Unsurprised that Lever was the prick loud enough to mouth off, I shrugged. "You don't have kids, Lever, so what the fuck are you worried about?"

His brow furrowed. "What you're saying is that the second we have kids, that's when our roles in the MC will change?"

"That's what I'm saying."

Murmurs spread among the crowd.

"You just wanna teach 'em Sex Ed, don't you?" Sin muttered in my ear, making me grin.

"Yeah. Do I need to bring out bananas and rubbers?" I mocked, smirking when he snickered.

"Some of our Old Ladies would prefer us to risk our asses to get the danger pay," Two Knives called out, which had a lot of brothers hooting.

"Don't blame your Old Lady either. Not with feet like yours stinking up the place," Junk groused.

"You sniff his feet a lot?" Lever mocked.

Junk retorted, "You can smell his fucking feet up in Maine."

"Fuck off, Junk," Two Knives grumbled. "I got those goddamn sachets you told me to buy for my boots."

Unsurprised that shit had gotten waylaid, I rolled my eyes. "Can we get things back on track?"

Junk sniffed. "You trying to tell me that Two Knives' feet don't stink, Prez?"

"I ain't saying nothing about his feet. I just want to make sure he keeps stinking out the clubhouse and not a prison cell, you get me?"

Junk shrugged. "I get you."

"Look, it's simple. You got kids, your role in the MC is going to change big time. You only got an Old Lady, that'll be considered when the council shares out jobs that are high risk. You make the decision to settle down, not me. I'm just thinking of the future."

"Why does it matter?" Lever derided. "I like things how they are now."

"Rex is right," Nyx rumbled, his glower dark enough that Lever's shoulders hunched in on themselves. "Half of us here grew up with our fathers going to jail for at least one stint. Some of them died; some of them were pieces of shit who we wished were dead. The only thing that got most kids through was the club."

"And that's the take from all this, brothers. The club is everything. It's our past, our present, and our future. I'm just the guardian for this generation, but there'll come a day when I'm buried in the backyard, much as you fuckers will be too, and it's them who'll rule the roost.

"For them, I'm going to make sure we have fat pockets, and that they have power in this town, enough to keep our people safe for many decades to come—"

"And if that ain't something worth celebrating, I don't know what the fuck is!" Link hollered, whooping and amping the crowd up until even the naysayers were cheering in my favor.

It wouldn't last.

We'd get complaints.

But it was time to grow up. I didn't have my dad to fall back on anymore. Neither did they.

Real or imagined, the safety net was gone.

The future was laid out there, terrifying in its complexity, but all I fucking knew was that I'd spent two decades apart from Rachel, and I wasn't about to compound that by wasting any time I had left in a jail cell or by ending up six feet under prematurely.

I had a life left to live, and so did the rest of my council.

I wasn't about to do anything to cut that short.

TWENTY-TWO

RACHEL

"Rachel," David Foundry crooned in my ear.

I grimaced. "David, what a pleasure. I didn't expect to hear from you so soon."

That was a lie.

I'd expected to hear from the Attorney General sooner rather than later, but preferably not today.

After a morning spent in court, then a ninety-minute traffic jam, I had a to-do list a mile long. Parker was sulking with me for not calling to dish out the gossip sooner, and Hunter had sent me mounds of information that I had to sort through before I contacted Dead To Me.

Today was not the day for this conversation, but it didn't seem like I was getting much choice anyway.

From the back of my car, around thirty minutes from home, I rubbed my forehead as he tutted, "I expected a 'thank you' by now. Currau Valentini is free, and already I've had some attorneys knocking on my door, trying to get their clients the same treatment..."

Thoughts racing a mile a minute, I realized that I *hadn't* thanked him.

Not once.

Holy shit.

Aurora had texted me that Currau was free, and amid the maelstrom that was my life right now, it had slipped my mind.

"I'm sorry, David. Truly." My voice oozed genuine apology because I felt it. I felt like shit, in fact. I didn't forget things like that. Ever. "Shall we meet up for lunch at Paginatis?"

His laughter was a hell of a lot more intimate than I'd have liked, but a meal on me at a three-star Michelin restaurant by way of an apology wasn't exactly small fry.

"I'd love that, but another time. You mentioned a certain someone would owe me a favor if circumstances were to pass where Currau Valentini was freed?"

"Yes," I said warily, and my wariness only grew as he detailed his 'requirements.'

After fifteen minutes of trying to butter the AG up, I ended the call with him and started another with Luciu.

I wanted nothing more than to dive into my house, to climb into bed, and sleep, but that wasn't in the cards for me today.

"Everything okay?" Luciu asked before I could utter a word.

As I started scanning the emails Hunter had sent me, multitasking so this interminable day would finally end, I muttered, "When I got your uncle out, I had to pull in a massive favor with the Attorney General."

"He's called it in now? So early?"

I hummed.

"What does he want?" he asked.

"Do you still have that cabin in Nevada?" I queried.

"Yes." If a man could sound wary with a one-word answer, then Luciu did.

Nerves high, anxiety well and truly amped up, I told him, "He wants that."

"Fucking corrupt bastard."

I grunted. "Like you didn't already know that. And let's be grateful that he is."

"You know what that cabin is?" he countered.

"A shelter made of wood? What's the problem? Go and build another one," I scoffed as I continued reading.

According to some of my ears on the ground, Eamonn Keegan's standing in jail was high enough that he had most of the screws (prison guards) in his pay—they danced to the drum he beat.

Luciu broke into my concentration by explaining, "It's a high-class resort for businessmen with certain proclivities."

For a second, I froze. Unsure if I'd heard that right.

"It's a brothel?" I hated that my voice was pretty much a squeak, but *fuck*. A brothel?

"Yes. It is. If he even knows about it, that means he has those kinks."

"You're into sex trafficking?" I growled, temper surging.

"These women aren't trafficked," he jeered. "Jesus, they're there because they make half a million a year.

"Plus, it's Nevada. That's not illegal there. The only illegal shit going down in that place is tax evasion because I highly doubt those ladies are paying the IRS all their dues."

I hoped for his sake his goddamn brothel was in one of the ten counties out of sixteen in Nevada where it *was* legal or he was screwed.

Which would be pretty damn fitting.

"Half a million?" I questioned dubiously. "What are they doing to earn that?"

"Keeping secrets, mostly," was his dry retort. "People wouldn't like knowing that their senator enjoys taking bright pink, ten-inch dildos up their ass while wearing a minidress and high heels."

"Christ. You know I have to work with the Attorney General, don't you? I'll never unsee that."

Hovering around David was bad enough as it stood, thinking of him like that was enough to make me puke, mostly because I could imagine him being into that scene.

I didn't kink shame, but the guy was slimier than a slug. Throw in his kinks, calling him a slug gave them a bad rep.

"You shouldn't have asked then," he drawled, but he quickly conceded, "He might not be into that, but only a select number of men are even aware of that goddamn cabin. They don't let the news out to just anyone."

"I'll bet," I grumbled. "Anyway, are you going to hand it over to him?"

"He can have it."

"I'll let him know."

I cut the call, but I felt skeevy as hell as I emailed David with the confirmation that his favor was about to be paid in full. Of course, I used loftier phrasing than that.

On edge that Luciu had a brothel in the first place, I knew I was being a hypocrite that that was my hard limit considering all the other shit he, as well as the Sinners, got involved in.

With a huff, I decided that diving into work would be my solace, and I unpacked most of the information Hunter had sent to me by the time we finally made it into West Orange.

Deciding to get this over with, I set my phone on speaker and hit Dead To Me's number.

Was it absurd that the sight of the name on the Caller ID had me sniggering to myself?

Dead To Me.

Like that was a name.

Jesus.

This really was my life now.

Rubbing my eyes, feeling like I'd aged a year since yesterday, I waited for the call to connect.

There were a couple beeps that reminded me of twenty years ago when a phone call went through an exchange to hit overseas, and then Dead To Me's smooth tones sounded in my ear.

"Rachel Laker, I didn't expect to hear from you this soon."

"I work fast. Especially when my friend's safety is on the line."

"What news do you have for me?"

"Do you want the long or the short story?"

"I want everything."

"I need reassurances that Hunter is safe."

"He's yet to leave his house. Plus, though this is no reassurance in today's modern world, I'm out of the country. He's safe for now."

That was as much of a warning as anything else.

Not feeling particularly reassured, I murmured, "I contacted the State Department, but they were useless—"

"Of course they were," she drawled.

"Three different connections, each one with an answer of their own. Only one got it right. Eamonn Keegan was released from jail in the new year."

"Gold star to them."

"Hunter was more useful in finding the information you required, but I have another source... He isn't much of one anymore, because he died in December. But according to this source, Eamonn Keegan's last attack in London was against the New World Sparrows."

Dead To Me hummed. "Intriguing."

"Apparently, the meeting was a conference between New World, Old World, and Eastern Sparrows."

"Three different varieties? I'd heard about the New and the Old World, but not the Eastern."

"Yes, they were new to me too."

"Keegan was against them?"

"According to this source, he worked actively against the Sparrows for a while before his arrest."

"Why?"

"I don't know. But I do know that when Keegan was in prison, his sister was murdered."

"By whom?"

"ECD."

Did I mention the rest of Bear's note? That he believed an 'underling' was behind the killing? Or was I borrowing trouble? She'd want a name, and when she asked for more info, I'd have no means of giving her that...

Before I could worry overlong, she told me, "Not good enough. I want more information than that."

My nostrils flared in outrage. "You only wanted to know if he was still in jail!"

"And if you thought that would be enough to appease me, you're not as smart as everyone says you are."

Jaw working, I muttered, "I'll get back to you."

"Lodestar might have that information. I'd hit her up first."

"Why don't you?"

"Then I'd owe her. Not you."

Impatiently, I snapped, "Am I going to become your *Ask Jeeves*?"

"God, it's years since I heard that name. We're both showing our age," Dead To Me jibed. "Where is Keegan now?"

"He entered the country in January. Officially, he's no longer in the States, but who knows if that's true."

"Find out. Lodestar will know."

Exasperated, I rubbed my brow. "Anything else?"

"The First Lady... Is she a Sparrow? I'd like confirmation."

I thought about the web of truths in Bear's room and was comfortable saying, "No. But she's in the ECD. Those Irish zealots—"

"I know *who* they are, and I know *what* they do." Dead To Me hissed under her breath. "You don't need to research this?"

"No."

"Fuck." A shaky breath soughed down the line. "Hunter's safe until I get back in two weeks. I'll be in touch regarding the murder of Keegan's sister. Don't call me; I'll call you."

A click sounded in my ear, and I knew she'd ended the conversation.

Oddly nervous, but equally relieved that that was over with, I exhaled. The way she'd sounded shaken about my certainty regarding the First Lady's ties to the ECD left me on edge.

Hell, who was I kidding? Everything about this situation set me on edge.

My water bottle beeped to tell me to rehydrate just as Emile pulled into the driveway. Relieved to be home, I dismissed him then, with a sigh, registered that neither Rain's car nor Rex's hog were there.

Grumpy because of that, I set my bag and coat in the hall, dumping them there for later, then trudged into the kitchen.

"I have a proposition for you."

God, I just couldn't catch a break today.

Seeing Giulia sitting at the table, I groused, "There'd better be no ice cream missing from my stash, Giulia Fontaine."

She grinned. "You can't deny the pregnant lady—"

Slipping out of my shoes and leaving them by the door, I quipped, "Say that to someone who isn't also pregnant."

"Shit. I lost my ability to barter with you, didn't I?"

"You did." I squinted at her. "What's the proposition? And why do we have to have this conversation after I've had a hellishly long day in court and have been stuck in traffic for ninety minutes?"

She blinked at me. "You must really love Rex if you put up with that commute."

For some reason, that had my cheeks burning with color. "I do love him."

Grunting, Giulia said, "I'm supposed to commute soon."

"You are?"

"Uh huh. If I want to do my apprenticeship."

"Oh, the piercing thing." I hummed. "Would you do my daith piercing?"

"I thought you were going to be dismissive."

"Why would I?" I arched a brow at her. "Well, would you?"

"Would I what?"

"Do my goddamn daith piercing?"

"You get migraines?"

"I do."

"After ninety minutes stuck in traffic, can't say I blame your head for rebelling. Anyways, yeah, I'll do it but it might not be for a while. What with the baby."

I shrugged. "I'd prefer you to do it."

"Indy's current piercer is good," she said honestly.

"I'd prefer you to do it," I repeated.

Giulia's smile was hesitant, but I saw that my loyalty pleased her.

If I had to have a needle stuck into me, I'd prefer it to be by someone who'd already had my back rather than a stranger.

If that made me insane that I'd prefer to have Giulia armed with said piercing needle, then so be it.

"Speaking of, I figured out a solution for your problem with Nyx."

"What problem?"

"Your concern that he'll stray after you give birth."

She grimaced. "I trust him."

I did too. At least, I trusted his cock. But his cock wasn't the part of his body that would get his ass sent up.

Still, I couldn't tell her that. Which made me feel bad. Goddammit.

And that grimace told me that she wanted to believe it but didn't feel like she could.

This was a mess.

Giulia was intuitive enough to have picked up on the fact that Nyx had hours unaccounted for—

"Kendra didn't leave."

Ah.

Shit.

And she'd left the same night that Nyx had been gone.

Giulia didn't know his ass had been in jail.

"Where did she go?" I queried.

"Don't know, don't care. But she's back."

"She's braver than me. Especially now you've taken command over your gag reflex."

Her lips twitched but she only asked, "What's the solution?"

"You don't really think he'd cheat on you, do you?"

"You're the one who brought this up."

"True. It was just an idea though."

"When Kendra left that night, I tried to call Nyx but he didn't answer."

Fuck.

"Probably on club business."

Her cheeks blew out as she released a deep exhalation. "Yeah. You're right. What's the solution?"

"Have him get another cock piercing near your due date."

Eyes widening, her smirk made a slow appearance. "What a brilliant idea."

"Is Indy's piercer a woman?"

"Sadly, yes. But Indy'll know a dude—"

"You think he'll be upset about having a guy pierce him?"

She smirked. "I think he deserves to be as uncomfortable as possible."

I really knew far too much about their relationship.

"He might not have done anything."

"He's Nyx. He'll have done something," she dismissed, "even if it isn't dicking down my arch-nemesis."

"Nah, Kendra's not your arch-nemesis. She's just a whore." I felt bad for saying that about Bear's daughter but even Bear had admitted she was alien spawn. "Not worthy of arch-nemesis status."

Giulia's eyes twinkled. "You're right."

"I often am."

She snorted.

"Go on then, hit me with the proposition," I said as I trudged over to fill up my water bottle from the refrigerator door then picked up one of the tubs of ice cream Hunter had sent me from the freezer.

Because I was feeling generous, *and guilty*, I stated, "Pick your poison."

"Vanilla." At my arched brow, she said smugly, "My taste in ice cream is the only boring thing about me."

Snickering, I grabbed us both a tub, picked up two spoons, and joined her at my kitchen table.

For a blunt woman, she suddenly stopped being able to maintain eye contact with me.

Swirling the spoon around the tub of ice cream once she'd opened it, she muttered, "I hate asking for shit like this."

"What do you need? A loan?"

Her head reared back at that. "Dude, my man's worth a fortune. I don't need dollars. I need a godmother for this kid of mine."

My mouth gaped. "You want me to be a godmother?"

She shrugged. "I like you. I've seen Rain around the clubhouse, and as much as he sniffs around the whores, he's always respectful. My kid, if anything happens to his dad and me, will be a hellion. You raised a Sinners' brat and made him normal. I want that for my baby. I want the best."

There was a compliment in there, I figured, still... "Axel raised him—"

"You dealt with the teenage years. You're alive so you survived it." Giulia bit her lip. "Well? Will you do it?"

My mouth worked, and my lips rounded as I started to figure out a way to get out of being asked—much as I'd done with Scott—but nobody was more stunned than me when I rasped, "Okay. But you can't die until they're seventeen at least."

Giulia beamed at me. "I have no intention of dying ever. So we're all good. But just in case some cunt clubwhore gets me in the back, I wanted to make sure I had shit arranged." She slapped her hands against the table. "Nyx's getting another couple piercings and you agreed to be my baby's godmother. This is a good fucking day."

I cringed. "A *couple* piercings?"

"He has a Jacob's ladder to midway down his shaft but—"

I held up a hand. "Do I need to know?"

"Shouldn't have asked."

"I was only asking if he needed more than one. You don't know if he actually needs punishing," I pointed out, even though he definitely deserved *something*.

"And I'll say it again—he's Nyx. He'll have done something to deserve it. Don't you worry. Like I was saying, I want his Jacob's ladder extended."

My nose crinkled. "TMI."

"Get used to it. We overshare. A lot."

"I'll remind you of that when Amara starts talking about Hawk's cock."

She smirked. "Amara guards Hawk and Quin's dicks zealously. She never talks about them. She's too possessive."

I huffed as I dug my spoon into the tub of ice cream. "No fair."

"Life ain't fair. Did you hear about the party?"

"The party? No." Confused, I asked, "When?"

"Tonight. Impromptu welcome home party for Rex. I'm surprised he didn't say anything." She cast me a look. "Unless he doesn't think you'd want to go..."

I thought about the day I'd had, the work still left to do before I could even think about sleep, and I almost groaned.

Silently, I ate a couple more spoonfuls of ice cream.

"You know you need to go, don't you?" Giulia asked softly.

"Yeah," I said on a sigh because she was right. "I know I need to."

"Hey."

I peered at her. "What?"

"This doesn't have to be like how Rene did things."

"What do you mean?"

"Rene was, well, she didn't have a career, did she? No shade to her, she was awesome—from what I remember, at least. But, like, the MC was her world. It isn't yours. Nor is it mine or any of the Posse's now. You don't have to run things like she did, you know, with your nose buried in everything."

"I don't?"

"No. That's what the Posse is for. I mean, you'll be like Rex's First Lady, but I'm the Second Lady, yeah? Then there's all the Old Ladies—they're not cats like the old guard. We're in this together."

Blinking, I nodded at her. "You're right." My mouth worked a second as a weight drifted from my shoulders that I hadn't even known was there. "You're right," I repeated.

She smiled. "My job isn't as important as yours—"

"Don't put yourself down," I immediately chided.

Her smile quirked up into a grin. "I wasn't, but I don't keep our dudes out of jail so I don't think I'm putting myself down, just being a realist. Anyways, you can rely on me to tell you when you need to do stuff."

"Like with tonight's party?"

She nodded. "Like with tonight's party. I figure this is the first time the Sinners will even know you two are an item. It's not like it's obvious. Sure, it might be the worst kept secret, but tonight would be a great way to kill two birds with one stone."

"Yeah," I mumbled.

"I know you're exhausted," she said commiseratively.

"I really am."

"But we changed the clubhouse now. There's a room off the bar where we can hang out after you do the rounds."

I yawned. "I think I should take a nap."

"I'll wake you up so you have time to get ready." She hesitated. "Rex really didn't tell you about this?"

"No. He's..." It was easier than I would have thought to admit to her, "I asked him to brand me but he's not sure."

Her brow furrowed. "Has to be because he knows you're not a fan of the club because that man is deee-voted to you." She coughed. "Hopelessly devoted, in fact."

I blinked.

Was that a *Grease* reference?

"It's not that I'm not a fan of the club. It's just that they're hard work. They do stupid shit and I have to get them out of it."

Case in point, Nyx.

Case in point, goddamn Harlow.

"Understandable. You know you can't get branded until after the baby, right?"

"Yeah, but I-I wanted him to know that *I* wanted that." Glumly, I dug out some more ice cream. "He has a ring though."

"How do you know that?"

"Long story short, Lily found it. Don't ask how."

"I won't. Though I want to know at some point."

I wafted my spoon at her.

"So you're too good to brand," she mused.

The phrasing put me on edge. "I'm not too good for the Sinners. I wasn't born into the club like you but I was definitely bred there."

"No need to get snippy," she chided. "If you acted like you were too good for the Sinners, do you think I'd have asked you to be the godmother for my kid?"

"Honestly? I don't even think about the logic behind your actions, Giulia."

A cackle escaped her. "You're a smart woman."

"That I am," I drawled.

"Tonight's a first step, then, isn't it?"

"A first step to what?"

"Proving to Rex that his wife can be his Old Lady and that his Old Lady can be his wife." She rubbed her hands together. "Go nap. I'll be up forty minutes before Nyx comes to collect me."

I didn't question the fact Nyx would be doing that when it was a short walk to the compound, just surprised us both by yawning again. Big enough that it cracked my jaw.

"You're still early days into the pregnancy, honey. You'll be exhausted faster than usual." She shooed me. "Leave the ice cream, I'll clear up. Just catch some Zs."

I figured it was a testament to how tired I actually was that I obeyed.

TWENTY-THREE

RACHEL

Giulia didn't seem to mind that I kept yawning. Neither did Indy. They just worked around the yawns.

I'd slept for two hours, but I felt worse now than I did before I lay down for a nap.

My eyelids drifted to rest on the crests of my cheeks, a move which they took full advantage of—Indy started sweeping shadow over the lids, while Giulia glued lashes on after the fact.

That I was slumped against my armchair didn't seem to bother them.

"You drug her or something?" I heard Indy mutter.

"If she wasn't pregnant, I might have thought about it, but nope, the kiddo did this for me."

I squinted at her. "Why would I need to be drugged?"

"Because Giulia's painting you like you're a scarlet woman."

Giulia tutted. "No, I ain't. We're making her look the part."

"Of a whore?"

"No such thing as a whore in modern society. Outside of club-whores. They're the fucking worst."

If Giulia had been a man, she'd have probably spat at that.

I was mostly glad she didn't spit on my Persian carpet.

"Nice to know you're a feminist when required," Indy sniped.

"Just because you can't sit down, don't give me none of your sass, Indiana Sisson."

"Why can't you sit down?"

Giulia cackled at my question. "Yeah, Indy, why can't you?"

"No reason."

The sister-in-law-from-hell snorted. "She'll find out soon enough."

Indy huffed. "Cruz is my Dom."

"Your Dom?" I repeated, my brow furrowing. "How do you..." I hesitated. "...do that after everything that happened to you?"

She paused in what she was doing and, slowly, reflected, "He liberates me from the memories. Takes the control away from me, and I trust him so I know he'd never do anything to trigger me."

"He spanks you?" I questioned, thinking about the last BDSM romance book I'd read, but that was far too long ago.

"Spanks? More like whoops her butt. You should see her wriggling around on her stool at work. Looks as if she has ants in her damn pants."

"Giulia," Indy hissed. "Shut the fuck up."

My hand snapped out, and I curved my fingers around Indy's wrist. "It's consensual?"

Indy rumbled, "Yes. Of course."

"No 'of course' about it. I just wanted to make sure."

She shot me a wary smile. "Thank you. For checking. But no, Cruz doesn't do anything I don't already want."

"I don't get it," Giulia mumbled. "Who wants the pain when there's so much pleasure to be had?"

"Says you with the guy whose dick might as well be a studded baseball bat," I mocked.

Indy whined, "Ew."

Giulia preened. "I can take every inch."

"TMI, Giulia."

"You started it."

"Did not," I grumbled. "I was making a point."

"If I really thought about it," Indy mused, "I could imagine Rex has Dom tendencies."

I snorted. "Not really. If he has, I terrified them out of him with my wailing and moaning."

"Not the good kind, huh?" Giulia queried sympathetically.

"No. The nightmare kind. Used to be if he tugged on my hair, I'd run for the hills." My nose crinkled. "I don't think I'd like being spanked anyway."

"You never know if you don't try it. You have to keep so many things under control, wouldn't it be nice not to have to think?" Indy mused. "I know I appreciate it. When Cruz takes over, I go into autopilot."

"Why would you want that though?"

She shrugged. "Less want, more need. Used to be that I'd fuck and I'd just lie there, and guys would get off, and I'd feel like a slut, but I was reaching for something I didn't understand.

"That happened with Cruz, but he didn't just let me lie there. He sees shit that no one else ever has. It's reassuring and annoying all at the same time."

My lips twitched. "I'm glad he makes you happy."

"He really does."

Smile fully blossoming, I tilted my head back. "You can finish painting me up like a scarlet woman."

Twenty minutes later, I actually felt like a scarlet woman as well.

My makeup was less neutral than I was comfortable with, and Giulia had somehow managed to find a pair of pants in my closet that I didn't even know I'd bought.

I wouldn't put it past her to pretend that she'd found them there when she'd purchased them for me but I didn't complain.

My exhaustion bought her my docility, and maybe that was what this evening required—if I was drunk on the need to sleep, I'd be able to endure a night of bad music, raucous crowds, intoxicated men and women bickering on the dance floor, and pretending to be interested when I really just wanted to climb into bed.

With Rex.

I tacked that on because the idea of spending the night in my lonely bed didn't sit well with me anymore.

Toeing into the heels Giulia had set out, I gave a final yawn as she primped my hair, sliding her hand over the crown to smooth out any stray flyaways, which was when Indy whistled under her breath.

"Surprised you're letting her get away with this, Rach."

"She's my Second Lady. Gotta have faith in her, don't I?" I mumbled sleepily.

Giulia, grinning wide, tugged me in front of the mirror on the back of my closet door.

I peered at myself, sighed, and muttered, "I'm too tired for Rex to fuck me over his desk."

"That wasn't the reaction I was aiming for."

"What? For Rex to want to bone me?" I asked around a chuckle.

"No. I wanted you to stand out so that everyone would know to back off."

"More like the Prez will want to claim me in front of everyone."

Indy cackled. "She has a point, Giulia. I'm not gay, and I think even I'd fuck her."

I snorted. "Thanks, Indy."

"Very welcome, Rach. You're owning your *Crybaby* moment."

I tugged on the pants, ruffled up the sweater, and complained, "More like my Sandy from *Grease* moment. Although I think Sandy's pants left more to the imagination than these do."

"Stop messing with the clothes," Giulia grumbled. "You won't be able to fit in these for much longer. And if you still can, then I need to work on fattening you up. This is your second kid; you should be showing more than you are. What did your OB/GYN say? You've been to visit one, right?"

"She said I'm underweight."

She sniffed. "No shit, Sherlock. Don't worry, I'll feed you."

"Pasta puttanesca?" I asked hopefully.

"As much of that as kiddo can stand before you puke." She patted my arm. "You look great, Rachel. Feel it?"

"I guess. I'm very..." I wafted a hand around my hips and chest.

"'Exposed' is the word you're looking for," Indy mocked.

I'd worn skimpier outfits to galas, but this wasn't a gala. I was going into a bar where people actively had sex. That changed the parameters of a scenario.

A part of me wondered why I wasn't freaking the hell out, but maybe I didn't have to wonder.

Maybe it was just faith—in Rex. In Giulia. In Indy, even.

Giulia shot her a dark look. "Hush. She looks awesome. I want her to go in there and turn heads."

"She'll turn heads, all right. Rex is probably going to get into a fight before the night's over."

I gave her a soft smile. "You think so?"

Indy snorted. "I know so."

The pants were drainpipe—clinging to the slender length of my legs with a closeness that only came from good tailoring. There was a crease so sharp running down the length that it looked as if I could cut myself. Tucked into that was a low-cut sweater that bared my shoulders and most of my chest.

Not unlike Sandy's rebellious outfit at the end of *Grease*, the sleeves hooked around my upper arm but the deep cut of mine made hers look innocent by comparison.

On my feet, I had a pair of red wedges, which made the black outfit all the sassier. Combined with the fact my lips were painted the same cherry apple red, and my hair was oiled back in a tight bun like the women in a Robert Palmer music video, I looked sexy.

It had been a long time since I'd aimed for that. Seemed weird that I'd be doing it tonight when I was more interested in climbing into my bed for anything other than sex.

Nyx called from downstairs, "Giulia! Where the fuck are you?"

She grinned at us. "He's such a gent." At him, she screeched, "Is it my fucking fault your hellspawn makes getting in and out of clothes impossible?"

Nyx, sensibly, didn't answer.

She tucked her hand in mine, grabbed Indy, hooked her arm through her SIL's, and dragged us down to the hall.

Unsurprisingly, Nyx didn't seem to notice me.

He glared at Giulia. "That dress doesn't fit."

"It does," she countered, jiggling her tits in the low-cut neckline.

"You want me to break bones tonight, baby, I will," he threatened, his tone darkening, as much as his gaze did.

Nyx obviously wanted to be in a bed too. Except he wasn't thinking about sleep.

"They shouldn't look at what they can't touch," Giulia practically purred, which had Nyx clenching his jaw.

"You shouldn't wear heels. What if you fall?"

"Going to be glued to you all night," she retorted instantly. "You won't let me fall."

His mouth tightened next. "Where's your jacket?"

"I'm running hot."

"You're running fucking something," he sniped. "You're goddamn trouble, you know that?"

She let go of both Indy and me and hurled herself at him. His hands went to her hips, hers went to his chest. "Just keeping you on your toes."

He grunted, and I chose to ignore the fact that he cupped her ass and practically demolished her in the hallway.

Indy and I, deciding that escape was the safest option, walked out together once I'd dragged on a coat.

"You think that was bad," I quipped as we maneuvered the hill and started toward the compound. "You should hear them when they argue."

Indy grumbled, "I already see way too much at work."

"They have more sex in a night than I had all of last year."

Indy taunted, "I figure this year will be different."

"I figure you're right," I teased, oddly warmed when Indy slotted her hand through my arm much as Giulia had done earlier.

"The whores are going to be there. Did Giulia tell you?" Indy warned.

"She didn't." My nose crinkled. "I don't think I have much to worry about."

"I'm not worried about you," she drawled. "I'm worried about Giulia. If Kendra's back, and if she sniffs around Nyx, there'll be hell to pay."

"Is that why she poured herself into that dress?"

"I'm thinking so. She's insecure with him right now. I don't get it. I've never seen Nyx like he is with her."

"Me either," I agreed, but on a sigh, I said, "When I was pregnant with Wynter, my body changed so much it was unrecognizable. I had other issues, after, you know, but even before then it stunned me. She's young, don't forget. We're more mature now. You remember how it was back then."

Indy's huff was impatient. "You're right." She knew it but didn't like it.

I got it.

It seemed futile for Giulia to be jealous, but when you were young and in love, the weirdest insecurities plagued you.

I'd been there, and I'd definitely done that and had bought several T-shirts. I had to think that Indy had as well.

I squeezed her arm. "I'll keep an eye on things."

"Stone and me too. We're on the lookout. Kendra's clearly got a death wish. She's been worse since Storm left."

I couldn't disagree—there was a reason Giulia was on the warpath, after all.

We finally made it to the compound, and the Prospect whistled at the sight of us.

Indy grated out, "Keep your eyes on the ground, boy. Our Old Men are waiting inside for us."

My lips twitched when his eyes didn't drop to the ground but bugged out in fear.

Sniffing, Indy tugged me forward toward the beyond loud clubhouse.

I'd heard remnants of it back at my place, but it was usually raucous. I'd gotten accustomed to it over the years.

"Did Rex really not think you'd realize there was a party going on?"

I shrugged. "I think he's not sure where to put me."

Indy tugged me to a halt. "You're not a doll. You don't need to be put on a shelf."

Her defense had me smiling. "I know. It's not a bad thing. It's more like he doesn't want to fuck up by bringing me into something that makes me unhappy."

She squinted at me. "Sounds dumb. But he's a man. Even if he is smart."

Humming my agreement, I was about to answer when a brother called out, "Well, bitches, don't you look fine..."

A soft voice rang out from nowhere, "Lever, you feel like losing your eyes? I got a nice vat of the good stuff just waiting to melt them down to soup."

Indy shuddered. "God, that shouldn't turn me on," she muttered to me.

I bit my lip to stop myself from laughing.

"Fuck off, Cruz. You can't be threatening my eyes—"

"You're using them to look at my woman and Rex's too. You really wanna be blinded tonight, you should carry on with this conversation."

Lever snorted. "Rex don't got a woman."

"Rex does got a woman," Cruz mocked, the bad grammar sounding even worse coming from a man of his intellect. "Rachel."

"Rachel? As in the snooty lawyer?"

My lips twisted. "Yes, as in the snooty lawyer who got you out of a solicitation charge last year."

"You paid for sex when it's on tap for free?" Cruz mocked, and some other brothers clearly heard because they came from somewhere on the veranda and started giving him shit.

I decided to cut him some slack—wasn't Lever's fault the clubwhores didn't have dicks, was it?

Indy and I headed up the steps toward the front door, and Cruz slipped his arm around her waist and I stuck close, knowing they'd take me to Rex.

In a pair of dark jeans and a bandeau top, Indy looked a lot more dressed down than me, but the emerald color offset her bronze skin and made her inky black hair gleam in the lights. She wore a muted nude lipstick, minimal makeup, but her black, cat-eye liner was on point.

Even above the music, because I stuck so close to them, I heard Cruz whisper, "You look beautiful, princess."

My lips curved when Indy, the woman I'd always considered hard as stone, melted into him.

Everyone had their kryptonite, didn't they?

I was glad Indy had found hers.

The party was in full swing by the time I'd hung my coat up in the vestibule in a cupboard whose purpose I didn't know, but it was acting as a coat rack tonight.

The place stank of beer and sweat. The music was too loud, the bar was too hot, and I was immediately miserable.

When Rex caught sight of me, that was worth all the misery, however.

He reacted like Nyx did.

I hadn't anticipated that.

He'd been sitting on the edge of the pool table, a 'Welcome Home, Prez' banner swaying overhead from the ceiling fans that brought some blessed relief to the still air in here. He'd clearly been watching Link and Lily playing a game, one leg cocked up slightly for balance. There were brothers around him, a couple whores too, and instantly, my own hackles were raised.

Much as his were.

It was then I realized that Giulia had been right to make me come here, to make me dress like this.

She'd understood the parameters of this world in a way that I hadn't.

Rex hadn't told me about the party. He thought he could keep this part of his life separate from ours, but that wouldn't work.

It couldn't.

Somehow, we had to unite the two halves so that we could both subsist happily in them, but me staying at home while he partied here would only cause mutual misery.

I'd already seen one relationship break down from taking this path, and though Rex was close to Storm, and he had to know this path was the wrong one, he'd still failed to share the news of tonight's welcome home party. He'd still taken the first few steps down this road.

Fool.

It wasn't often my man was that, but tonight, he'd definitely been an idiot.

When he saw me, he straightened up, his eyes flaring wide before they narrowed into slits. He stormed over to me, then, as if it'd do much good, he dragged off his cut and, before he even greeted me, tucked my arms into the leather vest he'd worn for decades.

It slipped onto me like it was silk.

The leather was warm, soft against my skin, but it didn't stop me from tipping up my chin, getting up in his face, and demanding, "Trying to cover me up?"

"What the hell are you wearing?" he croaked, his voice hoarse as his gaze devoured wherever it touched.

Adrenaline had eaten away at my fatigue. How he looked at me fired that burst of hormones that made me feel like I'd consumed liquid caffeine.

An hour ago, I could have yawned.

Now, I just felt the solid welter of the energy that stirred to life whenever I was around this asshole.

Fuck, I loved him.

And I'd missed *this*, and I hadn't even really had it in me to miss this side of things.

I'd never had this much guts as a teen, and I never would have had the balls to start shit in the middle of the clubhouse bar on his turf.

I smirked at him—in this situation I thought that was the sensible thing to do. "Don't like my outfit? Giulia will be disappointed. I think she picked it with you in mind."

"That fucking headcase," he ground out under his breath. "Did she want a bloodbath?"

His hand shifted, moving around to the back of my neck. He wasn't usually rough with me, but when he grabbed my nape, I half expected him to turn me away, to shove me aside and push me back the way I'd come and out of the door.

He didn't do that.

I shouldn't have been so foolish.

His fingers weren't like pincers; they drew me into him.

Closer.

Closer.

Closer still.

Until he kissed me.

It was carnal. It was feral.

It was perfection.

Around me, I heard the cheers and the hoots and the catcalls, but they might as well have been flies buzzing around my head.

The only thing I was aware of was Rex.

His smell, his taste, his strength.

Amid this room of outlaws, he was the worst and the best of them all.

And he was mine.

The desire to climb him like he was a tree hit me, but as he tongue-fucked my mouth, I didn't realize he was edging me toward the door, pushing me where he wanted me, and I was too far gone to even notice.

His mouth tore into mine, eating me up.

Rabid as if he were starving, he feasted on me and I was more than willing to be glutted upon. The difference was I didn't remain passive. I fought back. Kiss for kiss, bite for bite. The insatiable need wasn't new, but the desire to claim him was.

The desire for those bitches in there, even though they were no threat to me, to know who we were to each other was imperative.

Biologically so.

Maybe Giulia wasn't so immature after all.

Nails digging into his shoulders, I thrust myself into him, my tits rubbing up against his chest as my hips rocked, caressing his cock at every turn. The thick, solid length burned into my belly, just not where I needed to feel that heat.

The sudden silence and the pitch-black space were my first indications that I wasn't in the bar anymore.

Only, I didn't care.

I just wanted this kiss to never end. I needed it to carry on forever.

When he hefted me into his arms, I didn't argue, just clutched my knees around his hips, and as he moved forward, a soft scent hit my nose—*cedar*.

Fire.

Rex's office.

That was the only room in the clubhouse that had a fireplace.

He rested me on the edge of, what I assumed, was his desk, and his hands shifted to shape my back, my waist, then he rumbled, "Lean over the desk."

I didn't argue.

Every nerve in my body standing to attention, I twisted around, let my elbows rest on the surface, and I stuck my ass out. His fingers clawed at the fly of my pants a second before he dragged them down.

My panties were next. Both pooled around my ankles, baring me to his ravenous gaze. Those filthy digits then sought out my heat and I immediately spread my legs, my back arching as I moaned out my pleasure from that single rough touch.

I heard the sound of a zipper lowering, and that was pretty much all the warning I got.

His cock was there.

At my entrance.

I moaned, wriggled at his inexorable thrust, only stopping when he tapped out inside me.

His fingers rounded my hips, smoothing over my belly. One moved over the hard swell, the other shifted down, angling toward my clit.

"You think you can come here, dressed like that, and I'm not going to claim you in front of everyone? You think I can't fuck you when you look like a living wet dream? When you're finally fucking mine?"

I didn't answer, couldn't. I just groaned.

He started to move faster, harder. My ass slapped against his thighs, making his belt buckle jingle. The discordant noise ate at my nerves, but I pushed it aside as the hand that had shaped my stomach moved to my hip. His fingers bit into me there, controlling my movements, stilling them before it slid higher up. He grabbed me by the neck, pushed me down, then blanketed me.

It was at that moment that everything could have come tumbling down.

Grizzly had done that.

He'd torn at my hair as he'd fucked into me.

There'd been clumps that came free from how rough he'd been.

He'd laughed in my ear.

His stinking breath had filled my nostrils.

But Rex was *not* Grizzly.

He smelled of Calvin Klein, and while there was a hint of JD to his breath, I knew he'd been chewing gum because spearmint was prevalent in the air around us.

His fingers didn't *tear;* they caressed. They stroked. They teased and pleasured.

He didn't hurt me; he savored me. Drowned in me.

He didn't laugh; he groaned, his torment clear. A torment I'd bestowed upon him.

"You're walking sin, Rachel," he ground out as if he were in pain.

My heart, on the brink of skipping a beat out of fear, jolted back into its original pounding rhythm.

Rex.

Always Rex.

Mine.

Mine.

Unmistakable.

"My fucking heaven." He sank into me again, the flat of his thighs bouncing off my butt as he gifted me with another hard thrust that had me releasing a keening cry. "My personal goddamn hell."

"Rex!" I sobbed as the tips of his fingers went to work on my clit.

His movements turned wilder, shifting faster and faster while his forearm, clamped under my belly, kept me from bumping into the desk.

Just as my pussy clutched at him, he let out a hoarse yell, and the heat of him scalded me as I screamed out my own orgasm.

It seemed to go on for a lifetime.

My skin burned; my body ached—in the best possible way.

Every inch of me drowned in ecstasy as he imprinted me with a reminder of who owned me.

Another sob escaped my parted lips as he patted my pussy, because when he pulled out, his fingers went to my slit and he slid them through the mess we'd made together.

Once more, he retreated to my clit, and with his other hand, he pumped two fingers into me as he got me off again.

I cried out a final time as he pleasured me, until my bones were rattling, until every part of me vibrated with ecstasy, and then he gave me another physical signature on our non-existent contract.

In my ear, he whispered, "Mine."

Rex's.

King's.

No one else's.

Ever. Again.

TWENTY-FOUR

REX

"I need to have words with Giulia."

Rachel, still slumped against the desk, snorted then slurred, "You and whose army? She's a law unto herself."

I grunted under my breath. Not only because she wasn't wrong, but because I zipped my dick away and it did not appreciate being caged back up.

Fuck.

I wanted in her again.

Scraping a hand through my hair, I heaved a sigh at the sight of her. Even in the dark, she was fucking beautiful.

"Do you know how pretty you are?"

In the dim lights from outside, I could barely catch a glimpse of her outline which was a tragedy. Leaning over, I flicked on the light, just so I could imprint her on my retinas, but as soon as I turned it on, I switched it back off again.

Hugging my desk how she was, I knew I'd never be able to unsee her like this. Every time I came in here, I'd remember this moment, and hell, if that didn't paint a grin on my face.

She grumbled, "What's with the light?"

"Wanted to make sure I didn't forget this moment."

She huffed, and my lips twitched because now that I saw that she was close to falling asleep again, it was tough to remember the urge that had seen me dragging her in here like I was a Neanderthal hauling his woman into their cave.

She was pregnant.

She was tired.

She'd worked all day.

I grimaced.

Those were the reasons why I hadn't invited her to tonight's party, but damn, she'd livened up my boredom when she'd strolled in, looking like sin and the promise of heaven all at once.

I smoothed a hand over her butt, tweaked it because I could, and murmured, "We should get home."

"No, we need to show our faces." She yawned, straightened up some. "I really didn't intend to get fucked within five minutes of turning up."

"Good to know," I drawled, crouching down and helping her redress.

If there was cum on her pants, I'd probably cry. I needed to see her in them again. Maybe every year. On our anniversary.

Close to drooling, dick already hardening, I smoothed her panties along her legs, settled them on her hips, then drew up her pants and fastened the fly.

When she was decent, I felt my dick twitch as I said, "Going to be thinking of my cum drenching your pussy all night now."

"Is that a good thing or a bad thing?" Rach asked around another yawn.

"Mixture of both." She didn't sound pissed, just tired. I got to my feet, cupped her chin. "I was rough with you."

She leaned forward, pressed her face into my chest, and her arms slipped around my waist. "You were perfect with me."

I hadn't exactly lost control, because control wasn't something that often 'left' me, but I'd near as dammit let my total guard down.

Rubbing my nose against her temple, I murmured, "You didn't have to come here tonight. I know your schedule was rough, and I checked the traffic on the way over. You were stuck for at least an hour in the fallout from that pile-up on the 495."

"More like ninety minutes." She yawned. "Is that why you didn't tell me about the party?"

"Yeah, of course."

"Huh."

"Huh?"

"Thought you were doing a Storm."

"Hell, no. I just know you're sleeping more and figured that was because of the baby. With the extra workload, you need your rest."

"I do." She sighed. "But Giulia was right to tell me. If we do this, maybe I don't have to come again until I can hit seven PM without wanting to fall asleep?"

My lips twitched. "Wouldn't think you'd like to party here."

Rach shuddered. "God, no. This has never been my scene, but that doesn't matter. It's yours. You can come to my galas, and I can come here and act like your First Lady." She squeezed me. "Give and take. That's how we'll roll, no?"

I grinned into her hair, appreciating that more than she could know. "That's how we'll roll," I concurred.

When she tugged her arms free then grabbed my hand, I let her draw me out into the hall. There were brothers everywhere because it was my 'welcome home' party, and I received a bunch of claps on my back, and Rach got a lot of goggle-eyed stares as if the men couldn't believe she was here and that she was dressed like that.

Hell, I didn't believe it and I'd just fucked her in that get up.

We made it back to the bar, I grabbed us some drinks, we wandered around, talked to a few people, had a couple of dances, and generally just hung out.

I had my eye on the clock, just waiting until I knew we could step out without it causing raised brows, but as my internal countdown ticked on, Giulia fucking Fontaine had to wreck that.

Out of nowhere, I heard raised voices.

I wasn't unaccustomed to that, but these weren't men; they were bitches.

On the brink of wading in, Rachel pressed a kiss to my mouth and told me, "I'll deal with it."

Too stunned to speak, I just blinked as she disappeared into the crowd.

She was wearing my cut, so I wasn't concerned for her safety, but I was scared she'd end up getting hurt so I followed her through the mass of bodies toward the screeching.

When I realized it was Giulia and Kendra, I felt like groaning into my JD, but I'd admit, I hoped Rach was capable of containing this. I was sick of the fucking Posse and the shit they stirred.

"You fucking cunt, keep your goddamn hands off him," Giulia snarled.

"Where the hell *is* Nyx?" Rachel demanded.

"Getting sucked off by Peach—"

Though Kendra deserved it, I winced when Giulia snagged her by the ponytail and jacked her head all the way back.

"Fuck, that's hard enough to give her whiplash," Steel commented beside me.

One by one, the council joined me as Rachel attempted to adjudicate a cat fight.

"My man knows that his dick'd drop off if he goes near any of you bitches, and not because you're all diseased up to your eyeballs," Giulia sneered. "I'd fucking chop it off before I'd let any of you gnaw on it—"

Kendra's hand flew wide and she managed to score a hit—she slapped Giulia. Hard enough that her head whipped to the side.

Hell brewed in the she-devil's gaze, but that was more than enough.

About to wade in, to stop this now—no one touched an Old Lady, a fact that was backed by my council surging forward—Rachel jerked her hand up in a classic self-defense move. One second, Kendra was crowing. The next, she was clutching her nose. A nose Rachel had broken.

At my side, Link whispered, "I got chillzzzz."

I'd have laughed if I wasn't furious.

"It's electrifying," Steel whispered back.

Before they could break out into the song, T-bird-style, Rach proved she wasn't finished. Yet.

"You deserved that, Kendra," Rachel lectured, sounding like she was talking to a naughty schoolgirl and not a clubwhore who didn't know when to shut her fucking trap. "Things are going to change around here.

"Clubwhores have gotten away with shit for too long. You think you can talk smack to the Old Ladies and get away with it? You think you can slap one and there'll be no consequences? This is your final warning.

"Anymore shit moves like this, instigating fights, telling Old Ladies that you've been fucking their men when that's a downright lie, you're out on your ass."

Kendra glowered at her but shot me a beseeching glance.

Before I even had the chance to look away, Rachel had grabbed a hold of Kendra's wrist, and she squeezed down around her fingers, effectively pinching her broken nose.

As Kendra squealed in pain, Rachel intoned, "Don't look at the men. This is women's business."

There went my dick.

Before I had the chance to get more than a semi, Nyx appeared, his scowl making the crowd part like Moses and the Red Sea.

"The fuck is going on here?"

Rachel twisted around to glower at him, snagging Kendra by the ponytail to keep her in place when the bunny made to run off.

"Nyx, about time you showed your face. Kendra keeps on telling your pregnant Old Lady, your fragile, very vulnerable, Old Lady—"

"She does know she's describing Giulia, doesn't she?" Link questioned.

"I think so," I jibed, amused.

"—that you're fucking her. I thought you were going to deal with this."

Nyx's already dark scowl deepened. Blacker than black, he turned on Kendra and, in a tone so deadly that all his brothers stiffened, murmured, "When did I fuck you?"

She swallowed. "We always have fun, Nyxy. You know that."

"I told you last time that if you keep making shit up about me, Kendra, shit that upsets my woman, you'll start wishing you'd never been born when I'm through with you—"

"You'd never hurt me," Kendra whined, her voice nasal thanks to her injury. "Nyxy, don't say that."

"Stop calling him Nyxy," Giulia shrieked, her face bright pink and, Jesus, her cheeks streaked with tears. "He isn't your fucking Nyxy. He's *MINE*. No one else's."

"Baby," Nyx rumbled, his arm sliding around her waist so he could haul her against his chest. His hand smoothed up and down her back, granting more of a PDA to the crowd than I figured he ever had before, which made his snarl all the more threatening. "Kendra, I don't want to see your face around here until that fucking nose of yours is healed." He cast me a look, one that said, *'You're trying to protect this piece of shit?'* To her, he growled, "Get the fuck away from me before I throw you out."

Rachel finally let go of Kendra's hair, and with a sob, my half-sister scurried out of the bar, a bunch of bunnies following her, clucking and wailing all the while.

Pride filled me for what my woman had done, because *that* was a move that was First Lady material. I couldn't stop myself from dragging her into me, pushing thoughts of my problematic kin aside, and claiming another kiss.

Claiming her, period, until none of the dumb fucks in this room could mistake Rachel Laker as anyone other than mine.

TWENTY-FIVE

REX

Most of the clubhouse was still asleep when I set off for the motel the Sinners had bought after the blast. It was in the process of going through renovations but certain areas remained free from construction so that the clubwhores could live there and not on the compound.

I didn't know who had made that decision, but I didn't disagree with the idea. In fact, I thought it was fucking smart.

Keep the mice away so the Posse wouldn't play.

The reception building's facade was being taped so it could be painted, and that ran alongside deeper work going on in each individual room. In the background, I also heard the noise from the diggers where there was a pool being installed.

Curious about the progress of the renos, I took a short walk around the perimeter, where only the pool was being worked on as that appeared to have been subcontracted because my brothers were all recovering from last night's party and were sleeping off their hangovers.

The workmen clearly didn't recognize me, but seeing that the pool was underway, I didn't bother stopping.

When I made it to the clubwhores' digs, I knocked on the first door I came to.

As luck would have it, Peach opened it with a yawn, muttering, "Rex? You here about last night?"

As she knuckled her eyes sleepily, I grinned at her, leaning against the door to chat. "You look like you had a long one."

There was a lot of snoring going down in the background so I figured a brother was asleep in there.

Maybe even two.

Peach wasn't exactly discerning in her tastes.

"I did." Another yawn. "Good to have you back. I missed our games."

I shook my head at that—she knew I thought she was too fucking smart to get by on her back. "It's good to be home," was all I said as I peered at her. "How have things been in my absence?"

She raised a hand. "Gimme a sec to grab a jacket."

I nodded, watched as she ducked inside, picked up a jacket from the floor, collecting a pack of smokes from a side table dusty with cream powder I knew would be makeup, and a can of energy drink from the small fridge along the way.

I got mooned for my pains by the brother on the bed before he huddled beneath the blankets, the cold of the morning hitting him on the behind before he started snoring again.

Peach offered me a smoke and a draw from the can, but I only took a sip of the bright yellow liquid. I'd long since quit smoking.

As she lit up, she studied me over the Zippo lighter, muttering, "Lot of unease around the place. Girls aren't sure where they fit in now. That was *before* yesterday's speech."

"Heard about that, did you?"

She nodded. "We did."

No surprise there.

Shit often traveled back to the women. As much as Giulia begrudged the bunnies' existence, clubwhores were intrinsic to the ecosystem that was an MC.

They rarely got branded, but that didn't diminish the power they had over the men.

That fucker in the bed, whether he was a newly patched in brother—I'd heard there'd been a couple in my absence—or had been with us for twenty years, would have spread the gossip over pillow talk.

The brothers ran their mouths as much as the women did.

"I want things to change," I mused as I took a seat on one of the plastic chairs outside her door.

There were hundreds of sunflower seed shells on the ground, because I knew the bunnies ate those obsessively—kept them thin— and I figured this was where they'd all been hanging out now that the clubhouse was a trek away.

"It's an MC. Can't be an MC without clubwhores," she mocked as she took a seat opposite me, unknowingly mimicking my train of thought.

I didn't say that though. "Your time's coming to an end as a sweetbutt."

She shrugged. "I know. I'm not thinking about me."

"What are you going to do?"

"This ain't about me," she repeated, crossing her legs then folding her arms over her knees, hunching against the cold seat.

"Don't care. You're the only one I like," I mocked. "You want a job, I'll fix you up."

Her nose crinkled at the bridge. "Always figured we'd end up together. Stupid, huh? Didn't think I'd have to be thinking about this, thought you'd be like every other man and would give up on Rachel." Her lips pursed before she took a deep draw on her cigarette. "One thing I should hate about you is the one thing I admire too. Go figure."

"She's always been it for me," was all I said by way of apology.

I wasn't going to say sorry for loving Rach.

"I know. Just didn't think she'd come around. She's always been a stuck-up bitch. Never understood what you saw in her until last night." Her gaze turned shrewd. "You need an Old Lady as strong as you. That's definitely not me, even if I can hold my own with you at chess."

I reached for the can and pulled another sip. "Felt like she'd never come around. Glad she did."

"I am too. For your sake." She sighed. "I could work at the diner."

"I'll sort out a position for you there. Steel's in charge though. You and him never got along."

"Nah, but he's gotten better since he branded Stone." Clearly still tired, she rubbed her eyes. "Can I pay rent here?"

I shook my head. "Once the other rooms are refurbed, this section will be next, but I can help you find a place in town."

Her brow puckered. "You're too good to me."

"You've always been my favorite for a reason, Peach. We've been friends, ain't we?"

Her lips quirked up in a grin. "We have. I'm glad you think so too."

I shared a smile with her. "When you're ready, just tell me, okay?"

"I will. Won't be long." Her gaze fell out of focus. "I'm getting too old for parties like last night." She yawned again. "My head's banging."

"I'll bet. You didn't leave with Kendra?"

She snorted. "No. You know I hate her guts."

That was one of the reasons I liked her.

"She's been causing trouble with Giulia."

"I don't like Giulia, she's a bitch, but Kendra's really been getting under her skin."

"Giulia's..." How did I phrase it? "...a jealous cat by nature."

Peach nodded. "Man like Nyx, it makes sense to be jealous."

"Why? He's clearly devoted to her."

A smile danced on her lips again. "He's wild, Rex. You don't get it. Even if you feel like you domesticated him, it's still like having a tiger roaming around the compound. She'll feel better once she gives birth. Nyx'll like having a family."

Back in the early days, she'd been one of Nyx's bunnies. That she was fond of him was a given. Each of them had been fond of him in the aftermath, despite his having broken nearly all their hearts.

"But Kendra's been worse than usual. Giulia's not overreacting. I'd be jealous as hell too."

"Even though she's clearly lying?"

"Doesn't take much to nourish insecurity. Giulia walks by, Kendra goes, 'Boom, boom, boom,' in time to each of her steps."

"What the fuck for?"

"Saying she's fat."

"She's pregnant."

Peach jibed, "Don't mean dick. Not to women like Kendra. Being thin is their only commodity."

I sighed.

This was my half-sister we were fucking talking about, but it might as well have been an alien for all that she made sense to me.

Pointless spite was exactly that—goddamn pointless.

"What else has Kendra been doing?"

"Saying that she's been banging Nyx on the side, talking smack mostly. I think being pregnant has made Giulia more whacked up than normal so she's taking it harder than she would ordinarily. Don't like either woman but even I was glad last night when Rachel busted her nose."

I hid a smirk.

"Don't make out like that didn't get you hard as nails," Peach mocked, which had me grinning outright.

"Not saying nothing."

"Like every wise man." Peach shared the grin with me. "Anyway, why you here? You've come to throw her out?"

I scratched my chin. "Yeah."

She took a deep pull on her cigarette. "Interesting."

"Why?"

"Didn't think you would. You've always been soft on her. After all that shit she did with Storm, it stunned me you let her stick around."

"You knew about that?"

"We all did." She tapped her nose. "We girls stick together though. Only way to survive."

I clenched my jaw. "She raped him, Peach."

"I know." Her gaze darkened, her brow puckering as sorrow laced her features. "She wasn't the only one. A couple have over the years. They want a brand and they ain't afraid of doing dirty shit to get it." She sucked in a breath. "I hope he and Keira can make it work, but they won't be able to unless he gets clean."

"He's sober now."

She snorted. "We both know that don't last long."

"Nah, he's doing well. Seeing a shrink and all kinds of shit."

Pensive, she mumbled, "I'm glad to hear it."

I knew she meant it too.

"You should be more than a waitress, Peach."

Her lips quirked. "Wasn't ever in the cards for me."

I grunted. "Bullshit. You want to go to school, I'll make that happen too."

"You always were the best Sinner," she said with a teasing smile. "I'll think about it." With that, she got to her feet. "Kendra's in the room on the end. I'm gonna duck inside so I don't hear her wailing."

She retreated to her door, but as she passed me, she patted my shoulder. "I know this is goodbye in a sense, Rex, even if neither of us are going anywhere immediately, but I wish you well."

I stared up at her. "Same, Peach. Same. And I mean it. Whatever help you need, I'll make shit happen."

Something lightened in her eyes. "Thank you."

When the door closed behind her, I felt some of that lightness, too, because I knew she'd accept my offer of help.

That was one of the hardest things about being Prez and being me. I was a feminist, believe it or not. I didn't think I *couldn't* be a feminist when my woman was Rachel Laker, and having women believing that all they were capable of was fucking and cleaning for a living went against that.

What else was feminism, though, if it wasn't a woman's right to choose how she led her life?

Scratching my jaw, I got to my feet and ambled down the short path to the last room.

I knocked on the door, rested my shoulder against the wall, and stared down at the seating area I'd just left. Those fucking shells. Man, I hated sunflower seeds now.

The door opened, and Kendra's mouth danced into a smirk. Her face was busted up, and pride sank into me. Rachel had a wicked right hook. "You here for something that woman can't give you?"

I sneered at her, "You ask me that knowing full well what we are to each other?"

Her smirk dropped. "He told you?"

"In his will."

Thanks to the broken nose, her voice was nasal as she grumbled, "Even in death, he didn't have the balls to claim me."

"Not much worth claiming," I disregarded, ignoring her sharp gasp at my cruel words. "Last night just rammed that home. Why the fuck are you making waves, Kendra? Why are you messing around with Old Ladies and trying to shit on their relationships? Because it's fun? If you're that fucking bored, then I can get you some extra chores—"

Kendra's lips tightened. "I do it because I can."

I let those words resonate a second.

"You do it because you can," I repeated, my tone musing. "What makes you think you can?"

"I'm Bear's daughter. I'm untouchable."

A laugh escaped me because, I realized, she truly believed it.

"You ain't untouchable, Kendra. No one is. That's why I'm here." Even if last night hadn't happened, I'd still want her out. Storm... He deserved this. Her behavior had just put her higher up on my to-do list. "I want you out of this room tonight."

Her raccoon eyes widened. "You can't be serious. I'm your fucking half-sister."

"Don't give a shit. This is on you, for the stunts you pull and the decisions you make." I straightened up from the door when her hand darted out, her fingers tightening in my cut.

"You can't do this."

"Just watch me," I mocked.

"I know things," she spat.

"Sure you do." I winked at her. "Also sure you know that if you go to the cops, there's an empty hole in the graveyard just waiting for you."

"So I'm good enough to be buried in the graveyard?" she mocked. "Not good enough to be acknowledged in life, but in death, I will be?"

"Figure there's a pit that could be opened up. Don't need a marking to dump you in the ground."

Pain darkened her eyes. "You bastard. You mean that, don't you?"

"If you turn rat?" I grinned at her, but it was nothing like the ones I'd shared with Peach. "Bet your ass I do. Not gonna turf you out with nothing—"

"Aren't I the fucking lucky one?" she hissed.

"You are," I agreed, "because I'm only doing this for Dad. He asked me to make provisions for you in his will, and that's what I'm going to do." I reached into my jeans' pocket and pulled out a credit card. "Two grand will be deposited in this account on the first of each month. Consider yourself lucky that Dad asked me to look after you—"

I'd expected her to snatch the card out of my hand, but she didn't. She stared at it like I was passing her a snake.

"He didn't leave me anything, did he?" she questioned, the words coming slow, like she was thinking out loud. "I'd have been called in for the will reading otherwise."

"He asked me to provide for you," was my only reply.

Her gaze fixed itself onto mine. "Even in death, he reminded me how little I mean to him. A duty, a responsibility to bear... not good enough for my own inheritance." She swallowed, straightened up. "I'll be out by the end of the day."

Before she slammed the door in my face, she snatched the card from my grasp and left me staring at the number '69' on her door.

For all that she was a loose end, the weight off my shoulders came as a relief.

Kendra was trouble. I knew that without her making that threat.

This wouldn't be the last I heard of her, but I'd done as Dad asked.

It'd be the last favor I'd do for him.

Because the only safe place for Kendra to go was that empty hole in the graveyard...

Whether she knew it or not, whether she begrudged the fact he hadn't left her anything in his will, she'd be leaving the MC with her life.

That was more than she deserved for what she'd done to Storm.

RACHEL

"The mayoral election is wide open this year—" A groan went up around the table, and I ignored it, voice growing louder to carry over their noise. "—and after the farce with the Laceys, I think we're perfectly placed to install Joseph Ferrero in the township."

Their groans fell silent at that.

"Joseph Ferrero? *José?*" Link queried, his tone dubious. "The sheriff?"

"The sheriff," I concurred. "I know Miles Monroe and James Kinnock are casting their lots for donors."

Rex shot me a sharp glance at the mention of Wynter's adoptive grandfather.

Life could be ironic sometimes.

"Kinnock's into politics?"

"It isn't his first attempt, but die-hard conservatives are looking for an in, and he's that."

"Why doesn't that come as a surprise?" Rex grumbled.

"Kinnock," Maverick mused before he blinked. "Your kid's adoptive grandfather?"

"Yes."

The club knew what had gone down after the FAST gala between the Triads and the Kinnocks. I hadn't said anything, but when I'd shown up for this meeting, the council had been in session for a few hours if the state of the table was anything to go by. As well as the exhaustion in Rex's face.

He looked as tired as I felt.

I imagined the entire situation had been discussed, as well as the many open enterprises the MC was dealing with right now.

That was why I was here.

The mayoral election wasn't high on their list of priorities today, but someone needed to raise the topic.

"Can't we just pitch to some reporter that Kinnock couldn't raise a son who didn't try to sell his daughter off to pay his debts, so why should he be able to look after a town?"

I arched a brow at Sin. "You know that's our daughter you're talking about?"

He just grunted. "Take emotions aside, that's gonna cast immediate doubts on Kinnock's worthiness as a candidate."

"While putting Wynter in the crosshairs of a media shitstorm she'll never escape and humiliating my baby girl in public," Rex growled, fire sparking in his eyes. "What about that sounds like a good idea, Sin?"

That fire and that growl had no business whatsoever in making me wet.

Daddy Rex was fucking *hot*.

"He's not a strong candidate," I tried to assure them. "He's in his seventies—"

"Like that'll stop Americans from voting for him," Maverick mocked. "We like 'em old in our government. The older the better."

"It's almost like we have a fetish for ancient politicians," Link agreed before he shuddered. "One fetish I ain't into."

I rolled my eyes. "You like butt play, Link. That's the limit of your fetishes. Don't go around making out like you're into adult diapers or FemDom."

He whistled under his breath. "Can you imagine Lily as a Domme? Fuck, I could get into that."

My nose crinkled. "She has the disposition for it."

"Started bleating on about her fundraising ideas to you, has she?" he asked commiseratively. "I've heard all about them, and I tried to tell her that we're working at top speed but she's insisting she can control it."

I hid my grimace behind my coffee cup. "I don't like to dampen enthusiasm."

"Lily's definitely enthusiastic," he joked. "If you sit still long enough, she'll drive you to a hotel one day, give you a dress, and say, 'Here. Host the party.'"

My lips twitched because I could easily imagine that too.

"Not to disturb your chitchat," Nyx mocked, "but why the fuck would we want to lose our hold on the sheriff? He can't be both?"

"Because you own him?" The 'dumbass' was unspoken.

"José is good where he is. It'd be easier, surely, to get a new mayor than a new sheriff?" Link pointed out.

"Because there aren't many mayoral candidates, but I know you could maneuver Ferrero into the role. He's a great sheriff, aside from him being corrupt as fuck where the Sinners are concerned.

"He's pleasant, personable, and even the racist assholes who'd prefer to forget his heritage like him. He's that kind of guy. He visits the country clubs, blends in there, plays golf with the rich folk and dances with their daughters at the galas... He's perfectly placed in your pocket to make a great mayor who'll be proactive where the MC needs him to be."

"You've clearly been thinking about this," Rex mused.

I shrugged. "I'm surprised that you haven't, to be honest. The primaries are in June. He won the sheriff's elections so it's a good time to get him to make the shift."

"Who'd we get as the new sheriff? We need both in our pocket. It'd be helpful to have the mayor on our side for the new fronts we've inaugurated these past eighteen months, but it's not as if we're choir boys," Nyx countered.

"His Chief Deputy," I reasoned. "Farrow is as crooked as a fishhook. He and Ferrero deal well together. He'd be running practically unopposed, too, seeing as he'd have Ferrero's backing."

"You really have thought about this," Sin said.

"It's my job to."

"Who's Miles Monroe?" Steel questioned, shuffling those ever-present cards of his.

How Stone didn't toss them out when he wasn't looking, I'd never know.

"He's a deacon with the Evangelical church over by the town hall."

"He'd be a popular choice," Rex pointed out.

"He's a weirdo," I disregarded. "He gives off a creepy vibe. His congregation is probably hypnotized into going every Sunday."

"That bad?" Sin joked.

"Yeah, that bad. Makes my skin crawl."

"I think I know the guy you mean," Rex muttered. His eyes turned distant a second before he clicked his fingers. "Maverick, isn't he the one who goes to that brothel over in Hanover?"

"How the hell would you know that?" I demanded.

"He protested the construction of the strip club. We had to get him under our thumb or we might not have been able to get our licenses."

"Shit," I hissed under my breath. "He did. He was a major pain in the ass. How did I forget about that?"

"Plenty of other crap to be dealing with," Nyx dismissed, which, for Nyx, was borderline kind.

Especially when they could have told me I had pregnancy brain.

And I'd have had to kill them.

Maverick pulled up something on his phone just as a noisy howl sounded from outside. "Jax was the one you sent in for the photos, Nyx."

No one blinked an eye at the howl. No one other than Rex and me.

Nyx, oblivious to the howl, sighed. "Shit, I miss him."

"Me too," Steel ground out. "We lost too many in the blast."

"We did, and Jax was good people. Would have made an excellent brother," Nyx said bitterly, even as he was reaching for Mav's cell.

"What's with the howl?" I queried.

"Quin," was all Sin said.

Link chuckled. "It's that Newfoundlander that's got a crush on—"

"Shut up, Link," Nyx muttered as he swiped through the photos on Mav's phone. "I remember now."

Mav clicked his tongue. "Monroe gets off on beating his rent boys."

"The fuck are rent boys?"

Mav peered owlishly at Link. "Isn't it self-explanatory?"

"What? Have you been binge-watching *Bridgerton* with Alessa or something?"

"I don't know if they have male prostitutes in historical period dramas—"

Sensing this would start an argument, I jibed, "Can we get back to the matter at hand, please?"

"Not sure his congregation would appreciate knowing he's gay," Sin mocked. "The beating they'd probably be okay with."

I snorted but didn't deny that he was probably right.

I knew for a fact that under Monroe's leadership, marital abuse wasn't even a thing... It was, if anything, considered 'spousal discipline.'

I'd helped one of his parishioners escape an abusive home eight years ago when she'd come to me, begging for help to escape her father.

Parker had been loyal to me ever since.

"You remember Parker Henshaw?" I asked, trying to ignore the second howl from outside.

Jesus, were we in a doggy daycare and I just didn't know it?

Rex scratched his jaw. "Your executive assistant?"

"She was in Monroe's flock. If need be, I can prod her for info on him."

He nodded. "Thanks, babe."

I smirked, but deep inside, I couldn't deny that I liked hearing that term of endearment spilling from his lips. Especially as public as this was. "My pleasure."

What made it even better?

No one hooted or even batted an eyelash.

In this crowd, i.e., *Link,* that was a tough win, but I figured it spoke of the battle it'd taken to reach this high ground.

"As for Kinnock, I can lean on him," Sin muttered as he peered at Mav's phone, swiping through each photo with a glower. "We don't have to make it public what Jeremy did, but it can still be used as leverage."

"Maverick, dig up some other dirt on him, okay?" Rex ordered. "I don't want to use Wynter's situation for our gain."

Daddy Rex was beyond hot.

"Will do." He rubbed his forehead. "I have some treatments coming up, but Star will help out if I need her."

"Speaking of the witch, I'm not sure I like the idea of Lodestar working with the Italians," Steel grumbled.

"In the interest of full disclosure, I work with the Sicilians, and word to the wise, don't call the family Italians if you're ever dealing with Valentini. He won't appreciate it," I informed them. "An old friend was doing IT work for them, and he approached me regarding Lodestar being hired by the Italians. I agreed that he should pass on her name because I liked the idea of having her linked to both of you. It makes the flow of information easier."

"You should have talked to us about that," Steel argued.

"Why? It isn't like I have a say in what Lodestar does. My friend asked me if I'd heard of her, if she was good people—"

"And you lied and said she was?" Link teased, making my lips twitch.

"She's decent. In her own way."

His nose crinkled. "If you say so. She could definitely start a fight in a monastery."

I didn't wholly disagree with that.

"You *should* have told us, Rach, but I also like the idea of the flow of information being widespread. These last couple of months have shown us the importance of cooperation." Rex eyed Nyx. "Speaking of, we need to deal with the O'Donnelly situation."

Sin winced. "I don't know what the fuck Aidan Sr.'s game is."

I arched a brow, surprised that Nyx's arrest had clearly been under discussion prior to my arrival. They'd definitely been busy this morning.

"I can tell you what his game is," I drawled. "He's a desperate old man trying to wipe out some pieces of shit from the earth before he leaves it."

"Desperate?" Sin shook his head. "Nothing's desperate about that lunatic."

"I'm the one who spoke with him at the precinct when I got Nyx out. I'd know. I'm telling you, he was desperate."

"What makes you think that?" Rex asked quietly.

I tried to assimilate my impressions from that night and slowly verbalized, "This is personal for him."

"I agree," Nyx rumbled. "It is."

"You're not allowed to weigh in on this conversation," Sin sniped. "You were a moron for walking into that trap."

"It wasn't a trap."

Nyx's calm retort had me rolling my eyes. "Your freedom and incarceration were brokered by the same man. That doesn't mean he's friendly; it means he wants you beholden to him."

"He likes to have leverage over people," Sin concurred.

"In this instance, he wants certain people to die and, for whatever reason, he wants to control who does the killing."

Rex pondered my words then asked, "Did he ever mention a name?"

Nyx nodded, reached for his phone, and groused, "Am I allowed to speak, Sin?" He didn't wait for permission. "A couple. Mikhail Korolev, but the one that interested me the most was Francis Merriweather."

"You've heard from him since you were arrested?" Sin questioned.

Nyx just shrugged.

Steel shuffled his deck of cards at double speed. "Jesus, man, you should have told us."

"What was there to tell? He was being his usual asswipe self."

"Francis Merriweather," I blurted out. "How do I know that name?"

Maverick scowled. "I know it too. My fucking memory's shot though."

"Isn't he in Congress?" Rex asked slowly. "Jesus. He's a pedophile?"

For a second, we all let that sink in, then I rasped, "I think it's safe to assume O'Donnelly's targets will all be high profile. That's why he wants you beholden to him." Nyx's hands balled into fists on the desk, and at the sight, I murmured, "You need to tell Giulia about what happened. Kendra went AWOL that night, and she thinks you were with her."

"For fuck's sake," Nyx snapped. "What is it with her and Kendra?"

"I spoke with Peach yesterday," Rex replied, which came as news to me. "She said Kendra's been going out of her way to make Giulia miserable."

Nyx clenched his jaw. "I want her gone—"

"She is. I tossed her out yesterday. She won't be coming back."

My eyes widened—that was also news to me.

Rex shot me an apologetic look. "You were asleep when I got in last night."

I had been.

Dammit to hell.

Pregnancy was really messing with my mojo.

Link scratched his chin. "Maybe you should meet up with O'Donnelly? Figure out what his deal is?"

Rex nodded. "I've been thinking about that. Sin, I'll need you to arrange a meeting."

And there was the hope I'd never have to see O'Donnelly again going up in smoke. No way in hell would I let them do this on their own. With how volatile they all were, they'd trigger a war with our so-called allies.

"Will do."

"Last thing on the agenda—Bear's funeral," Rex murmured.

"It's under control," Link replied, grief shadowing his expression. "Lily has everything in place. She just needs a date."

"She arranged the funeral?"

Link shrugged. "Before she was working with Rach, she had a lot of time on her hands, and she has the money to get things organized with a lot of flexibility."

Rex swallowed. "I'll have to thank her for that."

"She just needs a date," Link said softly.

His mouth tightened. "Within the next two weeks?"

"Okay. I'll let you know the available dates."

"Storm will want to attend. I'll key him in once everything's confirmed." Rex rubbed his forehead. Before I could remind him that Bear had been no ordinary brother, he said, "The other chapters need to come as well. Damn. It'll need to be a show of strength."

Link nodded. "I'll coordinate that. Don't worry about it, Rex."

"Thanks, brother," was his tired reply.

"I promised Giulia that Grizzly and Dog's bodies would be removed from the cemetery." Nyx's tone was flat—I could tell he was still pissed at the thought of having to tell her where he'd been on the night of his arrest.

Rex cracked his knuckles. "Is the ground still frozen?"

"Thaw's in," Maverick confirmed.

"I want them out before Dad's burial."

"Rex!" I sputtered. "You can't seriously agree with this!"

His mouth was taut as he looked at me. "Sweetheart, one day, we'll be in that graveyard, and there's no way in fuck I'm having you share space with those pieces of shit—even in death. No," he growled, casting a look at his brothers. "I want them out. ASAP."

I guessed it was a testament to how I'd been raised that, as disturbing as his words were, they were also, I feared, some of the most romantic he'd ever uttered to me.

TWENTY-SEVEN

LODESTAR

The world had the annoyingly irritating habit of continuing to spin even when, beneath my feet, it felt as if the ground had been demolished.

Climbing to the top of that goddamn skyscraper had been a two pronged delight—I'd caught a cold as well as killed a murderer.

"Yo, you there?"

I grimaced. "I'm here, Cin."

Cin, AKA 'Dead To Me,' was one of my closest friends.

If a woman like me *could* have friends...

"You sure you want me to keep on giving Laker a hard time?"

My grimace twisted into a grin. "I sure as fuck do."

"Why?"

"Since when do we gossip about our jobs?"

"Since you asked me to do you a favor?"

"So I'm in your debt?"

"Forever and ever until kingdom come."

"With the state of the world, who fucking knows when that'll be. Hell, that'd just be the cherry on the cake, wouldn't it? Going to all this fucking effort for nothing?"

"Sounds like the story of our lives." Cin paused. "You sound... shitty."

"Snotty. That's what I sound like. I caught a fucking cold doing your job."

"Couldn't be in two goddamn places at once, now could I?"

I huffed because that was her fault, not mine.

We all had a process, and part of hers was to send a goddamn gift bag with balloons tied to it, 'Sucks To Be You' embossed on the front. She'd gotten such a fucking rep now, though, that she had to deliver the shit herself.

The first couple delivery guys she'd used hadn't been able to identify the real Cin, but she'd burned a false ID in the process and the threat of being caught wasn't a mistake she'd made again.

"You sure you got him?"

"I might not be the talent you are, but I'm still a fucking crack shot. Of course I got him. It's not fucking right, sending snipers after snipers. It's like a pig eating bacon."

"It's nothing like a pig eating bacon."

"Yeah, it is," I argued. "Cannibalism combined with that whole 'no honor amongst thieves' spiel."

"Well, we can agree on that. My only consolation is that some of the fuckers I've been sent to take out are nasty pricks."

"You're certain you're dealing with Eoghan O'Donnelly?"

"Sure as shit. He's the Whistler. As for Eagle Eyes—"

"Yeah. I know. He's with the Hells' Rebels. He interests me less."

"Why?"

"Because I have an active desire to keep most O'Donnellys alive?"

"Why?"

"What the fuck is this? Jeopardy?"

"You're doing weird shit, Star. Weirder than usual. Illogical—"

"Nothing I do is illogical. I like to keep people on their toes. If they aren't smart enough to figure that out, then that's on them. Not me. And since when did you care about my illogical games, huh?" I muttered even as I sent out a text to Amara.

Me: *Here's Liliana's location. Have fun.*

Amara: *This joke?*

Me: *I'm not laughing.*

Amara: *I will bring you back present.*

Me: *I don't need a gift. Just give the cunt what she deserves. That's gift enough.*

Amara: *Thank you, Star. I will never forget this.*

My lips quirked. Amara might be a lunatic, but she was honest about her lunacy. I appreciated that in a person.

"Why do you want Hunter Lachlan to think he has a hit out on him?"

"To keep him contained." I tutted. "Surely that was obvious?"

I checked my GPS tracker on Rachel's car. She was heading to a meeting with O'Donnelly Sr. with a couple of the brothers. I was curious how that'd play out and intended on listening in.

I felt like a spider, spinning silk, turning small webs into bigger ones. Webs that spanned a nation.

That, given time, would span the world.

I took a hit of coffee from my mug as Cin derided, "Nothing's obvious with you. I just trust your intentions. Not your methods."

"Why, Cin, that might just be the kindest thing you've ever said to me," I teased.

She made a barfing sound. "How am I supposed to help if I don't know what's involved in the plan?"

"The plan is convoluted."

"The best ones are."

I heard a soft shushing sound and realized she was rubbing her hands together.

That was the difference between her and me. She still enjoyed the subterfuge, the espionage. I didn't. I was fucking tired. Of everything. The bitch of it was, my work wasn't even halfway done.

Exhausted, I switched off my screen, wanting to take a break from the glare. With her in my ears, I tipped my head back and rocked in my desk chair.

The house was quiet for once; Kat was in school, Lily was out on her mission to make galas great again, Link was at his shop, and Tiff's mom, the cunt, had gone to a doctor's appointment.

As the silence sank into my bones, I visualized the plan.

Walking into Bear's motel room had come as a hell of a shock to me. Not because some of the information wasn't shit I'd learned a while back, but because he'd created a physical web that reminded me of my mental one.

His room conjured up the image of those kid's outdoor play areas. The kind that were shaped like a pyramid, and ropes were tangled together to create a climbing frame for them to reach the top.

"Hunter Lachlan has to stay out of sight for the next month at least," I mused. "Maybe longer."

"Why?"

"The DA got one of the Camorra to turn rat. They'll be making raids—"

"You're saving him from arrest?" Cin sounded disappointed that my maneuverings were for so basic a reason.

"He's important."

"Why is he?"

"The Camorra owns Vegas and a good chunk of the West Coast. His grandfather has more senators in his back pocket than the president. If De Laurentiis goes down for his crimes, Hunter will be the natural heir."

"So you want a strong Camorra?"

"I do."

"Okay. You really think they'll be able to take down the Camorra Don?"

"I've listened to their interviews with the rat. There's enough to Capone him, but the ADA on his case has a grudge against the family and he wants to bring him down on a host of charges. His hubris will bite him in the ass. A good defense will stop that from happening."

"You sound certain."

"I am. Hunter Lachlan's footprints are mostly virtual, but this rat found out about a murder fifteen, sixteen years ago. Hunter was behind it."

"Who'd he kill?"

I thought about Rachel. I thought about her fears and her hopes; shit she'd laid out for us all to see around that table in Lily's pink room.

"The brother of the ADA leading the case."

Cin whistled under her breath. "So it's personal."

"Sure as fuck is."

"Right, so, keep Hunter safe. Check."

"More than that, keep him under the radar. He's still in his apartment, right?"

"Apartment, more like a fucking stronghold," she grumbled. "If the evidence is there, then it's there, Star. You can't save him from that."

"Wanna bet?"

"Keeping him under the radar won't stop that, either."

"No, but De Laurentiis will work out a deal to spare Hunter. I can feel it in my bones. He'll go down and sacrifice himself for his grandkid."

"So... wait... the end goal you actually want is for Hunter Lachlan to be the next head of the Camorra?"

"Yup."

She whistled again. "That way, you're entangled with most of the East Coast Mob families and the West too?"

"Exactly."

Cin snorted. "You're a shrewd bitch."

"Aren't you glad you know me?"

"Most of the time. Not always. You're fucking mean with your intel."

"Always here when you need me," I demurred.

"Yeah, right. That's why I had to find out from Rachel Laker that the First Lady's in the fucking ECD."

My nose crinkled. "I didn't want you to know yet."

"Why?"

"Didn't want to compromise your loyalties."

"She's a fucking terrorist, Star."

"Aren't we all?"

She huffed. "My shit's technically sanctioned by the government."

I scoffed, "Which government?"

When she fell silent, I smirked.

Cin double-crossed the double-crossers like a pro.

"That's why you wanted to keep The Whistler safe? Because it would destabilize the Irish Mob?"

"Partly."

Partly because a strong Five Points was a strong East Coast network, and partly because it'd have broken Conor's fucking heart if his kid brother was killed.

The second I'd heard from Cin what was going down, random jobs, each with snipers at the other end of her rifle, I'd been on red alert.

Going so far as to overcome my fear of goddamn heights to take out the threat when Cin got stuck at Harry Reid because an unattended bag in Departures had housed an incendiary device.

"Star?"

"What?"

"You sound sick."

"Going up that skyscraper didn't help."

"You should get some rest."

"How can I? Got a lot of shit to do."

I rubbed at my tired eyes but rest was for the weak. I needed to listen into the meeting between the Five Points and the Sinners, then I had to monitor the situation in Edgewater.

That bag of bones that had once been Kevin Sisson had disappeared then reappeared a week later.

The records had been tampered with, but whoever had made their moves had made it look like human error about which fridge the corpse had been stored in.

So, no, I didn't have time to rest.

All that shit was at the top of my to-do list but the rest of that list made Everest look tiny.

Yawning, I mumbled, "Just keep Laker on her toes, okay?"

"I will. Anything in particular you want me to have her investigate?"

I shrugged even though she couldn't see me. "Whatever you feel like throwing at her, throw at her. Just remember that she's pregnant. Keep her stressed, but not enough to harm the baby."

I was still pissed at her for threatening Kat. I had to punish her somehow.

Cin snickered. "Star, are you turning soft in your old age?"

"Fuck off," I grumbled.

"I will, I will," she mockingly sang, making me roll my eyes.

"Are you in Vegas now?"

"Yeah, it's hell. You owe me for this alone."

I smirked. "I always repay my favors."

"That's the only reason I always come when you call," she said with a sniff, then her tone turned somber. "I'm seriously starting to think that someone in the CIA wants the First Lady dead, Star."

I was counting on it.

Just not yet.

I grunted. "Wouldn't be much of a loss. The president though... I like him."

"You would." She heaved a sigh. "I gotta go."

"Keep in touch."

"Will do."

As she ended the call, I thought about all the pieces I had out there on my great big chess board. Each of them was vital, and each could only be sacrificed or played in a particular order for my end game to be successful.

Hunter Lachlan at the head of the Camorra.

The head of the CIA disgraced.

Eamonn Keegan dead.

And, most important of all, the complete annihilation of the New World Sparrows, Old World Sparrows, and the Eastern Sparrows.

Only then would I have any peace.

Only then would I be able to have something I didn't even know I'd needed five years ago when I'd set off on this journey—a certain Fecker in my life.

TWENTY-EIGHT

RACHEL

"Everything okay?" I asked.

Wynter had shocked me by calling out of the blue, but mostly, I was just relieved she had. I was trying *very* hard not to be awkward.

Why was Rain the one who got all the charm in my family, huh?

"Not really. But I don't expect things will be easy, not with Dad still in the hospital."

I grimaced at Wynter's reply but tried to keep my distaste for her adoptive father out of my tone as I murmured, "Is there anything I can do to help?"

"I'm struggling with some of my ethics homework."

Surprised, I gushed, "Call me when you're back from school, and we'll talk. I'll guide you through it."

"Thank you," was Wynter's shy retort, but it was almost drowned out by the sound of the bell. "I'd better go. Lunch period is over."

"Speak tonight." I hesitated. "Stay safe out there."

"I will. Thanks, Rachel. Bye."

"Bye."

I scanned my screen for any missed notifications and saw a couple from Rex, one that was telling me he was on his way to

Manhattan, and another describing what he'd do to me if I did anything to agitate O'Donnelly Sr.

It involved his dick, several orgasms, and a potentially bright pink ass.

Before my conversation with Indy about her and Cruz's relationship, I might have taken offense at the idea of being spanked, but... with Rex, maybe I'd like that too?

He wasn't happy about my attending today's meeting, but he hadn't attempted to stop me from coming either.

That, more than anything, pleased me.

Nothing had changed on a professional level where our relationship was concerned. He hadn't started treating me differently because I was with him now. Aside from, of course, the odd 'babe' or 'baby' spoken in front of the guys.

I could deal with that. Being cosseted, on the other hand, would drive me nuts.

There were a few more messages, some from Parker—only just getting over her snit with me and that was thanks to a gift basket from Godiva—a couple from Susanne, my paralegal, and then one from Craig.

I pursed my lips at the sight of his name on my screen, and my thumb hovered over the message for a few seconds. One of the texts was a photo.

That I wasn't happy to hear from him saddened me.

I should have missed his and Scott's presence in my life, should have been grateful that he was reaching out.

Mostly, I was just wary.

I had a full schedule, was exhausted from that, had a new relationship, a new world, as a result, to maneuver, and they were just dead weight.

Because I was a sucker, the guilt from that realization had me opening the message.

Craig: *Meet Sarah. She was born last night at 4AM. 5lb. 4oz.*

She's a few weeks premature and has a couple of developmental issues. That's why she's in the incubator.

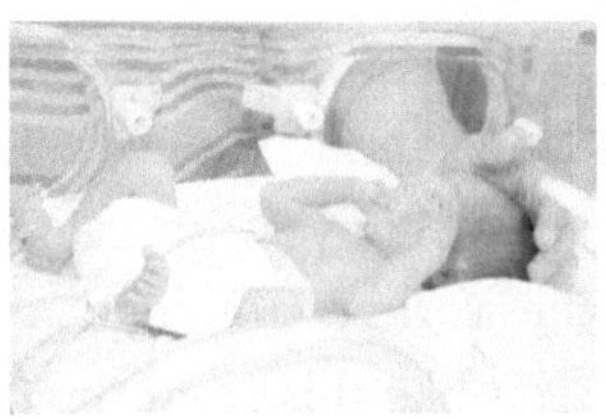

Craig: *Miss you xo*

I stared at the photo of the baby, her crinkled face, bright pink cheeks, the white of the blanket she was wrapped up in that was nuzzled against the mop of dark brown hair on her head and I wondered if she'd ever know the struggles her fathers had gone through to get her here.

Glad for them even if I was still cautious, I forwarded his first text to Parker and asked her to send a gift basket to them.

Then, to Craig, I merely replied:

Me: *She's beautiful. I'm so happy that you've finally gotten the family you've always wanted. Congrats xo*

The ticks didn't immediately turn blue, and I shoved my cell in my briefcase to handle that later.

We'd been friends for a long time, but Scott had been the one to say hurtful things, to be purposely antagonistic.

If that was the first move, it wasn't on Craig to make it. It was on Scott.

I decided that I'd reconsider the situation if Scott got in touch. If he didn't, then the ball was in his court.

With that settled, I felt somewhat better, and I decided to watch the traffic for the rest of the journey to the warehouse off the docks where O'Donnelly wanted to meet rather than spend it working.

I'd been doing that nonstop and I needed a break.

The car pulled up outside the building five minutes early, and as

I stepped out, Rex was there, moving into my space, his lips brushing mine in a greeting.

"You waited for me? How sweet," I teased, despite the fact that I loved this side of him.

The side that held my hand in public, who saw no shame in kissing me, and who sent me private grins as if we were in our own bubble that the rest of the world couldn't invade.

I knew he'd have been like this from the start, and I meant from way back when. I'd been the one to shove distance between us. But that didn't mean I couldn't appreciate it now. If anything, the distance of before made me enjoy it all the more.

He grabbed my hand and told me, "Not about to let you walk into that snake pit by yourself."

I rolled my eyes. "He's not going to hurt us."

"You've heard the rumors about the man as much as I have."

"We're allies."

"And getting Nyx arrested is how he treats his allies," was Rex's rejoinder.

"If you're going to have a shitty attitude with him," I remarked easily, "then you need to leave the talking to me."

His jaw clenched. "I'll let you take point—"

My brows rose. "You will?"

"Yes. But if you don't corral him, I'll take over."

He made O'Donnelly sound like a stallion with a mare in heat in the paddock next to him.

Refraining from rolling my eyes for the second time in as many minutes, I merely said, "Leave it with me."

He dipped his chin then called out, "Nyx? Harlow? We're going in."

"You brought Harlow?"

"Figured O'Donnelly would want to meet him. You think I should have left him in Jersey?"

"No. On the contrary. I think it's a smart move. I'm just surprised you brought him."

He grunted in reply, and Harlow and Nyx shouldered us as we stepped toward the outer gates of the warehouse.

Guards approached, armed with submachine guns—like we were in downtown Ciudad Juárez, for God's sake—but after Rex introduced us all, they guided us in without much fanfare.

Ten minutes later, after wandering what seemed to be the entire goddamn length of the warehouse, we were led into a room.

Unlike the rest of the place that was industrial in nature, this was an office, clad with rich wooden paneling that made the room warmer. There was a grand mahogany desk in here, as well as a board table of sorts, a large dresser loaded with photo frames, antique filing cabinets, as well as a seating area set before a fireplace.

O'Donnelly was behind his desk as he said, "Take a seat at the table."

Harlow and Nyx shuffled out from beside us, Rex did as well, tugging me along, but not before I greeted O'Donnelly with a nod.

He returned the nod as he got to his feet but he pressed a hand to the desk as if it were for support. His fingers, however, trembled, and he stumbled before he righted himself.

Quickly glancing away so he didn't realize I'd witnessed the show of weakness, I settled myself at the board table and waited for him to join us.

"There's coffee if you want it," O'Donnelly said as he shuffled toward the head of the table and took a seat. The relief on his face to be sitting, noticeable only because I was watching him, made me wonder if he had mobility issues.

"Thank you," I said pleasantly, straightening to drag the tray over toward me. "I'll play hostess, shall I?"

Nyx released the softest snort, and Rex cleared his throat.

Both of them knew I was the last person to play 'hostess.' O'Donnelly didn't need to know that though.

He smiled at me and said, "I take it black."

Nodding, I served us all coffee even though I wouldn't be drinking mine and, when the pleasantries were done, waited for him to take a sip before I said, "Thank you for agreeing to meet with us, Mr. O'Donnelly."

"Aidan, please. This isn't our first meeting."

"No." My lips twitched. "I have to say, you managed to rile up the clubhouse with your actions, Aidan."

"I like to keep people on their toes," he concurred, a gleam in his eyes as he slouched back in his chair. "Not that that was my intention here."

"No? We're supposed to be allies, O'Donnelly," Rex growled. "Getting my men arrested isn't what I consider friendly behavior."

I dropped my hand to his lap and dug my nails into his thigh. I knew it wouldn't hurt but it served as a silent warning for him to shut the fuck up.

"I wasn't dealing with Nyx as a Sinner. I was dealing with Nyx as a man."

"It's not as if they're separate entities." I frowned. "Do you allow your Five Pointers so little autonomy over themselves?"

"Depends. I give them leeway with certain matters. Family ones, for instance." Aidan shot Nyx a look. "Took your man long enough to agree to meet with me. I knew he'd stay dormant if I didn't push things." He glanced at Harlow. "Who's the boy?"

"He's someone I'd like you to meet."

Aidan straightened up in his seat. "Introduce yourself, boy."

"My name's Harlow Dresden."

Frowning, Aidan studied him. "Not wearing a cut, but still close enough to the MC that they trust you to be here... Curious. What's your story, Harlow?"

"My baby sister was kidnapped by a pedophile. He did... wicked things to her. The worst." His throat bobbed. "Then he killed her. He didn't go to prison—"

Aidan slammed his hand down against the table. "Jessie Dresden. Haune was one of your kills, wasn't he, Nyx?"

Nyx grunted. "He was."

"I remembered reading about the Dresdens. One of the girl's siblings was in the seminary if I remember right."

Harlow tipped up his chin. "My calling abandoned me in the aftermath of Jessie's death."

"Faith can be lost and found in the most random of circumstances." Aidan's lips pursed. "It's a sorry bunch sitting around this table. Aside from the lawyer and your President, of course, we've all failed to defend someone who matters to us. Someone who should have remained innocent but who was defiled.

"This isn't business between a Five Pointer and a Satan's Sinner. This goes deeper—"

"You can kill anyone you please," Rex interrupted, earning himself another bite of my nails into his thigh. "Why get my men involved?"

Ignoring him, Aidan turned his focus on Nyx. "I heard about your antics years ago."

"I know. I remember one of your sons telling me you were aware of my kills."

"A righteous cause is something to be celebrated, not denigrated." He drummed his fingers against the table. "It pains me to say it, but I'm an old man, and hunting is a young man's sport. But that doesn't mean I can't get my revenge and make my mark as well—"

"Why not just contact Nyx through the regular channels? Why go outside the bonds of our alliance, dammit? He's a man with a kid on the way, O'Donnelly. You're not just fucking around with his life here."

"I'm not fucking around with anything. The kind of hunger your man has doesn't abate, Rex. You have to know that. You've been feeding him kills for decades now.

"I understand your anger, but I don't appreciate being interrupted," he intoned grimly. "This had to happen outside of the regular channels."

"Why?"

"Because this is my key to heaven and it has to be free from the taint of the Five Points."

Whatever the hell I'd expected him to say, it wasn't that.

Harlow, apparently as stunned as me, blurted out, "You think the path to heaven is by killing pedophiles?"

Obviously, we were both on board the same 'Is he fucking crazy?' train.

"'*My God is vengeful against his foes; he rages against his enemies. The Lord is very patient but great in power; the Lord punishes. His way is in whirlwind and storm; clouds are the dust of his feet.*'"

Harlow swallowed. "Nahum 1: 2-8."

Aidan nodded. "He'll appreciate that my penance is, shall we say, active." Sitting up, he leaned into the table. "And in turn, so will yours be. A righteous kill. '*And thine eye shall not pity; but life shall go for life, eye for eye, tooth for tooth, hand for hand, foot for foot.*'"

I cast Rex a look, saw his glower had morphed into an expression of confusion. I couldn't blame him. The gossip about O'Donnelly Sr. being nuttier than a Froot Loop was clearly accurate.

"I will provide you with names. I will provide you with a secure location to avenge the victims in our past. The rest is down to you."

Nyx remarked, "I made promises—"

"And I won't ask you to break them. As your man says, you have a woman and a child on the way. I knew that already, and that was partly why I started things how I did. I wanted you to know that you're safe. Under my protection, you're untouchable."

"No one is untouchable," I warned.

Aidan's smile was patronizing. "Shall we have another round of 'Show & Tell?'"

I grimaced. "Let's not. I don't have time to waste sitting around in a police precinct on charges you can make disappear, but what if Nyx and/or Harlow do something you don't agree with? Your help is conditional." To them, I said, "When he gives you a name, he'll expect you to end them. If you don't, he'll have you over a barrel."

The leader of the Five Points grunted. "You're a suspicious woman, aren't you?"

"It's how I got where I am today," I mocked.

"What assurances can I provide that will satisfy you?"

"That's the point; there aren't any. Look, I shouldn't even be here, and I only am because Nyx is..." I sucked in a breath. Blew it out. Accepted the truth for what it was. "He's my brother. We're family, and I don't take kindly to my brother getting his ass landed in jail because you're on a crusade."

Aidan's eyes glittered. "Are you going to tell me that you're okay with a sitting congressman being a pedophile?"

"How do you know he is? What proof did you find?"

"Photos in his driveway."

"His driveway?" I repeated with a frown.

Nyx cleared his throat. "I think he means hard drive."

I glowered at him because he sounded like he was on the brink of laughing.

Nothing about this was fucking funny.

"And you, or whoever found the photos, just happened to fall upon that hard drive?"

"No. My son deals with that side of things and, admittedly, he went looking at my direction. But not for anything that's your business."

"How do you know he didn't plant them?"

"There's a reason I want these bastards to pay. My boy survived —" His nostrils flared. "My boy was—"

"Raped," Nyx said gruffly when Aidan appeared to struggle with the ability to phrase the unthinkable.

I knew how that felt.

"Yes. The bastard's dead, long gone, but this need inside me to make him pay won't die. I need to do something. I have to. I can't just stand by while other kiddies are hurt. Not when I can do something about it."

"You didn't think about exposing the congressman to the world?" I groused.

"For him to rot in jail? On my taxes?" Aidan derided. "I don't think so."

"As if you pay any taxes anyway," I said with a sniff.

That glitter made another appearance in his eyes. "You've got guts, Rachel Laker."

"We established that at the precinct that night," I countered, unimpressed.

"That we did," he grumbled. "My assurance is my faith. Something that's been knocked by the truth—my boy was raped by a priest." His mouth tightened. "For seven decades, I've committed a sin, confessed, and been absolved. I don't have that path open to me anymore. My faith has to change, and this is the way I want to do it.

"You are allies. I have no desire to break ties, not when we make a lot of money together. But this is separate to that."

"I believe him."

I scowled at Nyx. "You believed him the last time. You know, when he trapped you?"

"He didn't trap me. He showed me what he's capable of."

"That should scare you, not impress you."

Aidan's focus was glued to Nyx's. "She's right."

"Nothing scares me, aside from the idea of my woman raising my kid without me around."

And I didn't think that was because Giulia was as batty as Aidan —in her own particular way.

"I've been blessed with six sons," Aidan confessed gruffly, "and I've been further blessed to be around for every achievement and every failure. I'm not about to take that from you."

Harlow was frowning. "God won't absolve you of your sins if you take this path—"

"That's your belief, son, but that's not mine." Aidan's mouth set in firm lines. "You wouldn't be here if you didn't feel the need for vengeance."

"I do, but I'm willing to burn in hell for it."

Harlow's raw words had Aidan straightening in his seat. "That kind of bravery shouldn't go to waste."

"Why do I feel like I'm talking to myself?" I muttered under my breath.

I didn't expect an answer but I got one anyway. "They're all as crazy as each other."

Shooting Rex a look, I sighed. "This is going to happen whether we like it or not, isn't it?"

"Yeah." His expression was as bewildered as I felt sure mine was, but there was a measure of calm buried in his gaze, a calm that told me he'd sign off on this even if he thought it was insane. "If it's any consolation, I don't think he'll fuck them over."

"That's no consolation. 'Think' won't keep them out of jail."

But Nyx, Harlow, and Aidan were already deep in a discussion I had no desire to hear.

"Thank you for coming, Rach," Rex said. "Thank you for trying."

"I had to."

"You meant it, didn't you?"

I arched a brow at him. "Which part?"

"About him being your brother."

"Oh. That part." I swallowed. "Yes. I meant it."

His lips quirked up in a grin. "Glad you finally figured that one out. For someone so smart—"

"I'd watch how you finish that sentence, Rex."

That grin only widened, and *even though* this meeting was a mess, *even though* I'd heard more scripture now than I had in, well, ever, and *even though* I'd likely be defending Nyx and Harlow on counts of murder and vigilantism at some point in the future, that grin somehow made it all bearable.

Together.

That was what that grin said.

Together.

I wasn't alone anymore, and neither was he.

Nyx, and Harlow now, weren't just Rex's burden to bear; they were mine too.

Not much consolation, but I was the one who wanted his brand, and he was the one who didn't know if I could cope with what it represented.

This had to be a step down that path, didn't it?

TWENTY-NINE

REX

THE FOLLOWING WEEK

"Did you hear?"

"What in particular? The moans from across the hall where Lever's banging Enya? Gunner's puking from that curry he ate last night or—"

Link grunted. "You don't have to tell me how fucking noisy it is. I get it. But I meant 'the news.' About Monroe."

Deep into the accounts for the motel's construction project, it took me a minute to locate the name in my head.

"Monroe? As in Miles? The deacon Rach says is going to run for mayor?"

Link nodded. "I don't think he'll be running any time soon."

"Why not?"

"He just got arrested."

I blinked. "For?"

"Murder. Did Bear even know Monroe?"

"Dad? What does he have to do with it?"

"Kevin's body was riddled with Monroe's DNA."

"What the fuck? How's that possible?"

"I don't know. Just telling you what José told me."

"José made the arrest?"

"No. Edgewater cops did."

"That makes no sense."

"No, what makes no sense is that Nyx told me O'Donnelly got rid of the bones but they showed up again."

"What? You think he planted the evidence on Monroe? Why the fuck would he do that?"

"How the hell do I know? You said it yourself after that meeting with him—he's a headcase."

Well, that was true.

After sitting through a Five Points' fucked up version of a Sunday School lesson, I'd come face to face with the fact that Aidan O'Donnelly Sr. more than lived up to his rep.

By the time we left, I was thanking Christ that his sons were in positions of power because otherwise, we were all fucked.

"How would O'Donnelly even know Monroe?" Before he could answer, I raised a hand. "You know what... I'm not even going to worry about this. Nyx hasn't been sent up for it; that's all that matters to me."

"Just keeping you in the loop," Link said with a shrug. "They're getting ready to crack the ground. Rach's out there."

"Rach? My Rach?" I asked doubtfully.

"Unless it's her doppelgänger," Link mocked.

"Why's she there?"

"Looks as if Giulia strong-armed her."

"Why doesn't that surprise me?"

"Those two together..." He whistled. "Hell in heels."

He wasn't wrong.

Shutting my computer down, I got to my feet.

"Are the bodies out of the ground yet?"

"No. Nyx is still trying to get to them in the mini digger."

"Surprised there wasn't more resistance to this," I remarked as we headed into the hall.

"The men are uneasy about it, but no one really liked Grizzly. As for Dog, too many of the guys got sick of him sniffing around their women to really care."

Link was the best at keeping his ear to the ground, keeping me apprised of the morale in the MC. If he said there weren't too many grumbles, then there weren't too many grumbles.

"Why are they uneasy then?"

He shrugged. "Probably because they have guilty consciences."

I snorted. "Why?"

"In the future, will they be exhumed if some past crime comes back to bite them in the ass?"

"So, the key lesson here is don't be a rapist fuck and your skeleton can rest in peace."

He grinned at that. "I like that. I'm gonna steal it if I hear them bitching."

Rolling my eyes, I trudged outside, muttering my annoyance when I stepped in a pile of dog shit.

This wasn't the first time since I'd gotten back either.

"Since Quin came around, we got more animals than a zoo," I snapped.

He cackled. "Wait until you see the graveyard."

"Why?" I grumbled, swiping my boot against the gravel.

"You'll see. Nyx is in denial."

No longer trying to clean my boot, I started to lope over to the graveyard. It was definitely useful to have our own private burial site; especially when it came time for illegal exhumations.

I saw Nyx in the mini Cat, digging into earth that really should be left untouched but giving a fuck had long since left the building.

My woman and his, a couple of... No. *Wait.* The *whole* Posse was there too. They were joined by a tiny dog who hovered close to Giulia, and a couple yards away, there was a massive one. Big black fucker.

"Newfoundlander," Link chirped. "It and the chihuahua won't leave Nyx alone whenever he's in the yard."

"He's got the same whacked shit that Quin has? The Dr. Doolittle crap?"

"Nah. The juju is only with those two."

"Why?"

"Who the fuck knows."

My brow furrowed. "Isn't it dangerous to have two dogs off the leash when there's heavy machinery around?"

"Nah. You go anywhere near them, they dart off, otherwise they're like statues."

"Why the fuck haven't I seen them around?"

"You've been holed up in your office since you got back. If you'd been outside when Nyx is, you'd have noticed it. I think it's hilarious. The least dog-friendly humans are the ones the dogs are magnetized to."

"Magnetized is coming on strong—"

"*Magnetized*," Link repeated firmly. "If we don't make any sudden moves, they should be okay."

As our feet hit the lawn of the graveyard, leaving the gravel behind, I heard an audible clunk.

Nyx had uncovered one of the coffins.

The dogs in question yipped and barked before they scurried away, running into the land that bridged the compound with the Fridge.

"Rach, what are you doing here?" I questioned as I sidled up to her, a move Lily facilitated by edging over to Link. Sliding my hand into hers, I tugged her into my side.

"Giulia insisted," Rachel groused, her gaze on her phone after she reached up and pressed a kiss to my cheek in greeting.

"It's ceremonial. Therapeutic, too," was all Giulia had to say.

"This is not my idea of therapy," Tiffany chided, folding her arms across her chest as she huffed.

Because I didn't exactly disagree with her, I kept my mouth shut.

"Not everything that's therapeutic is in a textbook," Giulia grumbled. "Anyway, this was inspired by someone else."

"What the hell are you talking about?" I demanded.

"Saw it in the paper. Some fancy-assed graveyard in Brooklyn. A coffin had been exhumed and someone set fire to it." Her lips tightened. "Some people just deserve to burn."

"Everything okay?" I asked Rach softly when she jolted at Giulia's words.

"Yeah. It's fine." She shot me a weak smile. "You don't have to stick around. I'm sure you have plenty to do."

I did, but nothing was more important than her.

Gently squeezing her fingers as I recognized her attempt to distract herself from what was going on around her, I released my hold on her so she could go back to her work.

Sliding my arm around her waist in supportive silence, I watched as Nyx continued digging until Dog's coffin was revealed to us.

Behind me, I heard people congregating. There was the faint pop of Peach's snapping bubble gum, the sound of Zippo lighters flickering to life, low murmurs.

"Need someone to get down there, help me get the bindings under the coffin," Nyx called out over the engine.

Without waiting for a volunteer, I passed Rachel my cut then jumped down into the pit he'd made. Feet on the coffin, I angled to the side in the small space he'd created around it and did as he'd asked.

It was not only awkward, but messy. I'd need to be doused in bleach by the time I was done, that was for fucking sure.

After about five minutes, Link jumped down and helped me out. Two hands made lighter work of the task.

"Steel, grab the ends of the bindings," I hollered as I tossed them up toward the ground.

Rachel's gaze clashed with mine, and for the first time in a long while, I saw the ice in her eyes.

The wall was growing around her in the passage of milliseconds.

Her hands clutched at my cut, though her gaze returned to blindly staring into the grave.

I looked away, needing not to see that right now, and focused instead on helping Nyx get the coffin out of the hole, stabilizing it so that Link and I could jump out beforehand.

More minutes of grunt work passed as the earth did *not* want to give up its hoard, but we were out, still kneeling in the dirt though. Once the casket was free and clear, Nyx swung it around and settled it in an open lot with space around it.

Sweating from how labor-intensive that had been, I swiped the back of my hand against my forehead and turned to Giulia. "He's out. What next? This is your show, after all."

"Back the fuck off," she called out, loud enough for the devil himself to hear.

Grumbles sounded at her call, but I backed her up. "Move out," I shouted, watching as the guys did as I asked.

Rachel made to move, but Giulia snagged her arm. "No. You stay."

"No, I don't—"

"You're staying, Rachel," Giulia intoned, shooting me a warning glance when I started to argue with her. "She's staying, Rex."

I narrowed my eyes on her before I shifted my focus to study Rach's pale face. "Get on with whatever the hell it is you've got planned."

Nyx clambered down from the digger, pulling out a canister as he did so.

With a sigh, I watched as he doused the coffin in gas.

Giulia reached into her pocket and, to Rachel, murmuring, "You deserve to do this," handed her what looked to be a pack of storm-proof matches.

"I don't want to," Rachel said weakly, her hand still tightly clenched around my cut as she hugged it to her chest.

Her voice didn't match her regular Ice Queen routine.

That stuck out to me like a sore thumb.

For a second, I stared down at the now-empty pit, and I realized I'd fallen back on old habits.

She froze me out.

I allowed myself to be frozen.

Annoyed, I moved over to her side.

Today was not last year. Hell, it wasn't even last month. We were moving past this.

"He deserves to burn," I told her softly, not encouraging her, just trying to support her.

She turned to me, her bottom lip sucked in between her teeth as she nibbled it. Her eyes were bloodshot with tears that were on the brink of falling.

"I-I don't need this."

"Just because you don't need it, doesn't mean he doesn't deserve it," Nyx rumbled, stepping over to us. He slung an arm around Giulia, and when she nuzzled into him, I figured he'd gotten over his mad at her jealousy.

Them arguing and then boning each other until the early hours had been serenading me to fucking sleep for the past week.

They needed to find their own goddamn place.

Stat.

I watched Rach's hand shake as she reached out to take the matches from Giulia's grasp. "You don't have to do this."

"She does," was Giulia's stubborn retort. "She needs this. He took something from her, so she's going to take this from him."

I rolled my eyes at her drama. "He's not going to know—"

"He will," Giulia hissed, irritation snapping in her eyes. "He'll know because I don't have to be a believer to know that *this* isn't it. The people we love, who love us, they watch over us. They're here with us. And the only people Dog loved were in this clubhouse. So he's here. He's watching." She grabbed Rachel's arm again. "He stole something from you. Steal it back, Rachel. Let him burn. *Watch* him burn."

Rachel sucked in a breath and, carefully placing my cut under her arm, she opened the packet of matches with shaking hands.

Her gaze was fixed on the coffin; it seemed to absorb all her attention.

When she looked to be on the brink of doing it, I gently pulled her back. "Nyx poured a lot of gas over it, sweetheart. I don't want you anywhere near the flames."

She leaned against me, pressing heavily into me as if she were too weak to stand.

My brow furrowed because I was filthy, and she didn't appear to care even though she was dressed in one of her power suits.

It occurred to me, as we resettled at an adequate distance and she remained close, enough that I felt the tremors running down her form, that I was going to have to relearn my woman's reactions to things.

What I'd thought was her freezing me out, was her freezing the world out.

I was inside her icy walls now.

I got to see her tears.

Her weakness.

Standing straighter, I supported her as she finally struck the match and tossed it onto the coffin.

When the flames devoured the gas, the wall of heat had me dragging her further back as we watched Dog's corpse be eaten away by the fire.

Whatever remained, Cruz would deal with.

Regardless, Dog wouldn't have the honor of being buried among his brethren anymore.

It wasn't enough, could never be enough, but it was something.

Something was better than nothing.

When she turned into me, I cringed at the prospect of her coming into contact with the dirt that liberally coated me, but she burrowed her face in my throat, not seeming to care that I was sweaty and covered in mud, just wanting to hide from the world.

I held her tightly, relieved that I was in Rachel's inner circle now. No longer on the outside looking in.

Giulia reveled in the flames. She didn't lean against Nyx. If anything, she'd moved away from him, but she held his hand, her fingers tightly clenched around his as her father burned.

The spectacle seemed to last a lifetime, but probably only went on for fifteen or so minutes. When it was done, when smoke choked the air, I directed her away from the fumes and led her toward one of the benches in the graveyard.

She slumped against it as I knelt on the sparse patches of grass in front of her.

I didn't ask her if she was okay. *She wasn't.*

I just stayed there, hearing the world continue to spin behind us and acting as a barrier between it and her.

The digger started up again, rocking over the terrain on the path that was purposely built for this machine, on its way to the section where my father would be buried, where Grizzly was interred now.

Twisting around, I settled on my ass beside her, my back to the bench. She placed her hand on my shoulder, not wanting to lose the connection. I let my dirty paws hang over my knees as I watched Nyx, Link, and Sin this time, retrieve my uncle's coffin from the ground.

It seemed to take ages for Nyx to break through the dirt, but eventually, he cracked paydirt.

The only problem was that when Link jumped into the hole, he yelped. Loud enough to be heard over the machine.

"Stay here," I directed Rach, pausing only to catch her nod of acknowledgment.

Running over to the gravesite, assuming my brother was injured, I demanded, "Link, are you hurt?"

Sin shot me a grim look that I had trouble deciphering.

Peering into the hole, I saw Link was standing there, one foot in the mud; the other had landed on the coffin and it had splintered the weathered surface that was brittle and weakened after years of being underground.

Bits of wood littered the area from the force of his landing, but what didn't?

Bones.

THIRTY

RACHEL

I was pretty certain that I was going to faint.

Lightheaded was an understatement as I stared blankly at Rex while he told me his uncle wasn't in the grave.

"How's that possible?" I whispered, wondering why the words sounded as if they were coming from a distance when they'd spilled from my lips.

"We're going to figure it out, sweetheart, I promise." He grimaced at his dirty hand which hovered above mine. I could tell that he wanted to hold it, but he didn't because of the mud on his.

Uncaring about the filth, I clutched at his fingers and whispered, "Does this mean he isn't dead?"

He sighed. "I don't know what this means but I promise we'll figure it out, okay? Lily's going to take you home. You go and wash up, and when I get back, I want to find you in bed, napping, agreed?"

"I'm not tired," I said faintly. "And I don't appreciate being talked to like I'm a child."

His mouth turned down at the corners. "You need to rest."

I shook my head. "I need you."

Something flickered in his eyes.

Relief?

My brow furrowed at the sight, but before I could say a word, he told me, "Give me thirty minutes. I'll be home by then."

"Y-You won't. You'll get drawn into work." I didn't say that to make him feel guilty. Both of us were workaholics. But he still flinched as if I'd wounded him.

Reaching into his pocket, he hit the button on the side of his cell and said, "Set timer for thirty minutes."

I blinked.

"The second it buzzes, I'll be on my way home."

"Promise?"

"I promise." He squeezed my hand. "Go with Lily. For me."

Nodding shakily, I clambered to my feet, leaning heavily on Lily when she appeared at my side. Blindly, we walked out of the small graveyard. The wind whistled in my ears with each step I took, and my vision seemed to narrow, strange black walls settling at the edges. In time to my heart, my eyesight seemed to shrink.

Then, I heard stomping.

"Wait up!" Giulia called out.

The edges of my vision wavered.

"Rach!" Tiffany yelled.

"Rachel," Indy said gruffly as she rushed to my side—the stomping had been her running feet.

I swallowed, turned to her, saw her, felt her hand tighten on my arm at my other side.

More rushing feet, the rustling of feathers in a down coat, a swift breeze sending the sharp notes of a citrusy perfume to me...

The Posse was there.

Surrounding me.

My bottom lip trembled, and how the fuck I kept it together, I had no idea, but I did.

The silence of before abated as they started muttering among themselves. Amara and Alessa bickering in Ukrainian, Indy and Stone whispering about how to stop me from passing out—I must have looked as bad as I felt—Giulia, Tiffany, and Lily conferring on what to feed me.

A real group effort.

How ironic... that the first time I didn't feel like an outsider was here.

Now.

THIRTY-ONE

REX

"He was dead," Sin snapped. "I know what a dead body looks like."

I raised a hand. "Sin, calm the fuck down. He was dead. Okay. So where's his goddamn corpse?"

"I don't know. Fuck. I don't know." He shot me a raw look. "He needs to be dead. He has to be."

"Brother, you're not the only one who needs him not to be alive."

"Could Bear have moved him?" Link asked, his voice grim. That was as much a testament to the severity of the situation as anything else. Link was rarely anything other than playful.

"Without telling us?" I shook my head. "I can't see it."

"It'd make more sense than anything else."

"He'd have told us," I repeated staunchly.

Dad had kept a lot from me, but I didn't think he'd have kept this a fucking secret too.

"Does it matter?" Steel asked softly. "Whatever happened to his body, whether he's living it up in Boca Raton or is gracing some other grave, he's left us alone."

"Of course it matters," Sin yelled. "I want him dead. I want to know he's dead."

"I do too," I grated out. "How the fuck is Rachel supposed to have any peace if one of her attackers is still alive and free?"

"You say that like that doesn't happen all the time," was Steel's calm rejoinder. "Not everyone gets to enjoy the perks of having Sinners as family."

"She does though. She's my Old Lady, Steel. If anyone should know that her fucking rapist is worm food, it's Rachel."

Steel raised his hands, palms up, in surrender. "I don't see that there's any point in getting stressed. We've got plenty of other shit to be dealing with. The funeral, the fucking wake, Nyx and Harlow's first hunt, Giulia's about to pop—"

I rubbed my forehead, uncaring that I was probably smearing more dirt on it. "Where's Maverick?"

"Hospital," Nyx rumbled, speaking for the first time since this whole debacle with Grizzly had commenced.

"Alessa was here though."

He shrugged. "She'll go in later."

"I think she wanted to be here for Rachel and Giulia. That's why Lily came," Link added.

"Same with Tiff," Sin remarked gruffly, his hands fisted at his sides.

Whether she liked it or not, it seemed Rach had been inducted into the Posse.

At any other time, I'd have smiled, despite the headache that was roaring my way. But right this second, I didn't have it in me to fucking smile, not when the reality of our situation was grim.

"Unless Maverick can pull a rabbit out of a hat, we're not going to discover what happened to Grizzly," I rumbled, staring down into the empty pit as I faced the stark truth. "I don't want to say that, but it's true. We wouldn't even know about this if Giulia hadn't gotten it into her head to have the bastards exhumed."

"Ignorance is bliss," Link mumbled, shoving his dirty hands into his pockets.

"In this instance, yeah." The timer on my cell bleated. "Jesus, that went fast. I need to get back to Rach." I turned off the timer by handing it to Nyx who was the only one of us with clean hands. "Have Cruz get rid of any evidence of Dog's body, and, I guess, fill in both holes. While you're in the mini Cat, you can dig out Dad's space beside Mom."

Nyx nodded. "I was going to do that anyway."

"Thanks, man." I blew out a breath as he handed my phone back to me. "I doubt I'll return to the clubhouse today, but you can call me if you need me."

"We'll keep things at bay," Nyx rasped. "You can lean on us, Rex. We managed without you since Christmas."

My jaw clenched at the implied criticism, but before I could answer, Sin stated, "He meant no shade, Rex. Just that you've got Rach now. Things are different."

I tipped up my chin in understanding but made no comment other than to say, "I'll speak to you later."

As I headed toward the clubhouse and onward to the gates, I knew they stayed clustered together, discussing the situation, their eyes on me until I moved out of sight.

Mind whirring, I ran up the hill to our place.

Ours.

It still felt so damn good to call it that.

As I ran through the gates, I saw Rain and Harlow were sitting on the veranda. They didn't have their ears to the front door, but I could tell they were on red alert.

Frowning, I wondered if they were getting close.

I had plans for Rain after his service ended, and hanging around with a serial killer in the making wasn't a part of those goddamn aspirations. I still had hope that Axel's G.I. Joe brainwashing would die out before graduation and he'd want to become a cop.

If he did, his association with the club was a major strike against him to start with; I didn't need him contending with any extra weight around his neck.

I knew how that felt.

I loved Nyx. He was my brother. But handling his craziness was a full-time occupation, and honestly, it was only possible because I was Prez. Because I ruled over my particular roost and had the resources to manage Nyx.

Rain wasn't Prez material.

The thought made me feel disloyal, but that was how it rolled when you were a leader—the truth, even if it was painful, had to be in sharp focus at all times.

He was too intrinsically good for that. He could lead, but whenever I thought about his future, I saw him getting promoted, becoming captain of a precinct in the city somewhere. Not the leader of a bunch of outlaws.

"Why do you look like you've been playing in the dirt?"

I arched a brow at Rain. "Do you really want to know?"

His eyes rounded. "Club business?"

"Club business." I shot Harlow a glance. "It stays between brothers."

"Whatever," Harlow muttered with a dismissive shrug, which was clue enough that the second he found out what had happened at the compound, he'd tell Rain.

Fucking motormouths.

"Why aren't you at the clubhouse?"

"Nyx sent me away."

"Why?"

Rocking back in his seat on the outdoor sofa, Harlow blinked. "I don't know why Nyx does what he does."

Who the fuck did?

"You didn't do anything wrong?" I persisted, trying to figure out why his ass was here and not at the clubhouse.

"Not as far as I know."

Did Nyx just want him away while we illegally exhumed two graves?

There was no logic in that, though. Nyx and he were going on a two-man mission to slay pedos in the tristate area, but he couldn't know about something as basic as an illegal exhumation?

Grunting a dismissal, deciding that that truly was a problem for another day, I headed into the house without another word.

Hearing movement upstairs, I started up the steps but the door opened behind me and Rain stomped toward me.

I didn't even have a chance to swivel around before he was grumbling, "He won't say anything, but that guy Lever's being a dick."

One hand on the railing, I turned back to study him. "Most of the Sinners are dicks."

Rain scowled. "I know that, Rex." The 'duh' went unspoken. "I'm a Sinners' brat myself. I know how you roll. This is different. This isn't just hazing."

I folded my arms across my chest. "Explain."

His eyes drifted to my arms and the filth covering them. "I should have let you shower, but Harlow was worried you'd ask Nyx about why he was here—"

"He lied about that?"

Nodding, Rain said, "He's embarrassed."

My brow furrowed. "You got feelings for him?"

"What?" Rain scoffed. "No. I'm not into him, Rex. Jesus. You into Nyx?"

Lips twitching, I shook my head.

His gaze turned inward. "He's... I feel responsible for him."

Shit.

"Why?"

"Why do you feel responsible for Nyx?"

"I grew up with Nyx, Rain. There's a difference. When I first learned to walk, Nyx was the one whose building blocks I smashed. When I first learned how to ride a bike, he and I as well as Link, Steel, Mav, and Storm were the ones who were racing into town to try to steal porn magazines from the convenience store—" I waved my hand. "Most of my firsts happened with those dickheads around." I meant that in more ways than one. "You, on the other hand, barely know the kid."

"It doesn't feel that way."

"I repeat—you into him?"

"No, dammit." He huffed. "I'm just... It feels like we were supposed to be friends. It feels like I was supposed to have his back."

"You enlisting at the end of the school year?"

He swallowed. "Yes."

Dammit.

Still, becoming a soldier would look good on his resume if, after he came home, he wanted to be a cop.

Then, I thought about that slightest hesitation of his, and it had me asking, "You don't sound so sure."

"I'm not..." He heaved a sigh. "This isn't about me."

"It isn't?"

"No. It's about Harlow. I'm telling you, Rex, Lever is being a prick. He somehow got a hold of Harlow's goddamn Bible; the fucker won't give it back. Harlow used to wear a rosary. Not anymore. Lever grabbed Harlow by it and it broke. Right before he beat the shit out of him—"

My jaw worked—I hated petty fucking crap like this. I'd never understood why grown-assed men resorted to such childish games.

"I'll deal with it."

"You will?"

I saw and heard the hope in his expression and his tone, and I nodded. "I will."

"Thanks, Rex. Don't tell him I said anything? He's a proud man."

"Ironic considering he was gonna be a priest."

Rain's nose crinkled. "I don't think he'd have been a good one."

I didn't know why that had me barking out a laugh, but it did. After this shitty fucking day, I needed something to laugh about, and Rain had just given me a reason.

Going to slap him on the back, I stopped an inch away from making contact.

Rain grinned. "I appreciate you not getting me dirty." His gaze went to the ceiling. "Rach okay?"

"No. But she will be."

"You two together now? For real?"

I nodded, sent him a measured glance because I *should* have talked to him about this sooner—man to man. "You okay with that?"

"Would have preferred you to get together about ten years ago, but hey, it's reassuring that you're shit with women. You can't be good at everything."

Snorting, I said, "You're pushing your luck."

His grin turned cheeky. "Gotta be some perks to being your brother-in-law." To be on the safe side, clearly wary, he retreated a couple steps. Which amused the fuck out of me. "Genuinely though, I know you'll..." His smile abruptly died. "If anything happens to me, I know she'll never be alone."

Any amusement I'd felt, much like his, disappeared. "You ain't going nowhere, kid."

"People die all the time. It used to worry me. Her being so alone, you know? She only really talks to Parker and Susanne, but Susanne drives her batshit, and Parker's in Pennsylvania and she's kind of a hermit so—" He shrugged. "I dunno. I just, I knew that when I left, she'd be alone. I'm glad you got your ass in gear in time."

"Always did have good timing," was all I said, even though I got where the kid was coming from. More than he probably realized.

Rachel didn't know it, but as much as she'd been looking out for him since Axel's death, Rain felt like he'd been doing the same for her.

That was what family did.

"You don't have to worry about her anymore. I got a handle on things."

Rain stared at me. "That's not how it works when you have a sister, but I appreciate that you'll protect her." His gaze went to the ceiling again. "Someone hurt her, really bad along the way. She never said anything, but I know my sister. You're lucky I also know that you love her too much or I wouldn't have let you live."

I didn't disrespect him by so much as smirking at his threat.

As he nodded at me, his warning delivered now, he began to head for the kitchen.

"How would you have done it?" I asked out of curiosity once he'd taken one step through the doorway.

He peered at me over his shoulder. "I'd have fucked with your bike."

At that, my lips curved. "Axel taught you how?"

"What do you think?" he replied with an arched brow before he disappeared into the kitchen.

Letting him go, I filed the situation with Lever and Harlow away and strode up the stairs.

"About damn time," Giulia sniped, her hand on her belly as she waited for me in the doorway to Rachel's room.

"Rain ambushed me," I excused, glancing around and spying that the whole Posse had taken up residence in here. I frowned when I didn't see Rach. "She's supposed to be resting."

"She needed to shower." Lily moved over to me, and her hand went to my arm. "She's not doing so good, Rex."

Understatement.

"Leave her with me. You can all go."

Giulia grunted. "*Men.* She needs her friends around her—"

"That what you are, Giulia? Friends?"

She squinted at me. "You asking for some Ex-Lax in your dinner tonight, Rex?"

"No, just wondering what's going on here."

She stacked her hands on her hips. "The second she let us stay at her place after the blast, even though she values her privacy, despite the fact she hated having us around, was the second she stepped up and acted like a leader.

"An MC needs more than a Prez. Needs more than a council. It needs their women too—"

"Are you really gonna stand there and tell me what my MC needs, Giulia? When I've been a Sinner since I was fucking born and you're goddamn younger than me?"

"Well, I'm talking slow because clearly, you don't understand what's going on here. We're her people. That's why we're here.

"Even if we didn't like her, she's your woman—even if you haven't fucking branded her yet—" Her sniff was dismissive. "—and she's the First Lady. *But* we do like her. She's good people. And she's hurting. And this was supposed to fix that hurting. It was supposed to make her feel better, empowered—" Giulia burst into tears at that.

I wasn't sure who was more surprised—her or me.

Lily clucked her tongue and immediately moved over to her, tucking her under her arm and hugging her. Over her head, Lily murmured, "It's a very emotional time right now, Rex."

"I know, Lily. Trust me, I know."

Giulia wailed, "I wanted her to feel good and now she feels worse—"

I scowled at the bizarre tableau that was going down in my bedroom, and I rumbled, "Giulia, I agreed with you. We had no way of knowing this would veer so far off course we're in downtown Montreal." I heaved a sigh. "Look, I get it. She's your..." I hitched a shoulder. "First Lady. Your friend. She's my woman though. I'll fix this. Just leave her to me—"

"How can we though?" Giulia questioned around her tears. "You're useless—"

My scowl made a reappearance. "Giulia, I'm making allowances for the fact that you're very pregnant, but don't push me. I'm not useless. I'm Rachel's Old Man. I will fix this."

Amara grunted. "She has point. You waited long very to make her yours and even now, no ink. Where is ink?"

Tiffany cleared her throat. "What she means is that you haven't claimed Rachel yet, and that it took you a long time to even reach this phase in your relationship."

"Look, this isn't an episode of *Jerry Springer*. I don't need to excuse myself to any of you. Rachel and I took a long time to come back to each other, and I don't need you fucking critiquing our relationship.

"I haven't branded her because, one, she's pregnant. No ink when you're pregnant. Two, she wasn't ready for that—" I clenched my fists. "—I recognize that you care. In fact, I'm grateful you do. Rachel's always found it hard to make friends and to hang around with people, so I appreciate that you're looking out for her more than you know, but leave this with me."

It wasn't a request.

Giulia sniffled and wiped at her eyes. "If you fuck up, you'll have more than a laxative in your dinner, Rex."

I narrowed my eyes at her. "I'll know the first place to send the cops if I'm poisoned over my pasta, Giulia."

She sniffed. "Come on, Posse. Let's leave the man to work some miracles."

Shooting each other looks, a mixture of begrudging and unhappy ones, Stone and Indy were the last to leave the room.

Indy's shoulders hunched. "She might think she's too civilized to appreciate the fact that Grizzly and Dog were supposed to be dead, but there's comfort in knowing that your personal boogeyman can't come after you."

"I know, Indy. I know."

Stone studied me. "You need to get her to eat something."

"I will."

"Has she mentioned when her next OB/GYN appointment is?"

Shit. She hadn't.

"I'll take that expression to mean she hasn't."

"The last one got rescheduled," I excused, "but I don't remember the new date."

Carefully, she said, "I get the feeling she's scared of medicine."

"She's wary of doctors. I'll be with her for the next appointment."

Stone nodded. "Good. If this high stress continues as it's been doing since before you got back, you might need to take her there at some point."

My brow furrowed. "You're worried for the baby?"

"And the mother." Stone reached up and patted my arm. "Just watching out for her, Rex. No need to worry just yet."

Just yet.

Those words were like a death knell that I really didn't need to hear.

I blew out a breath in an attempt to remain calm, but Storm's words came back to bite me in the ass.

"The U.S. maternal mortality rate is the worst of any developed nation."

For the first time, I understood his terror.

As wonderful as this new life was, it wasn't worth losing Rachel.

"Hey, I didn't mean to frighten you," Stone said softly. "Just wanted to impress upon you the importance of monitoring her, making sure she takes the prenatal pills she'll have been prescribed, that she's eating plenty and getting enough rest."

I rasped, "I'll..." God, I'd barely been here the last couple days. "I'll do better."

Stone blinked, then her smile, when it appeared, was a genuinely warm, loving curve. She squeezed my arm again. "Just tell me if there's anything I can do."

When they left the room too, I closed the door behind them, locked it, then knocked on the bathroom door.

It opened.

I knew she hadn't been showering because I hadn't heard the pipes creak. But seeing her standing there, half-naked, like she'd been too weak to finish undressing, rattled the fuck out of me.

I took in her slender form, the bulge of her belly that was starting to thicken in earnest, the soft curve of her tits with the nipples that were starting to darken in color, all before she hurled herself at me.

Wrapping her in my arms, I held her as she sobbed, and I didn't say a word. I was just there. She needed to let this out. She needed to remember that she wasn't that same seventeen-year-old girl anymore.

This was not the past.

I didn't even allow myself to worry that all the great strides we'd made would be for nothing, that this would knock us off track.

She was letting me in. This was the new us.

So I hugged her as she cried, and afterward, I finished undressing her. She stood there, pale and wan, her gaze on her feet as I stripped off too.

Guiding her into the shower, I let the cold water blast onto me, using it to wash down my hands and arms first. I grabbed some soap, cleaned them up some more, which timed perfectly with the water getting warm.

I turned to her, saw she was watching me with rounded eyes. I didn't know why she was looking at me like that, and I didn't wait around to ask. Just gently tugged on her elbow and guided her under the spray.

Methodically, I reached for the loofah she used, splatted some of her soap on it, and carefully got to work. I smoothed it along her arms, over her shoulders, down her chest. Kneeling on the shower floor, I washed her legs then scrubbed her feet.

When she was clean, I stood up once more and went to work on washing her hair.

We did this in silence.

She just let me shuffle her around, and I took comfort in that level of trust.

I didn't feel frozen out; more like I was still inside that wall of ice, and she was just too out of it to communicate with me.

As I gently sluiced the shampoo through her hair, then conditioned it, I massaged her scalp.

When her eyes were closed, her head tipped back under the water flow, I tilted her face forward and pressed my lips to hers.

It was soft. Gentle. No urgency about it. Just a reconnection.

She didn't startle in shock, jolt like I'd hit her with a cattle prod. She sighed into the kiss, her hands coming to my chest—not to push me away—just to touch me.

I pulled back and made to turn off the water, but her eyes popped open and she snagged my hand to stop me.

Grabbing the sponge I'd used on her, she poured some of my soap onto it. It didn't take a mind reader to figure out her intentions, but that didn't mean they came as any less of a surprise.

Much as I'd done, she traced the loofah over my body, taking care to wash my arms and hands so they were cleaned to her satisfaction. She even angled my fingers into the light to check for dirt in my nails.

When she was done, she reached behind me and turned off the water.

"Luciu Valentini set fire to a coffin in Greenwood Cemetery."

My mouth opened, closed, then, and I had no idea why I said it, but I muttered, "Must be the season for exhumations."

Her lips twitched.

"Wait. Is that why you jumped in the graveyard when Giulia was talking about—?"

"Yes," she said simply.

Putting two and two together, I asked, "Are those the charges you had to get him off of when I was in LA? The one that the DA was being stubborn on?"

She swallowed. "Yes. I-I shouldn't have told you."

I shrugged. "Why did you?"

"I don't know. It was on the tip of my tongue."

"Anything you tell me is between us, and it's not like this breaks client privilege. Charges are public and you're on record for bailing him out. If I wanted to, I could have gone looking."

"It's just not something I should be talking about in the shower, after we just..."

"You can tell me *whatever whenever*, baby girl."

Her shiver had nothing to do with being cold.

Blinking up at me, her eyelashes all spiky from the water, she asked, "Do you think he's still alive?"

I didn't want to give her a trite answer so I opened the shower door and reached for a towel from the rail. Gently toweling her off, I murmured, "I think it's unlikely."

"Why?"

"I think bones weren't as easy to dispose of back in my dad's day. He didn't have a Cruz, and his men weren't the kinds of people who knew how to use chemicals to dispose of bodies. We had the pig farm, I guess, but..." I inhaled, annoyed at my rambling. "Dad wouldn't have fed Grizzly to the pigs."

"Did he never punish Sin for beating on him?"

Uneasily, I mumbled, "Do you know what happened?"

"I thought Sin beat him to death. He caught him in bed with his wife when he got back from a deployment, didn't he?"

I grunted. "Dad... had his own methods of punishing Sin."

"How?"

"Sin's my cousin, Dad's nephew. That comes with perks, favoritism. Dad never gave that to Sin. He had to get promoted the hard way."

"That's it?"

"By the time Grizzly died, I think Dad knew he was a liability."

Her hand snatched out to grab mine, and her nails dug into me. "If he *is* dead, why isn't his body in the graveyard?"

"I have no answer for that, sweetheart, and I wish I did. I just... Grizzly would have come back around by now if he were alive. You know the club was..." I didn't really know how to verbalize it.

But she did.

"It was his world."

I nodded. "Guys like that don't just walk away from everything. Even if it's the wise thing to do."

A shaky breath escaped her. "That's logical."

"We may never find out what happened to him, Rachel," I warned her.

"No. But you're right." She shot me an ashen smile. "I'd like to go to bed now."

I finished drying her, handed her one of the towels she put her hair in after washing it, and after I was dry too, I guided her into the bedroom.

As I tucked her between the sheets, she closed her eyes and whispered, "Don't leave me."

Hope and relief hit me like a bullet to the brain.

"I'm going nowhere."

THIRTY-TWO

MAVERICK

"You're shitting me."

Alessa sighed. "You say this often and I still don't know what it means. How can I shit you? It makes no sense."

Scraping a hand over my head, I shot her a sheepish glance. "I'll stop saying it."

"Good. It's impossible to shit a person. Amara is right. Our curse words are far more imaginative."

Grinning, I told her, "You'll have to teach me some."

"You say this because Hawk offered to learn." Her eyes narrowed. "You're playing a competition with him?"

"No. We just want our Old Ladies to be happy."

And to understand them when they grumbled under their breaths in Ukrainian if we did something to piss them off.

At least, that was *my* intention.

Alessa, though inordinately patient, got angry with me a lot.

Mostly because I never did what the doctors asked of me.

She dragged off her scarf and dumped it on the back of her chair before she plunked herself down. "The coffin was empty. I'm not shitting you."

"Can I have my phone?"

When the doctors had asked me to limit my screen time today, I knew she'd worked in cahoots with them. If I'd have known, I'd have brought a spare phone, well aware she'd take mine with her. As it stood, I was going to die of boredom. The treatments were tedious, and watching daytime TV was beyond excruciating—technically, I wasn't even supposed to watch *that* either.

My head wasn't aching as bad though. I knew the screens exacerbated migraines, but doing without them was impossible.

Not only did my brothers need me; coding—hacking—they were what I did.

Or what I used to do, anyway.

Lodestar had picked up a lot of the shit I did for the club, and while it had given me time to create my app that'd protect kids when they were online, I was starting to feel a lot less useful.

My identity was in crisis because my purpose had revolved around computers for so long, and what I could uncover for the club...

"Maverick?"

I jolted when I saw Alessa had her hand outstretched, my cellphone held in her palm.

Grabbing it, I immediately felt better and began scrolling through my notifications.

When I saw the message from Nyx asking me to look into Grizzly's disappearance, I couldn't deny my relief.

I'd suspected they'd go to Star for that, and though I wouldn't have blamed them, it would have felt shitty not to be asked.

"There's a problem?"

"No." I shot her a smile. "No problem."

"They asked you to find where this Grizzly is?"

I nodded.

She sighed. "I wish I could ask you not to work on this, but Rachel was so—" Alessa murmured something in Ukrainian. "So, so *sad.* I did not like to see her hurting. If you could find her answers, I know she would feel better about this."

"I'll do my best, sweetheart," I told her, snatching her hand and pressing my lips to her knuckles. "Did the doctors say when I'm getting out of here tomorrow?"

"Before noon."

I grunted.

Accessing the information I needed wouldn't be as easy on my phone, but I'd figure out a way to make the magic happen.

Rachel wasn't the only one who needed answers.

"I'll spend the night, yes?"

A grin creased my jaw. "You gonna monitor me, babe? Gonna get all bossy on me?"

Her eyes twinkled. "This I can do."

I hummed. "What'll you do if I get out of bed?"

"You will have to discover this if you do it," she said snootily. "But Giulia told me about this—"

"What are you talking to her about sex for?" I complained.

"She was talking. I listen. She's interesting."

Giulia was many things. Interesting? Not so much.

Alessa clucked her tongue. "She *is* interesting. She was telling me about this thing she called edging—"

I almost choked on my tongue. "Edging? You know what that is?"

She sniffed. "She told me, so *tak.*"

"Okay, what is it?"

"It's when you... when I..." Her mouth pursed. "What's the word for when a dick grows hard? I do not remember."

"Erection?" I chuckled.

"*Tak.* Edging is when you have erection and I don't let it come."

"My dick doesn't come. *I* come."

"There's a difference?"

"I mean, technically, yeah. My dick's attached to me." I scratched my head. "Why am I not surprised Giulia's been researching that?"

She shrugged. "Giulia knows many things."

Most of them psychotic, I felt sure.

"So, that's your punishment if I get out of bed? You'll edge me?" I smirked. "For how long."

"Full day."

I whistled. "Twenty-four hours for getting out of bed once? You're hardcore, babe."

Her smile was winsome. "Very."

Snickering, I shook my head. "What if I need to piss?"

"That is different." Her eyes narrowed upon me. "Unless you use it as an excuse. I will time you."

Rolling my eyes, I muttered, "Maybe you should just handcuff me to the bed and be done with it."

"Giulia also told me about this. Some men like this, *tak?*"

"Some men do," I concurred carefully, watching her expression.

Sex wasn't as much of a minefield as it used to be, but doing was different than talking ironically enough.

When I touched her, I knew she could differentiate between my hands and some creep fucker who'd used her in the past.

Words weren't like that.

They didn't allow for that kind of nuance. At least, not when her English often failed her during highly emotional conversations. It might've been easier if she were a native English-speaker, but she wasn't, and we had to work with what we had.

If that meant I was careful when I navigated chats like these, so be it.

Alessa's eyes shifted from mine to the bed and back again. "It's something you like?"

"The cuffs? I guess. If you liked it." I shot her a dopey grin. "I pretty much like anything we do together, babe."

That brought some of the warmth back to her expression. "I like very much as well."

"Good."

"Good." She bit her lip. "Men did this to me."

"Tied you down?"

The thought alone made me want to kill someone, but I knew she'd been through far worse than just that.

Not that that eased my anger any.

"*Tak*. I did not like it. I don't know why you would like it. It's not nice. To move is freedom. I would not tie you to the bed even if it meant I could get you to rest."

She said that so earnestly, my heart about fucking melted in my chest.

If anything, that was the danger here. Not my brain, but a heart that literally turned to a mass of melted sinew and muscle whenever she was around.

"Thank you, sweetheart." I reached for her hand and squeezed her fingers. "But whatever we do together, it comes from a place of love, doesn't it?"

She blinked. "*Tak*."

"So it's different. They bound you to the bed to control you, to take away your freedom. We wouldn't do it for that reason, would we?"

"I do not know."

"If we did it, it'd be to give each other pleasure. Not pain. Wouldn't it?"

It took her a while to process that, and I left her to it, checking my phone, wanting the words to really resonate without me pressuring her—even if that was only by looking at her.

Me: *Bear never mentioned to anyone that Grizzly might have been buried elsewhere?*

Link: *We asked around the MC, and no brother says Bear ever mentioned anything about that.*

Nyx: *Not surprising. Most of the Old Guard weren't in today. It was all younger brothers.*

Sin: *I'll head into town and go and speak with them. They hang out at Daytona a lot now. I can kill a couple birds with one stone.*

Me: *Bighead. Know you're good but are you that good?*

Sin: *Haha. You know what I mean, dipshit.*

Me: *:P*

Steel: *I just don't understand any of this.*

Sin: *How many fucking times? I'm telling you he was dead.*

Me: *He could've had a pulse.*

Sin: *I'm telling you he didn't.*

Me: *Okay.*

Sin: *Okay?*

Me: *Okay.*

Nyx: *Jesus, we get the picture. It's OKAY. FML. Whether he's alive or dead, his body ain't where we thought it was.*

Me: *How your mind works is disturbing, Nyx.*

Sin: *You only just got freaked out by him?*

Me: *Fair point. If he's alive, Nyx, his body is attached to him. I shouldn't have to explain that to you like you're Amara.*

Nyx: *Fuck off.*

Link: *Whatever's happening here, it can't be anything good.*

Me: *I disagree.*

Sin: *Why?*

Steel: *You just being difficult?*

Me: *No. Not at all. Bear and Rex had similar natures.*

Nyx: *Don't bring that up right now. Rex is still smarting about Kendra being his half-sister.*

Me: *Yeah, but I'm not bringing this up with him, am I? I'm talking to you, on a chat he isn't included in.*

Nyx: *True. What's your point?*

Me: *Even if Bear didn't know about all the shit Grizzly'd done in his time, and I'm talking about what happened with Rachel here, the way Sin ended him would have resonated with Bear.*

Sin: *What do you mean?*

Me: *On a scale of 1-10, how rational is Rex?*

Nyx: *10*

Link: *11*

Steel: *10*

Sin: *9.5*

Me: *Exactly. What's rational about his agreeing to exhume Dog and Grizzly just so that they're no longer in the graveyard?*

Nyx: *Not very rational.*

Me: *It's the height of irrationality, in fact. If that's Rex's reaction, why wouldn't it be Bear's?*

Link: *You mean you think Bear disposed of Grizzly before the burial because he didn't want him in the graveyard?*

Me: *Yeah. That's what I'm thinking. I'm going to look into it, see if his social security number has been triggered in recent years. Of course, that's if he kept his identity, which, let's face it, if he moved to fucking Dallas, it wouldn't matter worth a damn if he kept his ID as is.*

Me: *So, whatever whatever, I'll dig into this. But I don't think we have to worry.*

"You are right. We give each other pleasure. No pain."

Alessa's words had me jolting in surprise.

I quickly tapped out:

Me: *GTG.*

Then turned my phone over so I couldn't see the screen, just in time too.

Her brow had furrowed and she was moving to her feet, settling on the bed at my side. Realizing what she was about to do, I shuffled to the edge so she could join me.

With her curled on her side, she tucked herself around me, and as was usually the way with us when it came to moments like these, we sat in silence.

Sometimes, that was the easiest means of communicating.

Not because words and feelings were hard, but because reconnecting didn't need either.

It needed touch.

It needed love.

At moments like these, I didn't even need a cell phone or a computer to entertain me.

I just lay there with her, breathing her in, absorbing her as much as I could. Not just because my brain could trip a fuse and I'd be hurled back to Afghanistan, but because I loved her. Because I needed her imprinted on me.

I needed her to know she meant more to me than code.

Because she did.

This whole new identity of mine had one stabilizing force—Alessa.

She was my light through the darkness.

Which meant us lying together, breathing the same air, reconnecting, did more for me than any of the treatment the doctors put me through.

She wasn't a miracle in the flesh—she was just my reason for breathing.

THIRTY-THREE

RACHEL

I awoke to the sight of Rex sleeping at my side.

I awoke, bizarrely enough, without a scream lodged in my throat and without my heart pounding so hard that it felt like it could explode.

I awoke, not exactly feeling refreshed, but definitely feeling... okay.

Rex was hot.

Not just to look at.

In a bed, tangled in the sheets, he exuded a kind of heat that I knew in the winter meant I wouldn't need a heating blanket anymore.

That warmth sapped reality away from me. Drained me. Until my eyes closed again.

I was safe.

I was loved.

I was alive and living that life at long last.

Secure in that knowledge, I slept.

THIRTY-FOUR

RAIN

Rachel grimaced as she closed the door behind her which had me lowering the volume on the TV. "I need to speak to you."

I arched a brow at her. "It's too late for the birds and the bees. We covered that a while back."

"You'd better not have gotten a girl pregnant," she grumbled which made me smirk.

"Nah. Not yet."

She huffed.

"What's wrong?" I asked, studying her as I straightened up.

I was used to Rachel looking exhausted, but this was worse than usual. Especially when she bridged her fingers together and started wringing them.

"I need to tell you something."

Patting the cushion at my side, I said, "Come on. Take a seat. Whatever it is, it can't be that bad."

"It's not bad, exactly. It's something that I should have shared with you a long time ago but didn't have the guts to."

"You're entitled to your privacy," I told her softly, trying to ease her guilt. Rachel didn't wear that look well. She was too bullheaded for guilt.

"I am, but this is, I guess, I didn't think the day would come where it would be an issue. For most of her life, just thinking about her was painful, never mind talking about her."

"Talking about who?" I questioned, perplexed.

"When I was..." She swallowed, hesitated, restarted, "When I was seventeen, I was raped. It made things very difficult for me. For a long time, you were what got me through the day, and it made me delay some plans I had for college. Rex made sure I went—"

"That's what happened to you? That's why you were late starting college?"

I'd always known something had broken my sister.

I could feel the blood in my face draining, but I had to be strong. This was her pain, her truth, and she was finally sharing it with me.

God, I knew why as well.

I was a man now.

Not just an adult, but a man.

Fuck.

At school, I might have been dismissed as nothing more than a hormonal teenager, but Rachel was trusting me with her *truth*. At last.

"Yeah," she admitted, her face bowed as she stared at her fingers. "I started late, and because Rex, when, I mean, because he helped me, I was grateful and we hooked up."

"Okaaaay."

"I got pregnant, Rain."

My mouth rounded. "What?!"

"I went to college and I dealt with everything, and then there was an issue with my dorm and I moved into an apartment with some roommates—"

"Hunter and Rory?"

She smiled—it was the first sign of ease she'd shown since she'd come into the den. "Yeah. Hunter and Rory. But Rory was married back then, and her husband... he liked me." Rach said it in a way that made it clear she hadn't returned the favor. "He attacked me and afterward, I broke down—"

I stared at her blankly as I tried to process what she'd just said. When it hit home, I blurted out, "He raped you? When you were pregnant?"

"I know it's tough to believe—"

"No!" I snapped. "It's not that." I grabbed her hands. "I'm so fucking sorry, Rach. Men are such bastards—"

"Not all of them," she said with a wry twist of her lips. "I know a lot of good men too."

I shook my head. "I can't believe this." When I saw her expression fall, I squeezed her fingers. "No! I mean I can believe it but I don't want to have to."

Warily, Rach nodded. "I understand. I'm telling you this because—"

I didn't let her finish. "What happened with the baby?"

"After I was... you know, raped, I found it really hard to cope. I-I stopped eating and I lost a lot of weight. I was hospitalized for a while." I could feel my eyes growing larger and larger in my face. "I ended up, *we* ended up putting the baby up for adoption."

"You have a kid? I-I thought you meant you got an abortion."

"No. She's Rex's, Rain. I could never do that." She sucked in a breath. "I barely thought about her these past seventeen years, but recently, we, she and Rex and I, we reconnected."

"I have a niece?" I muttered blankly.

"You do. But she's a year younger than you," she said dryly. "So it's not like you have much authority over her."

"I have a niece," I repeated. "What's her name?"

"Wynter." Her smile twisted. "She's not had it easy recently. I tried to get her to come to the funeral, but..."

"Is that why you're telling me now? Because you want us to meet?"

"Of course I want you to meet! And no. I don't think she'll come.

She has time to change her mind but I don't think she will." She rubbed her brow. "I just... I wanted you to know. I hope you can forgive me for keeping this from you."

I was mad.

I wasn't going to lie.

But I'd been a baby, and she'd been traumatized, and, fuck, I had no right to be mad. To be sad, sure. For her. For my niece. For Rex even.

Life had fucked with them so much.

Gently, I squeezed her fingers and I told her, "Rach, whatever happiness you get, you've earned."

Her lips trembled. "Not sure life works like that."

"I know it doesn't, but I wish it did." I reached forward and hugged her. "Thank you for trusting me with your story, and thank you for telling me about Wynter. I can't wait to meet her."

She squeezed me back. "I hope... One day, I hope you get to catch up."

That one day had better be soon. There was no way in hell I was going to enlist without having met my niece.

My goddamn niece.

I was an uncle.

I grinned at her. "I'm gonna teach her everything I know."

For the first time, Rach released a heavy sigh and she shined a megawatt grin at me. "Wynter's seventeen, Rain. She knows about as much as you."

"Nah. I got a year's extra knowledge, that counts. Plus I'm an Eagle Scout." My chest puffed up. "There's plenty still to teach her."

She kissed my cheek. "Thank you, Rain. Thank you."

"Sis, you don't have anything to thank me for." I grabbed her wrist and tugged on her arm. "The men who hurt you, did Rex...?"

"They're dead," she said flatly. "You don't have to worry about that." She placed another kiss on my cheek and said, "I love you, Rain."

"Love you, sis," I rasped as she walked away, I figured, to go and cry in private.

I'd never seen Rach cry so much in my life, but the baby was messing with her something fierce.

"I'm sorry, man."

Jerking in surprise, I twisted around to find Harlow climbing into the den through the window via the veranda. "You heard?"

"Most of it. Was having a smoke out there."

"Those will kill you."

"Good," he said grimly before he sat down beside me. He was quiet a second before he rumbled, "We got more in common than we originally thought."

I swallowed.

He was right, and how I wished he were fucking wrong.

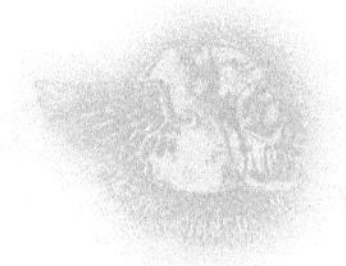

THIRTY-FIVE

RACHEL

THREE DAYS LATER

The pounding at the door had me grumbling under my breath.

Before the blast, no one came to my house apart from Susanne, and those were on allotted days and times so I knew when my space was being disturbed.

Now, it was a free for all.

I grabbed the door, pulled it wide, about to growl at whoever was darkening my stoop, but when I caught sight of Parker staring back at me, I blinked in astonishment.

"Parker?"

"Why do you look as if Justin Bieber has come to visit you?" she sniped, shoving herself through the door and pushing me inside. The second she did, she blew out a breath of relief.

"Justin Bieber's your guilty pleasure, not mine." I arched a brow at her. "How many drugs did you have to take to get out of the house?"

She waved a hand. "The CBD is doing something for me."

"Something or just giving you an excuse to eat gummies?"

A laugh escaped her as she hurled herself at me and dragged me into a hug. "You're such a bitch," she said affectionately.

"Well, you knew that without having to traumatize yourself by leaving your place." I frowned even as I squeezed her back. "Are you okay? What are you doing here?"

I knew she loathed West Orange.

Knew she was scared she'd see one of her brothers or sisters in town.

Hell, she wasn't only scared of seeing them; Parker was afraid of everything outside her home.

Literally *everything*.

"Bear's funeral's tomorrow."

"So? You didn't know him."

"No, but I know you, and I know he mattered to you, so I came here for moral support. Emotional too, but you're the ice queen and I figured you'd prefer for me to be here to help coordinate things."

This time, I shook my head. Had water got trapped in my ears?

"You're here to help coordinate things? How? This isn't a royal funeral, Parker. I mean, he might have been called a Prez, but there won't be an honor guard."

"Will there be a wake afterward?"

"Yes."

"Will there be food and drink and—"

"Yes, but there won't be servers." I frowned at her. "I wish you'd said something about visiting. I'd have told you not to come."

She rolled her eyes. "It's a good thing I stopped getting offended by the things you say a long time ago."

"You know it comes from a place of love," I chided, not even feeling guilty. Mostly, I felt confusion.

My hermit friend/EA was here to attend the funeral of a man she'd never met, all so she could coordinate the wake?

What did she think happened? Brothers lined up with silver trays loaded with bottles of beer to serve the council, and canapés of mini burgers and fried mac and cheese balls were dished out to the Old Ladies?

"I'm here now, so you'd best put me to good use."

Huffing, I asked, "Where are your things?"

She smiled at me. It was too bright. "I, um, didn't bring anything with me."

"What?" I spluttered. What in the actual fuck was happening here? "You came to stay and didn't bring anything with you?"

"Rachel?"

Twisting away from Parker, I sought Lily out. Peering at her, I asked, "Everything okay, Lily?"

"Yeah, but you have to get going soon."

I reached up to rub at my forehead. A thought occurred to me, and I turned to glower at Parker. "That's why you're here, isn't it?"

Parker's gaze turned blank. "Huh?"

"Hello?" Lily asked politely. And it was a question. She was silently asking who this was.

"I have an appointment with the OB/GYN. You came to strong-arm me, didn't you? Well, you didn't need to. Rex is coming with me."

Parker batted her lashes a couple times. "You caught me." She shot me a sheepish smile. "Well, don't worry, I did bring my computer with me so I can crack on with work while you're gone. Are you sure there's nothing to arrange for tomorrow?"

"No, it's handled." That was Lily. And she sounded put out.

"Lily, this is Parker. My executive assistant."

They shared a look.

"Hello, Parker." Lily's smile was pleasant.

Bland.

I didn't trust it.

Just like Parker's reason for being here. Why did she intend on staying the night and had brought her laptop along but not a change of clothes?

"Hello, Lily," was Parker's bright retort.

"What's going on?" I demanded, because something sure as hell was happening and I didn't like it. Not one goddamn bit.

"Nothing's going on," Parker grumbled. "Jesus, Rachel, you sure know how to make your best friend feel welcome."

Guilt hit me, but I was one of the best lawyers in the tristate area for a fucking reason.

"Are you guilt-tripping me?"

Parker's smile was sweet. "Would I do something like that?"

"Yes," I groused, but the lock at the door sounded, the handle twisted, and Rex appeared in the doorway.

"Rach, how many times have I told you to lock this damn door?"

"I did lock it. I unlocked it to let Parker in."

Rex arched a brow. "You're the assistant who executes, huh?"

Well, that was a weird way of phrasing it.

Parker's cheeks turned pink. "Well, something like that."

"Since when do you blush?" I demanded.

She glowered at me. "I do not blush."

"You're blushing now."

"I am not."

"Is this just playful bickering or can anyone join in?"

I threw my hands up at Giulia's intrusion. "This is a free for all," I sniped. To Rex, I muttered, "We need to get going."

"We do." His lips curved. "You get your keys—"

"We're not going on your hog?"

He shot me a bland look. "No?"

"It's a forty-minute journey," I pointed out.

"You're pregnant."

"You noticed."

"I did," he said somberly, but his eyes had teasing glints that surprised me.

I knew he was dreading tomorrow, and when my OB/GYN had called to reschedule my appointment to today, the day before the funeral, I'd been tempted to cancel but the news had actually cheered him up.

Ironic, considering I was dreading it.

In fact, the only thing I'd been looking forward to had been a ride on the back of his hog.

I'd missed it and hadn't even realized I did.

"Well? The baby's like the size of an avocado—"

"It's safer in a cage. Get your car keys. I'm not putting you at risk."

"So you'll put yourself at risk by riding the bike when I'm pregnant, and after, when the kid's born, but I can't be at risk for the nine months I'm pregnant... Is that your logic?"

He beamed a grin at me. It was utterly unapologetic. "Yes."

"Fucking men," Giulia groused. "One rule for us, one rule for them."

Parker shrugged. "I think he's being gallant."

Giulia hooted. "These ain't knights in shining armor, Parker. They're dark and downright dirty—"

"How did you know her name was Parker?" The room seemed to freeze at my question. "I knew something was going on," I growled. "Out with it!"

Rex said, "Rach, we don't have time. We need to get on the road."

I scowled at him. "Are you in on it?"

"In on what? I'm in on nothing, aside from the need to get you to the doctor's, aside from the knowledge that you'll do pretty much any damn thing to get out of today's appointment."

My lips tightened because he wasn't wrong. Not that he needed to know that. "I'm not that bad. I know I have to go."

"Well, stop procrastinating then."

Growling under my breath, I stormed toward my office to grab my purse and then redirected to the kitchen for the car keys.

Along the way, I tried to listen to whatever my 'guests' were talking about, but mostly it was Parker asking if she could help with the funeral.

Suspicions still locked and loaded, I shoved them to the side upon my return to the hall. Mostly because I didn't have an alternative—the nerves were starting to kick in.

I'd be having a quad screen and the nuchal translucency blood work taken today, and I was definitely anxious.

That was why I'd been looking forward to the ride. It'd have taken my mind off of things.

Goddamn overprotective men.

I shoved my keys at him as I approached and, halfway to the door, told Lily, Giulia, and Parker, "If you burn down the house while I'm at the doctor's, I'll make you pay to rebuild it."

Parker snorted. "You're such a weirdo."

"When two witches, and Lily, get together, I'm expecting a drama of *Macbeth* proportions."

Lily laughed. "Thank you, I think."

Giulia huffed. "Been called worse shit than a witch in my time."

Sweetly, I informed her, "I'm sure you have. I'll see you all later."

Rex opened the door for me, and I hovered nearby, just waiting for him to close it with both of us on the stoop.

That was when I heard a hissed, "You almost blew that, Giulia."

"Sorry, baby brain. I forgot I shouldn't know you—"

"Rach? You ready to go?"

Heading for my SUV, I waited for Rex to beep it and climbed in the passenger side. I could drive, and it was my car, but if I wasn't going to ride bitch, then I intended on dealing with a few pieces of work and I couldn't do that behind the wheel.

As I settled in, Rex did the same on the driver's side.

Once he adjusted the seat, we set off, and I pulled out a file from my purse and started scanning the document.

"So, that was Parker."

I shot him a look. "Yes, that was Parker."

"You didn't seem happy to see her."

"She was being suspicious."

As he slouched back, I wondered what it was about men that made them look so goddamn hot when they were driving. One arm on the door, the other over the wheel, all he had to do to make this better was to put the car in reverse with one hand on the wheel, hook his other arm behind my head rest, then look behind him.

The notion did interesting things to my body.

My very *stressed* body which shouldn't be focusing on his.

"That's overreaching, isn't it? Suspicious?"

"What are you? The prosecution?" I mocked.

He grinned at me. "Treat me like I am."

Further surprised by his good mood when he'd been somber this morning before he left for the clubhouse, I murmured, "Parker has agoraphobia."

"She can't."

"She does."

"*She can't.* How the hell is she here if she's agoraphobic?"

"Since she moved to Pennsylvania, I can count on one hand how many times I've seen her, and even then, I was the one who rode over to visit with her."

"Really?"

"Really."

He pondered that. "Huh. Okay, that *is* unusual."

"Thank you," I derided sharply. "My brain isn't addled just because I'm pregnant."

"Never said it was," he dismissed. "You're just being touchy because you're nervous about the doctor."

"I am. But I'm not being touchy. They're up to something." I cast him a glance, all thoughts of the doctor and the file on my lap forgotten. "*Are* you in on it? If you tell me now, I won't get mad."

"I told you that I'm not. What's the worst they can do? Help tomorrow at the wake? Parker was offering to coordinate things for us." He let loose a soft laugh. "I think she was disappointed to learn that it wasn't a royal funeral."

Amused, I said, "I told her the same thing."

"If she's agoraphobic, will she attend?"

"I doubt it. She also didn't bring anything with her. She's spending at least one night but didn't bring her stuff?" I tutted. "She must think I'm an idiot."

He cleared his throat. "I know that Giulia knows Parker."

My brow furrowed. "What? How?"

"From something she said when you left the room."

"What did she say?"

"That we wouldn't be serving afternoon tea at the wake. All three of them laughed like it was an inside joke."

I drummed my nails against the file on my lap. "Afternoon tea. You're sure that's what she said?"

"Yes, Rachel," he mocked. "I'm sure that's what she said."

"They're planning my baby shower."

"You can't know that."

"I can. Trust me."

Parker knew I hated stuff like that; dammit to hell.

"Guess she doesn't know you don't like group settings," Rex said carefully, shooting me a glance as he stopped at a red light.

Grimly, I said, "She knows."

"You dealt with the 'welcome home' party well."

I didn't exactly have a choice—not that I said that.

Knowing my place, my role, was one thing. Enjoyment was another.

One reason Parker and I got along so well was that we both had reclusive tendencies that meshed superbly together.

She had to know I'd loathe having a baby shower.

Still, it was odd timing. If she was here now, that implied they intended on having the baby shower soon, but near to Bear's funeral? That seemed unlikely.

I knew most people had a baby shower around six weeks before the due date, but the Posse did nothing the normal way. That was why Giulia was due in April but had hers after Thanksgiving.

I didn't imagine that the baby shower had consisted of diaper cakes or the regular type of gifts that you gave an expectant mom either.

"Why wouldn't she have brought anything with her if she planned to stay a few days?" I asked him, but mostly I was thinking out loud. "It's not like they're going to host a baby shower close to the funeral, is it? Something else is happening."

Rex just laughed. "You going into detective mode?"

"Damn straight."

Lips curving into an even deeper grin, he shook his head and settled back in his seat. He fiddled with the buttons on the wheel, and one of my playlists sounded through the speakers.

Sensing that he was going to leave me to my thoughts, I gave him the same courtesy. That was something I'd always loved about being with Rex—talking wasn't imperative.

He was pensive by nature, calculating too, but he was the kind of guy who strategized. He weighed the pros and cons of every action, and that required concentration and peace.

Leaving him to his thoughts, and me diving into mine, the ride to Manhattan barely took any time at all.

Only when we parked did my nerves revisit me, but when he bridged our hands together, I'd admit the feel of our fingers tangling, his arm rubbing up against mine, how he opened the door for me, how he said my name at the reception area for me, how he directed things—I needed that.

Control wasn't something I enjoyed being wrestled from me, but here, where my nerves were in full force, where sitting still as I waited for my name to be called was impossible, where I tried to gnaw off a part of my gel nails, where the scent of the doctor's office made my sensitive stomach lurch, I appreciated the calmness he exuded at my side.

The nail I tried to bite, he stopped me by tucking my hand into his. The knee that jiggled, he pushed his thigh against.

His arm slid around my shoulders, his scent filled my nostrils, and in my ear, he murmured, "I know you're nervous, but I'm excited. We made this kid together, Rach. Even though we didn't have a goddamn clue what we were doing, we made this beautiful perfect creation. Together.

"I can't do the blood work and I know I can't give birth, but I can be here. Whatever you need from me, you got it, baby girl."

I bit my lip at his words which soothed something raw inside me. "Can I be your baby girl if I'm having another baby girl of yours?"

His grin was cocky as he butted his lips against my temple. "You'll always be my girl, Rach. Ain't you figured that out yet?"

A soft breath escaped me at his words.

They settled in me.

Lodging deep inside.

I still whimpered when the doctor took my blood, and I cringed when she prodded me and poked me and told me that I needed to gain more weight, but Rex was there through it at all, and he made it bearable.

He listened and he asked the questions I was too nervous to ask, and he let me squeeze his hand hard enough that I felt sure I'd broken a finger by the end of the appointment.

It was one thing to be told you were loved by someone, but it was another thing entirely to be shown you were loved.

Despite his grief, despite his stress, despite the upcoming service, he didn't just show me I was and always would be his girl—he proved it.

THIRTY-SIX

REX

Shit was difficult that night, and it made what had happened earlier that day even fucking sweeter.

I couldn't goddamn wait to see our baby during a sonogram. Just listening to the doctor, discussing Rach's health, it all felt like a gift. A gift I hadn't been allowed before; one that I was given this time.

Blessed.

That was how I fucking felt.

Like she was my blessing. Like *they* were.

I tried to remember that when I heard the roar of a wave of hogs sound in the distance. There was no mistaking it. At any other time, the noise would've made me wonder if we were about to be goddamn sieged, but tonight, it heralded the beginning of a funeral procession.

A league of bikers who rode up from all over the States to attend the funeral of the late, great Bear.

It was cold out, but I had my window open to hear it.

It was an honor, after all.

One that, before, I'd never have questioned whether my dad deserved or not.

And it was that question that was painful. That had me sitting in the dark. That had me staring at nothing, ears pricking for the sound of more incoming bikes, rather than greeting the arrivals at the compound.

I already knew the clubhouse was in chaos. Just getting people somewhere to sleep was a nightmare in itself, never mind coordinating the parking of so many hogs in such a confined area.

I knew the council and their Old Ladies were on it, knew I didn't have to think about it, and it was a good thing because my headspace was definitely not on matters of housekeeping.

She found me sitting in her armchair in our bedroom. Her brow was furrowed, and I could tell she'd been arguing with someone. It was interesting seeing her with the other women. Her arguments weren't like arguments with me. She didn't get cold; she got hot.

If I didn't feel so fucking out of it, I'd have been on her faster than poison oak.

Her eyes were lit up, her cheeks a rosy pink, and her temper was sparking as she stomped inside, huffing all the while.

She loved it.

They challenged her, riled her up.

It was almost amusing that she didn't see that.

"Fucking Parker," she hissed under her breath.

My lips barely curved before she turned around, saw me sitting in the armchair, and, jumping a couple inches off the ground, she yelped in surprise.

"Rex!" She clapped a hand to her chest as if she could contain her heart. "What the hell are you doing here? Aren't you supposed to be greeting those noisy bastards you call brothers?"

"Just thinking."

"It's freezing in here," she grumbled, stomping over to slam the window closed then stomping over to me to stare down at me. "Are you..." She sighed. "You're not okay. What's wrong? What can I do?"

Now that had me smiling.

I grabbed her hand and tumbled her onto the armchair. Her butt landed on my lap, but she just resettled herself on there and leaned her back against the wing of the armchair.

I could no more stop myself from placing my hand on her belly than I could stop myself from taking my next breath.

When she didn't shove my hand away, I spread my fingers, trying to encompass as much of the bump as possible.

I could feel her gaze on me, could sense her curiosity, and despite the fact that I didn't want to discuss where my mind was at, I preferred hers to be busy because that way, she'd let me touch her here.

"You like that I'm pregnant, don't you?"

I'd thought she'd ask about why I was sitting here in the dark. I didn't think she'd ask me about the baby.

"I do."

Why lie?

"How come?"

"Wanted nothing more than a family with you since I was about sixteen. I guess I'm living the dream."

She blinked at me. "You belong in a romance novel."

I huffed out a laugh. "Good to know."

"No, seriously. I've seen less romantic talk in romance dramas than what you give me on the regular. Guys don't say stuff like that."

"You complaining or celebrating?"

"Neither. Just stating a fact." She tipped her head to the side. "I wasn't scared to tell you I was pregnant."

"No?"

"No. You might think that I was, but I wasn't. I was hesitant, but not scared."

"Because you had faith in me, or in yourself?"

She paused. "That's a good question. I don't think I had faith in myself. I just knew I couldn't relive what went down with Wynter. I guess I knew that I could support a child. The mechanics of it..." She grimaced. "...less so."

"The doctor's appointment was difficult for you."

"It was a nightmare."

"You dealt with it well," I assured her.

"Only because you kept me calm. You, well, it was better with you there. Most things are," she muttered under her breath. The kid in me who had been rejected by her a long time ago preened at that. But she didn't give me much opportunity to preen. "I always have faith in you. I know you won't necessarily do the right thing, at least, what I consider to be the right thing, but you have your own honor code.

"I knew you'd support me and our child—I don't just mean financially. You know I don't need your money."

"I know what you meant," I said gruffly, my fingers spreading wide again. "I'm glad you didn't think I'd be a piece of shit who'd fail in my responsibilities."

She snorted. "You're the most responsible man I know. Which is saying something."

"Considering I lead a bunch of outlaws?"

"Who are driving me crazy by riding their hogs toward our hill? Yes."

Smirking at her annoyance with the noise, I settled my head back against the armchair and murmured, "I love you. You know that, don't you?"

She sniffed. "Of course I know that. I love you too."

I liked how matter-of-fact she was about that.

It made it more cemented somehow. She wasn't breathless with joy; she was resolute.

That was our love.

Solid.

Unending.

"You know I'll never do you wrong like Dad did Mom, don't you? Even if..." I swallowed, pulsed my fingers against her belly. "Even if the unthinkable happened. I waited decades, baby girl. Ain't no one or nothing that's gonna beat what we have together—"

Her hand came up to cup my chin, and her thumb swiped over my mouth, putting a halt to my words.

"You don't have to say that. You're not your father, and I'm not your mother. They're not better or worse than us. We're not weaker or stronger than them. They are not us."

My jaw clenched. "It's hard to think about tomorrow, you know? Hard to think about what'll happen to honor him and I don't think he deserves it—"

"Bear was many things, but he never claimed to be a paragon of virtue. Your mother clearly forgave him, King," she said sternly, and I knew the use of my real name was a reprimand. "She wouldn't have let him back in the damn house if she didn't.

"Bear didn't find out about Kendra until after Rene died, but that doesn't mean Rene had no inclination that her man was cheating—women always know. Even if they wished they didn't. Men aren't smart. You do stupid things and are surprised when you get found out.

"So Bear didn't have to tell you in his letter for me to know that he was the kind of man who'd have apologized to her. Who'd have worked hard for a second chance. That's why they had many happy years together until life tore them apart.

"You know, cheating is the end for a lot of couples, but it doesn't always have to be. It can trigger a period of change. Can kickstart a rebirth. If love is there, it can always grow again. If it wasn't there in the first place, then there was nothing to lose—"

"What about Storm and Keira? What do you think about them?"

"You told me Storm was raped."

"He was, but Keira thinks he cheated."

Her brow furrowed. "Still?"

I shrugged. "Storm thinks he cheated. Why would he have told her otherwise?"

"You know, the way our society views consent is very disturbing," she mumbled grimly. "That he doesn't know..." She blew out a breath. "Do you want me to talk with Keira? Set her straight? She'll be coming for the service, won't she?"

"I guess."

"You don't know?"

"Storm tried to talk about it but I haven't been in the right head-space. But I don't think you should. It's a conversation for them to have, for her to understand that he was raped. But, in her position, what would you do?"

"I'm not in her position."

"I'm curious."

"Why?"

"I don't know. Just am."

"Storm loves her. Anyone with eyes can see that. She loves him too. Their situation isn't simple. He's a recovering addict, for God's sake. It's easy to understand why she'd be hesitant to forgive him."

"Would you forgive him?"

She shot me a look that cut through the bullshit, that told me she understood what I was doing and she wasn't going to fall for it. "You're not Storm. Neither are you Bear. This won't make you understand why your mom took him back."

"I don't think I'd want you to take me back. I wouldn't deserve—"

"King," she snapped, "shut up. You love me. You would kill for me. You would die for me. You would do anything to protect me. You would steal for me and beg for me—you are your father's son in that.

"Wouldn't *I* be the dumbass if, knowing your feelings are so powerful for me, I didn't recognize that something had broken down in our relationship to the point where you sought someone else out? I'm not excusing cheaters. I'm just saying not every relationship is the same.

"He fucked up. Your mom shut him out. That doesn't make it right what he did. Doesn't make what she did wrong. They fell apart but came back together. That's something to celebrate. There's joy to be found in that, not shame. He earned her forgiveness; there's no way she would have been as happy with him as she was if he hadn't.

"Look at the bitterness that's been sown between Keira and Storm—there was none of that with your mom and dad, was there?"

I licked my lips but had to concede, "No."

"No. Exactly. It takes a good man to admit that he was wrong. To work hard to become someone worthy of the woman he loves. But the real question here isn't why did your mom forgive your dad; it's why didn't he try to earn your forgiveness too?"

"He didn't betray me—"

"He betrayed your family. Let's face it, faithfulness isn't a common expectation in the clubhouse between an Old Man and his Old Lady, but your dad was different. And truthfully? He had such an impact on you, Link, Nyx, Mav, Steel, and hell, Sin, that it's no wonder you're all possessive jackasses with your women. You were raised in his image.

"That's something I have to thank him for because when I was at that party the other day, I suddenly understood why Giulia gets crazy jealous—"

"You do?" I asked dubiously, trying to imagine my icy Rachel being overcome with jealousy.

Nah, I couldn't see it.

"Trust me, it came as a shock to me too," she drawled. "But, my point is, he set your ideals in place, and now he's come along and taken a bulldozer to them. It'll take a while for you to forgive him, but don't let this one act take center stage. Don't let it take the full spotlight when he did so many other things that were good and kind and honorable."

"You do know why he was Prez, don't you?" I scorned.

Her lips curved. "I never imagined he was a Boy Scout. There was a reason he earned the road name Bear."

Frustration whirled around inside me. I wanted her to understand why I was riled up, but her cool logic eased me in a way nothing else could.

I wanted to hate on him. Much like—

Shit.

She was right.

It wasn't the man reacting here. *It was the kid.* The one who'd looked up to his father, who'd been taught to adore his woman, who'd been raised to be the pillar of strength in his household. Who'd seen the importance of faithfulness, had learned how vital loyalty was, and had registered how love couldn't really exist without either of those two facets.

He'd betrayed that kid—the one who'd listened as if God himself were talking when Dad gave one of his lectures.

I sucked in a breath, fighting the urge to cry like that little kid, and instead, I closed my eyes, counted to ten, sucked in a few deep breaths, and tried to get myself under control. "After, when you're ready—"

"After, what?"

"After you give birth—"

"Oh!"

"After you give birth," I repeated, "we'll head to Indy's place. It's time you got some ink."

She stilled. Hell, she was so fucking quiet for so fucking long that I thought my ears had stopped working.

"Rex, are you saying what I think you're saying?"

"Yes. It's time we got branded."

A soft breath escaped her. It was high pressure. More hiss than a sigh. "You're not asking?"

"No. Not that. Not telling, neither. Just discussing the inevitable."

Her mouth rounded. Then it shut. "I can't be angry with you about that."

I smirked in response then grabbed her other hand. With one set of fingers entwined with hers, the other on her belly, I rasped, "But... I will ask you this next question."

"Oh?"

"We've always been inevitable, but that doesn't mean we can take the link between us for granted. I want you to know, Rach, that I never will—"

She tutted me. "King—"

"I don't need another lecture," I teased, my voice still gruff but lighter than before. "I'm just saying that I'll always honor you and cherish you, Rachel. The day that I don't is the day you can toss me out on my ass, and I'll deserve it. Then I'll spend the next however long trying to figure out how to get you back because this *is* inevitable, sweetheart.

"So... will you marry me?"

She swallowed, and her silence might have stirred anxiety in another man, but not me.

This was right.

A blessing—*she was mine.*

I intended to be hers.

"You know I will," she whispered, her mouth catching mine in a kiss that tasted salty from her tears. "I didn't expect this," she mumbled as I tasted her, savored her. "I thought you wanted me to prove myself—"

"Maybe, the night of the gala, I did. But then I realized what a jackass I was. You've spent the majority of your career proving that you have what it takes to be my First Lady, Rachel. But that's not enough..." I sucked in a breath. "I want you to be my wife. I want you to own me as much as I own you. I want the fucking laws of the land to tie me to you so that there's nothing and nobody who can come between us."

She let loose a soggy laugh as she burrowed her face in my throat.

"I love you," she whispered. "I love you. I want—*that*. All of it. Every bit of it. I want my ring on your finger and my name on your skin."

I sucked in a breath. "Then that's what you'll have."

She clenched her arms around me, holding me tight, but that was nothing to how I held her.

As if she kept my world together.

As if she kept me tethered to this plane.

"Rex?" she whispered against my throat.

"Yeah?"

"Tomorrow, on the honor ride, I *will* be behind you."

My lips twitched. "A ride around the town is a helluva lot different than a ride into Manhattan."

"Just so you know," she said, a warning to her tone.

A warning that settled in my bones with just how right she was for me.

Before a funeral was probably the worst time to ask someone to marry them, but to me, it made perfect sense.

I didn't forgive him, but in this, in my actions, with my choices, I honored him—the father who'd taught me what it was to be a man, to be unafraid of looking weak because to love was not to be weak.

But I also honored her—the mother who showed me what strength was, who proved that power and position were nothing without the right mate at your side.

Here mine was.

My girl.

Perfection.

THIRTY-SEVEN

RACHEL

GEORGE HARRISON - MY SWEET LORD

This wasn't my first Sinners' funeral, though I sure as hell wished it would be my last.

The chaos—it was something I'd never remember. That'd always come as a shock next time there was a service.

Depending on the popularity of the brother, Sinners from all around the country would ride in to attend the funeral.

Because it was Bear, because he was the original Prez, because the other chapters only existed because of him, they were all here.

Hundreds of new faces—some brothers, some Old Ladies. The men had ridden down on their hogs, but the Old Ladies had driven here in cages so their kids could come too.

I was used to the chaos of arranging a gala, but this was so out of my comfort zone that I was beyond grateful for the Posse.

Rene would probably have been able to manage, but Rene had never had to arrange a funeral this size because this was unique.

Bear was unique.

It was clear in the brothers' faces. Some who'd probably never even met him. Regardless, the grief was the same. It was in their kids' eyes, the somberness on the Old Ladies' expressions...

Bear had mattered to so many people even though he'd quit the life years ago.

Rex was quiet for most of the morning in the run up to the service. He had been last night too. After he'd proposed, he hadn't taken me to bed. He'd just closed his eyes and fallen asleep in the armchair, and because I was oddly comfortable—odd because nothing about my position was comfortable—I'd managed to get some sleep too.

His sorrow and grief made him curt with everyone but me. Well, Wynter too. She phoned to give him her apologies for not being able to make it and to tell him that she wished she'd had the chance to meet her grandfather.

Though he was pleasant with her, I knew it hurt that she hadn't flown over. I'd made the suggestion, had offered to arrange a ticket, but she was being quiet. Something was going on, and she wasn't willing to talk about it.

I didn't know how deep the eyes Rex had on her could look, but after the funeral, when things had settled, I was going to have him delve deeper into the situation.

My instincts were on red alert with her.

They would have been with Rex too if his mind hadn't been split in so many directions that he didn't know which way was up.

At eleven on the nose, we headed outside. His bike was in the driveway for once, and I knew that was for ease. The compound was loaded down with hogs, after all.

I'd come back to the house to get changed after helping the Posse in the preparations for the wake and was wearing a simple black dress. Not ideal for a ride on the back of a bike, but it had to do. The unavoidable had happened—my pants and pencil skirts weren't fitting me right now.

The straps were a little too dressy for the event, but I wore a leather jacket that covered them. Rex wore black jeans, a black tee, a black leather jacket, and his cut. It wasn't a formal event, after all. Not for the Sinners.

"You okay, sweetheart?" I asked him softly. The place was ridiculously quiet in comparison to the clubhouse.

"I'll be better when today's over with," he said grimly as he climbed onto the back of his bike. He twisted and helped me settle behind him. "Let's give him the final farewell he should have had."

Going out in a blaze of glory and not in a hospital bed...

He didn't have to utter the words for me to hear them anyway.

The second I was settled, my arms around his waist, my inner thighs clasping his outer ones, he set off.

We headed down the driveway and out of the gates. All was quiet.

It wouldn't be for long.

West Orange didn't know what was about to hit it.

He revved his engine once he'd made it onto the road, and one hand settled on my knee as he called out, "Brace yourself."

In answer, I clasped him tighter, and he roared down the road.

The second he passed the gates to the compound, I heard hundreds of hogs start their engines, and Nyx, as VP, waiting at the gates, surrounded by the rest of the council, began pulling out.

If the situation had been different, if this weren't about Bear's death, it would have been exhilarating to be a part of such a massive flotilla of hogs. Instead, it was bittersweet.

Tears pricked my eyes as I turned my face into Rex's shoulder.

I knew Lily had arranged this, but I was surprised that Rex went along with her plans, mostly because at the end of our road, there was a hearse waiting. But when I saw inside the vehicle, I got it.

Instead of flowers, there were photos.

It must have taken Lily a long time to collate so many and to arrange for this.

Each picture was clipped onto a little stand so it stood up and wobbled with any movement. They were at different heights, some short, some tall, so that Bear's coffin looked to be covered in them.

I could only imagine what they depicted.

Smiling Bear, angry Bear, drunk Bear.

A thousand different expressions, not a single damn one capable of showing the real man and his mettle.

And as these processions were meant to, it traveled at a snail's pace.

Maybe that made it all the more impressive.

Rex and I led the procession, and behind us, the others fanned out. Hundreds of bikes, cages at the back, each following the hearse, traveling around the town that Bear had pretty much bought and sold, crossing streets that were loaded with people, each of them pausing to gawk at the majestic spectacle in front of them.

My throat ached and my eyes burned as I tried to contain my grief. It was difficult. So difficult. I wasn't sure if I'd ever seen anything more beautiful, and I ended up sniffling my way around town.

We completed a full circle and the hearse guided us up our private road and back to the clubhouse.

There was clearly some prearrangement here, because when the hearse crossed from public to private land, the driver held down his horn, and so did Rex, as well as Nyx and Link and the others, and the rest of the hundreds of bikers too.

The cacophony made my heart pound.

It was a celebration of the rebel. A man who'd manipulated laws for his own gain.

When we finally made it onto the compound, the noise still bellowed back to me. It should have given me a headache, but there was such a sweet joy in hearing it.

It was a reminder that we weren't alone in this.

We were all grieving.

Rex pulled up in his regular spot, and I climbed off and hovered by his side, grateful to get there first so no one could get a flash of my panties.

Rex remained seated, his shoulders hunched, his back loaded with tension.

I pressed my hand to his nape, and I leaned over him to whisper, "King, I love you. I'm here. We can do this together."

His hands tightened around the handlebars, but he nodded. Once. Then he climbed off the bike.

Silently, I held out my hand.

Silently, he accepted it.

Together, our fingers clasped in each other's, we walked toward the hearse.

"It's beautiful," I whispered as I got nearer to the quilt of color that were the photos.

There had to be over two hundred, minimum.

Rex's hand covered mine before he released his hold on it. "I'll see you by the grave," he rasped, and, nodding, I kissed his cheek.

As I stepped away, the Posse were there. Lily and Giulia linking arms with me, talking about something Rex had asked to be added to the ceremony, Stone, Indy, Amara, Tiff, and Alessa joining arms with them until we were an awkward collective, walking toward a narrow space.

We didn't let it stop us.

No one spoke as we settled around the grave site.

We just stood there, watching. From the corner of my eye, I watched as a couple dogs peered through the fencing as silent spectators.

Keira drew my attention away from them as she shuffled toward us, while brothers and the few Old Ladies from this chapter book-ended us. Then came the other chapters and their women.

The tiny space was filled to the brim. But people just moved around the fence, cushioning the graveyard with the respect Bear had commanded.

I held up well.

Until a song blasted through the private cemetery.

I'd have been able to cope with Black Sabbath, or some other heavy rock band, but when 'My Sweet Lord' whispered along the wind, I pressed a fist to my lips and choked back a sob.

Eyes burning for real now, I remembered the last time I'd heard this—Bear and Rene's vow renewal.

The pain shredded me as I thought about them then. So happy. So united. Not knowing she'd be torn away from her Bear soon afterward.

Tears poured down my cheeks as a song that should have been happy, triggered the purest pain inside me.

God, King.

My King.

This must be killing him.

But he must have been the one to pick it.

It wasn't a Sinners' song.

It was the song a husband selected for a beloved wife. The song a son played to commemorate parents he'd adored. Was that what Rex had added to the ceremony? Because of what we'd discussed last night?

I hoped it was.

I hoped our discussion had brought him some peace.

Mouth trembling, I watched when, finally, he was there; Storm, Nyx, Steel, Link, Maverick, and Sin at his back as always, while they carried Bear's coffin toward us.

It was a testament, I thought, to men who rarely showed emotion, who killed and hurt people for a living, who thought nothing of committing the worst crimes... that their faces were twisted into grief-stricken grimaces.

As a unit, they walked Bear toward his final resting place—beside the love of his life, a love that had transcended even death—next to his Rene.

REX

HOZIER - TAKE ME TO CHURCH

The service hurt.

The aftermath hurt.

Shaking hands with all my brothers hurt.

Talking to people who'd respected my dad hurt.

Dealing with business associates hurt.

It all fucking hurt.

It didn't goddamn matter that he'd been dead since December 25th.

It didn't matter that I'd had months to mourn.

It was a raw open wound in my fucking soul and no one, no one, apart from the woman standing at my side throughout it all, understood.

Because she knew what secret I was keeping.

We'd freed him together, after all.

When Aidan O'Donnelly Jr. showed up, his hand outstretched, it took me a second to realize that a Five Pointer, one who wasn't Declan, had shown up for the ceremony.

I shook his hand and rasped, "I'm grateful you could make it."

"Even in the city, we know what Bear got up to," he

remarked, sympathy in his eyes. "Men like you and me, Rex, we see a side of our fathers no kid should ever have to see. And in the aftermath, we have to handle the kind of business that no kid should ever have to inherit." He reached out and clapped a hand to my arm. "If there's anything we can do, you know to get in touch."

Before he could step away, his fingers tightening around the cane in his grasp, I rumbled, "Your father's insane."

He tipped his head to the side in surprise at my statement. More because he knew I wasn't saying it to insult him or his parent. This was an opportunity I didn't realize I'd be afforded, but he was right— I'd inherited a business that no grieving kid should ever have to deal with.

That I'd inherited it when my dad was still alive didn't matter.

"He is," was all Junior said. "What's he done now?"

"Is he good for his word?"

Junior's brow furrowed. "What has he promised?"

"For certain acts, an amnesty."

"From NYC's finest?"

I nodded. "Is he capable of following through with that offer?"

"In the city, yes. On the East Coast, it depends."

A slow breath gusted from my lips. "I appreciate your candor."

"If you want to talk about it, in a safer, more private setting, I can make arrangements." He dipped a hand into his coat and pulled out a card. "My direct line. You don't have to go through Declan to reach it."

I palmed the card then pocketed it without a second's glance. "Thank you. I'll be in touch."

He bowed his head and stepped back and limped away. Only pausing when MaryCat hurled herself at him, hugging him tightly. Junior surprised me by embracing her in return, and Digger and the other man shared a look over her shoulder.

The trio shuffled off together, prompting me to realize he was attending alone. I knew he had a girlfriend, but she wasn't with him.

For her safety? I couldn't blame him; if I were attending his father's funeral, I wouldn't bring Rachel.

The card burned a hole in my pocket, but it came with relief too.

Harlow and Nyx were only in the preparation stages, but I needed to nip this in the bud, fast, if O'Donnelly Sr. tried to get them out of the city and beyond the influential reach of the Irish Mob.

There came a point where the council and their Old Ladies, Storm, his Keira, Cyan, and Rain were the only ones in the graveyard. Lily moved over to us then, and she held out a picture for me.

I gritted my teeth when I saw the happy, smiling faces of my mom and dad, dancing to that goddamn song. Which, like twisting the knife in the wound, was when it came on again.

A choked sound escaped me and I accidentally crumpled the photo in my hand. But Lily and Rachel shared a glance, and somehow, Rachel translated, because all of a sudden, she was in my arms, and she was prompting me to move.

Around us, each Old Man and Old Lady, hell, even Rain and Cyan, tumbled into the other's embrace and started dancing. Nothing more than a shuffle, but it was a dance, nonetheless.

I got it.

I did.

A celebration—a full circle.

I'd requested that the song be played as we brought his coffin into the graveyard, but I hadn't asked for this.

Fuck, *this* hurt.

I wanted to howl out my grief. My anger. My sorrow. My bitterness. My fucking loss.

But I didn't.

I just let my woman hold me, I just shuffled to 'My Sweet Lord' like my mom and dad had done once upon a time, and I vowed that no one would touch my woman, not without the entirety of the East Coast feeling my wrath.

No one, no fucking one, would take Rachel from me.

That was more of a vow than I'd make to her in a church.

THIRTY-NINE

REX

I should have known Kendra would show up.

Maybe I should even have thrown her out, but I didn't.

He was her dad too, though it pained me to admit it.

She skirted the edge of the ceremony, the edges of the wake. I tracked her with my gaze, making sure she went nowhere near Storm or Keira, but she actively avoided them so it made it easier to relax. Her chameleon act was so good that, after a while, I forgot about her.

People drank and ate, smoked and vaped. Kids snacked on ambrosia salad and ran screaming through the clubhouse and out into the yard. Women congregated together and gossiped; men bitched in small clusters.

A few of my dad's original club—no one from his council had survived—were all seated, getting drunk on whiskey.

I watched it all with a distance that would have been disturbing if the sense of numbness wasn't appreciated.

Maybe that was why I saw it.

Just out of the corner of my eye—a movement in the hallway.

No one expected much from me, that was the only relief. No

conversation, no chitchat. They let me wander from group to group, not saying anything apart from dipping their chin in greeting.

It provided me with a reverse kind of anonymity. Everyone knew who I was but they were going out of their way to give me space, that meant when I turned into the hallway, I moved into the room silently.

It meant that I saw, with my own eyes, what Rain had told me.

"You bastard," Harlow was spitting, struggling against the hold two of my brothers, Anchor and River, had him in. His arms windmilled, spinning faster and faster until Anchor and River were struggling to contain him.

Opposite, sneering and laughing all the fucking while, Lever had a book in his hand. He tore out a page and dropped it to the floor where there was a pile of dog shit—the strays had clearly taken advantage of the open doors.

Goddamn Quin.

"Need a few more sheets," Lever cackled as he raised the book just a couple of inches, which was when the light gleamed off the silver copperplate writing on the front of it.

Holy Bible

This time, the shredding of paper ricocheted through the room like a bomb blast.

Despair etched into his expression, Harlow ceased struggling, watching with distraught eyes as Lever broke so many unspoken fucking rules that I couldn't even begin to count them.

Harlow had come here for acceptance, for help, and *this* was what he was given.

I wasn't a religious man. Not because of what I did for a living, not because you couldn't attend church and be a brother—some guys actually drove over to Hanover to attend church there with a pastor who didn't know their rep. It just wasn't in me to believe in a higher power.

Religion wasn't scorned here, however.

You could do whatever you wanted—liberty was celebrated.

So to see Harlow's liberty being scorned, to see a text that he held dear, that he believed to be holy, being destroyed simply because Lever was a prick, because he wanted to belittle Harlow, made something inside me snap.

The numbness that had infected me ever since the ceremony, making me grow colder and colder, had put everything on ice. The emotional pain was buried away, deep in my soul.

But all that pain exploded to the surface, no longer content to be buried away, tearing to the fore as he crouched down and went to pick up the shit with the pages that Harlow held so dear.

It hit me like a red wave.

I stormed into the room, ignoring the ground out, 'Fucks,' from Anchor and River who immediately let go of Harlow. They dropped him so fast that he rocked back on his heels, actually falling to the ground with a dull thud without their unwanted support before they backed away.

It was too late for them.

Too fucking late.

Lever, still cackling, peered up at me, his face dropping at the sight of me.

He knew he was doing wrong.

He knew he was pushing the club's limits.

Before he could get out, "Prez, I—" I grabbed him by the hair and slammed his face into my fist. Jerking him to his feet, ignoring the punches he tried to land on me in self-defense, I beat into him over and over again.

The few punches he landed, I didn't feel.

When his hands slapped at me, his nails scoring into my flesh in an attempt to stop me, I didn't feel a thing then either.

His grunts became cries, his pleading became sobs as I smashed his fucking face into pieces.

Cartilage shattered, blood vessels ruptured, bones crunched beneath my fist, blood and drool sprayed me as I beat into him, and I still didn't stop.

Over and fucking over, that red wave of fury held me in its grip.

"Please," he said on a soft sob, but where was his mercy?

Why should I give him any?

I dropped him to the ground and he cried out with relief, great shudders wracking his frame. Only, he was wrong—we weren't done.

I knelt down at his side, not looking up when I heard the hushed whispers of a crowd that was watching me, not looking up when I heard Nyx muttering something to Storm and Link.

Unluckily for Lever, he had all my attention even if I was aware of my surroundings.

"You think you can pull your stunts today of all days with no repercussions?"

I grabbed his chin, staring at the mush of his flesh, the features that had blurred under the pounding of my knuckles. It was a credit to him that he hadn't passed out.

"You want me to stop?" I crooned.

He sniffed and bleated, "I'm so sorry, Prez, so sorry. So sorry, so sorry."

Over and over again, he apologized.

But it was too late for that.

The second he'd torn those pages out, it was too late.

I pinched his chin between fingers that would ache in the morning and whispered, "That didn't answer my question."

His mouth trembled, the torn and bleeding lips shaking as he stared at me. "I-I need you to stop, Prez."

I nodded. "Pick up the shit, Lever."

His gaze drifted to the pieces of holy text he'd been using. He went to pick up the sheets, but I grabbed his hand, twisted his fingers around, not stopping until the appendage flopped back and he was screaming.

"Jesus Christ," someone hissed behind me.

Knowing that his consciousness would be fading, I grabbed his hair once more—he didn't even yelp, that was how much pain he was in—and I pressed his face nearer to the shit.

"Eat it."

"Rex, fuck," Nyx snapped.

I lifted my head to stare at him, his jaw clenched at whatever he was reading on my face.

Storm stepped closer. "There are kids watching."

"Then their mothers should take them away," I growled. "And if they don't, that's on them, not on me. I will protect every Sinner under my roof, even if it's from another brother." To Lever, I snarled, "*EAT IT!*"

"He's gonna pass out—"

"Link, he's gonna spew first," Sin said softly, amusement lacing his words. He knew what this felt like. Knew what I was going through. "He's lucky to get out with his life."

Maybe Lever heard him, maybe he recognized the truth in what my cousin said, because he opened his mouth and, gagging, bit into the turd on the floor.

There were a couple gagging sounds from behind me too, and the stench wasn't pretty, but I held him in place by his hair, making sure he ate every fucking bite. He sobbed throughout it, sniffling and retching with each swallow.

Only when he was done did I lift him up.

But my hand tightened on his hair as the other went to his chin.

In one swift move, I snapped his neck and let his body fall to the ground.

A stunned gasp swept among the crowd, and I peered up and saw brothers were watching me.

Rachel was too.

She stared at me.

I stared back.

Unapologetic.

She swallowed.

Then, she stunned me.

She didn't run away.

Inevitable—the word drifted through my mind. Through the numbness.

Her eyes on me all the while, her shock clear, her distaste clearer, she intoned, "Cruz, I think we need your assistance."

Her words shifted me into movement. I got to my feet, collecting the Bible as I did so, and I moved over to Harlow who was watching me in bewilderment, his mouth rounding as I approached.

Without looking at either of them, to Anchor and River, I rumbled, "Help Cruz deal with his body. No pay for the next four weeks."

I got two garbled, "Yes, Prez," when Nyx and Storm, who had a firm hold on their arms, kicked them to trigger their answer.

"Let them go," I said grimly.

Nyx and Storm listened to me.

I held out my other hand.

They frowned.

"Your cuts."

Anchor whispered, "You want us to give you our cuts?"

I didn't reply, just waited.

"Think you should be grateful that's all he's asking for," Sin said snidely.

That got them moving.

I tossed the leather on top of Lever's corpse.

"Destroy them with him."

"No!" Anchor bit off. "This ain't right. We didn't do nothing."

I shot him a look. "Doing nothing is sometimes the worst thing you can do. But you didn't do nothing. 'Nothing' I could forgive. You held Harlow down.

"What fucking club is this, Anchor? You think you can do whatever the fuck you want? You can. With *your* liberty. Not with another brother's.

"He's a Prospect; I can see that you're about to throw that at me. Prospects get treated like shit, and I can handle that. It's fucking pathetic to me, but I get it. Men are pathetic. So I let you haze them and I let you give them the disgusting jobs and that's fine because there'll be plenty worse asked of a brother along the way. But there's a fine line between hazing and this bullshit.

"I tell you what, you can earn back your cuts. You wanna belong to this club, you can learn how to be a brother again. Consider yourself Prospects."

Sin, chuckling, snagged the cuts. I didn't need to turn around to know that he was ripping off their patches. "I'll keep a hold of these until I think you deserve 'em."

With that, he tossed their patches on top of Lever.

Ignoring him, and still holding the Bible in my hand, I flicked to the beginning of the book.

God made you beautiful, but your soul is so much more stunning than your face.

I love you. Thank you for being my brother.

Jessie.

I'd had a feeling, and as usual, my gut was right.

Staring down at the inscription, I asked, "You want a patch?"

Harlow was quiet for too long, so I finally looked at him.

His eyes were wide as they clashed with mine before he stared down at the Bible in my hand, flicked a glance at Lever's corpse, shot a look at Nyx, then returned his focus to me.

There was no escaping the ugliness of this scene.

But he didn't want to.

He retrieved the Bible from my hold. "Yes."

Nodding, I found Nyx's gaze and said, "Make it happen."

"Sure, Prez."

Not Rex. Not King. Prez.

That was who I was at that moment.

Anyone who thought I was weak because I was strategic, diplomatic, even, was wrong.

I stepped away from the mess and I called out, "Celebrate my father's life, enjoy our hospitality, but remember that he started all of this. We're outlaws to the rest of the world, but inside these walls, we're brothers. Brothers don't disrespect each other."

My fist flew into Anchor's face, and the other soared into River's gut.

As one grabbed their nose and the other dropped to their knees, I drifted away, leaving Nyx and Storm to clear up *my* mess for once.

FORTY

RACHEL

The deadly silence in the clubhouse entryway was all the starker for the rowdiness of before.

The corpse on the ground snatched my total attention, until I realized Rex was... *leaving.*

Eyes wide, I grated out, "Cruz, are you going to deal with this?"

"Yes, Rachel," he said calmly.

"Rachel, go," Nyx urged me. "We'll handle this."

"Who the fuck is she?" someone muttered behind me.

I stood up straighter, my shoulders flying back as I declared, "I'm your First Lady."

I didn't wait for a reply.

I rushed out of the clubhouse and saw Rex, from the back, kicking the stand down on his hog.

"King!" I shouted, running over to him, trying to get there before he took off. He remained in place, frozen until I reached him, my arms sliding around his waist from the back as I pleaded, "Please, don't leave me."

A hard breath escaped him. "Are you frightened of me?"

"No."

It was a difficult truth to admit.

But I knew what he was capable of, knew that his control was strong and that it took an act of God to break that control.

How fitting that thought was considering what had triggered that... I couldn't call it a fight.

It was one-sided.

An evisceration.

Swallowing, I repeated on a whisper, "No."

"Grizzly, Bear, Sin, we all have it. We all share this fucking temper—"

"I know you do."

"You do now," he said grimly, his tone still as cold as ice.

Fuck, that was *my* job.

He wasn't supposed to freeze me out. Especially not anymore.

I squeezed him, then I threw out the words that might have meant the end for us: "You killed my mom, didn't you?"

He tensed.

"If you lie to me," I rumbled, "I'll walk away. Here. Now."

Snarling, he twisted around in my hold. His hands went to cup my cheeks, and though the position might have been threatening, I went toe to toe with him. Head tilted back, chin tipped up as I glared at him defiantly.

But there was no need for that.

No need for defiance. Not only because I knew Rex would hurt himself before he hurt me, but because he gave me the answer I'd known without needing to ask.

"She was going to leave you."

I swallowed. "She did that a lot."

"She was going to take Rain and leave you behind." He shook his head. "She did that before I was around. No one leaves you, Rachel. No one."

Tears pricked my eyes for the ten millionth time today, but it wasn't from the pain his words caused, just from his devotion. From his love. It wrapped me up so tightly that it'd have strangled another woman, but for me, it was perfect.

Still, I had to choke out, "Rain's going to leave for the army. You're not going to kill him, are you?"

"She wasn't coming back," he said grimly. "Rain will. Whether it's in a fucking coffin or in a cage, he'll come home. No one leaves you, Rachel, no one. Not on my watch."

The tears spilled down my cheeks at that.

Behind me, I could hear the grunts as Anchor and River collected Lever, while Cruz, Storm, Nyx, and whoever the hell else got roped in, stomped around on clean-up duty.

But they ignored us, much as we ignored them.

I placed my hands on his waist again, letting one shift around to slide up the center of his back.

"Come home with me."

He shook his head. "I need to ride."

"I want to come with you."

"The road—it's too cold. It's—" He heaved a sigh and pressed his forehead against mine. "Your safety, I can't compromise—"

"My safety is with you," I told him. "I want to come with you."

He gritted his teeth but slowly nodded. I didn't think my words convinced him; if anything, I thought he didn't want to be without me.

Rex pulled back to climb onto his bike, and I was almost certain he'd ride off without me, but he didn't. He stayed there, as still as death, waiting for me to get behind him.

The instant I was settled, I squeezed his waist, and he took off.

He didn't go right toward the road but left toward our place. I almost argued but he'd never have heard me over the roar of his engine.

As we pulled up outside the house, he rasped, "I promise I won't leave without you. Go and change into something more suitable. Leather, if you have it."

I ambled off the back of the hog, and because I trusted him, just kissed his cheek.

He didn't let me down.

As I rushed into the house, I didn't keep my ear cocked for the sound of his bike. I just changed into a sweater, dragged on a leather jacket, and deep in the back of my closet, I found the leather pants I'd bought years ago for rides with him.

They still fit me in the legs, but not around the waist or the hips, but it was better than nothing if we took a tumble.

I dragged them on, leaving the zipper gaping wide, then pulled on some ankle boots. Absentmindedly, I grabbed two hair ties. One tied my hair back, the other I looped around the button on my fly and fastened my pants that way—I remembered that trick from the 'good' old days.

My mind tumbled from thought to thought as I changed.

The repercussions of killing a brother in front of so many, the knowledge that Rex had killed Mom, the aftermath of another death in the clubhouse—they blurred into one, fading as my urgency became directed on getting ready fast enough.

Once I was dressed, I rushed down the stairs, practically burst through the door, then ran over to his side. He'd moved the bike around so he was staring out of the gates. When I climbed on behind him, he waited for that squeeze before he took off.

We rode for hours.

Hours upon hours.

It was cold and exhausting, but I clung to him as my mind raced and he burned off his temper, as he let his rage slip through him, as he grieved in privacy and let the wind take away his emotions—emotions that a man like him, in his position, wasn't supposed to have.

That he let me be there was, I knew, yet another turning point.

Another bend in the road of life that we had to work through together. Because, if I didn't bend with him, move with him and the bike he steered, we could crash, and I'd spent enough of my life like that.

Tonight, with its many revelations, should have torn us apart, but it had brought us closer together than ever.

I was ready for the open road now.

STORM

"You fuckers know how to throw a welcome back party."

"Technically, it was a wake. Had nothing to do with you."

I smacked Nyx in the side before I hauled an arm over his shoulder and dragged him into me. "Last time he lost it like that was—"

We shared a look.

"Yeah."

"Think she knows?"

"Maybe." Nyx shrugged. "You saw how Rach went after him. Not exactly his finest moment. She still ran toward him, not away."

"I thought he was inspired."

I grunted at Sin. "You fucking would. Sick fuck."

Sin grinned at me. "Making him eat the dog shit was just fucking epic."

"You taking pointers?" Link queried. "Because that's a whole pile of messed up, Sin. If you start doing that, so help me God, I'm gonna get holy water and drown you in it."

I had to grin. "I heard you gagging. For someone who eats so much ass, you'd think you'd be used to the smell."

Link supplied me with another gagging sound that had us all howling. "They wash it first, Storm," he mumbled, clearly scandalized. "Lily is very hygienic."

"Glad to hear it," I joked.

"You may have ruined eating ass for me now, jerk-off."

Fuck, it felt good to smile.

The day had been hard, the week had been harder, and the goddamn month and start to the year hadn't been fucking easy either.

I needed a break.

Coming home felt like that, but mostly, what perked me up was that Keira had danced with me in the graveyard.

I wasn't sure if she would, but she had.

I could still feel her in my arms, could still feel the slickness of her tears through my shirt.

Did it make me a fucking sap that I regretted it when they dried?

Yeah, I thought that might be the official definition of a sap.

While the murder in the hall had been impromptu, it was just another welcome home. A reminder of the man who led us, who had honor and who believed in duty, who lived his life with respect.

I'd missed these fuckers.

Didn't matter that we were always on the phone to each other, I missed them and regretted that my visits home were just that—visits.

"When are you bringing Cruz onto the council?"

Nyx frowned at me. "Why do you ask?"

"You know there's no room," Steel retorted.

Cruz watched Anchor and River haul Lever's corpse into a bathtub, then he dragged out his chemicals, completely aware he was at the center of our attention as he got to work.

"He deserves it. The shit he does for the club?"

"Giulia's been on at me about this. Has Keira gotten you to talk to me—"

I snorted. "If you think Keira wastes her words on club business, you're fucking mistaken."

He shot me a look. "She still giving you a hard time?"

"Things have been better since Rex visited."

"Why?"

"I get the feeling they had a talk."

Nyx whistled. "Rex and his talks."

"Doesn't give them often, but when he does, they pack a hell of a punch," I agreed.

Link, who'd finally stopped gagging, asked, "Where do you think they went?"

"Just for a ride. They'll be back. He was a ticking time bomb," I mused. "You saw how he was ghosting around the place, listening in, not talking... He only does that when he's about to lose his shit.

"Lever was just enough of a dumb fuck to do something disrespectful on a day like today."

"Think we should watch out for another explosion?" Steel queried.

I arched a brow. "Why are you asking me? You know him as well as I do."

Steel sniffed. "You were in his house when Bear made Rex pay for losing his temper."

"True." I hitched a shoulder. "Bear wasn't cruel."

More often than not, he'd made us go running around the compound together. That wasn't a punishment for me. Some days, running was the only time I'd felt free as a kid.

"Not saying he was, just saying that you've seen the aftermath of shit like this more than we have."

"That's why I know he'll go for a ride then come home."

What was a ride if not a better version of running?

I shoved my hands into my pockets, watching the chemical steam start to rise from the bath where Cruz was at work. He was wearing a gas mask, which was creepy as fuck. I hated those fucking things. They made people look like they'd been bitten by were-ants.

"You heard that Rach's pregnant?"

I nodded at Link's question. "I heard. Also heard about you getting arrested, fuckface," I directed at Nyx.

He shoved me. "Fuck off."

"Are you seriously going off on this crusade?"

Nyx reached up and twisted his neck until it cracked. "Rex ain't the only one close to blowing his top."

"Thought you made a promise."

"Did. Ain't breaking it."

"It's a sidestep, ain't it?" I queried, tone doubtful.

"Indy didn't want my ass in jail; she wanted me to protect my family—I'll be able to do that."

"Because O'Donnelly can keep the cops away...?" I let the words fall flat. "No one's that powerful. Not forever."

"Maybe not everywhere in the US, but New York's his playground. Since the Sparrows were drawn out of the woodwork, the Five Points have been consolidating power." He stared at Cruz who was busy destroying evidence. "Going out of my mind. Last couple months have been rough."

Link sighed. "He ain't wrong. Been one hit after another. This ain't exactly gonna be great for morale. Rex came back from Cali with change in mind. People don't like change, never mind MC brothers."

He wasn't wrong.

Neither was he right.

"I don't think this'll be bad for morale," I disagreed. "It's a sign of strength. Brothers forget what Rex can do because he don't do it often. A reminder's always good. Plus, when you patch in Harlow, he'll be a brother too."

"He ain't made to be a brother," Steel said grimly. "He ain't got the stomach for it."

"He can grow a stomach," Nyx rumbled. "Give him time."

"If it were anyone else, we wouldn't bother," was all Steel said.

"Well, that's the point. He isn't anyone else, is he? He's Jessie Dresden's brother, and he saw us kill Samuel Haune. He has leverage over us, but we have it over him too."

I cast Nyx a glance. "You like him, don't you?"

Nyx grumbled, "I don't like anyone."

Link let loose a laugh as he hijacked Nyx and dragged him into a noogie. "You know you love us."

"Fuck off," Nyx snapped, shoving him away before he folded his arms across his chest again. "You're my family. I don't have to like you."

I snorted. "You say the sweetest shit."

Nyx just flipped me the bird.

"He's not all bad," Sin stated.

"Who? Nyx?" I teased.

"Well, him too. I meant Harlow. He's smart."

"He is?" Link questioned.

"Very. Got talking to him about some shit from the Bible one day last week—"

"Since when were you into religion?"

"He didn't try to ram it down my throat," Sin said, ignoring Steel. "He just explained what he was reading and drew a parallel to today. He'll be good in an admin role around the club."

"Speaking of, I finally got some men trained up for the strip joint. Nyx, you okay with me bringing Hawk deeper into managing the day-to-day security—"

"Ain't my say you need," Nyx interrupted.

Sin grimaced. "Been asking you for so long now, I forget I gotta consult Rex first. Sorry."

"Don't be."

I eyed Nyx. "You don't miss acting as Prez?"

Nyx shook his head. "No. I'm not made to lead."

"Bullshit. You are. You're just not meant to be the one who has the final say. All these dipshits here look up to you, don't they? Sin just fucking did it in front of us."

Nyx wriggled his shoulders. "You going somewhere with this?"

"No. Just saying you should watch yourself. No one is untouchable."

"Ain't that the point?" he countered grimly.

I sighed. "I just want you with your family, Nyx. Don't want you torn apart from them like I was before Keira agreed to bring Cyan to Ohio."

"Giulia'd never let Nyx catch a break," Link mocked.

"Fuck off, Link," Nyx grated out. "Stop saying shit about her like that. She gets it. She gets me. Yes, she's a whack job, and yes, it's funny, but I'm just as crazy as she is, and she accepts me. She's my fucking life—"

"If she was, wouldn't you be able to stop with this hunting shit?"

Nyx set dead eyes on me. "When Giulia found out her dad was a rapist, she asked me if the buzzing in her head would go away. I couldn't lie to her, so I told her that it didn't. *And it doesn't.* It blankets everything, all of my senses until I feel like it blinds me and deafens me. Until it's on my fucking tongue, on my skin, in my nose, tainting the very air I breathe.

"Indy asked me to make a promise to be there for my kid, and I'd rather die than leave Giules alone to raise our baby, but the truth is, some fucking days, that buzzing is so goddamn loud I could claw it out of my head with a hammer.

"My woman knows what I'm going through. She feels it too. What fucking use is a father who sticks around only to claw his skull open with a hammer when his kid is ten? What fucking use is a man who can't function because all he can fucking hear and see is his sister being mauled by a monster?" He grabbed my shoulders and shook me. "I know what you're doing and I know it comes from a good place, but you took drugs to escape, and you're having to find a way out of that. And good for you, man.

"I'm proud of you. Fucking proud. Every day you're clean is a day I celebrate, and knowing you're doing what you can to get back with Keira makes me even fucking prouder. You're fixing your mistakes.

"But that's what I'm doing too. I'm not addicted to the kill. I do it to function."

"You don't think some days I took drugs to function too?" I saw the hell in his eyes and knew I was wasting my breath.

Nyx released a shuddery breath. "Hunting's my anti-depressant."

"You did well as acting-Prez. I know you did—maybe if Rex gave you more responsibilities," Steel started but Nyx stopped him.

"No. I don't want that. I'll stick as VP, and I'll be good at it, but the hunting... O'Donnelly means it. He knows how this feels. He has that fucking buzzing too. He has demons who haunt him. He'll keep me safe. You don't have to trust him, but I do. Because he knows how this works. He knows the only escape is taking that final breath—"

"Why are you talking like this, man?" Sin demanded. "You got too much to fucking live for."

"That's the exact reason. Because I need you to get on board with this. I need you to see that I'm going through with this because I feel safe in doing so, and this is a low-risk way of me living my life, of being there for my woman and kid."

There was so much I could have said, so much I wanted to, but I wasn't about to beat a dead horse.

Instead, I grabbed him by the nape, and I shoved my forehead against his. "You need to get out of town fast, come straight to Ohio. You hear me?"

"I hear you."

"Fucking promise me, Nyx."

"I promise," Nyx rasped.

I shoved him away. "Guess that's the only reassurance we'll get."

And, in the grand fucking scheme of things, it wasn't much of a reassurance at all.

FORTY-TWO

PARKER

BAZZI - MINE

I peered out onto the driveway when Rachel left, zipping away on the back of Rex's bike.

She hadn't even noticed that I was sitting on the veranda.

If she had, I knew she'd have been surprised.

It was taking every ounce of strength in my being to stay seated. Not to move. To stay still.

"I can do this, I can do this, I can do this," I whimpered in a rush, my hands curling around the edge of the seat until the wicker bit into them.

Tucked away in the shadows, I was properly placed to see a couple called Digger and MaryCat amble through the gates. Their baby was cute, and I'd agreed to sit for them while they went to the clubhouse. What else was I going to do? It was a great excuse for me not to leave the house, after all. But when I'd heard the music start up, a longing so raw had me facing my fears and forcing myself to drift outside to listen to the roar of sound.

I almost wished I'd been able to attend the ceremony—it had sounded wild. Alive. So unlike the funerals I'd attended as a child.

As MaryCat and Digger returned, their arms clinging to one another, a piercing longing shot through me.

I was so alone.

It was my own choice—but that didn't diminish how horrible it was to require that as a basic survival instinct.

Before they reached the house, someone called out, "Digger, you know where Storm went?"

"Think he headed to the Fridge with the others, didn't he?"

"Ah, shit."

The soft drawl of an accent had me peering through the darkness to the faces that were illuminated in the moonlight.

My brow furrowed as I saw the stranger when he hunched his shoulders and turned to glower at Digger.

He was on the thinner side, but his face was beautiful.

His cheeks were full, his brow wide, and his lips were soft even when they were pursed in irritation. But in his eyes, there was a kindness that I didn't think I was mistaking.

His hair flopped onto his forehead in a way that made my fingers crave to stroke it back, to touch him.

"What's wrong?"

"Wanted to talk to him about the arrangements for tomorrow."

"So late? Jesus, Sweet Lips, you're taking this too seriously. Go back to the clubhouse, get laid, and get drunk."

Sweet Lips?

That was his name?

I mean, he *did* have sweet lips. That was no lie but I didn't think road names were supposed to be complimentary. Why would the one called Nyx be called Nyx when that was a goddess' name and not a god's?

The MC brothers were strange, that was for sure.

Digger didn't wait for an answer, just buried his face in Mary-Cat's hair. He said something that had her chuckling, and it made it too awkward for me to tell them I was there, listening in, so I let them go inside, and I watched as Sweet Lips kept his hands stacked on his hips in annoyance, glaring over at Rachel's place.

As he approached the veranda, I tensed up.

When he climbed the stairs, rumbling, "Eavesdroppers never hear good of themselves," I thought my heart was going to combust.

"I wasn't eavesdropping," I said on a gasp. "Honestly! I was sitting here the whole time. I didn't hide on purpose."

Now he was under the veranda's canopy, much as they did for me, the shadows hid his expression. I heard a rustling sound, tensed up, then he muttered, "Want one?"

I squinted at him and barely saw the faint gleam of the wrapper in his hand.

"Cow Tales?"

He hummed. "My favorite."

Swallowing, I said, "Thank you but I'm fine." I really wanted the candy, but that would have required me to let go of the chair beneath me. That was impossible—my fingers were soldered in place now. "I haven't had anything like that in years."

I heard the wrapper shred beneath his fingers. "I couldn't live without candy. I'm guessing you heard my name? Loving candy is how I earned it. What's yours?"

Huh. Sweet Lips from the candy. Clearly, the brothers didn't recognize how truly sweet his lips were.

"I'm Parker." Nerves hit me. "I'm Rachel's assistant."

"Interesting."

"Interesting, how?"

"Just is. She shocked a lot of folks at the clubhouse tonight. There were plenty of mutterings about her."

"About Rachel?" I demanded with concern. "Why?"

"You're not with the MC, are you?"

"No."

"Can't tell you then, sweetheart."

I huffed. "She's my boss, but she's also my friend. Is that why she and Rex went racing off?"

"They came here?"

"They did."

"Interesting."

"Stop saying that."

"I can't. It *is* interesting."

Huffing out a breath, not realizing that I'd stopped clenching my fingers around the chair, I muttered, "Is that the only adjective you know?"

"You asking that because I'm a biker ergo I'm stupid or because I keep saying shit's interesting and I won't tell you why and you're being bitchy because you're curious?"

"Ergo?" Of everything he had to say, that stuck out like a sore thumb to me.

He shrugged. "It means—"

"I know what it means. I work for a lawyer. If you know what that is, then, you know another word for interesting."

"Might do, but that won't ease your curiosity." He clucked his tongue. "Your hands stopped clenching around the chair. You can relax again, honey. I ain't gonna hurt you. Might look mean but I'm not gonna bite."

I blinked. "I didn't think you would."

"No? Most people see the cut and nothing else. You want some candy now?"

Biting my lip, I told him, my voice rawer than I'd like, "If I take the candy, then I'll have to let go of the chair, and if I do that, then I might run inside."

"Why? Because you're scared of me?"

A hard laugh escaped me. "I'm scared of everything."

"Huh. That sounds annoying for you."

"You've no idea." I gnawed on my lip again. "Could you maybe feed me the candy?"

God, I really wanted that treat.

"You'd be okay with that?"

For candy, I would.

"More than okay."

"I got clean hands," he told me as the crinkling of another wrapper sounded loud in the silence on the veranda.

"I doubt it."

He paused. "Huh?"

"Do you know how many different types of bacteria live on your palms?" I pulled a face he couldn't see, explaining, "I used to be a germophobe."

"Is that something you grow out of?" he queried as he passed me the treat, placing it on my lips. "Bite down so that I can drag off the wrapping without touching it."

Well, hell, how considerate was that?

Doing as he'd bid, I savored the treat. The sugar hit me fast.

"Better than an orgasm, I swear," I mumbled once I was done chewing.

"Honey, I love candy, but you've been doing sex wrong if you think it's better than an orgasm."

I refused to blush. "I very likely have," was my prim retort. "And yes, I weaned myself off of being a germophobe. I had too many phobias. It was getting tiresome to juggle them all."

"Huh." He paused a second, grabbed another piece of candy and, before he ate it, asked, "How many phobias do you have?"

"Now? Two. Back then, it was like sixteen or something."

He coughed. "Sixteen?"

"Yeah." My nose crinkled. "See why it was tiresome?"

"I mean, maybe. If one of those was you being scared of sharks, it's not like you see a shark every day in New Jersey, is it?"

"I live in Pennsylvania," I corrected.

"They have sharks there?" he asked around a laugh.

"Only in aquariums," I retorted, but I was smiling. "I just don't go to them."

"Smart. So that's one of the phobias you still have?"

"Yes. I used to know someone who was terrified of frozen custard. Can you imagine?"

"I really can't," he said somberly before he cleared his throat. "So, you're scared of being outside, huh? Agoraphobia?"

I bit my lip. "Yes."

My voice was so tiny a frickin' mouse could have uttered that confirmation.

"Sitting out here's being brave for you, isn't it?"

"Very. Just being here period is too."

"Ah, yes. You're a Pennsylvania girl. You came for the funeral?"

I didn't correct him. Unfortunately for me, I was Jersey born and bred. Only unfortunate because my goddamn family were from here too, and I didn't like associating with anything to do with them.

That was why I'd moved.

Also why I'd stopped eating hoagies, and they were my favorite fucking thing in the world. Even more than candy.

"I sort of did."

"Sort of? You didn't know Bear? Not that I really did. He was before my time."

"No. I only know him through my boss."

"So, why'd you come?"

I grimaced. "My roommate failed to tell me that she'd have collectors coming around to grab all our furniture as payment for her debts."

He stilled. "That's really shitty."

"Right?" I demanded, still beyond pissed, and he was the first person I'd told about this. The person I *could* tell, Rachel, had so much on right now that I didn't feel like I could add to her stress.

"They took all your possessions?"

"Apart from my computer."

"How did you salvage that?"

I sucked in a breath. "I ran off with that, my phone, and my wallet."

"That's all you have to your name?" he questioned, his shock clear.

Trying not to cry, I whispered, "It is now."

"Fuck! That's not right. Not at all. Come on, we'll go there now and I'll get your stuff back."

My eyes flared wide in bewilderment. "What? No! I couldn't ask that of you."

"Jesus Christ, Parker, that's disgustin'. I don't have an Old Lady anymore—" Did he sound bitter about that or was it just me? "—got nothing to spend my cut on. Let me help you."

I knew if he'd seen me in the light, I'd have looked like a fish out of water with how my mouth was opening and closing the way it was, but what in the frickin' fuck?

"I can't ask you to do that," I denied.

"You didn't ask me. I offered."

"Because it wouldn't be fair to you. You don't know me. R-Rachel would help if I asked—"

"You haven't told her? Or is she a bitch who'd let you be tossed out on your ass without a damn thing to your name?"

"She's a bitch but not in that sense," I muttered, my fingers tightening around the seat again. He somehow knew because his hand settled on mine. His warmth was... *Goodness.* I blew out a breath. "And she'd help me if I told her. I had clothes and stuff delivered today and she didn't say anything."

"Why haven't you told her? And why the hell didn't she say anything when you practically moved in?"

"Because she's pregnant, which is super stressful for her, and then there's this situation with Bear and Rex and everything. Business is crazy right now."

"She shouldn't be too busy for friends."

My nose crinkled. "You don't understand what being pregnant means for her. She's terrified of the doctors—"

"You bonded over phobias, didn't you?"

"Jerk."

He chuckled. "Couldn't resist."

"And we did talk about my staying. She told me I could have the spare room for as long as I needed."

"Do you think she meant for the next decade though?"

I couldn't stop myself from laughing, but I jolted when his fingers pried mine off the chair, and he soothed, "There." He gently squeezed them. "Let me help you."

"Why would you even want to?" I questioned weakly.

"Because I've been in bad spots and I'd have liked someone to help me out."

"You're a Good Samaritan?"

"The very best kind. I wear leather."

Snickering, I tugged on my hand. "You don't need to—"

"What? Wear leather? Trust me, it suits me."

I couldn't stop myself from grinning. "You know what I mean."

"I know I don't have to help you out. Doesn't mean I won't."

I bit the inside of my cheek. "It's not safe."

"Why isn't it?"

"They weren't..." I swallowed. "They weren't like agents from the bank."

He paused. "Loan shark?"

"Yes," I whispered.

I could sense his mind racing, but the first thing he asked was, "Did they touch you?"

"No. They broke down the door and went straight into her room. When I realized what was happening, I was too scared to confront them, and when they were removing the TV, I grabbed the things I need to work and got the heck out of there."

He gently squeezed my fingers again—it was a soft pulsation that was oddly reassuring.

"Workaholic, huh?"

"What?"

"You didn't grab clothes or pictures of your family or your first dog—you saved *'the things I need to work,'*" he quoted.

My brow puckered. "I need to work to pay for the things that were taken."

Though he hummed, and that felt like a judgment in itself, he only said, "Fair point. Are you scared I'll get hurt or are you too scared to leave the veranda?"

I exhaled softly. "Both."

"Well, you don't have to worry about my being hurt. They might call me Sweet Lips but not every part of me is sweet."

"Good to know."

He chuckled, and it was low, and deep, and dark, and... I gulped.

"Now, the getting off the veranda thing, lemme see, have you ever been on the back of a bike?"

"No," I yelped. "And I don't want to either."

"Sure you do," he said easily. "You can never feel freer than when you are on a hog."

"I don't like feeling free. I like feeling—"

"Caged in?" He scoffed. "I don't think so. Your fear is a cage, and your apartment, or whatever place you're trapped in, is a construct of that fear."

Huffing, I muttered, "You a therapist or something?"

"Nah, just watch a lot of daytime talk shows."

"You're a strange kind of biker."

"Honey, we're all strange." If it were daylight, I figured he'd have winked at me. I almost resented the darkness because it meant I missed it. "Will you let me help you?"

The interest of moments ago faded to be replaced by soul-sucking fear. "I-I don't think I can," I whispered, feeling the panic overtake everything else.

I didn't realize I was breathing hard, that I was on the edge of an anxiety attack until he was on his knees in front of me, breathing with me, both his hands on mine now—when had I let go of the chair entirely?

My body tensed with the urge to get up and run inside, but he was there, and he smelled good—leather and aftershave—and his breath scented of vanilla, and his hands were rough but warm, and—

My breathing edged out.

"You're doing so well, sweetheart. Come on, just breathe with me. Take it easy, take it easy."

His soft words settled deep inside me, in a place they had no business settling, in all honesty, but settle they goddamn did.

The gentle pressure of his fingers, the softness of his words, the praise in them, the desire to help—*who was this man?*

The spots in my vision stopped dancing, and my heart slowed down so I didn't hear the rushing of my pulse in my ears.

"—doing so well, Parker," he repeated. "Just take it nice and easy. We're in no rush—"

I choked out, "Who are you? Why are you being so kind?"

"Ah, honey, that you even have to ask me that tells me you're used to men being fuckers." He graced me with another gentle squeeze. "Can I bribe you with Cow Tales to get you on my bike?"

The bribe didn't work even though we both gave it our best effort —I was actually feeling sick of candy by the time he ran out.

But for an hour, he tried to get me off the veranda. He *really* tried. He didn't lose patience once. I wouldn't have blamed him if he had. I was annoyed with myself. And as I cried through my exasperation, that was when I found myself sitting on his lap, being held by him.

This was insane.

Crazy.

Lunacy.

And it was also the start of something I could never have anticipated when I'd rushed out of my apartment two days ago in a fit of terror so strong that it blanketed my agoraphobia, making me do what would have been impossible a week earlier.

Fate, I'd realize later, had a weird way of working out...

FORTY-THREE

REX

"Do you think Quin knows this place isn't a sanctuary for dogs?"

I cut Nyx a look. "That chihuahua just won't leave you alone, huh?"

He huffed.

Because that was all he had to 'say,' my lips twitched in response.

Ever since the funeral, the dogs had become more of an issue. It was clear they were starting to believe this was their territory, and as a result, Nyx had two buddies that followed him from the compound to Rachel's place.

I returned my attention to the window where the Newfoundlander was staring right back at us, jowls loaded down with drool, tongue lolling out of the side of its jaw. And where the big brute was, Lucifer's chihuahua was close by.

"How many still to leave?"

"A couple from Montana who stuck around because they were too hammered to ride back. Storm's chapter."

"I'd prefer them to stay," I admitted.

Link chuckled. "Then they'd be the New Jersey chapter."

Sighing, I said, "I know."

I missed having Storm around. When he wasn't getting high, he was one of the few who could keep up with me. In the last couple years, getting high had been his MO though.

Ohio had done him good. Becoming Prez had been even better for him. Now he just needed to get back with Keira.

"You think they'll make a go of it?"

I peered at Link who shuffled up beside me. "I dunno. I hope so. She danced with him at the funeral, didn't she?"

Link cleared his throat. "Wasn't sure if you noticed that."

"Couldn't have blamed you if you didn't," Nyx said, his tone forthright. "It was a tough day."

Hell if he wasn't right—and I didn't like agreeing with Nyx about anything.

On principle.

I rubbed my chin. "I think she wants to be with him."

Link heaved a sigh as he raised an arm and leaned against the wall.

The rev of an engine drew all our attention, and as he took in the flashy green hog that had graffiti styled into the bodywork, Link muttered, "I don't like that dipshit Angelo. Who the fuck gets named after a *Teenage Mutant Ninja Turtle* and then shortens it?"

"Are you more offended that he isn't going by the full moniker Michelangelo or that he's named after a *Teenage Mutant Ninja Turtle* when he's a Sinner—" Before Nyx could finish his question, he was yelling, "That dumb fuck!"

I didn't even see what was happening until it was too late.

The fucking chihuahua.

It came prancing out of nowhere, heading straight for the Newfoundlander.

Which just happened to require crossing into Angelo's path.

"Fuck!" I shouted, dragging the window open and yelling, "Angelo! Stop your fucking bike!"

But he didn't hear me over his engine, and apparently he was fucking blind because he didn't see the dog.

Until it yelped.

Nyx got clipped as he dragged it into his arms, and he fell back on his hip, the chihuahua yipping its outrage all the while.

"Goddammit, stop biting me! I just saved your ungrateful ass," Nyx boomed.

Link coughed. "We shouldn't laugh."

My lips would've twitched if I wasn't too busy yelling at Angelo. "What the fuck do you think you're doing riding when you're still drunk?"

That could be the only reason why he hadn't seen the animal.

Sure, it was tiny, but no way should he have failed to spot it.

"Huh, Prez?" Angelo questioned, shooting me a dopey look that just confirmed he was about to ride home under the fucking influence.

Nostrils flaring in outrage at his idiocy, that was apparently what it took for Angelo to finally realize he'd pissed me the fuck off.

I figured news had spread about Lever because he pretty much leaped off his bike and darted over to help Nyx who pushed him away, yelling, "You fucking asshole. Didn't you see the goddamn dog in front of you?"

Angelo had the grace to hunch his shoulders. "I'm sorry, man. It blended in with the road."

"The yellow dog blended in with asphalt and white stones?" Nyx punched him in the shoulder even as he was holding the dog by the scruff because it kept on trying to bite him. "You fucking high or something? I get that you were drunk, but it's either that you're jacked up or you need goddamn glasses."

Content that Nyx was gonna rip him a new one, especially when I saw him demand Angelo's keys, I left my VP to it, monitoring the altercation until I heard Nyx punish him.

Angelo, head bowed, slouched toward the clubhouse to help Giulia in the kitchen—might not have seemed like a hardcore punishment, but she was a bitch when armed with a cleaver.

Nyx, still holding the chihuahua, grabbed his cell from his pocket and tapped out a text. I half-expected it to make a phone ping in here but it didn't.

"Must be texting Giulia," Steel mused, watching everything from the table.

He had an ice pack on his eye because he'd apparently gotten into a fight with one of the Ohio Chapter about a game of cards. *Asswipe.*

Nyx hobbled across the path toward the compound. His limp was definitely pronounced, and from how he was holding himself, I didn't think he'd only hit his hip on the way down.

"Think he's okay?" Sin asked. "He's just healed up from that beating at the precinct."

"Angelo was going fast enough to clip him badly," Maverick pointed out, and how the hell he'd noticed that when he was doing something on his computer, I'd never fucking know. "Reckon he'll be bruised. Nothing broken unless he landed funny on his hand."

Seeing how Nyx was holding the dog with one while texting with the other, I figured he hadn't landed badly on either wrist.

The second Nyx set it beside the Newfoundlander, the chihuahua went for his boots. So, clearly, it was okay too.

Snorting, I murmured, "I didn't know I needed to see this today. Better than a show on TV."

"Well, much as I agree you needed something to cheer you up, I promise this wasn't scripted," Sin mocked, shaking his head as Nyx had to detangle the 'beast' from the cuff of his jeans.

"Not sure you can be 'cheered up' after a funeral," Maverick mused. "You just have to get out of the headspace, don't you?"

I shrugged. "Woke up in a piss-poor mood, but Rachel was puking so, in the grand scheme of things, I chose life and made her some tea rather than stay wallowing in bed."

Link grimaced. "She's still getting sick?"

"The doctor said it'd get better now she's in her second trimester. Got her results back from her latest bloodwork—everything's fine," I said with no small amount of relief.

"Fuck, you and Nyx are gonna be dads. It's insane."

"I'm already a dad," I said tonelessly.

"Yeah," Link groused, "but you've been a dad for like five minutes to me. I gotta get used to the notion. It's freaking me the fuck out."

I snorted as I picked up my cell. Seeing Wynter hadn't texted me this morning, I sent her another.

Me: *You doing okay, sweetheart?*

I knew all wasn't well with her, not with how quiet she'd been recently, but I was waiting for her to come to me about it. It was hard going. I wanted to fix shit, but it wasn't my place unless she made it mine.

Deciding I'd talk about it with Rachel tonight, see if we agreed we should push Wynter to talk about whatever she was going through, I turned around as Nyx limped into the office.

"Did you see that fuckwit?" he growled.

"I thought you dealt with the situation admirably," Sin said with a hoot, earning himself the bird Nyx flipped him.

When my VP slouched in his seat at the council table, he grunted, "That hurt like a motherfucker. I just knew I was gonna land on the goddamn dog so I had to twist out of the way. Otherwise, there'd have been no point in me trying to save the little bastard from Angelo."

"Did you get Giulia to give him the shitty jobs in the kitchen?" Mav asked, his gaze drifting from his computer to look at Nyx.

"She says she's got plenty for him to do," he said with no small degree of satisfaction.

"You know, any other Old Lady," Steel mumbled, "I'd say that wasn't much of a punishment. Definitely not one worthy of drunk driving, but I wouldn't wish Giulia on Satan."

Nyx's lips cocked up in a grin. "Yeah, she puts the Satan in Satan's Sinners."

Though I rolled my eyes, I watched as he rubbed his hip then checked out his wrist, stretching it as if it were tender.

"You okay?"

"I'll be fine."

"You should adopt those dogs," Mav commented. "The Newfoundlander would be a good guard dog."

"What'd the chihuahua be? A lapdog?" Link teased.

"Not if Nyx wants to keep the one ball he didn't give to Giulia when he branded her," Sin joked.

"Fuck off," Nyx muttered.

"You're moving out of our place this week, aren't you?" I asked Nyx. "Might not be a bad idea. They're clearly attached to you."

He scowled at me. "You kidding me? What the hell would I do with two dogs?"

"Give 'em somewhere else to shit other than here?" Link pointed out cheerfully as he sank into his own seat at the table.

Nyx grunted. "Great."

"Ask Giulia," I encouraged.

"I don't want pets."

"To be fair, you didn't want an Old Lady, and now you've got one of them *and* a kid on the way."

Nyx glowered at Sin. "You looking to get your ass kicked?"

"Seeing as you're hobbling around, now'd be a good time to get into it."

Though I snorted, I pivoted to give Maverick my attention. "Mav, you're the one who called a council meeting today. What's going on?"

"I checked Grizzly's SS number. His death is officially recorded and since that date, his SS number has been inactive."

I blew out a breath. "You think that means he's really dead?"

"I do. We just don't know what your dad did with his body."

"That doesn't feel like closure. He could be living under another identity. Social security numbers aren't exactly hard to come by," Steel pointed out, tilting his head and rubbing at his chin when the ice pack started dripping.

"That's the best that I can do," Maverick said with a shrug. "I've looked as deep as I'm able, but it's like hunting for a needle in the US.

"Bear went ahead with everything as if Grizzly *were* dead. The undertaker bill was paid; public records were updated. Bear legally filed him as deceased. That's not something I imagine he'd fake. Not sure why he'd even go to as much effort as he did."

"Who the fuck knows what Dad's capable of now," I groused, staring back out the window, watching as the Newfoundlander settled down on the ground and the chihuahua climbed on him and lay down in his fur.

Though I'd heard it yip upon Angelo's approach, it appeared to be okay.

"You need to remember who your dad was," Link griped, drawing my attention away from the dogs and over to him. "He made mistakes; ain't we all made 'em in our time? Won't we make plenty fucking more before we die? What he did don't take away from how good a dad he was, Rex. And he wasn't just your father. You're dissing on the man who was like a dad to all of us—"

"He has a point," Maverick muttered.

"He does," Sin agreed.

"Dead on," said Steel.

"Yeah," Nyx rumbled. "Bear fucked up, but you need to let it go, Rex."

My mouth pursed tight, so fucking tight I must have looked like a goddamn prune.

Rationally, I knew they were right. Feelings, however, weren't always rational.

And I couldn't dismiss their words, not without dismissing their worth to my father.

He *had* raised us. Been there when these dipshits' dads had either fucked off or done fuck all.

I didn't want to hurt them, nor did I want to argue with them, so I just shut my goddamn mouth.

Fortune favored me because Lodestar changed the subject. The door slammed inward and, unapologetic as ever, she stormed in.

In her hand, she had a plastic file and she slapped it on the table.

"That fucker is on your dad's murder board, Rex."

"Which fucker?" I demanded, too accustomed to her inherent disrespect of my rules to care that she'd stormed into a council session.

"Francis Merriweather. The pedophile Aidan O'Donnelly Sr. wants Nyx and Harlow to kill—"

"Have you been listening in on council meetings again?" Steel groused.

She ignored him. "He's a fucking Sparrow!" She balled her hands into fists and rammed them into the table. The boom jolted most of the shit on its surface, making them, in turn, rattle. "You know what that goddamn means, don't you?"

It hadn't been outside the realms of possibility, not with all the shit the Sparrows were into, but until now, I'd never heard anything about this... From her horror, she hadn't come across it yet either.

Jaw working, I grated out, "The NWS dealt in kids too."

Lodestar shot Nyx a look. "I want in on this deal you've got going with the Five Points."

Fuck.

I attempted, "Lodestar—"

Nyx spoke over me, "You got it."

She dipped her chin. "Tell me when, where, and how, and I'll help."

With that, she strode out as quickly as she'd stormed in, bringing war to our door. A war that, in all honesty, was impossible *not* to get behind.

RACHEL

Parker peered around the office door. "Want some tea?"

"If I pee anymore, I might as well just work out of the bathroom."

She snorted. "You could have kept it simple and *polite* and said that you didn't want any."

"Since when do we not overshare?" I shot her a sweet smile. "Oh, wait, since now seeing as you're lying to me about that baby shower I know you're organizing."

Parker folded her arms across her chest. "You're paranoid, do you know that?"

"Oh, I'm sure." I sniffed, but before I could pepper her for more information, my cell rang. When I saw Hunter's Caller ID, I snatched my phone and snapped, "Have you been avoiding my calls?"

Recognizing the tone, Parker backed out of the line of fire, gently closing the door behind her.

"With a greeting like that, who could blame me?" Hunter intoned, sounding grimmer than usual.

"Are you or are you not related to the De Laurentiises? The *Camorra* De Laurentiises?"

I still couldn't believe that this was news to me.

That I'd learned it from Dead To Me pissed me off more than anything.

And that I hadn't been able to get in touch with him since her call was beyond annoying.

He heaved a sigh and I chose to believe that it *sounded* guilty. "You could have asked Lodestar that."

"Why would I ask her when I could just ask you? You're one of my best friends—I should know little things like you being a part of a crime family."

Another rough exhalation sounded down the line. "It's not my fault I've got blood ties with the Camorra."

"No, it's not your fault, but you could have goddamn told me. That's why you have the hit out on you, isn't it? What the hell have you done?"

"Nothing. I haven't done anything," he grated out. "Nothing worthy of a hit at least, goddammit. You have to understand, Rachel, I never asked for any of this.

"My parents broke away from that side of the family when they moved to Sicily when I was a small kid. I didn't even know my grandfather until he approached me after college and invited me to live in Vegas. I came because what the hell else was I going to do? Follow you and Rory around the country?

"He promised that he wouldn't get me involved in the business. That he just wanted to get to know me. The bitch of it is, he meant it. It's only these last two years that I've even gotten a pinkie muddled up in their trade, and that's simply because he's old and sick.

"Now, he's going to be on fucking trial too—"

My ears pricked at that. "What? Why didn't you call me? I can't practice law there, but I could advise. I'm sure he's paying for the best, but another set of eyes on a mob case is never a bad thing."

"He's old school," he muttered, his tone *finally* apologetic.

"My ovaries make me less capable of getting him out of this?"

Hunter grunted. "Yeah. Otherwise I'd have had you on the next plane out here. The idea of him dying inside is hell. But I don't know if that's gonna happen or not. He's done plenty of worse shit than what they're charging him for. I don't want him to go to jail, Rach. I love the cranky old bastard."

It was very common for criminals involved in organized crime to be Caponed, and the reason for that was the DAs had a brilliant success rate in getting powerful men behind bars on the simplest of charges.

Take Luciu Valentini—his ass could have rotted for a couple years in prison for that desecration of a burial site.

He'd done plenty worse, but that was what could have had them locking him up and throwing away the key as they found 'ways' to extend his time inside.

I didn't often fear the counts of murder one, but the pathetic charges packed more of a punch than most could imagine, and took a great deal of skill to maneuver out of.

"So, you think the hit on you is because you're the natural heir?"

"I mean, I assume so. I genuinely haven't done anything worthy of being targeted by a hit man. Not since... you know. I've kept on the downlow. It has to be because of who I'm related to."

I released a soft sigh. "Send me what you can from your grandfather's case?"

"No. You have enough going on. How's my niece or nephew?"

"They're making me need to pee a lot, and I'm not even that big yet."

"You're in an oversharing mood."

"I'm tired," I admitted. "This week has been rough. Bear had his funeral, and Rex..." Jesus, Rex had been at his lowest.

"How are things between you and him?"

"We're together."

"You are? Really?"

"It's awesome." I knew I sported a dopey smile. "Which is saying something because it hasn't been easy."

"I'm glad, Rach. So fucking glad. I appreciate that you're willing to take the time to check out my grandfather's situation, but honey, he's got enough lawyers on the case to fill out a football team. They can't work miracles, and neither can you.

"But, what you can do, is try to take a step back. You're pregnant now. You need to chill out more."

"If life would accommodate that, I would." Worry hit me even though he'd just told me to calm down. "Are you safe?" Dead To Me was still a threat.

"Yeah. I have everything delivered in, and my place is secure. Granddad saw to that."

My brow puckered. "He did?"

"He's paranoid. Has been ever since the Fieris took down the Valentinis."

Knowing the intimate details of Currau Valentini's case—where he'd been accused of killing his entire family so that he could take over as Don, but was, in fact, only the patsy for the Fieris—I didn't exactly blame Hunter's grandfather for being cautious.

Strange things, *horrific* things, happened all the time in this game.

It wasn't a safe world to inhabit.

"Keep me updated?" I asked softly.

"I will. You too. I promise I'll be better about communicating."

"You'd think for a man who was stuck at home you'd have more time on your hands."

Hunter chuckled. "You would, but I'm busier than ever."

"I'll let you get on with your day. Stay safe, Hunter."

"I will. If Dead To Me gets in touch, tell me what she wants and I'll get it to you."

"Will do. Speak soon."

As we hung up, I pinched my bottom lip.

Everyone had secrets; logically, I knew that. But was Rory aware of who her childhood friend was related to? Were her brothers?

Somehow, I didn't think so, which was going to be a massive problem if, once this BS with the hitwoman was over, Hunter still intended to claim Rory this year...

But that was tomorrow's problem.

I had enough shit to deal with today without worrying about that, and worry was an understatement because when everything fell apart, both of them would come running to me. Somehow, *some-frickin'-how*, they'd both expect me to fix things for them.

"That," I mumbled under my breath as I reached for an antacid for the heartburn that was incoming, "is a nightmare waiting to happen."

FORTY-FIVE

REX

When I woke up and she wasn't there, I stared blankly at her pillow, almost as if looking hard enough would let me figure out her location.

A yawn escaped me, tiredness had my eyes drooping, but I wanted to know where she was so I could check up on her.

Her sleep wasn't perfect; the nightmares weren't going anywhere, but she seemed better at dealing with them. At least, I hadn't woken up with her punching me in the past week, so I considered that massive progress.

With another yawn, I got to my feet, rolling off the bed before I could fall asleep. I dragged on my boxer briefs, trudged out into the hall and down the stairs.

When I found her in the kitchen, I smiled, noticing she was diving into one of the endless tubs of ice cream her friend Hunter had sent her.

She caught me watching her in the doorway, and she waggled the tub at me. "Want some?"

About to say no, I blinked when I realized I actually *could* eat some.

Yawning yet again, I moved toward the table as she shifted from her chair. Accepting the silent invitation, I seated myself then smiled as she perched on my lap.

She dug into the tub then twisted to let the spoon hover in front of my lips.

I opened, let her feed me, and savored the taste of the frozen treat.

"Did you know that you don't eat as many sweets when you're sad?"

Finishing the bite, I pondered that. "Really?"

"Really." She peeped at me from under her lashes as she enjoyed some ice cream. "Thought you might go into withdrawals."

"You're sweet enough for me."

"That was so sugary you gave me diabetes."

"Can you catch it with words?" I teased, lips quirking before I opened them to accept more ice cream.

Her eyes warmed with her smile, and it had heat unfurling inside me. "You can catch anything with words."

A single solid truth unfurled inside me and it had me pressing my mouth to her temple and telling her, "Not sure how I'd have gotten through these last couple weeks without you, baby girl."

She shrugged. "That works both ways."

"I doubt it." I swallowed. "Thank you for sticking by me."

She'd seen me do things she shouldn't have had to see. Things I'd have preferred her to be in the dark about.

"I don't consider it sticking by you."

"No?"

"Where else would I be? Why would I leave?"

"A lot of women would be scared."

Snorting, Rach retorted, "Why would I be scared of you? For you? Hell, yes. But not *of* you." She clucked her tongue as she scraped the last couple spoonfuls of ice cream from the container.

"You've seen too much violence in your short life."

"Some people attract it, I think," she mused. "Like shit and flies."

"Which are you?"

She shoved me. "I'm the honey and the bees."

"You picked the metaphor, not me," I teased, sliding my hand up and down her arm. "What woke you up?"

Her smile was oddly bright. "Grizzly," she chirped. "But I got him this time."

"You got him?"

"I did. They forced me in the living room—" She said it without tensing up and with such ease, I had to blink. "There was nothing to grab, but I remember I was eating ice cream when they came in." Rach grabbed the spoon she'd just been using and studied the handle. "I should have stabbed one of them with it."

My brows rose. "That's what you did in your nightmare?"

"Yeah. Made me crave ice cream." She pulled a face. "Weird, huh?"

"Nah." I wished she *had* fucking stabbed them. That'd make both of us feel a hell of a lot better. "I'm just glad you're dealing with the nightmares better."

"You like not being smacked in the gut whenever I close my eyes around you?"

"Well, I didn't want to say anything..." I drawled, which made her snicker.

"Such a gentleman."

"Only for you."

"The best kind," she said on a hum, angling her head back so that she could rest it against my shoulder.

Taking that for the invitation it was, I pressed my mouth to hers, gracing her with a gentle peck before I licked her lips, savoring the remnants of the vanilla ice cream she'd been eating.

She tasted better than that.

Letting my tongue explore her to my heart's content and given my body's craving for her, I reached around her waist to shape her curves, cupping her tit, squeezing it gently as she nipped my bottom lip and started to give as good as she got.

Tender affection surged into urgent need before that was swallowed up by a hunger so fierce we were both slaves to it.

Twisting around, our mouths still united, she moved to straddle me. Her weight shifted, and I felt more pressure on my lap. She angled her hips, rocking them slightly as she began to grind into me.

No way in hell was I going to complain.

She dragged her fingers through my hair, pulling away so that she could move down and suck on my throat, nibbling the sinews before tonguing the area.

I wasn't as sensitive as I knew she was, but when she grazed me with her teeth, I gritted mine and let my hands finds her hips.

With her wearing an oversized tee, I took immediate advantage and dragged at the hem, tightening it about her waist, clenching the soft cotton in my fist, even as I tugged it up.

With that one hand, I supported her, encouraging her to grind down harder against my dick, but I also exposed her ass to anyone who might look through the door.

It was a stark reminder of where we were.

"What is it about this goddamn kitchen and us?" I groused.

A laugh escaped her, and I felt the curve of her lips against my pulse as she slid her tongue over the throbbing flesh. "Where better to feast than here?"

God, I needed to taste that smile.

Moving one hand to the back of her head, I snagged her ponytail in my fist and tilted her face down so I could kiss her.

Thrusting my tongue against hers, I swallowed her groan as I reached between her legs and found her slick and hot and ready for me.

Rubbing her clit with my fingertips, I breathed for her as she froze atop me. Her heart pounded and she seemed to quiver in place, her legs throbbing with tension as she used her tiptoes to stay upright.

When she began to writhe against me, I grinned and murmured, "So wet for me, baby girl."

She shuddered as I slid my hand down so that the butt of it was rubbing along her clit and I could thrust a finger into her.

She was always so fucking tight that I hissed with need. No wonder she had a chokehold on my dick when this was the only place it wanted to be.

Gently testing her bottom lip, biting it hard enough to leave imprints, I pressed down on the front wall of her pussy, finding that spongy tissue that'd make her squirm even more on top of me.

Of course, that was when, upstairs, there was a noise.

This fucking house really was turning into a hostel.

Both of us stilled, our eyes wide, lips locked again, my finger inside her as footsteps sounded, a door creaked.

Slowly, I kept up the grinding motion of the heel of my hand against her clit.

A muted sob escaped her and I watched—*I fucking watched*—her eyes blur. Reality faded and delirious pleasure overtook them.

Enthralled by her, I continued with my teasing, keeping it slow, too slow to do much for her, but enough to hold her on the edge.

I didn't want to fucking know who was doing what upstairs—I still wasn't sure if Harlow and Rain were into each other that way—but when the sound of steps on the staircase drifted toward us, she mewled against my mouth and my hand sped up.

I kissed her to swallow the noise, but I was ready to cover her ass, just waiting for whoever it was to burst into the kitchen—especially with the light on.

Talk about an open invitation.

It could've been Parker, Rain, or Harlow—even with Nyx and Giulia gone, it was still a full fucking house.

But we were in luck.

Whoever it was, and I'd bet it was Harlow because he avoided people like they had the plague, he moved over to the front door and pulled it open.

Just as a light flickered on outside, her pussy clamped down around me, and she tore her mouth from mine to push her hand to it to still the cries.

As she tensed up when the pleasure hit, I let her grind down harder, to the point where my dick felt the pressure and started to get jealous, even as I was enjoying watching her get off.

When she was done, she pressed her forehead against mine and panted as if she'd run a race.

But we weren't done.

I retreated, dragging my finger out of her slit, enjoying her hissed breath brushing up against my lips, all while I delved between us to drag my cock out.

She knew what I was doing because she angled her hips, tilted her ass back, and let me find her gate.

Gracing me with a choked cry as she slid down onto me, gravity did me the favor of impaling her on my cock.

Each inch was hard won because her cunt was clutching at me, not about to welcome me after she'd come, but she was the one who was squirming to fill herself up with my dick. As for me, I just sat back and enjoyed the show.

When her ass was sitting on my lap, her knees digging into my hips, I grabbed her butt cheeks and spread them apart, letting my fingers dip in so I had a firm hold on her. She'd have yelped as I surged to my feet, but she was aware enough to know her limits, and her mouth notched itself to my shoulder. Fuck if that didn't feel good when she bit down.

The pressure of her sinking onto me was so intense, my eyes almost rolled into the back of my head.

Each footstep was a sweet torment as I aimed for the stairs and slowly walked us up the steps. Each one was bittersweet. The jolt of each thrust had me seeing fucking stars but concentrating on not falling was a pain in the ass.

This was definitely not one of my better ideas.

Except, she was as into it as I was, and the way she kissed me and clung to me made me feel like we'd never been closer.

I didn't speed up the stairs, just kept it slow, and that seemed to drive her even wilder. By the time I made it to the top, she was panting and her writhing had me burning to fuck her hard.

As I walked us down the hall toward our room, when I closed the door, she cried out, "Oh. Dear. God. King, fuck me. Please. Fuck me, fuck me, fuck me!"

The chant was the best song in the world.

Taking advantage of our privacy, I dragged her shirt off, realizing that it was one of mine at the last moment.

Loving that she was wearing my stuff, I thrust my tongue into her mouth to shut up that chant of hers before I shot my wad too soon. The sound of my woman, desperate for our union, was like setting a bomb off in my brain.

I pressed her onto the bed, positioned her legs so that her knees were spread wide, resting against the mattress, and I placed my palms on the backs and used that as a fulcrum.

Then I gave her what she asked for.

Her hand snapped to her mouth as she cried out at the first, fast thrust, and the sight of her, pussy full of my cock, lips spread wide, tits shaking, her curves on full display, was the most beautiful fucking thing I'd ever seen.

Unable to stop myself from touching her, I kept one hand pinning her knee down and the other shaping her tit, pinching the nipple before I moved back to her pussy.

She was so fucking wet, and I tested how full she was with the tips of my fingers, putting pressure on my cock but also on her slit.

Her back buckled at that, and she let loose a hoarse grunt that set off a cataclysmic wave of pleasure inside me.

The second she detonated, I did too.

Fast and hard, I pumped into her, not stopping until her pussy ceased that soul-sucking clutching that milked my dick to the point of exquisite agony.

Both of us slick with sweat, I collapsed on top of her and rolled us over so that I was underneath her and she was on top of me. My dick was still inside her, and the feeling of connection was so damn good that I took the first deep breath of, what felt like, the week.

She nuzzled into me, and I curved my arms around her after I dragged the duvet half over us.

My eyes drifted to a close as I felt her soft breaths turn into the little puffs of air that were her precursor to sleep.

As weird as it was to think this right now, a solid truth resonated around in my brain and I couldn't escape it.

If this was what heaven felt like, no wonder Dad had wanted to go home to Mom.

Living without this again was untenable.

Living without her would be hell.

I hugged her tighter to me, only letting up when she wriggled against me in protest.

"King?" she complained sleepily.

"Sorry, baby," I whispered. Gaze stark, I stared up at the ceiling where the reflection from the light on the veranda gleamed slightly. "Get some rest."

She hummed. "You too."

I pressed my lips to her forehead. "I will."

As she did as I asked and finally got some rest, I stayed like that for a good, long while. Enough that I saw the light flicker off outside, enough that I heard the door open, enough that I listened to the creaking of the stairs as Harlow returned to his bedroom.

It should have been easy to fall asleep, but my mind was churning.

Because of him, because of Dad who I fucking missed even as I was furious with him, because of Wynter, because of the MC, because of every-fucking-thing.

Life was never still. I knew that. It was always in motion, and Harlow was a reminder of that. He'd brought chaos back into my world, after all. My temper hadn't snapped in years until I'd watched Lever destroy something that mattered to Harlow just for the sake of it.

But Harlow was no longer a Prospect; he was a brother. He was another soul I had to protect, another man who'd become family...

Gently, I rubbed my hand up and down Rach's back, taking and finding comfort in her.

Chaos might have darkened my door, but finally, she was mine.

My ring, which didn't fit, would be on her finger the second it was resized. I'd been carrying that fucking thing around since I'd bought it when she was seventeen—just before everything had gone to hell.

When the baby was born, Rach would wear my ink, and I was scheduled in with Indy later this week for some of my own so she'd have official protection from the club.

Into the maelstrom, we'd come out swinging, and by having her at my side, that burden was so much easier to bear.

Not just an Old Lady, not just the First Lady, but the *only* lady worthy of reigning over this slice of hell with me.

FORTY-SIX

RACHEL

I woke up entangled with him.

My body responded first, jolting in surprise, then the scent of us was an intense reminder. It was getting easier; every day, another step forward, another step away from the chokehold of the past.

I sighed into a smile then rubbed my nose against his arm.

"Morning."

His voice was deliciously low, a soothing grumble that further pleased my drowsy senses.

"Good morning," I whispered back, pressing my lips to his pec as I leaned up slightly to stare at him. With my thumb, I traced the curve of his cheek, just below his eye which was red. I didn't mention it. Just asked, "Bear?"

"A lot of things."

I nodded then planted both hands on his chest and propped my chin on them. "Anything I can help with?"

"As if you don't have enough to handle," he scoffed.

"Hey, work is work. You're not work. You're mine. You fix my stuff; I fix yours. That's how this is going to be, isn't it? If not, I'll write a memo so that you don't forget in the future because this is definitely how it's going to be."

His mouth quirked up at the side. One arm slid behind his neck so he could tilt his head without straining, and the other stroked over my head, tucking a couple strands of hair behind my ear.

"That guy Harlow and Nyx are planning to kill..."

"The congressman?"

"Him. He's a Sparrow."

A soft breath whistled through my lips as the ramifications of that hit home. "Jesus."

"I mean, it wasn't outside the realm of possibility. Maybe just wishful thinking. They sold anything that moved. Hell, for all we know, they trafficked men too. Everything's a commodity to them."

"Kids..." I gritted my teeth. "Lodestar found out?"

He nodded. "It was in the stuff in Dad's room."

"How the hell did Bear uncover so much stuff and we weren't even aware he was on a personal crusade?"

"No idea. He managed to hide a lot over the years." He grunted, but there was no bitterness in it. Just a slowly building acceptance that Bear wasn't exactly the man he'd believed him to be. "But speaking of Dad Maverick said Grizzly's filed as dead and that Dad had paid all the dues to the undertaker."

I refused to feel relieved. "So he's really dead?"

"Grizzly is," he confirmed, but that slight hesitation in his voice let me know that it was a good thing I hadn't gotten my hopes up.

"If he's living under another name, like you said, he'd have shown up by now and he hasn't." That was the only comfort I could find and I was going to embrace it wholeheartedly.

"Then there's Wynter. She's quiet."

"She is," I agreed softly. "Do you think she's okay?"

"I think she's too proud to admit that she made a mistake in staying."

I bit my lip. "I have no right to say this, no right to want this—"

"You're her mother. You have every right in the world."

"I gave her up."

"In devastating circumstances. We'd have been together if it weren't for Dog and Grizzly, and as for the other, it'd never have happened. Period."

Something about his grimness had me asking, "You wouldn't have come to college with me. It could still have happened."

"I wouldn't have let you go alone. It'd *never* have happened."

I paused, his resolute tone hitting me harder than he could know. "You'd have come with me?"

"Of course. Four years ain't a lifetime, and Brown wasn't all that far. We could have come back for weekends," he dismissed, unaware that at that moment, if I'd had *any* doubts, they were annihilated. Dragged away with the obviousness of his devotion.

This man just kept on showing me how much I meant to him.

How much *we* meant to him.

Fuck, I was gonna cry.

I was so sick of crying.

This baby was turning me into a fountain.

It was tough to keep the emotion out of my voice with the power of what he'd just said ramming into me as hard as his body had done last night, but I eventually rasped, "I don't need you to make me feel better, Rex. I'm just saying that I know I gave up the right to want her with us, but it doesn't stop me from wanting that all the same."

He blinked at me. Slowly. "Let's go get her."

"Huh?"

Abruptly, he sat up and I plunked on the sheets, twisting to gape at him.

"She needs us."

She did.

I could feel it.

I didn't think I had much of a motherly instinct, but what I did have was blaring sirens in my head.

Wynter was withdrawing.

Distance might be at play, but I didn't think so. Still, she had school and it wasn't as easy as just going to grab her—

"You're overthinking this," Rex rasped, his tone urgent.

"I'm not," I countered.

"You are. You're probably thinking there's barely any time left to the school year and that she needs to focus on her finals, or that she's pulling away because there's a country between us, but Wynter isn't like that. She was relieved we didn't just dump her. She *wants* to know us."

I bit down harder on my lip as his urgency united with mine.

I was a cool, logical thinker. Reason was my friend, even before Rory, Hunter, and Parker were, but—

"Okay. Let's go."

Something flashed in his eyes, something I couldn't define, but I rushed to my feet, grabbed the tee he'd hauled off last night, and darted into the hall.

Without any ceremony, I shouted, "Parker?!"

In the silent house, my shout might as well have been a yodel in the Alps. I felt like Julie frickin' Andrews, only this hill wasn't alive with anything other than dark and dirty bikers.

"You hollered?" Parker grumbled, staring up at me from the bottom of the stairs. "You know I'm not in Pennsylvania anymore? You don't have to yell—"

"Rex and I need a flight to LA. ASAP."

Her eyes widened, and I was grateful I'd filled her in on *everything* that was going on when, her tone urgent, she demanded, "Is something wrong with Wynter?"

Technically, no.

"Yes."

Her expression turned fierce. "I'm on it."

"Thank you," I whispered, relief settling inside me.

This felt right.

So right.

I blew out a breath as I rushed into one of the separate bathrooms, hearing the shower come on in ours.

Washing up as quickly as I could, I tucked myself into a towel and darted out into the hall.

Parker was already leaning against the wall, waiting for me. She pounced the second I was out of there.

"You have two hours to make your flight because First Class boarding allows for twenty minutes before takeoff and I upgraded your precheck accounts with the TSA so you can rush through security—"

I listened to her drone on with the details and, relieved, I nodded. "Thanks, Parker."

"When do I book the return flight?"

"I'll let you know." I cast her a look. "Are you going to be okay here?"

She rolled her eyes. "Of course."

"If you need any food, just deliver in, or get Rain or Harlow to pick something up—"

"You don't need to organize that for me. That's kind of my job," she teased.

I shot her a sheepish glance.

For all that I was pissed she was arranging a baby shower with the Posse behind my back, I didn't want to leave her in a lurch.

Something was going on with her, something she didn't want to share yet, but I'd done all I could—had opened my doors, invited her to stay with us for as long as she needed. She'd talk to me about this when she was ready.

"Anyway, go! You need to be on your way outta here. Traffic's insane at this time."

She wasn't wrong. "Shit!"

I rushed into the bedroom and found that Rex was already dressed—without his cut, probably for ease with airport security—but he was on the phone, clearly leaving orders for Nyx. I ignored him and got myself dressed.

Ten minutes later, he was done, so was I, Parker had breakfast smoothies ready to go, and we were racing out of the driveway and onto the open road.

Rex downed his liquid breakfast, but my stomach churned with nerves.

Steering with one hand, he pressed the other to my lap and murmured, "Drink the smoothie, Rachel. You need to eat."

"It's stupid to be nervous," I said on a rush. "We've got the flight to be anxious too—"

"You don't have to be anxious. If Wynter were in danger, she'd contact us. But she isn't. Something's going on, something I want to fix, but physically, she's safe. I've been checking in with her guards three times a day. She's safe, baby," he repeated.

Physically wasn't the only way you could damage someone, though.

I didn't say that, just forced myself to drink the smoothie I didn't want.

We made it to JFK with hardly any time to spare. Even with First Class priority boarding, we cut it close, and I was sweating like crazy when we settled in our seats.

I forced myself to eat, but I didn't bother with the entertainment options, just scrolled through some work documents Parker had sent to my email during the ride to the airport.

Rex was quiet in the seat beside me, and when he fell asleep, I was grateful—I didn't think he'd gotten much rest last night and he needed it.

When we landed, we hired a car and Rex drove us to Burbank.

Settling in the rental, that was when the reality hit me.

I was about to meet my daughter for the first time in seventeen years.

My fear for her overwhelmed any panic I might have felt, however, but I wished I were only anxious about her liking me.

Traffic wasn't on our side again, but eventually, we made it to her academy.

Only when we were parked outside did Rex send Wynter a text.

From the corner of my eye, I saw it.

Rex: *Guess who's outside?*

It took a few minutes for her to reply, and in those moments, I started gnawing on my thumbnail.

Wynter: *What?! You're outside?*

Rex grabbed my hand and tucked it in his to stop me from biting my nails as, with his free one, he typed:

Rex: *Surprise!*

Wynter: *OMG. School's out in fifteen.*

Rex: *We're not going anywhere.*

Wynter: *WE? Rachel's there too?*

Rex: *She is.*

Wynter: *And you didn't think to tell me you were coming yesterday? I'm not even wearing anything nice!!!!*

Shocked at her answer, at her eagerness to meet me, I sucked in a sharp breath.

Keen understanding fused into his expression but he simply squeezed my fingers.

Rex: *Don't worry. We're not exactly dressed up.*

Wynter: *!!!*

Wynter: *Do you think she'll like me?*

A soft sob escaped me.

My kids were killing me with this making me cry shit.

Rex raised my hand and kissed my knuckles.

Rex: *I know she will. She'll love you.*

Wynter: *I hope so. OMG when will the bell rinGgggg-GGGGgggg?!!!! AGH.*

"She's excited," I whispered, unable to believe it.

He knotted our fingers together, as just holding mine was apparently no longer enough. "She is. I knew she would be."

I swallowed. "I-I was still half-certain she hated me."

"No. I don't think she ever hated us. She was angry, but the truth helped ease that."

He sat up straight in his seat as the bell rang, and he peered out of the windshield, staring at the front doors for her.

When she appeared, wearing baggy jeans, an ill-fitting tee, and neon pink sneakers, my lips curved with joy.

He released his hold on my hand, opened the door, and stood beside the car, arms folded across his chest as he waited for her to spot him.

I saw the moment she did.

A smile lit up her face, bright and filled with joy, and she ran across the way, down the path toward the parking lot before finally crashing into him—hard enough that he jerked back a few steps until he braced himself and hugged her with a fierceness that made my ovaries melt.

Seeing as they'd already gotten me into plenty of trouble because of him, I figured it was too late for them to melt, but they did it anyway.

I was too happy at the sight of *their* happiness to be nervous, and I stepped out of the car. I felt a tad awkward, waiting for them to notice me, but when Rex shot me a wide grin over her shoulder, I knew, from that grin alone, coming here was the right move.

West Orange was loaded with memories he wanted to escape.

Here, it was a blank canvas, and Wynter gave him something only a daughter could give a man as loving as mine.

He pulled back from her, stared into her face, and said, "You look tired."

"King!" Wynter whined. "That's the first thing you have to say to me? Why is that always your first greeting?"

She had a point, I thought with a smile.

"Would you prefer me to ask if you're hungry?"

She snickered at that. "I'm always hungry."

"Don't I know it," he teased before he angled his chin toward me. "Rachel's there, Wynter."

Her head didn't whip around, but slowly, she took a deep breath. Whatever was in her expression made Rex nod encouragingly at her.

With another deep breath, she turned around, and that was when I first set eyes on my daughter.

God, she was beautiful.

The best parts of Rex and me.

The very best.

She was...

I didn't know what to do.

Did I shake her hand?

I wanted to hold her. I wanted that so badly—

But she was shy. Naturally.

I had to be the adult.

Jesus, adulting sucked.

Shooting her a smile that was probably just as shy, I stepped forward and gently placed my hand on her shoulder. She bit her lip as she peeped a smile back at me, at long last, and I released a shaky breath.

"I'm so nervous," I admitted with a self-deprecating laugh.

She blinked then, incredulously, questioned, "You? You're nervous?"

I shrugged. "I can't help it. I want you to like me, and that makes me feel as if I'm back at my high school and not at yours." My nose crinkled. "I wasn't very popular."

"Rachel's always been difficult."

Shooting Rex a glare, I had to laugh at yet another of his grins— this time, it was utterly unrepentant.

It did my heart good to see him like that.

Rather than focus on Wynter and me, I turned it around on the one man who'd brought us together.

"See that grin, Wynter?" I queried, pointing to her father. "That's been in short supply the past couple weeks."

Our daughter's eyes rounded. "Oh, King. Your dad. Of course. I'm so sorry I couldn't be there." She bit her lip. "Rachel offered to get me a flight but I just…" She hunched her shoulders. "It's hard right now."

"You don't have to apologize for not attending," he tutted, hauling his arm around her and tucking her into his side. "But I want to know what's going on with you."

She squirmed in his hold. "Nothing's—"

"Wynter, don't lie to me. We've already been through too much together, haven't we?"

Ducking her head, she heaved a dramatic sigh, but, when neither of us filled the silence that fell between us, she mumbled, "Mom's started drinking again."

Ally was an alcoholic?

Rex's eyes narrowed and, to me, he mouthed, "I picked great parents for her, didn't I?"

Though I winced, I shook my head at him in silent reprimand. Just in time, too, because Wynter peered at him.

"You're *really* here. I can't believe it," she whispered, the wonder in her voice making me choke up.

He shrugged. "I knew something was wrong, and I wasn't about to wait for you to confess because you're as stubborn as Rachel. I'd have been old and gray by the time you told me anything—"

"Shut up, you," I quipped. "Like you're not stubborn?! Ha! Don't let him BS you, Wynter. He's as obstinate as we are. And, anyway, what's wrong with being obstinate? It's great when you're ambitious."

"You're really here and you're *really* bickering in front of me," Wynter breathed, her eyes wide with delight.

Her joy surprised me into blushing.

Rex chuckled. "Look at those cheeks. Brighter than a stop light." He squeezed Wynter's arm. "What do you say we go and grab something to eat, huh?"

Wynter bit her lip again. "I'm supposed to go straight home."

"You're not working at the coffee shop anymore?"

"Dad had a…" She swallowed. "He shouted at me and said my grades were really bad because I was working too many hours."

Rex's grin faded and his fury blossomed on his face. "He shouted at you?"

He made it sound like he'd aimed a gun at her.

"He didn't mean to. He's in a lot of pain," she excused.

Untangling them, Rex cupped both her shoulders and stared straight into her eyes. "We both know that when you say he shouted, he'll have done something else because you always make excuses for him. No one, *no one,* sweetheart, has the right to talk down to you.

"You are *my* daughter, and I don't care if I've only just turned up and he's been there for you all your life, you are *mine* and no fucking one talks down to you, do you hear me?"

Her eyes were big in her suddenly pale face but at his words, she crumpled. Her arms slid around his waist and she burrowed into his hug.

I knew what a hug from Rex could do.

It made you feel like he could fix every problem you had. It made you think he could move mountains. Then, when he hugged you back, you knew he *would* fix every problem you had, and that he *would* move mountains. *For you.*

I didn't have the same power as Rex, but it didn't stop me from stepping closer to her and embracing her from the back.

Maybe she was too old for this but—

She dislodged one arm from around his waist and twisted it back to hold me too.

It was awkward, but it was beautiful. So beautiful.

I started crying—*again, goddammit*—but I buried my face into Rex's shirt to hide my tears.

My family.

I was with my family.

All of us.

Here.

When I'd never anticipated anything like this.

When I'd prepared myself for a lifetime of solitude. Of hookups with Rex, of work, of—

Nothingness.

Was it any wonder I cried quietly?

I'd expected nothing and had gotten everything.

I didn't know what I'd done to be so lucky, but I wasn't dumb enough to question it. I just embraced it and considered myself blessed.

FORTY-SEVEN

REX

It took a lot longer than I'd have liked to get the full story out of Wynter.

Her shyness around Rachel faded every time we started bickering, and without us conferring on it, we bickered a lot so that she'd grow accustomed to it faster.

In barely any time at all, she had the confidence to join in.

Circumstances and concerns aside, with my two girls sitting opposite me in a restaurant, a spread of tacos and taquitos in front of us, I didn't think I could be fucking happier.

This was living the dream.

I didn't think it was possible for there to be more clear-cut proof that I was meant to be a family man. That *this* was what I'd been wanting, hell, *waiting* for all along.

It made it a fucking pleasure to sit back against the booth, to watch them both talk about AP History, to get pumped for information on Greek philosophers, to discuss her math paper, to talk about band practice...

This was what we'd missed out on.

This.

And it hurt, but in the best possible way because 'better late then never' was starting to become my motto.

So when, after all that good stuff, her fingers covered in guac as she dove into the nachos that had just arrived, she murmured, "I don't want to be here anymore," my heart kind of broke.

Rachel instantly blanched but she was reactive. "We can take you home if you're ready—"

"Huh? Oh. No!" Her cheeks flushed. "I meant, not *here*. I meant, you know, like, um, Burbank?"

The relief that hit me was like a smack to the fucking face.

I released a soft breath and said, "Kid, preface that better next time. You about broke my heart."

Her eyes rounded. "I did?"

"You sure did."

"But—"

"We're very aware that any time you grant us is a blessing," Rachel said softly, gracing Wynter with a smile that hit her eyes and made her ten times more beautiful than the knockout she was.

My woman as a mom was the hottest thing I'd ever fucking seen in my life.

"A blessing?" Wynter frowned. "Really?"

"We never thought we could have this," I said gruffly, reaching for my soda. "So, Rach has it right—this is a blessing." Wynter gnawed on her lip but I didn't want to overwhelm her, so I just asked, "What's going on, kid? Why don't you want to be in Burbank anymore?"

"I'm ready to come home, Dad."

For a second, I could only stare at her.

Dad.

Fuck. **DAD**. She'd called me 'Dad.'

Rachel swallowed, then seeming to realize my brain was fried upon hearing that label that mattered so fucking much to me, rasped, "We'd love for you to come to Jersey."

Maybe because she was always so practical, her immediate acquiescence—which was very impractical—made me step up. "Kid, I want you home with us. Make no bones about it. But you ain't like me—what about school?"

Wynter's shoulders hunched. "I took my SATs."

My mouth rounded. "What?! You didn't tell me. Is that why you've been stressed?"

"Yes." She bowed her head. "I didn't do so well."

"Well, you took it junior year," I pointed out, wondering if that was why Kinnock had shouted at her to get her to quit her job. "There's time to retake it if the scores were that bad."

Clearly wanting me to shut up, Rachel kicked me under the table. "What did you get, honey?"

She sniffled. "Fifteen hundred and ten."

I shot Rach a look and mouthed, "Is that bad?" I hadn't taken mine so I genuinely didn't remember. It didn't sound bad, but maybe shit had changed since I was in high school.

Rach was shaking her head though. "That's... ninety-ninth percentile?"

Wynter swallowed. "I was aiming for top marks."

I snorted. "You're so like Rachel it's insane."

Rachel shushed me. "It depends on the school you want to go to, I guess. Harvard's out," she admitted with a grimace.

"It's out with fifteen hundred and ten?" I groused. "What do they want? Blood?"

Her glance was worried. "Yes. I'm sure a blood sacrifice would help too."

See, this was why I was over this bullshit.

Rach had once told me I had it in me to be a politician, but I *didn't*. Not because I lacked the smarts or the skills, but because I lacked the patience for these ridiculous social constructs that meant nothing to me.

Wynter bit her lip. "I want to go to—" She paused, sucked in a breath, then blurted out, "I want to cross-register with Juilliard and Columbia. They have a program—"

Rach's eyes started glistening. And I got it. Damn if my heart didn't squeeze in my chest. "You want to come to the East Coast?"

Wynter's chin bobbed. "I do."

Rach reached for our kid's hand. "We can work toward that. You still have a year until graduation," she pointed out.

"Thank you," Wynter muttered before, miserably, admitting, "My mom doesn't even care what my score is."

"I'm sure that's not true," Rach tried to appease.

"She got clean years ago, but whatever the Triads did to her, it made her start drinking again. She's too busy sleeping off her hangover so that when she goes to visit Dad, he doesn't snipe at her for being drunk."

Wow. Healthy.

"And Dad, when he found out, you'd think I'd gotten nine-hundred on the tests or something." Her bottom lip quivered and, sniffling, she swiped at her eyes. "He was really mean."

I reached for my cellphone and typed out:

Me: *You got that fucker Jeremy Kinnock off the transplant list like I asked you?*

Lodestar: *Yup. I tagged him as a low priority.*

Me: *Good.*

Lodestar: *No 'thank you?'*

Me: *You know I'm grateful. Wouldn't put up with you otherwise.*

Lodestar: ¯_(ツ)_/¯

Grunting under my breath, I asked, "You only have, what? Six weeks left in the school year?"

"I know it's nothing—"

"If you come back with us, I can set you up with remote learning. You'd need to fly back for finals, but you could stay with us."

Wynter's eyes rounded. "I could do that? You'd want me there?"

"Sweetheart, I didn't want to leave you in January, so you can guarantee I want to take you back with us now."

She gulped. "Really?"

"Really."

"Are you sure you want to do this? You seemed to want to stay to support your mom and dad while he's sick," Rachel remarked, her tone cautious.

I wanted to snap at her and ask her why the fuck she was putting obstacles in our way when *this* was the reason we'd traveled like crazy people today, but I knew it was the right thing to do.

"Dad barely talks to me, and if he does, it's about school and how I should have gotten 1600. He wants me to go to Stanford, and he wants me to do what he's doing, but that's not... I don't want that. I didn't want it before King, I mean, Dad came—"

Excuse me while I fucking preened.

Dad.

"I'm not a teacher. I'd be so bad at doing something like that, but he insists, and I just feel horrible because I can't yell at him when he's in a hospital bed and he's almost dying."

"You said it yourself, Wynter. He *will* die if he can't get a transplant," she pointed out. "I don't want you to feel bad for leaving—"

"A month ago, I went to get Mom some coffee because she was slurring her words. When I came back, I heard him say that he regretted marrying her, that I'd ruined his life because I'd brought Rex into it." She peeped a look at me. "He was speaking as if I were the reason he'd gotten hurt, when, if anything, I'm the reason he didn't die. Because they'd have killed him if it weren't for you, wouldn't they?"

Temper surging, I wasn't certain how I managed to keep a rein on it as I stated, "If a man pays his debts, there's no reason to kill him. It's when that changes there's a problem, and considering how he offered payment in kind, I'm going to assume that things weren't looking great for him."

"Rex, you're upsetting her," Rachel sniped.

"No. I'm not. Real talk shouldn't hurt."

"It usually does," Rachel countered.

"I needed to hear that," was Wynter's soft reply.

"What did your mom say?" I questioned.

"She didn't say anything." If a breadstick could be snapped bitterly, then she did it then. "She didn't defend me, even after everything he's done. Everything he's put us through. I just don't understand her.

"I thought this would bring us all together. When you came here, Dad, I realized that I was kind of hard on you. That was wrong of me. S-So, when—" Her mouth worked as she struggled to get her words out.

"You thought that if King was worthy of a second chance, then your dad was worthy too," Rachel supplied, her hand coming to rest on Wynter's shoulder.

Head bowed, she nodded and her chin butted her chest. "He was... I didn't want to get to know you. But you were... You made me realize I was closed off. So I thought Dad, I mean, Jeremy, would appreciate a chance to turn things around too, but it hasn't worked out."

"Then he's the fool, honey," was Rach's soft rejoinder.

Wynter shot her a grateful look.

The temptation to visit Kinnock's hospital room and to deliver on my last promise to him was strong.

But I didn't have time to waste on that bastard.

He'd had his second chance, and he'd fucked it up. Now *my* family would reap the benefits of his mistakes.

So, I gritted my teeth together, and I rumbled, "Tomorrow's Friday. You can skip a day and we can make arrangements to fly out over the weekend."

"Parker can handle that."

Wynter frowned. "Who's Parker?"

"My assistant," Rachel answered then, to me, asked, "You can deal with the school and set up some remote learning?"

"I pay the bastards enough," I grumbled, "that they should bring the exam hall to Jersey."

A soft snort escaped Wynter. "Not sure that's how it works."

I grinned at her, but Rachel murmured, "Your father's used to getting his own way. He's the Prez of his club. That means that what he says, goes, and what he wants, he gets. It's very bad for him. I make it a point to make sure I don't always say yes, just to keep him real."

I chuckled. "Oh, that's why you're so ornery, is it?"

Rachel's eyes were twinkling. "For sure."

Wynter's laugh was stronger than before. She was more at ease. I could feel it.

"I really do want to go back with you," Wynter whispered, her gaze darting between us both.

I half-expected to hear a 'but,' only it never came.

"One thing Rachel didn't tell you is that when you're the Prez's kid and the Prez's woman, that means you get your own way too." I winked at her. "We can make this happen if you're ready for it. We can even get you a goddamn piano if that makes it better."

Her eyes definitely lit up, but she admitted, "I-I feel bad but I'd be leaving for college soon anyway and it's not like being here is—"

"Is what, sweetheart?" I asked when she broke off.

"It's not like they want me around," she said on a rush. "So I'd prefer to be with people who do want me around, you know?"

I reached over and patted her hand. "I'll make it happen."

Rachel shot me a measured glance. "You'll need to get Ally to sign off on her leaving the school *and* the state."

Simply arching a brow, I repeated, "I'll make it happen."

My little girl shot me a shaky smile. "Thank you, Dad."

TEXT CHAT

Dead To Me: *You got any information for me?*

Rachel: *No phone call?*

Dead To Me: *Miss the sound of my voice?*

Rachel: *No. This can be traced, can't it?*

Dead To Me: *Everything can be, but I wouldn't worry about that. Do you have information for me?*

Rachel: *Keegan has been out of the country since January. He was seen in a restaurant in Manhattan.*

Dead To Me: *Which restaurant?*

Rachel: *Verdi. I've exhausted all my sources and that's the only information I can find on his location. Clearly, he came out of hiding to go there.*

Dead To Me: *You asked Lodestar to help out?*

Rachel: *She's busy right now. But she was the one who got me the intel on Keegan being in Verdi.*

Dead To Me: *What about who killed his sister? You found out anymore on that?*

Rachel: *What I have comes with no guarantees.*

Dead To Me: *Meaning you can't prove it?*

Rachel: *I have no way of being able to do that, but an underling supposedly killed Keegan's sister.*

Dead To Me: *In the ECD?*

Rachel: *Yes. My source believed that the reins slipped free of Keegan's grasp while he was in prison.*

Dead To Me: *Anything else to tell me?*

Rachel: *Keegan... He's the uncle of Aoife O'Grady.*

Dead To Me: *Who's that?*

Rachel: *Come on. You have to know. She's a Manhattan socialite and she just hit the news with the brownie that went viral.*

Dead To Me: *Interesting. Okay. I'll be in touch.*

Rachel: *That's it?*

Rachel: *Dead To Me?*

Rachel: *Is Hunter still safe?*

Rachel: *Dead To Me?*

FORTY-EIGHT

LODESTAR

A WEEK LATER

When I barged into the pink room, most of the Posse, apart from Giulia, twisted around to stare at who'd intruded upon their space.

Tiffany shot me a smile and asked, "You're joining us today, Star?"

I grunted and slouched toward the remaining empty seat around the table.

I refused to feel touched that they'd left a chair out for me when I'd only attended their group meeting the one time. Especially when I wasn't here to talk.

"Communicative as ever," Indy mocked.

Stone chuckled. "Leave her alone. She woke up today and chose peace or I'm sure she'd be chewing us all a new one."

"What's with the dog?" I asked, staring at the ugly chihuahua at Giulia's feet.

When it bared its teeth at me, I bared mine right back.

Giulia's cheeks flushed. "It won't leave me alone."

"I told Nyx was your spirit animal," Amara said around a chuckle. "You bite first, ask later questions."

"Giulia's got a dog that really needs to go to the vet. We get it,"

Stone sniped. "Rachel, dammit, I want to know what happened in LA."

Rachel settled her gaze on me, and without us even having to utter a word, I knew she knew I was there for her.

Slowly, her eyelids drifted down in silent assent, confirmation we were on the same page, before she murmured, "We took Wynter home, and Rex explained to her mom that she was coming to stay with us for the rest of the school year."

"Did she take that badly?" Lily asked.

I snorted. "How else could you take that? What do you expect her to do? Thank them?"

"The home situation wasn't great, Star," Tiffany chided.

"In my experience, few home situations are. But we make do. Is Wynter okay now?"

"She's settling in," was all Rachel said. "She's spoken with her parents a couple times, but the calls end in arguments. Her mom's drinking too much."

"Ironic considering that's what's killing her husband."

The Posse blinked at me.

"He has cirrhosis of the liver and needs a transplant," I explained. "That's why Wynter's dad's in the hospital."

"How do you know that?" Stone asked.

I scoffed. "Like he didn't consult you about that." I got my answer when she flushed. "Rex wanted me to get involved."

"Do we even want to fucking know how?" Indy groused.

Amara chuckled. "I hope he has you fuck with list. How you say new organ list. Bastard deserve to die." She kissed her fingers. "Self-destruction. Perfect."

I rolled my eyes but confirmed or denied nothing.

"Anyway, I just hope Wynter isn't going to regret how things ended with her dad," Rach murmured.

"What happened? How bad was it?" Giulia questioned.

"It was awful. She's such a sweetheart, and he didn't even look at her. Didn't even say goodbye. I'm glad that I told Rex to wait by the car, because I think he'd have beaten the shit out of him which would have been hard to explain away as self-defense when the man's still in casts.

"I never imagined how bad it could be to be frozen out like that."

Another snort escaped me. "How ironic considering your nickname was Ice Queen."

Rachel's mouth pursed. "Trust me, I know. I didn't realize how devastating it was to be on the other side of that."

"We rarely know the damage we cause," Tiffany assured us. "But it's good that, after some self-reflection, you picked up on it. In the future, you can try to make sure you have a better way of communicating your issues and that freezing someone out isn't a coping mechanism you constantly fall back on."

This time, I didn't roll my eyes, but I felt like doing it.

Psychobabble bullshit.

"So, she's staying with you long term?"

"I think so," Rachel answered Alessa. She sounded excited. That surprised me. "I hope she does. It's great having her around. She's talking about attending Columbia and cross-registering with Juilliard."

Stone laughed. "It's a good thing you and Rex are loaded."

Rachel grinned. "It is, but it's worth it. She's excited and I am too."

"How's Rain taking it?"

"He's acting like he's ten years older than her and not just a year." Her grin widened. "It's hilarious."

"You look happy," Stone mused. "It's good to see."

Rachel shrugged. "I feel happy. I didn't realize that she was what we were missing."

"How's the baby?" Giulia asked.

"Fine. I gained some weight so that'll shut the doctor up at my next appointment. How about you?"

"I'm ready to pop," she said miserably. "But it's all good."

Tiffany cleared her throat. "Rachel, Giulia's dealing with some guilt about what happened in the cemetery. She's finding it hard to express herself—"

"Tiffany, dammit to hell. I told you not to say anything."

"And I told you that repressing this is bad for you. Plus, Rachel doesn't resent you, do you?"

"Honestly, no. The last month has been so chaotic, it's just one extra piece of baggage to deal with."

"That's the point," Giulia muttered. "I wanted to ease you of that burden. Instead, it made it worse."

I watched as Giulia, for the first time since I'd ever met her, actually looked apologetic.

It wasn't a great look on her.

Rachel shot her a smile. "It came from a good place."

"Some things are meant to be left in the past," Indy mused. "Digging them up is just asking for trouble."

"You'd know," she said sympathetically. "Has that PI been sniffing around again?"

"No. The cops have left me alone too."

I snickered. "That's because I left a nice trail of breadcrumbs for them both."

"How?" Rachel demanded. "You'd better not have fucked this up, Lodestar."

"Fucked what up? There was nothing to fuck up," I sniped. "I just laid a trail for the PI to pick up. David went traveling around the East Coast, don't you know? Stayed in a couple motels, and there's even CCTV footage to prove it."

Rachel demanded, "You doctored motel records and CCTV footage?"

I hummed. "Picked nice anonymous places with heavy foot traffic so he'd just be one small needle in a large haystack for the staff to remember."

"You didn't have to do that," Indy said softly.

"Sure I did. You deserve to not have that hanging over you. If I could find Grizzly, I'd solve that too."

"Look at you being Ms. Problem Solver," Stone mocked.

"I know. It's weird that I'm being helpful."

"Very weird," Giulia agreed. "And there's really no lead on finding Grizzly?"

"I'm going through Bear's murder board with a fine-tooth comb. If anything comes up, I'll let you know, Rachel."

"Thanks, Star."

"Anyway, are we not going to talk about the fact that you're wearing an engagement ring and that Rex came in for ink this week?" Indy teased.

Rachel blushed. It was almost nauseating how happy she was, but fuck, after what she'd been through, she deserved it.

"Let's see it," Tiffany crowed, and she snatched Rachel's hand and peered at the diamond. Snow white. As cold as Rachel used to be.

A fitting gem for her, especially when combined with the two rubies bracketing the Princess cut.

Fire to warm up that ice.

"What ink did Rex get?" I asked.

"Scales of justice," Indy murmured. "Rachel's name on one of the scales, Sinners' brand on the other."

"The scales were tipped?"

Rachel's blush deepened at Stone's question. "They were. My name's on the lower one."

"As it should be," Giulia said, her tone stout. Her gaze clashed with mine. "Star, you know what's happening this week, don't you?"

I arched a brow. "Many things, I'm sure."

Including a visit to Kat's school.

Her bully needed a broken arm.

Another one.

"Nyx's going into the city with Harlow."

Rachel frowned. "He's talked about that with you?"

"Yes."

"And you signed off on that?"

"I have," Giulia answered as she reached for her glass of water. "I understand."

"I don't." Indy's tone was grim. "He made me a promise."

Rachel questioned, "Has he spoken about it with you?"

"No, because he knows I'd call him out on his bullshit, and he wouldn't be able to do this without feeling like a piece of shit for breaking that promise."

"He isn't breaking it. He's just helping Harlow."

"Ever heard of the term 'aiding and abetting' or 'conspiracy to commit murder?' Because I'm no lawyer, and I've heard of those," Stone bitched.

Giulia scowled at her. "Harlow can't do it on his own. He needs to learn how to leave no footprints behind."

"Since when were the Sinners running a school for serial killers?" Stone sniped.

Giulia hissed, "Stone, I get that you're attacking my man on his sister's behalf, but I'm okay with this. I trust him."

"You shouldn't," Indy retorted. "If he can break a promise to me, he can break a promise to you."

"You do know that this plan is sanctioned by the head of the Five Points, don't you?" Rachel threw out there.

"Like that means anything," Indy said bitterly.

I derided, "It means more than you fucking know. Aidan O'Donnelly Sr. has one of the best hackers I've ever met as a son, and he has him jumping through hoops on the regular to meet his demands.

"Throw in the fact that his empire has been built over decades, and there isn't a war he's waged that he's lost—you're an idiot if you discount the level of influence he has."

Rachel sighed. "I hate to agree with Star, but she's right. I've seen his influence in action. It's beyond impressive. Borderline disturbing. The way he can make the authorities dance tells me there's something very flawed with our justice system."

"What are you talking about?" Indy demanded. "How have you seen the Five Points' influence in action? Are you their lawyer?"

"No, thank God. I have enough problems to handle without adding their bullshit to the mix."

"Nyx told me about the speeding charge, Rachel," Giulia murmured quietly.

Rachel's eyes widened. "He told you?"

"He did."

Giulia's tone was bizarrely calm.

It was so bizarre, in fact, that it sent chills down my spine—which was a fucking feat in and of itself.

Giulia had the temper of an agitated scorpion.

That she was chilled was just proof that pregnancy was all kinds of wrong for the female body.

Wishing I had some Cheetos, I settled back in my seat for the show, watching as Giulia leaned down and started stroking the dog which, from her wince, immediately bit her.

"Nyx got caught speeding?" Indy queried, her confusion clear.

"Nyx got *arrested* for speeding," Giulia clarified.

"I didn't even know that was possible," Indy derided. "The guy's killed dozens of people and the club's managed to keep his name clean, but he gets a record for fucking speeding? I think I went down the rabbit hole and let me tell you, it's whacked down here."

Rachel cleared her throat. "It was a trap."

"Like a speed trap?" Stone asked, as perplexed as her friend.

"No, like a trap to get him arrested." Rachel rubbed her brow. "It was, essentially, a game. Aidan O'Donnelly Sr. wanted to prove that Nyx could be caught red-handed and he could make the charges disappear."

"How was he caught? Killing a pedophile?" Tiffany questioned, her forehead furrowing.

"Killing a rapist." Rachel's tone fell flat. "I'm sure we're all in agreement that the bastard deserved to die."

"*Tak*," Amara intoned grimly. "We very do much agree. Bastard need to rot."

"Well, he is," Rachel remarked. "He's rotting as we speak."

"You mean to tell me that Nyx was caught killing a rapist, and all he got charged for was speeding? Did I get that right?"

"You got that right," Rachel confirmed. "Reckless driving and excessive speeding, to be precise. Insane, I know, but true, nonetheless. All because O'Donnelly wanted to prove he could protect Nyx from jail."

Indy blew out a breath. "That kind of power is insane."

Almost as insane as the man himself.

Not that I said that. I just kept watching the show.

"It is," Rachel agreed before she warned, "There's no certainty with this situation, Giulia. It could still go wrong."

"The moment you told me that my dad had raped you, I knew what Nyx felt," Giulia said flatly. "If I weren't pregnant, if it weren't for this kid, I'd be going with him."

"You're nuts," Indy rasped. "If a man has that much power, there's no saying what he could do. And what if he has a falling out with Nyx? What then? He could twist everything around. All the evidence he's thrown out could make a miraculous reappearance—"

"No, that won't happen."

"How the fuck do you know?"

I turned to stare at her. "Because I'll make sure it doesn't."

Indy's frown faded. "Why would you do that?"

I got to my feet. "Because he's family."

Not sticking around for a discussion, I bypassed the feral dog, strode out of the room, and headed into the kitchen.

Hungry, I grabbed some Cheetos, but I didn't return to the meeting, just stayed looking out of the window onto the pool.

It was a beautiful property, but soulless.

A little like me.

My cell phone buzzed.

Conor: *You're quiet. What's going on?*

Me: *Not much.*

Conor: *Bull.*

Me: *I need you to promise me that whatever shit your dad tangles Nyx up in, we can get him out of it.*

Conor: *Of course we can. You're not really worried about that, are you?*

I stuffed my mouth with Cheetos.

Me: *I can't have his kid being raised without a dad, Conor.*

Conor: *It won't come to that. I know what you're willing to do for family, Star. But it isn't necessary.*

Me: *Just like it won't come to you standing in the window to make a sniper think you're your brother, you mean?*

Conor: *The glass was bulletproof. I was safe.*

Me: *Pfft.*

Conor: *Don't 'Pfft' me. You know I'm right. You know I was safe. Helluva lot safer than you with your ass on top of a goddamn skyscraper. The wind could have blown you off.*

My lips twitched.

Me: *Have you ever read Roald Dahl?*

Conor: *No.*

Me: *Shame. That sounds like something that'd happen in one of his books.*

Conor: *I doubt it. I just googled him. Skyscrapers weren't as massive in his day. BUT, Nyx is safe. Dad means him no harm, and trust me, those aren't words I type lightly.*

Conor: *Never thought I'd see the fucking day where Dad meant someone NO harm.*

Me: *Is it all set for Friday?*

Conor: *Yup.*

Me: *Good.*

Conor: *What's going on with you?*

Me: *Nothing. I'm eating Cheetos.*

Conor: *That wasn't what I meant.*

Me: *GTG.*

I didn't just get out of the conversation because I didn't want to talk about what was going on with me; I heard footsteps in the hall.

When I moved away from the window facing the pool, I felt the buzz of another message from him but I ignored it.

Rachel, unsurprisingly, was the person in the hall. "What did you want to speak with me about?"

"Audrey Diane Linchester Newton."

She blinked at me. "Mouthful."

"Big one," I agreed.

"Who is she?"

"The daughter of the president of Cayman Credit Group."

Her brows shot up. "Okay. What about her?"

"There's a sex tape of her I need to leverage."

It was interesting watching her go into a deep freeze. Her soft lips flattened, and her eyes narrowed into slits. "Why?"

Her disapproval was clear. Not that I cared.

"Cayman Credit is home to one of the Sparrows' bank accounts. Another of their accounts in Switzerland routes money to them, and from there, I believe it goes into individual bank accounts. I'd like to know who the recipients are for those transactions."

"Your intent?"

"To hand them over to the US Attorney."

"The evidence will be inadmissible in a courtroom."

"That's what Savannah Daniels is for. She can put the names out in public, where they can be hung, drawn, and quartered, and the government can go to work in taking the individuals down once they pull their heads out of their asses. Do you have a problem with that?"

I could pretty much see the thoughts racing behind her eyes.

She hated this.

Did she think I was a goddamn fan?

Did she think I wanted to leverage a woman's pain, her humiliation, her suffering, *her body* for this?

Her hands balled into fists at her sides. "I hate this."

We shared a look.

"They need to be destroyed."

"So we'll destroy Audrey instead?"

"Collateral damage," was all I said, aware I sounded like a bitch, but I was trained for this.

Trained to not care.

That was what made it all the more bittersweet—I *did* care. Like cracks appearing on the top of a frozen lake, humanity was starting to slip into my nature.

It was why I was here.

I could handle intimidation tactics, didn't care if my life was endangered, but she'd threatened Katina. *That* I couldn't abide.

Her nostrils flared. "If you do this, I want results."

"I'll get them."

She stared at me until I felt the frost connecting us both. That was when she ground out, "Do it."

HARLOW

RADIOHEAD - BODYSNATCHERS

I should have felt sick to my stomach.

I should have wanted to run screaming for the hills.

But the second I walked into the warehouse and saw the body-shaped bag on the floor, a great welter of calm overtook me.

To reach this point, I'd taken a path I could never have imagined stepping upon when I was younger. A path Jessie would never have wanted me to take. But for all that it was so wrong, it felt right.

I felt calm.

At peace.

It had been so long since I'd experienced this level of serenity that it was almost as if I'd been forsaken.

"You get the top. I'll deal with the bottom," Nyx rumbled, breaking into my heavy thoughts.

"How did they get him?" I asked as I studied the heavy-duty liners that shrouded Francis Merriweather's body.

Three thick lines of duct tape kept everything in place. There were the tiniest of breathing holes that had been popped in the plastic canopy shielding his mouth to grant him some air, but I had to figure that was why he was so still—there wasn't enough oxygen for a mouse, never mind a man.

"Why do you need to know how they got him?" Nyx asked. "He's here, ain't he? S'all that matters."

"I want to know how much time we have."

"Good question."

The booming tone was so chipper that it had me withholding a shudder.

I truly felt as if Mr. O'Donnelly Sr. was the devil himself.

Nyx and I didn't have the best of relationships. He tolerated me as he taught me how to clean up a crime scene, Cruz helping out with the chemicals and the deeper explanations as to how things worked. When I asked questions, he answered to the best of his ability, and throughout the hazing, he, Cruz, and by the end, Rex, had been kind to me.

They didn't like me though.

I regretted that.

I'd never fitted in, and even in the MC, it appeared as if I wouldn't.

"You have about three hours before his security detail realizes he's not in his girlfriend's bed where he should be."

"Where's his girlfriend?"

"Do you really care?" Nyx aimed at me, making it clear he didn't.

"She's dead?" I rasped, his tone prompting me to assume the worst.

"Figure she's bound to be."

"You'd be right. She's the patsy."

Turning to O'Donnelly, I murmured, "Won't her family be hurt in the fallout?"

"She shouldn't have shacked up with a married congressman then," was O'Donnelly's retort.

Nyx tried to pass me a knife. "Just get on with it. This is what you've been waiting for, isn't it?"

"No one else was supposed to get hurt."

"You wanted the freedom to do these things," Nyx retorted. "Freedom is expensive."

Clenching down on the side of my cheek, I nodded my understanding.

Throughout the weeks of hazing, of Prospecting, of cleaning up their shit—literally—of learning how to dispose of a body in a pinch, of learning how to make a crime scene spotless, this was what I *had* been waiting for.

And to be honest, it was coming sooner than anticipated.

I'd gone to the Sinners' clubhouse hoping to get help, wanting to know how the MC navigated these waters.

I'd watched them infiltrate Haune's home. I'd seen them lynch him. I'd observed cameras on the sides of buildings drift out of shot as they passed through a street.

They were ghosts.

Living ghosts.

I'd wanted that power, and now that it was here, within reach, I didn't know how I felt. Not when someone had died to make this happen, to give me what I'd craved most.

Agitated, I accepted the knife Nyx handed me.

A weapon, no longer a tool.

Notching the tip into the plastic, I slid it along the black wrapping and through the tape, uncaring if it scored the flesh beneath.

As the sides parted, a man was revealed to me. I'd never even heard of him until I'd searched online for his name, but he was naked apart from a pair of pajama pants.

The same duct tape bound his hands and ankles. His eyes were closed and his mouth slack. His skin was faintly blue from asphyxiation.

"Nyx tells me this is your first kill," O'Donnelly murmured, making me jolt as I hadn't realized he'd moved so close to me.

With his hands on his knees, he loomed above Merriweather. The pine tones of his aftershave overpowered the air around me.

"It is," I confirmed.

"The seminary wasn't atonement?"

"No." I scowled at him, insulted by the question. "It was *not*. I felt a calling."

I still did. It had just shifted directions now.

O'Donnelly nodded. "It wasn't strong enough to counter this though, was it?"

"You trying to stop him or help him?" Nyx sniped.

It was then I realized just how insane Nyx was because he wasn't scared of O'Donnelly.

At. All.

I was terrified.

More of the man who'd crouched awkwardly beside me than of what I was about to do.

O'Donnelly recognized it too. He shot Nyx a smirk, one that said he appreciated my brother's lack of fear.

Straightening up, he raised his hands and said, "Heaven forbid I distract you." With a glance around the warehouse, he continued, "This'll be where your kills are brought."

"They'll always be brought to us? I thought you didn't want to include the Five Points in this business?"

"I don't, and I never said I used my men to bring him here, did I?" was O'Donnelly's cold retort. "How I get them to this warehouse is none of your business. Just know it's clean and won't be easy for the authorities to trace. This is my home away from home. I ain't about to taint it by giving the cops a reason to sniff around the place." He wafted a hand at me. "Make it entertaining."

The knife slipped in my palm as I stared down at the congressman.

What he enjoyed made my skin crawl, and when I thought about the death certificate in my father's office, when I'd read about everything Samuel Haune had done to my baby sister, it made it easy to ask, "Do you know what stigmata is?"

I didn't exactly direct it at Nyx but he was the one who answered, "No."

"I wasn't asking you."

O'Donnelly released a soft laugh. "How very, very perfect for a man of God. I know what it is, son. You want to play with him before he dies, do you?" The laughter turned into a cackle as he called out, "Jonesy, bring out the St. Andrew's Cross."

"You have a crucifix on hand?" I sputtered.

O'Donnelly murmured, "I have a great many things on hand." He slapped his own together. "This is perfect, more perfect than I could have imagined."

"Will someone tell me what the fuck stigmata is?"

"It's a phenomenon that befalls the ardent believer. They're ailed with the plights of Christ as he died on the cross," I explained to him, the rightness of my words making gooseflesh wave up and down my spine. "A crown of thorns, a stab wound to the side, marks of the nails at the hands and feet."

Nyx rolled his eyes. "Only a Catholic would come up with this shit. That's how you want to kill him?"

My hands curled into fists. "That's how I want to kill him," I confirmed.

"Fucking weirdo," Nyx grumbled, "but it'll stink less than what Giulia likes."

"What does she like?"

"Fire. You ever smelled burning flesh before?"

I reared back in disgust. "No. How could I?"

O'Donnelly snorted. "Give it time, boy. Your repertoire will grow."

At that moment, I had the choice to walk away.

Merriweather was unconscious, nothing had happened other than kidnapping which, granted, was a felony, but we could dump his body somewhere...

The man O'Donnelly had called Jonesy and a few others brought out a cross on a kind of trolley—as if it were an everyday occurrence. Something that was only compounded when I heard them talking about the last Lakers' game of the season.

O'Donnelly was talking to Nyx; their focus wasn't on me.

My heart started pounding.

I should walk away.

This wasn't my place.

Jessie wouldn't want this.

She'd been so proud when I'd been accepted into the seminary—

The man's eyes popped open.

He stared at me as I stared at him, only his were dazed and bloodshot.

All I could think was that they looked like any other person's eyes.

There was no malevolence in them; no hint about what he was capable of. No hint about what he'd done or would do in the future if I didn't stop him.

No sign of his wickedness.

I raised my hand and it was unerringly steady.

I released a breath as I pressed the tip of the blade to his forehead. His eyes widened as he realized what I was about to do. He started to roll his head to the side, his struggles weak and limp from what he'd endured just getting here, but Nyx appeared and he helped me out by keeping him still. His fingers snagged in his hair, pinning him in place.

There was no walking away.

Not because he'd seen me, not because he knew what we looked like, but because those eyes weren't loaded with the evil that would have warned people of his true nature.

They were just irises and pupils and sclera.

My hand moved of its own volition.

Merriweather released a sob that morphed into a terrorized shout when the tip of my blade dug into the flesh of his forehead, which was when Nyx released a shaky, relief-soaked sigh.

We shared a glance, one loaded with understanding for the first time, a connection drifting into being as we reveled in the spurt of

Merriweather's blood, of his bone and cartilage crunching beneath the force of my hand.

His screams rang in my ears as I made three vertical slices. One at either temple, then a final one in the center.

Those screams nourished something inside of me that had been starving.

A welter of relief flooded me.

It drowned the ache in my soul.

My sister.

Jessie.

So innocent, so pure.

She'd dreamed of becoming a ballet dancer, had loved K-Pop, and was lactose intolerant—a fact she always forgot when she wanted ice cream.

Her laughter had filled a room with joy.

Such a good heart, so kind, and all of that snatched away by a man just like Merriweather.

A man who craved her purity, her innocence. Who lusted after something that was never his to possess.

The congressman's screams merged with the one that had escaped me upon the news of her death, one that echoed inside my skull as if her body had been discovered yesterday.

His and mine rioted together in my ears as I slid through each vertical slice with one long one that joined them altogether into a crown.

"The crown of thorns to mock the good Lord's claim of authority," O'Donnelly practically crooned.

"Why are you doing this?" Merriweather sobbed, his terror and pain easing my suffering.

"Because you need to die for what you've done," I whispered, taking that knife and tracing it along his ribs.

"The blade ain't long enough to find his heart from that angle," Nyx muttered, ever pragmatic.

I stared at him. "That's the final step. The killing blow."

He shrugged, mumbling, "You religious headcases, I swear to fuck."

"Let the boy have some enjoyment, Nyx," O'Donnelly chided, clapping his hands together. "You saying you never had fun on a kill?"

"Only if I learned any details of what a sick fuck like this one had done to a kid beforehand."

That had me frowning. "How did you know those details?"

"I didn't get my kills delivered to me," he scoffed. "The MC had to 'collect' the pieces of shit. This is part of O'Donnelly's entertainment." Nyx peered at the older man over his shoulder, his scorn confirming that he was crazy to butt heads with a man like O'Donnelly—the devil himself. "Didn't realize you'd be here to take in the show."

"An old man has to get his kicks somehow."

Nyx grunted and, to me, drawled, "Well, come on then. You've clearly been planning this in your head for a while. Your first one's always shaky. You never bring the right equipment—"

"You really don't, do you?" O'Donnelly mused. "I remember my first time. I got their piss all over me."

Nyx frowned. "Do I even want to know?"

"Stripped him. I learned to always keep the pants on." He nodded. "Sage piece of wisdom for you there, boy."

"I'm not a boy."

"To me you are," O'Donnelly retorted. "What do you need? I've got an arsenal tucked away in this warehouse. A whip? Christ got scourged before his death. We don't have a lance, but I'm sure I've got a sword somewhere—"

"How the fuck do you have a sword?" Nyx demanded.

O'Donnelly tapped his nose. "Got it from a pawnbroker."

Rolling his eyes, Nyx asked me, "You want a sword?"

"A sword?" Merriweather slurred. "My God, are you crazy?!"

O'Donnelly's foot kicked back, and it lodged into the congressman's belly. He coughed and spluttered, choking and hacking as

O'Donnelly told him, "Don't take the Lord's name in vain in my presence."

Blinking, I just said, "I'll take the sword."

"Jonesy, you heard the boy. Get me that silver sword O'Leary brought me in '86."

"Now, you gotta decide," Nyx said, as if O'Donnelly hadn't just asked for a sword like it was an umbrella on a wet day, "whether you want his mouth taped or not. If you want him to talk to you, then you'll hear his screams—"

"Best part if you ask me," O'Donnelly quipped.

Aside from an annoyed grunt, Nyx ignored him, continuing, "— they always make some noise. You can't escape that. But if you don't want them to talk, then we can duct tape his mouth."

I swallowed. "I want them to confess."

"Then deal with the screams you will." Nyx peered back at O'Donnelly. "This place good for that?"

"Soundproofed better than a concert hall." O'Donnelly raised a brow at me. "You know what he could confess to. Are you ready for that?"

"I was going to be a priest. I'd have heard worse sins in the confessional."

"You would if you were serving in Five Points' territory," Nyx said wryly.

O'Donnelly quipped, "I wish I could say he was wrong, but he isn't.

"Merriweather likes little boys, Harlow. A confession would bring that filth into the air. Does he deserve to confess?"

"Confession means nothing without atonement. True atonement and repentance," I said softly, wondering if he knew that. Wondering if, like so many, he just thought he could say a couple Hail Marys and that was that—into heaven he'd go.

"And what if they atone?"

How could he?

Still... "Some sins can't be atoned for," I murmured as I sliced the sign of the cross into Merriweather's saggy pec, unaware that O'Donnelly blanched when my attention was on the screaming man in my control. "Some sins require an eternity of damnation—"

"Look, I get that this is *your* thing, but it ain't mine. Can we get a move on? You're killing my buzz," Nyx growled.

His words shook me from my thoughts. "Sorry."

"Yeah, you should be. Bringing religion to my party," he grumbled. "I'll let you crucify the fucker, but let's keep the claptrap to a bare minimum, yeah?"

I bit the inside of my cheek again. "It isn't claptrap. I'm willing to burn in hell for this, Nyx."

He appeared unimpressed. "Life's a fuck-ton more terrifying than hell, Harlow, and demons get their ideas from humans."

"I hope you're wrong about hell," O'Donnelly rasped. "It's easy to think that when you're in the middle of your life. When you're approaching the end, your perspective shifts."

"It *can* shift. There ain't no god gonna tell me that we're not in the right here." Nyx slammed Merriweather's skull down against the concrete floor which stopped his wailing. "Your God's the one who brought this sick piece of shit into the world, and we're doing him a favor by taking out his mistake."

O'Donnelly's mouth popped open as if he wanted to argue.

But slowly, his lips sealed to a close.

His silence, I thought, spoke louder than words.

FIFTY

RACHEL

THAT SAME EVENING

"Giulia wants to see you."

Frowning, I asked Parker, "Huh?"

"She's in the kitchen."

I tensed. "Is this about the baby shower?"

"You mean the one that isn't happening?" Parker retorted, tongue-in-cheek.

Glowering at her, I got to my feet. I wanted to bitch about her still being here, but I kind of liked it so I kept my mouth shut. She shoved her nose into everything, and it made my office less quiet.

My place was full again and, surprisingly, I liked that too.

It was official—this baby had given me a personality transplant.

With Rain, Rex, Wynter, Harlow, and Parker under my roof, it should have felt cramped, but it didn't.

It felt right.

I headed out of the office, down the hall, and walked toward the kitchen. Half expecting she'd have dived face first into the cake Wynter had baked last night just because—who baked 'just because?' My daughter, that was who—instead, I found Giulia sitting at the head of the table, her hands clutching the sides, her face pale.

My brow furrowed as I walked over to her. "Nyx'll be fine, Giulia," I tried to assure her. It might have been a half-lie, but she looked as if she needed the affirmation.

A slow breath drifted from her. "I did as you said."

"Huh? What about?"

"The piercing."

"The piercing?" My brain didn't want to work. I wasn't thinking about body modification in the regular sense right now; not when I was well aware that, at this very moment, someone in my family was likely torturing a US Congressman. "What piercing?" was a safe question in comparison to *that*.

This time, a sharp breath was expelled from her lungs. "On Nyx's cock."

I blinked, then realizing what she was talking about, I burst out laughing. "You got him to get his dick pierced again?"

"Bet your left tit I did," she said on a low mumble. Her hands clenched around the desk, and slowly, she turned to look at me.

Well, she was definitely being weirder than usual. Especially seeing as Parker had made it seem so all-fired important that I sought her out. Nyx's cock piercings might be her priority, but they weren't mine.

"I know you overshare, Giulia, but that seems pretty random to me. What's going on?"

"They're coming eighteen minutes apart."

I frowned. "What are?"

Her gaze locked on mine. "Contractions."

"Contractions?" I yelped. "What the fuck? You're going into labor?"

Her face scrunched and it had nothing to do with my reaction.

"Holy shit, we need to get you to the hospital! PARKER! Oh my God, where the fuck are you?"

"You need to stop hollering at me. Especially when I'm down the hall—" Parker grumbled, her focus on her cellphone. That small smile died as she froze when she looked at me. "Rachel, what's wrong? What is it?"

"I'm going into labor."

"SHE'S GOING TO GIVE BIRTH!" I shrieked. "She can't give birth in my kitchen. How will we clean that?"

Parker snorted, her regular expression of, 'throw at me what you will, I can handle it' settling back into place. "Plenty of Lysol and elbow grease." She wandered over to Giulia and rested a hand on her shoulder. "I helped my mom a couple times—"

"A couple? How many kids did she have?" Giulia breathed, her head bowing as tension hit her.

Fuck, I remembered that. *Hell*—that was what giving birth had been.

Nurses and doctors touching me when I didn't want them to, and it wasn't like I could stop them. I wanted the baby out, and I didn't want to be pregnant anymore, and they had to help me—

"Rachel, I need you to focus," Parker told me calmly. "You're not giving birth. This is Giulia. We need to concentrate on her."

Rex hadn't been with me when I had given birth. He'd been outside. The doctors at the facility hadn't let him in.

God, he'd be with me when I gave birth this time, wouldn't he?

I didn't realize I'd said that out loud, but Giulia was the one who rasped, "Of course he will. Anyone who tries to stop him will probably get a busted nose for even attempting to keep you two apart."

I gave a rough exhalation. "Right. You're right. He'll kill them." I nodded quickly, swiftly, *panickedly*. Far more panicked about the labor than the idea of Rex having to cut down a hundred people to get to me.

"Rach, we need to focus on Giulia."

"I know," I said shakily. "I know. This isn't about me. This is about her." I staggered over to the kitchen table and stumbled into my seat. "Giulia, this is about you," I informed her.

She shot me a smirk. "You don't say. Parker, how many brothers and sisters do you have?"

"Nine."

"Holy shit. Your mom gave birth ten times?"

"She did." Parker blew out a breath. "I can help until you're ready to go to the hospital."

"You can't come with me?"

"Parker doesn't like leaving the house."

Giulia frowned at me. "Me neither. People suck."

I snorted, and her reaction made my heart stop racing so damn much.

"She means I have agoraphobia, Giulia."

"You do? That's inconvenient, huh?"

"You've no idea."

Giulia's hand let go of the table, and she pulsed the digits at me in a silent request. I studied that hand and slowly bridged our fingers together.

"I want you with me at the hospital."

I could literally feel the color leaving my cheeks. "Okay," I said weakly. *Was it too soon to pass out?* Trying to be brave, I whispered, "Not sure how much use I'll be, but yes."

Parker derided, "She'll be as useful as a house made of toast, but she'll scare all the doctors for you so that'll be good."

"I won't scare the doctors," I grumbled.

"You will."

"I won't."

"You will."

"I won't!" I grated out, scowling at her.

She grinned. "There's some of the regular Rachel. Come back to me, bitch." Her phone buzzed, and I watched her fight the need to check her notifications.

On the brink of demanding who the hell was texting her all the damn time, I crinkled my nose then yelped in surprise when Giulia squeezed my hand. "Ouch!"

Giulia hissed through a breath. "Sorry not sorry."

Parker patted her shoulder. "It's all good. Okay, we need to get you to the hospital."

"You're coming?" I pleaded, though I knew the answer and hoped guilt-tripping her would make her change her mind.

"No. But I'll get you ready."

I shot her a desperate look and she shot me one back as our two phobias collided in a jump hug.

"Rachel, do you know where I put my tablet?"

Wynter's voice was like a dash of cold water in my face.

I turned to her with wild eyes and answered, "Your what, honey?"

"My tablet?"

"Your tablet? Are we talking vitamins?"

"No." She chuckled before, with a disinterest that even in my state I recognized was totally fake, queried, "Also, do you know where Harlow is?"

"I've no idea, sweetheart."

Her brow puckered as she took in the scene. "What's going on? Are you praying?"

Parker laughed. "No. It might look like a prayer circle but Giulia's going into labor."

Wynter scrunched her face. "Ew. At the table?"

"Like mother, like daughter," Giulia muttered.

"We have our solution, ladies and gent... Well, *ladies*. Wynter can go with you to the hospital," Parker said brightly.

"Uh, no, I don't think so—"

Before she could back off, Parker had stormed over to her and was dragging her to the table. I didn't blame the kid. I'd have run off as if the devil himself were at my back too.

"What about Nyx?" Parker asked. "We need to get him."

"He's—" Giulia ducked her head. "—busy."

"You're giving birth," Wynter pointed out. "Shouldn't he care?"

I swallowed. "It's a really urgent project."

Just a little thing called murder.

"More urgent than his kid coming into the world?" Wynter was definitely not impressed by that. "You're breaking up with him, right?"

Her hand clenched around mine. "No, babe, I'm not."

"If he can't make time for labor, when can he make time—"

I grimaced at my kid, because she definitely wasn't wrong, but it wasn't like Nyx could just waltz out from wherever in the city he was.

At least, I didn't think O'Donnelly would be happy about his game coming to an abrupt halt thanks to Nyx's Old Lady going into labor.

"Honey, I know it's weird, but trust me, if Nyx could be there, he'd be there."

"Did he get arrested?"

"Wynter, sweets, ya gotta shut your trap," Parker butted in. "Let's focus on the mom, not the dad, yeah?"

Wynter mumbled, "Maybe if he were here, then I wouldn't need to be."

I'd have laughed, but it was beyond me. My hand snapped out and I grabbed hers and held her in place.

"Now it really does look like a prayer circle," Parker teased, making me realize Giulia was clutching her hand again.

"What do we do?" I rasped.

"We need to get Giulia into the car and on her way to the hospital," Parker repeated kindly—*kind* for once because she was too hard-core to be kind.

I figured she knew I was about to lose my shit because the brain that could cope with the workload I had, suddenly couldn't deal with the to-do list that had one item on it. *Get Giulia to the hospital* was apparently too much for it.

I swallowed. "I can drive her. Yeah, I can manage that."

"Will you come into the labor room with me?"

My eyes about crossed. "You want me in there with you? Not Lily? She's made for stuff like that. She's so sweet—"

"No! You're going to be my kid's godmother. He should see you before anyone else."

"Even Nyx?"

Even I lost my patience at that. "Wynter, drop it." Was it hot in here? It felt hot in here. "I'll, sure, yeah, okay, fine, right, I can do that."

Parker snorted.

It took us ten minutes to get Giulia to the car, and when Wynter was in there with her, I said, "I'll be two minutes."

Before Wynter could grumble, I slammed the door behind her, well aware that the child lock in the backseat would stop her from running.

Parker, watching us from the front door, eyed me warily as I rushed toward her. I grabbed her hand, and she tensed, expecting, I thought, for me to drag her outside. I didn't. I dragged her inside.

"You get that dickhead outta whatever pit he's in and you get him to that hospital, do you hear me?"

Parker countered, "Thought he was away on business."

She didn't know the specifics.

I did, but I was past caring.

The labor room.

Jesus Christ, she wanted me in the labor room?!

Nyx would just have to handle O'Donnelly.

"I'm not going to be the one in that labor room with Giulia, Parker," I screeched. "You get him there!"

She scowled at me. "How do I do that? I don't even have his number!"

"Log into my computer and get the number from there. Call him. If he doesn't answer, CALL AGAIN. Do. Not. Stop. Calling. Until. He. Answers. PARKER, do you understand me?"

She huffed. "I got it as well as a perforated ear drum. I'd ask if you need a Valium but I don't think the baby'd appreciate it."

"Not sure it'd appreciate me passing out either." My mouth

watered at the prospect of a Valium too. I grabbed her shoulders, squeezed and shook her. "What's your job?"

Parker smirked. "My sworn duty is to get Nyx to the hospital."

"Not just the hospital. The labor room, Parker. He has to take over for me—"

"Where's Rex? Can't he find his man?"

My mind almost caved in as I clutched at the love of my life who always had a solution. "That's right. Call Rex. Tell him. He'll make it happen."

"Can't you call him?" she complained.

No way could I drive and talk on the phone at the same time while Giulia was sitting beside me about to give birth.

"Wynter can." My head bobbed. "Yeah, she can. Okay, you try Nyx, and we'll speak with Rex and—"

"Rachel?" Parker murmured as I stood in place for a good twenty seconds, torn so many ways that I could only freeze.

"Yes?" I breathed.

Her tone was kind again—it was a testament to my panic that I wasn't freaked out by it—as she said, "We need to work on a labor plan for when your time comes." She patted me on the head, *literally* patted me on the head. "Now, go, before she gives birth in your SUV and you're the one pulling the baby—"

I didn't let her finish that sentence.

TEXT CHAT

Rachel: *Where the fuck is Nyx?*

Rex: *He's coming. I am too. I won't be long.*

Rachel: *You'd better not be. Oh my God, Rex, this is horrendous.*

Rex: *You got this, baby girl. You fucking got this.*

Rachel: *I really don't. All I keep thinking is how the hell am I going to cope when it's our turn?*

Rex: *I'll be there, and we'll do it together, sweetheart.*

Rachel: *You know, when I was in the hospital the last time, they restrained me.*

Rex: *Those cunts. I will NOT allow that to happen this time.*

Rachel: *No, I know you won't. I-I just need to get over it.*

Rex: *They traumatized you, but we don't have to do it the same way, baby. We can have a home birth. I'll hire the best goddamn doula, and Stone will be there, and we're not far from the hospital. We can make it work.*

Rachel: *I like the idea of that, not going to lie.*

Rex: *I'll make it happen. But I GTG. Less typing, more driving. Be there in fifteen.*

Rachel: *Thank you. I love you xo*

Rex: *Love you. Always, Rach. You got my fucking soul in your hands.*

TEXT CHAT

Nyx: *Brothers, meet Samael. 9lbs 1oz. 23 inches.*

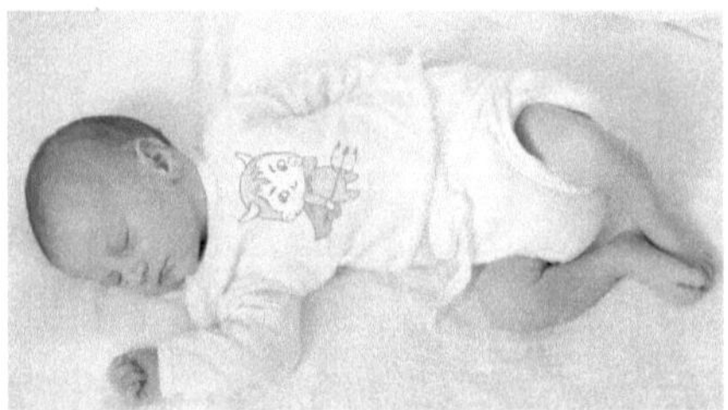

Nyx: *Giulia's sleeping but she got through it like a fucking champ.*

TEXT CHAT

Nyx: *Posse, meet Samael. 9lbs 1oz. 23 inches.*

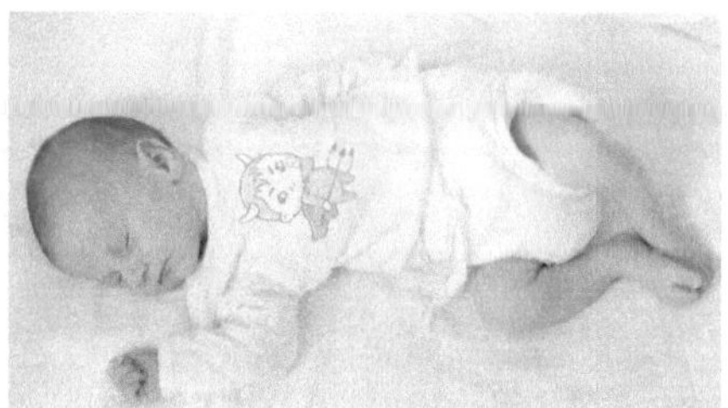

Nyx: *Giulia wanted me to tell you that childbirth sucks, and...*

Nyx: *Well, I ain't gonna tell you everything she wanted me to say because your men'll have MY dick.*

Nyx: *But she's safe, well, got through it like a pro, and this little monster's already stolen her heart from me.*

Nyx: *This once, I don't mind. :D*

FIFTY-ONE

LODESTAR

"Hello, priest."

When he jumped a clear six inches in the air, I didn't bother rolling my eyes.

"I'm not a priest."

Unimpressed, I said, "You need to work on growing some balls, kid. I know the church emasculated you, but you're not doing the Lord's work anymore, are you?"

"What the fuck are you doing in my room?"

Was it just me or did he sound scandalized?

I sniffed. "I wanted to talk with you."

"About what?"

"Not tonight."

He released a shaky breath. "Good."

"Although... How'd it go?" I queried as I snapped a light on.

He frowned, his eyes adjusting to the sudden blast, but my eyes were used to shifts in lighting so I took him in faster than he could me.

A few specks of blood spattered his face, his eyes were wild, and his expression was calm.

This far, Harlow made me think of James Dean. Mooching around the place, his face tortured, his pain clearly on display for everyone to see.

You didn't need to know what it was to be aware that it was heinous.

He was the ultimate rebel *with* a cause, and I was a sucker for that. Especially with eyes so blue that—

Okay, we didn't need to get into that.

Not only was he far too young for me, but I already had a man I was pining over. One who made Harlow look like a little boy.

My hands curled into fists at the thought.

Would I ever get to kiss Conor?

"He died," was his simple answer, but I jerked as he tore me from my thoughts.

"Did you make him suffer? Did Nyx get his hands dirty?"

Like he was in a daze, slowly, he shook his head. "He promised his sister he wouldn't murder anyone again."

I knew he'd killed that rapist, but that didn't count. Under the circumstances, I'd have condemned him for *not* killing that scum-sucking piece of shit.

"He kept his promise?"

His answer mattered more than he could know.

"He did."

That shouldn't have satisfied me, but it did.

I liked a man with honor, even if I had none myself.

But Nyx's actions meant that my presence here was necessary— I'd had faith in him, and it had paid off. That meant it was doubly important I kept his ass out of jail.

"Was the guy dead by the time Nyx got called to the hospital?"

"No."

And he'd left to go and be with Giulia.

Awww. Nyx really *was* growing up.

Now he had a son to drive him crazy as well as a batshit Old Lady.

Seeing the photo he'd sent everyone, the baby in a onesie that had a tiny devil on the front, had made me realize I needed to check in with the priest.

Changing the subject, I asked, "You feeling fucked in the head?"

"How does that feel?"

I thought about that. "Like you want to scream?"

"I've been feeling like that since Jessie... No. Tonight, I don't want to scream."

"Ah, so you're feeling blissed out, huh?"

When he didn't reply, just sank onto the side of his bed and stared blankly at the wall, I figured I had my answer.

Softly, a couple minutes later, he said, "I'm feeling more relaxed, yes." He turned to look at me, and it was kinda creepy and kinda hot. But then, I'd always liked the freaks. "What are you doing here? You're Lodestar, aren't you?"

"Should probably have started with that question before you admitted to committing a murder," I drawled, amused when he tensed. "Yeah, I'm Star. I'm here because..." My amusement faded. "There'll come a day when I'm not around anymore—"

"Why? The club relies on you, doesn't it?"

"It does, but I'm on a mission of my own."

He swallowed. "Oh."

Figured the priest'd get that better than most.

"I won't be sticking around to say bye—" Apart from to Kat, but he didn't need to know that. "—but what you're doing, *your* mission, is something that I'm interested in. You'll never go down for taking the trash out. Ever. So, if it happens again, when it happens again," I corrected, "and if I'm not here, you get in touch and I will facilitate your hunt."

"It wasn't like that. The body was in the warehouse when we showed up."

My nose crinkled. "Where's the fun in that?"

"It was..." The priest tilted his head to the side. "Is that what was missing?"

I shrugged. "Hunting's half the fun."

He released a shaky breath. "Fine."

"Fine?"

"Yes. When, the next time, if you're not here, I'll get in touch. Will you leave me an email address or something?"

I handed him a scrap of paper with a scrawled web address on there.

"Contact me through the site."

His brow furrowed. "wherepriestsgotogethigh.com?"

I smirked. "Just a joke."

Gaze somber, he studied me. "Not everything is a joke, Star."

On edge, that somber gaze turning weird, turning knowing, I commented, "I don't need converting, buddy. Just wanted you to know that even if I'm not around anymore, you can depend on me to keep your ass away from the electric chair." I reached up and pointed to the places on my chin where there were specks on his. "You got blood on you. Go and clean up."

He didn't get to his feet, just gave me a slow nod before he rumbled the creepiest shit ever: "Go with God, Star."

Hiding a shudder, I sniffed. "God can't help me, priest."

MAY

REX

"Fuck."

A soft laugh escaped her. "Does that mean I'm doing it right?"

I peered down at the witch sitting on her knees between my legs and mumbled, "You don't have to do anything other than breathe on it by this point and I'll consider it a world-class blowjob. But yeah, sweetheart, you're doing A-grade work here."

She slipped the tip into her mouth and left sucking kisses around the head like I'd asked her to before. All while her eyes were locked on mine.

"Overachiever. A-plus." Around a groan, I muttered, "Roll your tongue around the underside. Yeah, there."

My hips jerked up and I quickly grabbed the base of my cock so I didn't thrust into her mouth too deep.

She circled the edge, underside the glans, then waited.

This 'asking for direction' shit shouldn't have been so fucking hot.

I drew in a sharp breath, stared up at the ceiling. "Suck."

She did.

I groaned.

"Flat of the tongue around the circumference, then gently prod the slit."

God.

"More spit," I rasped.

She hummed and suddenly, the glans was flooded with a hot slickness that made me want to shoot my load.

"Let go now before I come. Trace the vein on the underside with your tongue."

Her breath washed over me as she moved down the vein, sucking nibbles that had me clenching my fist around the base of my dick.

When she reached my fingers, she pressed a kiss there before she started back up again.

That little dose of tenderness made it so much fucking sweeter knowing she was the one doing this to me.

I hadn't had a blowjob in decades, and if I didn't go blind by the end of this, I'd consider it a win.

"Gather spit and move your tongue—" I broke off to gasp when she took the initiative.

As she followed the veins around my cock, her movements were slicker now, easier, because of the added lubricant.

"Now, put the tip back in your mouth and go as deep as you can. I like suction, not speed."

At least, I thought I fucking did.

Jesus, I didn't even remember.

Either way, she listened.

I lowered my chin to my chest, watching her lips tighten, her cheeks suck in, and I couldn't stop myself from reaching over and letting my fingers trace the indents. When she shuffled to the left, I got a feel of my dick in there too.

Grinning, I told her, "Less messing around, more sucking." She rolled her eyes but listened, and I hissed, "Fuck."

It was ten times more guttural than the last time.

"Take your shirt off."

Her eyes widened and she shook her head.

"They won't come in," I assured her.

She moved down my cock and back up again; that vacuum-like pressure felt so fucking good until she released me with a pop. "I'm not getting naked."

I huffed a breath. "They're not coming in here."

"Your ears aren't working because your brain is in your dick, but they're arguing." I gritted my teeth when she pressed a kiss to the glans and whispered, "You taste so good."

My eyes flared wide. "You like that?"

She nodded, her tongue peeping out to thrust into the slit which made her moan. "Can I suck it harder?"

"Fuck," I snarled. "Yes."

"Let go," she whispered, her fingers stroking over mine.

"No, I don't want to thrust too deep—"

"You can let go," she told me, her eyes on mine as she suckled me. The slurping sound that came next had me tightening the clench of my fingers before I slowly released it.

When my cock flopped back and onto the flat of my belly, she released a soft laugh and I watched as a globule of spit sank from her pretty red lips and down onto my dick.

I reached up and cupped her chin, my thumb moving over her mouth. "How is this still red?"

She shot me an amused smile. "Disappointed?"

"No." Maybe.

"Stain." She reached down and jacked my cock fast enough to make me clench my jaw. "Stops it getting on my teeth for meetings."

I blinked at her, completely clueless as to what she was talking about. Especially when my gaze shifted to the red-tipped fingers that were circling my dick, to the other that moved to her shirt. When she dragged her tits over the neckline, I had no idea why she didn't just take the damn thing off, but I wasn't about to complain.

Her tits were perfection.

Fucking perfection.

I groaned and reached for one, cupping it in my palm then

squeezing her nipple. She tensed and moaned, reminding me they were very sensitive right now, and I rolled it instead of pinching, enjoying her guttural groan because I timed it with the first suck she took on my cock.

"Is your mouth wet enough?" I instructed gruffly, and watching her nod when her lips were full of me was the picture I wanted on my screensaver. "Then move your head up and down and suck as hard as you can."

When she complied, my brow puckered as I clenched my eyes closed. The pleasure rammed into me, and I gritted out, "There's spit on my balls. Use that to lube your hand so you can rub them together."

She released a soft moan that made my heart stutter.

"Next time, I want you to touch your clit when we're doing this," I rumbled. Hell, I'd wanted her to do that this time, but she'd insisted on her lesson first.

Another moan was her answer.

"Twist 'em. Gently! Not like you're juicing a fucking orange," I yelped, which made her snicker. "Just, ya know, in your palm. That, that," I rattled off, my ass clenching as my hips rocked.

"You like that?" she whispered as she pulled back, blowing a stream of cool air down the length of my pulsating dick.

"Yeah, I fucking do, baby girl."

She groaned. "I like it when you tell me that."

"You do? You like knowing that your mouth is sinful? That I'm trying really fucking hard not to come right now?"

"Oh God, yeah, I do."

I growled, "Get those hot lips back on my dick, baby. I want you to taste my cum. You good with that?"

Her nod was hesitant, and I wanted to celebrate that nod. I knew what it meant. Another step forward.

"Thank you, sweetheart. You're sucking me off so fucking well, Rachel. No one could make me feel like this, no one. Only you.

Always you," I ground out, then I bit off, "FUCK," when she placed pressure on the glans with her teeth.

She pulled back, and just when I thought I'd fucked up, she moved down to my balls and I groaned, "Jesus," when she sucked one between her lips and palpated it with her tongue.

"Next time, I'm gonna eat you out as you do this."

"Thought the next time I was gonna rub my clit as I did this," she teased when she came up for air.

"We're gonna do it all."

"Got a lifetime ahead of us to check it off the list," she agreed, softly releasing a breath as she sucked the tip.

"Fuck, we do," I moaned as she went back to gently twisting my balls.

"I want you to come, Rex. I want your cum in my mouth, and I want you to get pleasure—"

I grabbed her ponytail and tugged *gently* on it. "Baby girl, I'm so fucking close, you've no idea."

She grinned at me as she tongued that vein on the underside again. "I'm doing it right?"

My eyes nearly crossed. "Yeah, you're doing it right."

"Good."

Suddenly, a gush of warm spit drenched my cock, and she slurped as she began to move her head. Faster than before, clearly more confident in what she was doing.

Somehow, that, more than anything fucking else, was what got to me.

Was what had me rocking my hips. Was what had me bucking in her mouth as I strained to find the release I'd been denying myself throughout this lesson.

When she bobbed her head faster, I hissed out a long breath before I reached up and grabbed some of my fucking hair and pulled on it so I didn't do that to her.

I choked out a, "Fuck, baby girl, like that, like that, please, fuck, don't fucking stop—" And her mouth tautened around me.

I was a goner.

I didn't have the wherewithal to worry if she was okay. I just fucking exploded in her mouth and she took me.

All of me.

And that was when two things happened.

One—I was reminded my woman was often right.

Two—the door to the den off her office, her sanctum sanctorum, popped open.

I had moments to react, and I grabbed a blanket and managed to shove it over us both so her tits and my dick were *not* exposed.

Wynter and Rain didn't notice. They were too busy bitching at each other about something or fucking nothing and I had no clue what to goddamn do.

"You're a hypocrite! How can you want to join the army to spread peace? Peace isn't spread through war, dumbass."

It was safe to say, Wynter and Rain argued a lot. I figured it had helped her settle in, though, because settle in she had.

It was almost like we'd never been without her, which was fucking awesome.

"Because humans suck—"

How right he was.

Rachel, the little witch, gave my dick a quick suck.

"—and sometimes, they only respect a show of strength."

As they argued, I saw her head bobbing which triggered a whole host of new fantasies, and then she was out from under the blanket, her shirt righted, her lips wet, and her hair mussed.

She twisted around as if nothing had happened, quickly straightened her ponytail, and leaned back against the sofa with her phone in her hand.

I felt like I'd had a bullet between the eyes, but she looked as if she'd been working—but had been pulling at her hair because it was definitely mussed. But in a natural way. As if she were stressed.

The kids were used to that look.

"Rachel, for fuck's sake, would you tell your brat that the army can do good?" Rain demanded, finally glaring at his sister.

"Aren't you talking to the wrong person there, Rain? I'm with Wynter on this one," she said coolly.

So fucking coolly that I had to remind myself she'd just swallowed every drop of cum I'd given her.

That was when I realized this might have been for the best.

The aftermath—it was rushed, and she couldn't panic, and it was over with. Nothing to discuss. Nothing to dissect.

Where I could have killed my kid and my brother-in-law a moment ago, suddenly I wanted to thank them.

"Rex, talk some sense into them," Rain argued.

"Why? I don't want you to enlist either. And if you're going to join the army, why can't you go to college first and enlist as an officer?"

Rachel shot Rain a smug look. "See? That's the smart move, Rain."

He grated out, "When are you three fucking off to Cali again?"

"No parties," I grumbled.

"What are you? My dad?"

"Tomorrow. So Wynter's not jet-lagged for her finals on Wednesday," Rachel intoned calmly.

"What's with the blanket, Dad?" Wynter asked as she moved over to the sofa and plunked herself down beside me. *Well, this wasn't weird at all.* "You gonna nap?"

I shot her a bland smile. "Yeah, honey. That's what I'm gonna do."

Rachel snorted. "Not in here you're not. I thought we were talking about Farrow's election and the upcoming primaries?" Her smile was a taunt in and of itself.

I narrowed my eyes at her in a silent promise.

Her response?

A wide grin and my ass buzzed when my phone received a message.

Rachel: *Told you they'd barge in.*

Rex: *You did. Little fuckers. Why can't they just get along?*

Rachel: *They're making up for the years apart.*

Rex: *If you say so.*

Rachel: *Did you hear Rain say he was taking her into town?*

Rex: *I did.*

Rachel: *Good. I need you to fuck me.*

Rex: *What if you sucked my dick dry?*

Rachel: *That was my intention, but I'm sure you'll rise to the occasion.*

Rex: *How wet are you?*

Rachel: *So goddamn wet my panties are drenched.*

Rex: *Fuck.*

Rachel: *Hard already?*

Rex: *Stop being smug.*

Rachel: *:P*

Before I could reply, the sound of a hog's engine roared outside. Wynter shrieked and rushed over to the window to stare out into the yard.

Harlow was getting used to a bike the club was lending him. Link had nearly shit a brick last week when the hog had come back scraped up because Harlow hadn't put the kickstand down properly.

Rachel pinched my leg and texted me:

Rachel: *Stop glowering at her. She can't help that she has a crush on him.*

Rex: *Of all the goddamn brothers, she had to have a crush on the one who kills pedophiles for a living.*

Rachel: *You're the one who said it was time he started riding a bike.*

Rex: *So it's my fault?*

Rachel: *I think the crush was there. The Harley just made it worse.*

Rex: *FML.*

JUNE

RACHEL

NANCY SINATRA - THESE BOOTS ARE MADE FOR WALKIN'

"You are not talking about the primaries, Rachel," Parker warned me. "*You are not!*"

"I was talking about Rain's graduation ceremony," I lied.

"Bullshit. No talk about the primaries! Or about the fundraiser next month either." Her eyes flashed with temper. "I won't allow it. No work. Just play."

"You mean you won't allow me to talk about things that interest me at the baby shower you knew would bore me senseless? The baby shower I knew you were organizing even though you repeatedly lied to me about organizing it?"

She squinted at me. "Do you or do you not like afternoon tea?"

"That isn't the point. I love afternoon tea, but you still lied to me." I huffed. "You all did. Traitors."

Utterly unapologetic, most of the Posse beamed smiles at me. Giulia, who was nursing baby Sam, outright grinned at me from across the way.

Honestly, I'd seen more of her than I ever wanted to see of another woman thanks to Nyx taking his sweet ass time in arriving at the labor room.

I was just grateful I didn't need to be there for the whole thing. The miracle of life might be grand for a lot of women—I was okay with sitting it out.

"Suck it up, buttercup," Giulia chirped. "And have some fun."

"I'd have more fun if I could have one of those glasses of champagne," I said wistfully to Lily and Amara who, interestingly enough, were the only ones in the room who'd listen to me talk politics.

José 'Joseph' Ferrero was on the ballot after Rex had twisted his arm. I didn't need to know how literal that twisting had been.

Ferrero hadn't shown up to the press ops with a cast so I figured Rex hadn't been violent.

"Not long now," Lily soothed.

Giulia hissed under her breath. "Stop biting, kid. They're not detachable."

"What do you expect when you name a baby after a fallen angel?" Tiff demanded.

"Samael's a beautiful name," Giulia argued, staring down at her kid who was wearing a onesie that declared to the world 'Mommy's Little Demon.'

"He's channeling rage today," Lily teased as she moved away from me and rubbed the tufted dark hair on top of Sam's head.

Because I had no interest in Sam, and Giulia didn't hate me for it, I stayed away from the pooping machine and dug into a small parfait that, I couldn't deny, tasted damn good as I texted Rex:

Rachel: *You suck.*

Rex: *Why?*

Rachel: *What was all this, 'I'll be there through it all, baby girl'?*

Rex: *I will be.*

Rachel: *Then why am I the one dealing with this baby shower on my own?*

Rex: *I meant the labor room. Doctor's appointments. Shit like that. Not being in an enclosed space with the Posse for an indeterminate length of time.*

Rachel: *Pfft.*

Rex: *Enjoy? :P*

Rachel: *I don't think so.*

Huffing under my breath, I sought out Wynter and found that she'd tucked herself away in a corner with a stack of cakes, earbuds in and her phone tipped in a way that told me she was streaming something. Knowing she was comfortable helped me relax.

I'd already heard her playing the Bosendorfer Imperial baby grand Lily owned and determined that was the piano Rex and I would be buying her for our place too.

I couldn't wait to hear her play at home.

Watching the others coo over Sam, I said to Amara, who wasn't overly fond of kids either, "Did you get Azael and Baal checked over at the vet?"

Giulia and Nyx had taken the chihuahua and Newfoundlander in and had also graced them with the names of fallen angels.

I thought Azael's was the most fitting—one of the most evil of fallen angels, it fit the current Azael's nature.

Baal was less 'Duke of Hell,' but he definitely was a lord in stature.

"*Tak*," Amara told me, as she'd been the one to take them as a favor to the new mom. "Both are well, but Azael has arthritis."

"Is that why she's such a bitch?"

Amara grinned. "I think she is born bad bitch."

I snorted at her. "Would you do me a favor?"

"Of course."

"Could you get me some more cake?"

"*Tak*." When she returned with a massive slice of strawberry shortcake, she made me love her even more by asking, "Think you Oliver Farrow will elected Sheriff?"

"I don't see why not. The other candidate is weak, and Farrow has Ferrero's backing."

"Ferrero's name is hard to say."

I crinkled my nose. "Sorry. Joseph is easier for you?"

"I'll call him Iosef."

"Fine. The primaries look set to be a landslide win though. I told Rex Joseph was popular enough for his backing to count. I'm just glad he listened."

"Jesus, woman, are you still talking about work?"

"What do you want me to do, Parker?" I grumbled, glowering at her from over my shoulder. She'd swooped in like a sneak to catch me unawares. "Talk about babies?"

"Well, it's a baby shower. You're supposed to."

"Glass ceilings were meant to be broken, darling," I drawled which made the others laugh.

We were sitting in Lily's pink room, the chairs clustered together around several trolleys housing teapots for Giulia and me, then champagne and coffee for everyone else. There were at least twenty sets of stacked plates that were eponymous with afternoon teas. Each was loaded down with finger sandwiches, cakes, pastries, cookies, even small savory Danishes.

I wasn't going to lie about the food being awesome, but I didn't have a clue about babies and Parker knew that. So did the others at this point because I'd thought the diaper cake was made of actual cake and I'd gone to cut it.

Twenty minutes later, one of Lily's housekeepers knocked on the door, and Lily got to her feet and spoke with her.

"Oh, good! She came! Invite her in."

"Who did?" I queried.

When Rory appeared in the doorway, I surged forward and, grinning all the while, rushed over to hug her.

She squeezed me back and said in my ear, "This totally isn't our scene."

Relieved that I wasn't alone in feeling like a fish out of water, I hugged her tighter. "Thank you for coming."

"I wouldn't miss it." Then, with an expression of utter loathing, she grimaced and declared, "Go on, you can ask me."

My lips twitched at her melodrama. "Ask you what?"

"Hunter informed me last night that he's going to be the baby's godfather." Her nose crinkled as she wafted a hand at my stomach.

Because, yes, I'd forgotten where the baby was. Not.

"So?"

"So we both know you're going to ask me to be the godmother. Which makes no sense as you're not religious but go on, ask me."

"Are you in a good mood?"

"Good enough that I'll say yes to things I don't particularly want to do."

Snickering, I said, "I'm surprised you spoke with Hunter."

She shrugged. "I do from time to time."

Rory made it sound like such a hardship.

I shook my head at her.

Dead To Me had been quiet since our last text chat, and I wasn't about to complain, but I hadn't spoken to Hunter since I'd gotten the information over to her. I was glad to know he was still safe.

"You know you like him," I grumbled.

"I don't have time to like anyone," Rory muttered, peering around the room. "They don't look like Old Ladies."

"What did you expect them to look like? Hookers?" I retorted.

"No," she said with a surprised laugh. "I just didn't expect them to have a twenty-million-dollar house and to have a— What the hell kind of dog is that anyway? A horse?"

"A Newfoundlander."

"Yes, well, I didn't expect for there to be a Newfoundlander guarding a stroller all while everyone's eating cake and drinking tea."

"Only Giulia and I are drinking tea. Everyone else has champagne and coffee."

Her eyes flared wide with relief. "There's champagne? Give it to me! I need some!"

Laughing at her dramatics, and so fucking grateful she'd come—I wouldn't have expected her to, which made it all the sweeter that she had—I went to get her a flute of champagne. She looked more in need of it than I did.

Her change of career had come with consequences, and she wore those consequences in the bruised shadows that had made an appearance below her eyes.

On the brink of introducing Rory to everyone, I heard a bit out, "She's carrying my brother's kid. I think I'm invited."

The happy atmosphere immediately froze.

"Tell me that wasn't Kendra," Giulia growled.

"Is her," Amara snapped.

"Who's Kendra?" Rory asked me under her breath. "Rex has a sister? Or is the daddy not who I thought?"

"She's his half-sister." I rubbed a brow because this was definitely unanticipated. "I thought she'd left West Orange," I said to no one in particular.

"She did. Keira said she drifted over to Ohio until they turfed her out down there," Tiffany replied.

"Let me in, you fucking bitch! I'm the baby's aunt!"

"Over my dead body," Giulia lashed out, bolting upright, which made Sam start bawling.

"Giulia, calm down," I retorted. "I'll deal with this."

"I will. You pregnant," Amara inserted. "Should not get stressed. Is my pleasure to hurt her."

"Too late, babe, I'm already stressed," I said with a snort. "Seriously, leave this with me."

I headed over to the door, and just as I opened it, something hit the wall beside my head.

A stiletto heel?

I stared down at it in bewilderment before I peered at the hallway, finding Kendra hopping around on one shoe as she tried to take that off as well.

"Using heels as a weapon has to be a new low for you, Kendra," I said coolly.

The housekeeper excused, "I'm so sorry. She wouldn't take no for an answer."

"No, that seems to be your 'go to' default, Kendra, doesn't it?"

I surged forward on a pique of temper, faster than she expected, because my hand tightened around her arm and I was hauling her outside before she knew what I was doing.

She shrieked and almost went flying but I kept her upright, because if she was going to be tipped on her ass, then it wasn't going to be by accident.

"What are you talking about, Rachel?" Kendra sniped, dragging her arm out of my hold as she snatched her shoe from my grip. "I have every right to be here. That's my niece or nephew you're carrying."

"You have no right to be here," I retorted. "We are not and never have been friends, and this isn't about the baby, it's about me. Trust me, if it was about the baby, I wouldn't be attending either." *God, talk about boring.* "You are not welcome, Kendra."

"That's being made clear to me," she sneered. "I don't have to listen to you. You might be the big, almighty First Lady but I ain't in the MC anymore."

"Firstly, why would you even come here with that attitude? Secondly, you say that like that improves your chances of safety if you mess us around. If anything, it's the opposite, and that you haven't realized that yet tells me how dumb you are." I got in her face. "On Giulia's behalf, I'll tell you that you're not welcome here. On Storm's, I'll tell you that the only place where you *are* welcome is hell."

Her cheeks pinched. "I love that man—"

"Love?" I shrieked. "Love? You have to be kidding me. You took advantage of him when he was high. I've heard all the sorry details."

"If that's what he told you, he's lying. He loved every minute of it." She sneered at me. "He came, didn't he?"

I saw red.

This kid was making it happen more and more often. Tears having given way to temper now, a temper I was less and less inclined to control.

Whatever she saw in my face had her reaching out to smack me first.

In retaliation, I grabbed her hair, that swinging fucking ponytail that drove me crazy because she tossed her head about so much, and I dragged her back by it.

She must have known what I was going to do though, because she scratched her nails down my cheek. I hissed at the sting, felt the tears in my skin, and that only exacerbated my fury.

With her head dragged back, to the point where her balance was shot and she was almost falling over, I spat in her face.

I had no idea where that came from.

But I did it anyway.

"That's for Storm." I jerked my knee up and aimed it between her legs. "That's for Giulia because she'll always choose violence." Though she cried out, she tried to punch me in the belly, but I grabbed her hand before she could connect and I twisted it to the point of spraining the joint. "Now, I'm going to tell you, very politely, to get out of town. I do that because I loved your father, and so, out of respect to him, I won't tell Rex. If he knew you tried to punch my stomach, you'd be leaving West Orange feet first. So, heed my warning, Kendra, and don't make the mistake of coming back."

I let her go and watched as she crumpled to the floor.

I knew she had nowhere to go, but I also knew that she was more than capable of getting a job that didn't involve her lying on her back.

Before I could pity her, she grated out, "Storm wanted me—"

The red of before was nothing to the crimson wave that settled over my features. But before I snapped, she scurried away, finally realizing that she was outmatched.

As she ran off, behind me, I heard cheers.

I twisted around and saw the Posse were watching, clapping and hooting. Parker had wide eyes, so did Rory and Wynter, but the Old Ladies weren't surprised.

To them, I was this Rachel. The Rachel who waded into fights and who defended her friends.

Because that was what they were now—friends. *And* family.

Parker and Rory only really knew the lawyer and so, for the most part, did Wynter. But I refused to be ashamed. Downright refused.

I was the Satan's Sinners' MC's First Lady and that was that.

TEXT CHAT

Rachel: *Total disclosure, I just got into a fight with Kendra.*

Rex*: Are you fucking kidding me? She's back in WO?*

Rachel: *Yeah. Not for long.*

Rex*: You sent her off?*

Rachel: *Goddamn straight. At least it livened up this baby shower.*

Rex*:* LMAO.

Rachel: *You'd better not have been in on this.*

Rex*: I wasn't. I swear. If I'd known, I'd have told Parker not to bother.*

Rachel: *That was what I needed to hear. You'll be rewarded in heaven for knowing me so well.*

Rex*: I expect rewards before then. ^^'*

Rachel: *I'll bring you some of this strawberry shortcake. It's to die for.*

Rex*: Baby girl, you'd better be messing around.*

Rachel: *Nah, it's top-tier cake.*

Rex*: Rachel!*

Rachel: *What? BTW... I'm officially Posse now.*

Rex*: That I knew about.*

Rachel: *You did?*

Rex*: Yeah. Giulia told me she was making you Posse. I'm not sure what it entails.*

Rachel: *I think it'd have been more fun if I could drink.*

Rex*: Lol. Everything's more fun with a drink.*

Rachel: *I don't think even that would have made the baby shower more bearable.*

Rex*: LMAO. Stop being a big baby.*

Rachel: *Why? I'm carrying one. Doesn't that mean I can be a brat? Don't you want to spank me out of my funk?*

Rex*: Rachel... don't put ideas in my head.*

Rachel: *;) Why not?*

JULY

REX

"Fuck, are you okay?" I demanded as the video call connected.

Storm looked wrecked, and I didn't fucking blame him.

Today had been a shitshow, and it was a miracle that it had ended how it had.

Storm granted me a shaken nod. "I nearly fucking lost them, man."

"That bitch," Link ground out. "She'd better be rotting in hell. What's the point in being one of Satan's Sinners if she ain't?"

He had a point.

We were all in on the video call, dealing with the aftermath of the clusterfuck that had gone down in Coshocton.

"Kendra got mixed up with Sticky, Hook, Grim, and Doc. They set fire to one of our warehouses, had all the guys riding over to deal with that mess. When I got the call they had Keira and Cyan, I headed out by myself.

"I was fucking lucky that North had come over." He rubbed his eyes. "The men came racing to my place, though, once they got the Code Red message. They had my back."

"Of course they did," I said gruffly. "You're their Prez."

"No. Grim sowed a lot of dissent amid the MC." His jaw clenched. "I seriously thought I was fucked. Keira got Kendra though. I can't say I'm sorry, man," he directed at me.

"You're kidding, right? Rex hated her more than the rest of us did," Nyx retorted. "And that's saying fucking something."

Sin leaned forward. "Do you need Cruz to come down and get rid of the bodies?"

"I got it handled." Storm's eyes were round with remembered terror. "I nearly fucking lost them."

"But you didn't," I said, my tone sharper than I'd like, but I wanted him to snap out of this. He hadn't lost them. They were alive and well, and I didn't need him spiraling. That was a surefire way for him to lose his girls. "They're safe, and they're with you, and you have a fucking future now that cunt's dead."

Giulia had told me how, at the baby shower last month, Kendra had tried to punch Rach in the belly. If I'd had an ounce of sympathy in my being for her, it had faded at that.

Dad had asked me to give her some kind of legacy, and I'd complied. He hadn't asked me to be charitable.

"I'm gonna go, man." Storm still looked spaced out, and it had nothing to do with his drugs of choice. More like a whacked combo of fear and adrenaline. "Fraction, Cyan's dog, is with the vet—"

"They hurt him? Those fucking bastards!" Nyx growled.

I shot Nyx the side-eye. "You caught what your brother's got?"

"Fuck off. You don't kill the dog. It's like the fucking law."

"It really ain't," Link muttered.

"Well, it goddamn should be."

"Storm, you get going, man. We understand. Give our best to K and Cy, yeah?"

"Will do. Thanks, brothers." He paused, then his brow puckered. "It might be nothing, but..."

"But what?" I probed when he fell silent.

"When I was working Hook over, he mentioned something about

an expensive necklace being hidden in a secret safe on the compound here."

"What about it?" I asked.

"They had hidden safes there?" Maverick queried in surprise.

"Yeah, they did shit differently than Rex. Butch was a prick. They didn't split their cuts fairly." Storm scraped a hand over his head. "I only ask because Hook mentioned something about it being stolen from a crime family in New York. You heard anything about that?"

I shook my head. "I haven't. Has anyone else?" When I looked around the table, I saw everyone seemed to be as confused about it as I was. "You think it's a big deal?"

"I gotta find it first, if it even exists. I just... I thought it was curious, that's all.'

"Sin, you could ask Declan, right?"

"Sure. I'll text him when we're done."

"Great. I can get Rach to ask around with the Italians. If anything comes up, I'll let you know."

Storm nodded. "Thanks, Rex."

Link said, "I heard you're gonna brand Keira."

My brows lifted. "You are? And she wants that?"

"She does." He swallowed. "It's time."

"Fuck, that's awesome news," Nyx rasped.

"It goddamn is," Steel rumbled.

"Yeah. I got my Old Lady back, and that cunt nearly stole her from me." Storm's jaw clenched. "Okay, I'm going. Speak soon, brothers."

The video call ended, and most of us rocked in our seats now that his face faded from the TV screen on the back wall.

"I wasn't sure that'd ever happen," Sin said slowly.

"Me either," Nyx replied.

"I knew," I murmured. "They just needed to get their heads out of their asses."

"Yeah," Link agreed. "They had a lot of shit to work through, but what the fuck is the point in loving someone if you can't do that together?"

He was right.

Which was terrifying.

Steel cleared his throat. "A necklace in a hidden safe? What is this? A Nancy Drew story?"

From the looks of relief on all our faces, the lot of us were grateful for the change of subject.

"He wouldn't have brought it up if it weren't important," Maverick pointed out as he rubbed his temple. It was a common thing to see. Those goddamn headaches of his. If I could take them away from him, I would. "That's fucked up what happened. Hijacked by ex-Sinners, almost goddamn killed, his family nearly—" Mav blew out a breath. "We're lucky today ended the way it did."

Slowly, I nodded. The main emotion I was feeling right now was relief. Seventy-five percent of that was aimed at the fact that my brother and his family were safe. The other twenty-five was aimed solely at the fate that had been delivered unto the half-sister from hell.

How goddamn horrendous was that?

Kendra was dead.

She'd never done anything wrong to me personally. It was only her existence that was an affront—

I really shouldn't have felt relief, but I'd never claimed to be a good person.

Shit, I'd have to tell her mom.

Goddammit to hell.

Pinching the bridge of my nose, I ordered, "Be ready to ride over to them, Link, Sin, in case there's more unrest in that chapter."

"What the fuck about me?"

I shot Nyx a look. "What about you, dipshit? You really okay with leaving Giulia and Samael right now?"

His mouth rounded.

Nyx had a habit of forgetting his new circumstances, then, when he remembered, he looked like he'd been whacked on the head with a baseball bat, followed by...

Yeah.

The dopey grin.

I almost shook my head at his contented look.

It was starting to creep me the fuck out, and I knew I wasn't the only one. At least it always shut him up.

"Speaking of unrest, I've been meaning to bring this up with you, but I'm thinking about promoting Cruz to the council." When there was no arguing, and I meant *zero*, I raised a brow. "I expected some criticism."

"Why? He keeps our asses out of jail for the most part," Sin said with a shrug.

"There's no position for him," was all Steel had to say.

"That's the only issue? How about we fucking make one? He's our Reaper, ain't he?"

Nyx's lips twisted. "We'd need to get him a patch."

"Seeing as you're domesticated now, I'll leave that with you."

He flipped me the bird. "Fuck off."

Shooting him a grin, I murmured, "Got nowhere to fuck off to. Harlow still doesn't have his patch. We can have a dual celebration."

"Sounds good to me. I'll make the arrangements," Steel, as Secretary, confirmed.

Sin said, "I wanted to talk to you about that actually. It didn't feel right partying so soon after Bear..."

Everyone nodded their understanding.

"So... we're agreed then?" I got a bunch of nods and had to admit I was taken aback by the lack of blowback about making a new council position out of nothing.

Cruz was one of the best men I knew, but these fuckers were argumentative dipshits. I'd expected to have to bring forward my A-game.

Looked like that wasn't necessary.

A fact that was cemented in place when Maverick, moving onto other business, remarked, "José flew through the primaries—totally whooped Kinnock's ass. He's set to be the next mayor. If that's the case, I don't think we'll have any issues with Farrow becoming sheriff. Rachel was right to push this—we'll have the town hall and the sheriff's department in our pocket."

"She's smart as fuck, that's why." I'd been slow off the mark with this being election year. I was almost ashamed of how myopic I'd been and was beyond grateful my Old Lady was hot shit. "I'll be meeting with him in a couple weeks."

"You need to bring up him lifting the noise ordinance in the city limits," Sin rumbled. "Couple of guys got fined for that last week."

"I will. Anything else?

"There are zoning issues with building houses on the compound. It's listed as agricultural right now, but it needs to be residential. Plus, the quotas need adjusting. The plot's limited to six houses, but Giulia and me aren't the only ones who want to live here."

"Consider it handled."

After, we discussed the strip joint which was raking us in so much dough that Maverick was having to offset a lot of the income to offshore bank accounts so we didn't need to pay Uncle Sam more than he was worth. Then we discussed opening another on the outskirts of West Orange's border with Verona.

After that, we conferred about what had gone down with Storm when Digger called to give us another update. Which was when it became clear that we'd almost lost Storm in today's fuckfest.

It was bad enough losing him to goddamn Ohio, never mind to a graveyard.

As the late meeting came to a close, I muttered, "I'll speak with Cruz in the AM about a promotion. He might not fucking want it."

"Nah, he'll want it," Nyx disagreed. "Did you hear about Indy getting through to the finals on that TV show? We got the news earlier today."

"I did. Rach told me." I tapped the ink on the side of my throat. The scales of justice—if they were sentient, they'd have hated being on my skin seeing as I was beyond shady. "Good thing I got to her before she's mega famous," I teased.

Nyx grinned, but he looked proud as fuck. "Yeah. Got myself a back full of Indy Sisson's artwork."

"Shame you're not a swimsuit model so you don't get to show it off to the general public," Sin joked, which, of course, led to him and Nyx duking it out as they left my office.

I didn't bother rolling my eyes as, one by one, they started to leave. Link, on the way out, told me about Lily going Bridezilla with their wedding which was gonna be a 'white wedding,' Steel bitched about Stone's shifts which were fucking with their 'fucking' time, until finally, Mav and I were left in peace.

Arching a brow at him when he made no move to leave, I asked, "You got something to bitch about too?"

"Nah. Alessa's perfect. If you wanna kill someone, you can off my doctors, though. I'd be okay with that."

"They're trying to fix you. I ain't killing them until you're on the path to being healed."

He shot me a look loaded with disbelief. "That ain't gonna happen, Rex. You know that, don't you?"

I frowned at him. "Fuck off. Don't be living your life like that. We gotta be positive."

"I ain't living my life negatively. You kidding me? I wanna be around until I'm at least eighty. Alessa's totally gonna be a GILF."

I chuckled. "Pervert."

"You know it." He grinned at me. "I just meant you can't fix what's fucked, just gotta deal with it. There'll be good times and bad, but I know she'll see me through."

"Just like you will with her. Hell, just like we all will. We got your back, brother."

"I know you do." He scratched his chin. "You remember Drew?"

"The school shooter?" I blinked at the change of topic. "What about him?"

"He turned seventeen two days ago and ran away from Shady Pines."

Hissing under my breath, I argued, "How could they let him get out? He was fucked in the head."

Mav shrugged. "His records show he was an exemplary patient and he was in there on a voluntary basis anyway. School's out so I don't think he's a risk."

"He ran away for a reason," I pointed out, but I didn't let him answer as an uneasy feeling settled inside me. "Watch out for him."

"I will."

"Did he ever email that address I gave him?"

"Nope. But I'll carry on checking the inbox."

"Thanks, man. Appreciate you keeping on top of that."

"It's what I do." Gathering his laptop, he asked, "You think Giulia will be pissed when she finds out North is back on the radar and he turned pussy and went to the Ohio chapter and not back here?"

I winced. "Fuck, never thought about it that way."

He hummed. "Something to watch out for."

"Ain't there always in this fucking job."

His lips twitched. "Rach okay?"

"Yeah. Had more bloodwork done. She and the baby are fine. Late August/early September's when she's due. I'm shitting myself."

He laughed. "'Course you are. That's how you know you love her."

"Didn't need to be terrified to figure that out." I rolled my eyes. "Anyway, I'm going home. You?"

"Nah. Alessa's in the kitchen. She's making some Ukrainian thing for dinner tomorrow and it needs a whole night to prep."

"No offense, bro, but I'll be glad when Giulia's back in the kitchen."

"Mav's grin was sheepish. "None taken."

TEXT CHAT

Rex: *Kendra's dead.*

    Rachel: *Keira told us. How are you feeling?*

    Rex: *Relieved.*

    Rachel: *Understandable. She was trouble.*

    Rex: *Yeah, she was.*

    Rachel: *You okay?*

    Rex: *I'm fine. Just... We almost lost Storm, Rach.*

    Rachel: *Trust me, we've had that meltdown too. It was a close call. Too close.*

    Rex: *I swear no one will ever get to us, Rach. I promise you that.*

    Rachel: *You can't promise that, and regardless, I wouldn't change anything.*

    Rex: *You wouldn't?*

    Rachel: *Well, you know I always thought you were meant for the White House, but I can settle for being a White Lady of the Dark House instead.*

    Rex: *Lol!*

    Rachel: *:P*

    Rex: *BTW, Storm asked me about something one of the traitors* *told him. There's a secret safe in the Coshocton clubhouse and it contains a necklace that was apparently stolen from a New York crime family.*

Rex: *I know it sounds like something from a crime show, but Storm wouldn't have brought it up if he didn't think it was legit.*

Rachel: *You want me to ask the Valentinis?*

Rex: *Please.*

Rachel: *Will do. Hey, guess what Wynter did today?*

Rex: *Figured out how to solve world hunger?*

Rachel: *That's on tomorrow's agenda. She called me Mom. It was by accident, but damn, it sounded good.*

Rex: *She can have two moms, Rach.*

Rachel: *Hush. I don't need her to always call me that. It was just nice, and I knew you'd get it.*

Rex: *I do, but I don't think you should limit yourself to only hearing it the one time. She'll surprise you. You'll see.*

Rachel: *Maybe. Anyway, what time are you coming home?*

Rex: *Got José coming in to see me, and after that, I'll be back around twelve.*

Rachel: *I'll wait up.*

Rex: *You need your rest.*

Rachel: *Need you more.*

Rex: *You decided on what your ink's gonna be?*

Rachel: *Planning ahead, are we?*

Rex: *Don't see why not.*

Rachel: *It's gotta be a crown, doesn't it?*

Rex: *Thought that'd be too cliché for you.*

Rachel: *Nope. Some stuff is just meant to be. Plus, Indy's designing it so you know it'll be cool.*

Rex: *Nyx was crowing about her heading to the finals.*

Rachel: *Something to be proud of. His back is worth a fortune now and he probably didn't pay her because he's family.*

Rex: *Nah, Nyx is always fair. He pays her double.*

Rachel: *Color me impressed.*

Rex: *So, a crown? I like that actually.*
Rachel: *So you should. :P*
Rex: *Gonna suck it every day.*
Rachel: *LMAO. Suck it?! You could just kiss it.*
Rex: *Where'd the fun be in that?*

AUGUST

REX

As was tradition when a brother had an Old Lady, she was the one who sewed his patches onto his cut.

For Cruz, next time he earned a patch, I thought I'd have to get Giulia to sew it on the sly because Indy was definitely not a seamstress.

My lips twitched at the sight of the Reaper patch that was kinda skewed, and *a lot* in danger of falling off. Still, Cruz kept peering down at it on his chest before he'd beam a grin at the room.

It was hard not to grin back when he was so fucking happy to be promoted onto the council.

When he'd shrugged into his cut, the MC had roared its approval by stomping their feet and hauling him into a crowd surf which had the potential to go disastrously wrong.

At my side, baby Samael, who was strapped onto Nyx's chest in a carrier that had a skull and crossbones print, cooed, proving that he lived up to his name. Somehow, Rach and I were his godparents—God help us.

"Thanks, man," Cruz told me as he was returned to the bar. "Can't fucking tell you what this means."

Oh, I knew what it meant.

His mom was a goddamn FBI agent, a crooked one, and we were bringing him onto the council anyway?

It was a testament to the faith we had in him, the trust we felt.

Cruz more than deserved his place on the council, and the Sinners would be so much better for it.

Rachel, the only Old Lady this close to the bar, was leaning against the counter at my side. Her belly was getting bigger, and it was getting harder every fucking day not to stroke it and touch it. It still freaked her out, but she was doing well, apart from backache that crippled her some days.

As I turned to her, she handed me the cut she'd sewn—I got my confirmation Giulia was gonna be the club seamstress—and I shouted to the crowd, "We got a brother who's been walking around without a cut or a hog. Today, we rectify that. His hog's finally outside, and now, his cut's here, in my hands, just waiting for him."

Cheers from the crowd had me grinning as Nyx called out, "Harlow, where the fuck are you? Get your ass over here!"

Becoming a brother hadn't made Harlow more popular. People still floated around him, and he drifted through the club like a ghost. But he'd started helping Maverick and he was brilliant with the ledgers, and mostly, he hung with the council which was A, unusual, and B, surprisingly not all that annoying.

Even if Wynter's googly eyes on him were starting to piss me off.

Harlow, his shoulders hunched, trudged over to the bar. Raising the cut, I saw his eyes widen at the letters on the back.

I knew he'd hate it, and that was my confirmation, but Nyx had chosen his road name, and I couldn't deny—he *was* Priest.

When I handed it to him, I joked, "You'll always be our priest now."

"You want me to watch over your souls?" he mocked, with more ease than he'd shown since the last hunt—the eve of Sam's birth. Proof that he felt more settled now he had his hands on something tangible that told the world he was a brother?

I'd done him dirty by not arranging for him to get patched in sooner, but shit had been so crazy in the run up to today that he was fucking lucky we were celebrating at all.

"Nah, our souls were fucked a long time ago," Link boomed, which earned him a laugh from the crowd.

As Priest shrugged into his cut, I announced, "The past has shaped us, the present inspires us, and the future will see us soar—we're the goddamn Satan's Sinners and here's to reigning over West Orange for the next fifty years!"

As the cheers were overtaken by loud rock, and a party stirred into being, I drifted over to Rachel and asked, "You wanna go home?"

"No. I'm pregnant not decrepit."

I grinned. "You're going to stay even though you don't want to be here because my question was an affront to females everywhere, wasn't it?"

"Exactly," she grumbled.

Laughing, I shook my head as I slung my arm around her shoulders and took a moment to peer around the room.

Indy was currently being carried away to only God knew where with Cruz's hands all over her ass in a way that told me he wasn't reading the room, because Nyx might have turned into a cinnamon roll for Havoc—I was calling Sam that because he was a pain in the fucking ass—but when it came down to his sister, he was as protective as ever.

So, yeah, Cruz was *definitely* feeling brave.

Either that or fucking lucky.

Catching sight of Priest, with his head tipped back how it was, I could see he was on the brink of tears, and I knew they were more emotion than the fucker had displayed in months.

After a few, Rain showed up, and I watched him trace the gleaming neon skull patch on the front of his cut while Rain chewed his ear off until, out of nowhere, Wynter turned up too. He jerked in surprise when she cried, "Harlow!"

The tears were a distant memory, soon to be replaced with a gleam as Wynter oohed and aahed about his patches.

"What's she doing here?" I groused.

"I told her she could come. She's nearly eighteen, Rex."

I scowled. "'Nearly' is the keyword in that sentence. You know what goes down at these parties. Why the fuck would you let her come?"

"I attended them when I was younger than she was," she pointed out.

Splitting my scowl between her and Priest, I muttered, "And I didn't like that either."

Rachel snorted. "Leave them alone. You can't stop her from liking him."

My growl had her chuckling. "I can stop him from liking her."

"Leave them alone," she repeated. "Maybe he'll keep her in the tristate area. Let's not encourage her to leave for Stanford, huh?"

"She wants to go to Juilliard."

"She won't if we try to break them up. She'll run from us too," she commented, making me huff.

On the brink of arguing with her, I watched as her eyes lit up when the Old Ladies arrived and started clustering around her, so I decided I'd be a good Old Man and would let her have her fun. Especially when MC parties weren't her thing.

Letting her go with a kiss that had the MC hollering and hooting at us, with Lily and Giulia shepherding her over to the smaller den just off this one that the women had claimed, I leaned back against the bar.

Nyx had stormed over to the stereo and turned it down because of Havoc, and anyone who grumbled about it getting quieter in here received a death stare in return.

"Nobody fucking smoke while Sam's around," he snarled when a brother tried to light up a cig. "I'll be leaving soon. You can give yourselves cancer when he ain't in the bar."

Ignoring the scowls, he moved over to my side and gave me the reason I was putting up with having Havoc here all the fucking time —he stared down at the kid like he was his savior.

Maybe he was.

Maybe Havoc was what it'd take to get him off the path he'd been on for so long.

I knew Wynter had changed me, and I knew having her around was shaping the man I was becoming, never mind what the baby would do.

Why wouldn't Havoc do that for Nyx?

Neither of us said anything as we stood together, that powerful bond of solidarity which existed between us, linking us as always, coming into being.

In silence, we watched over the crowds, me trying not to stare at what Priest and Wynter were getting up to, until, gradually, most of the council moved around us. Nyx sniping at Cruz when he showed up, wiping his mouth, Link shooting the breeze with Maverick, Steel snapping at Sin because he'd confiscated the ever-present deck of cards...

Good times.

The best.

I was on the brink of relaxing, finally having accepted an over-large measure of JD that Quin had handed me because I'd started growling when Wynter and Priest began dancing together, when I saw lights in the window, coming from the gates.

Nyx immediately tensed up. "What's going on? Who's at the gates?" he snapped. "Everyone's already here. Nobody should be showing up at this time."

"Sin, go and check," I ordered, but I wasn't worried. The lights weren't flashing red and blue, so that was all that mattered.

Sin didn't need me to prompt him though; he was already on his way. Five minutes later, he returned, dragging a scrawny kid by the back of his collar.

Straightening up, my eyes widened in surprise. "Drew? What the fuck are you doing here?"

"Who the hell's Drew?" I heard Link mutter behind me.

Maverick heaved a sigh. "It's a long, fucking story and it starts in New Mexico."

PRIEST

SEX & CANDY - MARCY PLAYGROUND

Wynter's hands flittered over my cut, oohing at the Sinners' patch, aahing at my name.

She smelled of citrus fruits and spice—like mulled wine.

She rubbed against me, her hands touching my shoulders, brushing my arms as we danced.

Now, I had the true meaning of temptation.

Temptation of the flesh.

Of the *heart.*

I shuddered as I was faced with the very real realization that everything in my life that'd happened to this point—all the trauma, all the misery, all the broken vows—could have been to bring me here.

Now.

To this point.

Was God granting me peace?

Or testing me further?

RACHEL

"I need some information on a Warren Kieran Winchester. He's local to New Jersey."

The sound of Dead To Me's voice in my ear was not a welcome one.

With no further threats and no calls, I'd been hoping that she'd forgotten about Hunter.

Naive, but I had enough shit on my agenda without her adding to it.

Trying to get ahead of myself so that I could have at least a couple weeks off after I gave birth was already feeling like an impossible feat without this BS.

"Who the fuck's he?" I growled.

Dead To Me tutted. "Why do you think I'm asking you?"

And like that, she cut the call.

Hissing under my breath, I rang Hunter.

"Rach, today's not a good day. My grandfather's in court. It's the closing arguments for the prosecution; the jury's about to go into deliberation."

Though I grimaced, I said, "I'm sorry, Hunter, but it's Dead To Me. She made a call and you know we have to get her some answers."

"For fuck's sake," he grated out. "What does she need now?"

"She wants some information on a guy called Warren Kieran Winchester. He's based in New Jersey."

I heard a scratching sound and knew he was taking note of the name.

"I'll get something back to you by the end of the day."

"Thanks, Hunter."

He didn't reply, which was a testament to how stressed he was.

Ironically enough, if I were his lawyer, I'd have been thrilled. The best part of the job was closing arguments.

I shoved thoughts of Hunter aside because I had a massive list of things I needed to accomplish before the day was out, and I never expected that only four hours later, I'd hear from him again.

When his name flashed up on my Caller ID, I answered, "That was fast."

"Yeah, it was easy. He's interred at Windy Ocean Pet Cemetery."

"Huh?"

"You heard me right."

"Windy Ocean Pet Cemetery?"

"You got a pen? I'll give you the address if you want."

"The fuck is she asking us about dead pets for?"

"Who the hell knows? At least this time it was an easy task."

He had a point.

"What a weird name for a pet."

"Heard of weirder. Do you want the address?" he asked hurriedly.

After I jotted down the address, I told him, "Best of luck today with your grandfather, Hunter."

"I appreciate it, Rach. Thanks for everything."

Sending the info over text to Dead To Me, relieved that that was off my to-do list, when she called me five minutes later, I ground out, "I got you the information you asked for. I have a job, you know?"

"You did. But it's not enough. I need you to go to the grave."

"You want me to visit a pet cemetery for you?" I spluttered.

"I can't go. I'm out of the country."

"What do you need to know?"

"I want a picture of the tombstone."

Utterly confused, I snapped, "You're asking too much."

"To keep Hunter De Laurentiis alive?" She tsked. "I thought you'd do anything to make sure he was safe."

I gritted my teeth and tried not to let my newly-found red hot temper get the better of me.

"Fine. I'll get the photo to you tomorrow."

"No. Tonight. I need it ASAP."

I didn't answer, just slammed the phone down on the desk. When that wasn't good enough, I slammed it a couple more times, actually satisfied when I heard the screen crunch under the pressure.

Striding out of my office, I hollered, "PARKER."

"For fuck's sake, Rach, my office is next door to yours," she groused.

I grumbled, "Why are you still here again?"

She'd finally told me about the loan sharks, but that didn't mean I was going to cut her any slack. That was how she and I rolled, after all.

It was also why she'd moved in.

I'd gotten her out of the house once, and I considered that a win as well.

Her lips twitched. "You like having me around."

"Uh-huh," I drawled. "Right. I'm going out."

Her brow furrowed. "You have no appointments scheduled."

"I do now."

"Do you want me to call Emile?"

"No. I won't be long."

I didn't hang around to say goodbye. I was too pissed. If I'd been thinking clearly, I'd probably have second-guessed shit, but I didn't.

My ice-cold nature of before had melted under pregnancy hormones and too much sex.

Volatile wasn't the word.

I typed in the address to Windy Ocean Pet Cemetery on my phone, pissed now at the state of the screen, but I took off a moment later.

It wasn't far, a fifteen-minute drive max, but I bitterly resented each moment I was away from my desk.

When I got to the cemetery, I headed to the small office.

It was hard to be polite when I was so mad, but I gritted my teeth and lied, "I'm hoping you can help me, ma'am. My dad's dog was buried here, but he never told us where he interred Warren before he died too—"

The older woman's distress on my behalf was so genuine that I felt bad for manipulating her. "Oh dear, that's so tragic."

Before she could ask any questions about who'd registered the burial, information I didn't have, I prayed the name was strange enough to trigger a memory. "His dog was called Warren Kieran Winchester." A fucking mouthful for a dog. It made Giulia's choice of pets' names look normal.

And bingo—I was in luck.

A soft smile graced the older woman's mouth. "Oh, I remember him! How could I forget a name like that? Your father said he named him after his brother but he called him Grizzly for short. He was so angry about his death."

Whatever she could have said, I never expected that.

For a moment, I felt my heart surge in my chest until I was sure it would explode through my rib cage.

It couldn't be...

Could it?!

Grizzly was probably a common pet name.

But why would Dead To Me have sent me here if there wasn't something suspicious going on?

"Grizzly, yes," I choked out, unsure about what was going on, just knowing that I felt as if I were dangling on the edge of a precipice that'd lead me only the fuck knew where. "Such a waste. So young."

She nodded. "I remember because... well, Warren was one of the first to be interred here, and you'll call me an old fool but Winchester? It reminded me of those fine Winchester brothers."

Grizzly.

This couldn't be a coincidence, could it?

"Here we are," the receptionist said before she drew out a map and circled where 'Grizzly' was buried. "It's not far from here," she assured me, then her gaze took in my very pregnant self. "Do you think you'll be able to manage? It's ever so hot out."

"I'll be fine," I rasped, just wanting to get out there and to understand what the fuck was going on. "Thank you so much for your help. You've been so kind."

We parted, and I almost stumbled outside as, following the map, I rushed over to the burial site.

It was a pleasant place, massive. There had to be tens of thousands of graves here, and that made it harder to find the specific plot but find it I did.

There was a wooden cross atop the burial mound, with a small silver plaque that read:

'Grizzly'

<u>Warren Kieran Winchester</u>

'An animal in life, an animal in death.'

A shudder rushed through me.

This was no coincidence.

My stomach plummeted as did I. My knees caved out and landed in the soft lawn and I hovered there, shaking, until I had the strength to text Rex:

Rachel: *Rex, does the name Warren Kieran Winchester mean anything to you?*

Rex: *Warren Kieran were Grizzly's first and middle names. Winchester was my grandmother's maiden name. Why? And how do you know that?*

Rachel: *Dead To Me asked me to find out some information about him. Hunter located him in a pet cemetery. You have to see what I'm looking at.*

I didn't bother sending him a photo, just started a video call.

Turning the camera toward the plaque on the grave so it'd be the first thing he saw, I watched as Rex's eyes widened and, out loud, he whispered, "'Grizzly' Warren Kieran Winchester 'An animal in life, an animal in death.'" He sucked down a breath. "How the fuck did you find that?"

"I don't know how Hunter uncovered the info, but I'm here, and... this *has* to be Grizzly, doesn't it?"

Rex scrubbed a hand over his face. "'An animal in life, an animal in death.' Yeah, that sounds like him, and it sounds like some kind of punishment my dad'd mete out."

Relief swelled inside me, but I dampened it down to whisper, "I just don't understand why Dead To Me wants to know—"

Before he could answer, I received an incoming text.

Dead To Me: *You're welcome.*

A soft gasp escaped me, and that was when the tears started.

I had my closure, and because I'd been so busy, I'd never even realized that I'd been missing it.

Ten minutes later, more relief hit me when she sent one last message:

Dead To Me: *Goodbye.*

LODESTAR

THAT SAME DAY

Cin*: She's at the cemetery.*

Lodestar: *Good.*

Cin*: I don't understand all the cloak and dagger shit.*

Cin*: And Star, I'm a fucking spy too. Why the fuck couldn't you just tell her you knew where her rapist was buried?*

Lodestar: *Because we don't have that kind of relationship.*

Lodestar: *Plus, she's smart, and she'd know that something was going on.*

Cin*: That might be the first time you've ever complimented someone.*

Lodestar: *Yeah, what can I say? She's a clever bitch.*

Cin*: Should I be jealous?*

Lodestar: *Lol. Yes. You should.*

Cin*: Charming. What's with the pet cemetery anyway?*

Lodestar: *Her father-in-law buried his brother there.*

Cin*: Huh. In a pet cemetery?*

Lodestar: *Yep. The fucker deserved an unmarked pit.*

Cin*: Why?*

Lodestar: *Rapist.*

Cin: *Bastard.*

Lodestar: *Exactly. From his notes, I don't think her FIL knew his brother had raped her, but in his diary, he talked about some shit he'd done to his ex. He called him an animal.*

Cin: *So he buried him in a pet cemetery?*

Lodestar: *Didn't want him in the family plot.*

Cin: *You say that like it makes sense.*

Lodestar: *Does to me. Animals belong together.*

Cin: *People bury their beloved pets in graves. Isn't he tainting the graveyard with his poison?*

Lodestar: *Shit.*

Cin: *You don't like it when I'm right, do you?*

Lodestar: *No.*

Lodestar: *You can stop making Laker's life hard now.*

Cin: *Did you need any of the information she gave us?*

Lodestar: *Nope. Kept you informed though, didn't it?*

Cin: *Anyone ever tell you you're really bad at sharing?*

Lodestar: *I'm a typical only child.*

Cin: *That you fucking are.*

Lodestar: *Anyway, thank you for your help.*

Cin: *Any time. I'll wait on your call. Don't cut me out, Star. I'll be pissed if you do.*

I set my phone down on the desk as I stared at Conor's rig.

It was a beauty.

The entire place was.

It'd be better if he were here, but that wasn't to be, and being around his stuff felt right.

Homely.

And I hadn't had a goddamn home since my mom's murder.

I slipped the thumb drive onto the USB dock and transferred over the folder I'd stuffed full for Conor.

There were terabytes of information within that folder because that was how much shit Bear had collected over the years. And none of that was from the photos he'd used to store data in either.

The hacker behind that clever steganography I'd yet to find.

Regardless, for someone who was old school AF, how his mind had worked, how he'd gathered intel—*impressive.*

I was giving out compliments to more than just Rachel.

Because of Bear, I had access to more names, to different factions, knowledge about initiation practices. There were banking details and breakdowns on the hierarchy within organizations like the ECD and something called the United Brotherhood—a Russian body of bankers. An elite Russian version of the Masons.

I'd also uncovered private information.

Like where Bear had buried his brother.

I couldn't let Rachel live in fear. Not when I had the answer in my grasp. But giving her the runaround was imperative to keeping Hunter Lachlan on the downlow...

Conor's rig beeped when the TBs of data had finished uploading. I transferred it into a folder called *noxxioustar* and tucked it within a couple random dozen subfolders on his desktop. I wanted him to have the information, just not be able to gain access to it yet.

Once that was complete, I delved into his security system and set up an alert that would trigger an email being sent to him with the video of my presence in his apartment.

Checking the calendar, I picked the date I could potentially die.

It was creepy, but necessary.

Anything could go wrong, *everything* could, in fact.

My loyalties were torn between the past and the future, but there was no way I could leave Conor out in the cold.

I picked up a pen, grabbed a piece of paper from the printer, and wrote:

> I know you'll be pissed at me for breaking in. I know
> you'll be doubly pissed at me for fucking with
> your security system. I know you'll be TRIPLY
> pissed at me for leaving, but no matter how
> pissed you are, I want you to know something:

<u>You've brought joy to my life, Conor.</u>
I don't think you realize that.
I wish this didn't have to be goodbye, and if I think
    that it is, it makes me want to cry.
The Japanese use 'Sayonara' to mean 'Goodbye
    forever,' or 'Goodbye, I don't know when I'll see
    you again.' It's why they don't use it often.
I don't know when it'll be, I don't even know <u>if</u> we
    will meet again, I just hope that we do.
So, sayonara, Conor.
Yours,
Star
Ps. My dad's band is always a good place to start
    looking for clues. You'll never know what you'll
    find with their name on it.

Call me crazy, but I picked up my phone and took a picture of it.

There were very few people that were worthy of a second thought from me, but I knew if I didn't take a photo of my note, it'd haunt me. I'd second guess what I wrote and would think about it to the point of distraction.

Now I could regret what I wrote, knowing that I'd definitively written it, and I could cringe every time I reread it.

I peered at his security camera, folded the note in half, then tossed it in the trash, knowing that when he saw this video, when it arrived in his email, he'd look immediately in there.

He didn't allow his housekeeper in his office, and from the dates on the couple newspapers in his trash can, I knew I was safe to put the note there. He *could* find it before the end of September, but I didn't think so.

And if he never found it, then... It wasn't meant to be.

It was harder than I'd like to let go, but it pushed me into standing once I'd collected my USB drive, and then, it hit me.

The misery.

The finality of everything.

Pressing my hand to the headrest on his desk chair, I sucked in a breath and closed my eyes—*the air scented of him.*

This was his space.

I could have given this USB drive and this note to him so easily. Could have visited and we could have shot the shit, but...

No.

I couldn't do that.

If I did that, I'd stay.

And I couldn't stay.

There was too much unfinished business to finally, *finally* bring to a conclusion.

I'd told Kat that I would be going away, and that she had to keep it a secret between us. Then I'd come here...

With the two people who owned my heart taken care of, I slipped into the shadows.

Well aware that I might never get out of them again.

HUNTER

THAT SAME DAY

"Hunter, it's Stan."

Rubbing my brow, I mumbled, "Hey."

"You sound grim."

"I feel it."

My grandfather was going to die in jail.

That was a fact.

"What's wrong?"

"Nothing. Why are you calling? I thought you were using Lodestar for your hacking now?"

Stan grunted. "We're old friends, Hunt. I can call for something other than help."

I arched a brow. "Cut the bullshit. We *are* friends, but we don't have that kind of friendship."

"Aurora..."

I straightened up. "What about her?"

"I think you should come and see for yourself."

I scowled. "I don't think Rory would appreciate that."

"I think she might."

If she did, then that meant... Fuck. That meant something was really wrong.

It killed me to even think it, but Aurora never wanted me around. Only if things were bad would she want me close.

Clenching my fists, I rumbled, "I can't just drop everything, Stan."

"I know, man. I know."

He fucking didn't.

With Grandfather in prison, I was—

Jesus.

I was the head of the fucking Camorra.

What kind of sick joke was this?

"What's going on with her?"

"Overworking, mostly."

"She does that anyway."

"She's unhappy, Hunt," Stan said softly. "You're the only fucker who can make her smile, even if she's in denial about that."

His words nourished something inside me that had refused to die out no matter what she did.

Aurora and I—we weren't second chance, best friends to lovers.

We'd *been* best friends.

We'd been close as fuck.

Now we were just nothing.

And that fucking hurt.

My tone pinged with an incoming message.

I pulled it away and read Rachel's text.

Rachel: *Fantastic news. Dead To Me says that's the last time she'll contact us.*

Somehow, that made less sense than any-fucking-thing else.

Dead To Me had asked for the most irrelevant information imaginable.

I'd heard great things about her, but after our interactions, I was disappointed.

Which was saying something when I was the one who'd die if I fucked up.

But, without her watching me through a set of crosshairs, and with Grandfather in jail now that his case was over, I could go to New York. Not for long. A week, tops.

Me: *You're sure you can trust her assurances?*

Rachel: *YES.*

Me: *Thank you for being the go-between on this, Rach.*

Rachel: *I love you, Hunter. I'll do anything to keep you safe.*

I released a breath.

Why couldn't we have fallen in love with each other?

I knew what we felt was fraternal. An incredibly strong bond, but nothing romantic.

Not like what I felt for Aurora.

Fuck, she consumed me and I hadn't even seen her in years.

Me: *Love you too, Rach.*

"Hunter?"

"I'll catch a flight tonight."

"You sure? Tomorrow's—"

"It doesn't matter." I'd read in the papers about the society wedding of the decade taking place in the Victoria Hotel tomorrow. I could easily pack for a black-tie event. "I'll be there."

SEPTEMBER

REX

The second Lisandra Sommer was placed in my arms, it *wasn't* like everything shifted. As if the universe had come together to create a perfect moment for my small family. But it was definitely up there as one of my top five of all fucking time.

Beside me, Rachel was cringing as the doctors did some whacked up shit to her body, and I was left cringing too because I knew she'd never let me live it down that, when I'd seen the baby crowning, I'd wobbled on my feet.

I'd killed men.

I'd tortured them.

My hands were dirty and they had no right to be holding this tiny precious body... and I'd fucking wobbled when I'd seen she was finally coming home to us.

Because giving birth wasn't normal. Some people could tell me it was the most normal thing because everyone was born, but not to me. It was beyond science fiction and there was no fucking one who could tell me otherwise.

When they took Sommer away and weighed her and cleaned her

up, returning the swaddled bundle back into Rachel's arms, I sank down heavily in the armchair beside her bed.

A little over eight months ago, I'd been sitting here, in this hospital, next to someone else's bedside.

A little over eight months ago, shit had felt hopeless.

I'd felt hopeless.

Lost.

But as I looked at Rachel, as I thought about what she'd gone through to get us to this point, as I pondered how fucking brave she'd been during labor, how she'd held up and done us proud by coming to the hospital when there'd been complications with the home birth—I knew I was found.

And that, because of her, and the girls she'd gifted me with, I'd never be lost again.

LODESTAR

This was it.

The day had come.

I watched as the First Lady herself read the message I'd just sent her. The two small ticks had turned blue.

> I'm a nurse at the hospice where Michael Byrne is
> dying. He gave me your number and begged me
> to message you. He wants to speak to you before
> he dies. He says he knows something about a guy
> called Cheile that Alan would be interested in
> hearing.

I could almost imagine her panic.

The First Lady was a *cheile*, after all. Part of a terrorist organization that had been working for decades to unify Ireland.

Alan, her husband, was POTUS!

Of course she'd be shitting herself at the prospect of her one-time lover and her current hubs getting together over Michael's imaginary deathbed.

It sounded like something from a spy novel, but life was funny like that.

One minute, you were reading something in a book, the next, you were on social media watching the practices of a secret organization unfolding before your eyes.

The second she clicked into my message, the worm I'd infected the SMS with went to work. It bypassed all the security on the device because I had no intention of reading her private correspondence.

It affected her GPS tracker and the call function.

From my desk in the building opposite Conor's—call me a sap—I waited.

And I waited.

Did she take my bait?

Would she?

I needed her to if I was going to draw Eamonn Keegan, AKA 'Dagda,' out into the open.

He was skilled.

For someone who'd been in prison for decades, his abilities were envious, and I couldn't run up against him if he stayed in hiding.

"Come on, bitch, *bite,*" I whispered under my breath, my knees jumping as I rested my elbows on them so that my entire being jiggled.

Michael Byrne was dead. I'd watched Conor kill him earlier this year and he'd agreed that I could take a sound bite and put it on the dark web in a place where the ECD would catch wind of it.

Eamonn Keegan knew, because of me, who had killed his sister.

Eamonn Keegan knew, because of me, that he'd been betrayed by his own side.

Now the First Lady was going to deliver him to me and I could scratch one thing off my bucket list—*butcher the motherfucker who took Mom away.*

Who ruined everything.

Who set me on this path.

Who destroyed my father.

Who shattered our world.

Who took the light out of it.

An alert pinged on my computer.

Surprised to note that the worm *had* infected her emails, I determined that if I ever saw Maverick again, I'd congratulate him.

This malware had monstrous capabilities. Especially when a quick trace revealed that it had inserted itself into the footnote of her correspondence, infecting whoever opened her message.

"Jesus Christ."

Intrigued, I saw the emails flooding out from her Mail app and watched as they received replies.

When a private jet was booked and paid for on the Davidson's family account, I realized they were keeping this on the downlow.

Then a man called Eric emailed her, and I learned that he was in charge of her security detail.

The terminology was civilian, but I reasoned he had to be with the Secret Service.

If they were talking off the books like this, did that mean he was a *cheile* too? Or was he a Sparrow?

God, as if life wasn't complicated enough.

I went with my gut and used the worm to access Eric's phone. The second it opened up to me, as simply as turning the page in a fucking book, I knew I was right.

He *was* ECD *and* at the top of the tree in the Secret Service.

Shit moved fast after that.

I tracked the jet in question after I hacked into the local airfield's control tower and watched as it flew over to New York.

Because I had nothing better to do, I spent the two hours of that flight listening to the air traffic controllers.

The jet landed with no issues.

Then, there was swift movement across the city.

She was visiting the hospice.

A sweet kind of bitter joy hit me.

My plan was working.

I saw her stay at the hospice for twenty minutes, and then I had all the confirmation I needed.

She made a call and I listened in.

"Wondered when you'd deign to pick up the fucking phone, Elizabeth. Didn't realize it would take nearly six goddamn months."

Did I recognize that voice?

I felt sure that I did.

"I have more important things to be doing than speaking with mobsters," the woman sniped.

Mobsters.

Jesus.

That low, gravelly tone—I'd heard it at the meeting Rachel, Rex, Nyx, and Priest had had with Aidan O'Donnelly Sr.

"So why did you decide to call me back?"

"You heard that Eamonn Keegan is out?"

"Old news. He's been sighted in New York though. Your husband's immigration policy really is as weak as they say it is."

A hiss escaped her at the insult. *"Michael's gone missing."*

His reply was belligerent. *"And?"*

"What do you mean, 'And?'" she snarled. *"You're supposed to protect him."*

"How the hell am I supposed to save him from cancer? If the bastard discharged himself to go and slit his wrists in private, well, he did the world a favor, didn't he?"

"You're a heartless bastard, Aidan," Elizabeth growled. *"You didn't have any men guarding him?"*

"Not my job."

"You made a deal."

His voice throbbed with anger as he intoned, *"I made a deal with Michael, sure, but if he wanted guards, then he should have gotten his cheile friends to look after him. I'm not his nanny, Elizabeth."*

"You mean you don't know where he is?"

"I didn't say that I didn't know where Michael is, now did I?

Funny how you're calling me. Someone whispered something in my ear recently about the pair of you.

"Imagine how surprised I was to find out you and Michael had a thing. Wonder what the president would have to say about that..."

There was silence down the other end of the line. "*Do you, or do you not know where Michael is?*"

"*Even funnier that this is the first time you've asked about him. His cancer's terminal,*" he droned. "*Thought his little woman would care about that.*"

"We had a falling out," Elizabeth bit off. "*He's supposed to be in a hospice, but there are no records of him—*" She hissed under her breath. "*Where is he, Aidan?*"

Well, I had my confirmation.

How the fuck was Conor's da involved with this?

Was it simply the obvious? The man believed himself to be more Irish than an Irish national and he'd never left the fucking US. Was he with the ECD too?

"*Information like that comes at a price,*" he taunted. "*I'll be at Greenwood Cemetery at three. I'll meet you at my brother's grave.*" He gave her directions on how to reach it. "*If you want answers, I'll see you there. And don't even think about bringing your guards along.*"

"*How am I supposed to get away from them?*" she snapped.

"*Not my problem. You want to know where your* lover boy *is, you know where to find me.*"

And as that call came to an end, another started from Eric to someone listed only as 'Private.'

"*Eamonn? She's heading to Greenwood Cemetery. Will be meeting at Padraig O'Donnelly's grave.*"

"*Time?*"

"*Three PM.*"

My plan was working. It was fucking working.

Eamonn Keegan was going to be in Greenwood Cemetery at three!

I had options—call this in, protect the First Lady, probably get a badge of fucking honor, rewrite my life, get on the right path.

Wait, watch how things unfolded, take my rifle to Greenwood, see if Dagda showed up, shoot him.

Options.

A future.

The First Lady would survive, Dagda would be shot for treason, and Aidan Sr. would... Well, I didn't know what the fuck would happen to him, but knowing the Five Points, he'd get out within the hour.

Did he deserve that though? After he'd let that rapist attack an innocent woman just to tangle Nyx in his web?

The obliteration of the past.

The First Lady—traitorous scum—would die, and I'd free my country from that toxic presence in the White House. I could shoot Dagda, watch him die through my scope. My mom would be avenged...

Where would Aidan Sr. fit into that? He was ECD but clearly unfriendly with the First Lady.

Would Dagda keep him safe?

If I didn't protect him, would Conor ever forgive me for that betrayal? Their relationship was fucked up, but whose wasn't with their parents?

Mind whirring, still unsure, I packed my shit together and, beginning the race to Brooklyn, well aware that today could be my last day on this godforsaken planet, I sent out a text:

Me: *It's on. Greenwood Cemetery. Three PM. I'll send you my coordinates when I get there.*

Cin: *On my way.*

OCTOBER

RACHEL

LADY GAGA - BORN THIS WAY

I grinned at my new ink, proud to finally have my brand and beyond excited to show it off to Rex. I'd wanted to do this on my own so that, A, it came as a surprise, and B, he could look after Sommer.

A girl needed a break every now and then.

"I don't know why you wanted it there," Giulia mused, staring at my chest in a manner that would have been creepy if she hadn't already seen my tits before.

Hey, we nursed together, and she was the only reason I hadn't given up on breastfeeding Sommer after I'd nearly lost my shit when she refused to latch. Nothing funky.

"Why wouldn't I want it there?"

"You know they say it's the new tramp stamp, don't you?"

"I've never been a tramp in my life, and even if I were, I think that's very sexist of you to say, Giulia."

She sniffed. "I'm not the one who goes into fancy courtrooms." She grabbed the neckline of her shirt, jerked it down. "Matching ink, baby."

I laughed at the sight of one of Indy's mandalas right between her tits, just low enough that a bra would cover it. "And here was me thinking you'd turned into a bitch."

"I didn't turn into anything." She winked at me. "I was born that way."

Indy snorted. "Since when would a fancy pants lawyer go into a courtroom with her tits out?"

Giulia mused, "You have a point. You'll just have to contain yourself, Rach."

Laughing, I shook my head at the pair of them.

Indy gave me the aftercare instructions, and once I settled my bill, I stared at the certificate and the photos on the wall of her prime-time feature that had made her famous and had put the tattoo shop on the map.

"I'm grateful you could fit me in."

"Her schedule's rammed solid," Giulia said proudly. "We even have some crazy asses flying in from France to get matching tattoos."

"Hey, they appreciate my genius," Indy mocked, but she was beaming.

I couldn't blame her.

She'd won her competition, had been featured on several shows, and now, she and Cruz were planning on moving out from above the shop and were going to build a place on the compound once Nyx and Giulia's home was complete.

I went to use the restroom, and on my way back, I greeted Amara and Quin, who was busy with another client. Amara was helping him, but every task he gave her she completed with such a look of love in her eyes that it warmed my heart.

She was so crazy that it was easy to forget that she could love so fiercely.

"I need you guys to come around sometime this week," I told them upon my return, trying not to sniffle. Sommer had made me such a sap.

"Why?" Giulia asked suspiciously.

She still didn't trust me not to retaliate for the baby shower.

"Because Rex and I decided on a date and I need to plan the ceremony."

I totally *was* working on a way to get Parker and her back, but she didn't need to know that.

Indy and I shared a bland smile—she was in on it.

When the next client came in, I left Giulia and Indy to it and headed outside.

We'd had a cold squall, but the sun was shining today.

The US was in chaos. The First Lady had been assassinated while visiting a mobster's grave at Greenwood Cemetery, and this wasn't information available to the public but I knew Aidan Sr. had died that day too.

I wasn't sure if that relieved me or not. He'd been a monster. Unconscionable. But there'd been something I liked about him. Something raw and real.

Amid the manhunt for an assassin who'd murdered the First Lady, the country had locked down over the Sparrows and deep investigations were being made into all aspects of government as President Davidson, grieving, his approval rating never higher, weeded the wheat from the chaff.

For all that America would never be the same again, my family had come together.

Wynter was at a charter school a couple towns over, Sommer had finally started to sleep at night, Rain had been a doofus and had enlisted after the First Lady's death, and as for Priest, I didn't want to think about him.

Somehow, he'd become family.

And Rex hated it because Wynter only had eyes for him. Well, him and the baby grand that had finally arrived after months of our being waitlisted.

Apparently, she was like her mom in more ways than just her smarts.

My phone buzzed.

Parker: *Are you still in town?*

Me: *I am.*

Parker: *Fair warning, Rex is looking for you.*

Me: *Why do I need the warning?*

Parker: *I've been told not to disturb either of you, lol.*

A grin creased my jaw.

Me: *Well, you have your orders for the afternoon then, don't you?*

Parker: *I'll make sure I wear earplugs.*

Me: *LMAO. Sorry not sorry.*

I snorted as I tucked my cell back in my purse.

The limpid sun warmed my bones, but what really heated up my blood?

The sight of Rex, holding our baby, sitting in the passenger seat of the SUV he loathed and that I'd ridden to Verona in after my last OB/GYN appointment.

"How did you get here?" I queried as I climbed in.

"Nyx gave me a ride."

I jibed, "You two are holding up under the strain of having to roam around West Orange in cages pretty well."

"We're modern bikers," he told me with a grin.

He was joking but it was true.

Sommer had attended more council meetings strapped to her dad's chest in a baby carrier than I could count. God only knew what she was learning, but hell, why shouldn't she?

She and her older sister would inherit all this craziness, wouldn't they?

Why shouldn't one of our daughters be the future Prez? Because Sommer was definitely *it*. No more kiddos for me.

He arched a brow at me. "You look militant."

I just smirked at him.

"Uh oh, Sommer, baby, Momma's got that dangerous glint in her eye," he teased before he continued, "Come on, show me the good stuff."

Well aware he thought I'd go for somewhere safe like my wrist, hip, or shoulder, a breathless anticipation hit me when I dragged down my nursing shirt just enough to expose the crown between my breasts. I watched his eyes widen and knew, at that moment, I'd never been sexier to him.

And trust me, the first seven weeks after birth, nothing sexy was going on. Just climbing into pants in the morning was a frickin' feat.

He reached forward and, uncaring that we were in a parking lot, that people could peer into the car, traced his fingers around the lines, careful not to touch the ink itself.

The crown was masculine in design, tipped on its side to reveal all eight points. It was black and gray shade, with the only color coming from an unknown light source, meant to represent the sun, which beamed along its spikes, and which made the icicles decorating each one gleam all the more.

"It's fucking beautiful," Rex rasped, and when I smiled at him, he reached up and traced the curve of my mouth. "Please tell me your OB/GYN signed off on—"

"Why do you think I got my ink today?" I teased. Starting up the engine, I murmured, "I think you need a very long nap, Sommer."

"I agree," Rex said, his voice almost a growl. He cupped my chin and drew me toward him. "Baby girl, it's time to go home."

TEXT CHAT

Lodestar: *Vana, I want you to know something.*

    Savannah*: About the Sparrows?*

    Lodestar: *Not just about them. About us too.*

    Savannah*: Okay, hit me with it. What have you done and who do I need to bribe?*

    Lodestar: *Like old times?*

    Savannah*: Yep. Remember when you tried to sneak off with that band who was on the starting lineup for noxxious?*

    Lodestar: *I do. It didn't go down well.*

    Savannah*: And that was with me helping you, lol.*

    Savannah*: I watched them play at Madison Square Garden last week. They went straight to the top.*

    Lodestar: *Thought Aidan Jr. would have put you on lockdown.*

    Savannah*: No. Aidan and I were there to meet with someone.*

    Lodestar*: Business?*

    Savannah*: Always.*

    Savannah*: Anyway, what's up?*

    Lodestar: *You might not hear from me for a while.*

    Savannah*: As long as last time?*

Lodestar: *Maybe longer.*

Savannah: *Shit.*

incoming call

Savannah: *Star, pick up the damn phone.*

Lodestar: *No. I don't want to talk. I need you to know that everything I'm doing, it's for a reason.*

Savannah: *This sounds like a suicide conversation.*

Lodestar: *A, what? Jesus, Vana. Can't you just let me get this down?*

Savannah: *No. Not if you're trying to give me an interactive suicide note via text.*

Lodestar: *I don't want to die.*

Savannah: *Good. That's half the battle.*

Lodestar: *That doesn't mean some people don't want me dead.*

Savannah: *Babe, some people want ME dead. Isn't that how we know we're doing it right?*

Lodestar: *That's your sparkling personality.*

Savannah: *Bitch. Why did I miss you again?*

Lodestar: *:P*

Lodestar: *You'll be receiving a package in the mail soon. There's a lot of info in it for you. You should be able to trigger hell.*

Savannah: *I don't hear from you in months but you always come back bearing gifts. You do know I'm always the last person who messages in our chats, don't you?*

Lodestar: *Sorry.*

Savannah: *No, you're not. And if I get to trigger hell, you'd better be around to see it. We always liked reigning over our personal hellscape, didn't we?*

Lodestar: *The shit our dads got up to was more like paradise than what we waded into, Vana.*

Savannah: *Crazy how they were hedonists and we dove deep into this batshit world, isn't it?*

Lodestar: *Typical second gen trying to prove themselves.*

Savannah: *Think we've proven enough?*

Lodestar: *No. I haven't.*

Savannah: *Then I haven't either. We're in this together.*

Lodestar: *I want you to be happy, Vana.*

Savannah: *I am. Aidan makes me very happy. He pisses me off too, but that's to be expected. I want you to have this, Star. I want you to be happy.*

Lodestar: *Happiness isn't for people like me.*

Savannah: *Bullshit. You can have this as well. We can keep on waging this war together, fighting from the trenches, and we won't stop until we win.*

Lodestar: *I love you.*

Savannah: *I love you too. But that's not what I needed to hear. What's going on with you?*

Savannah: *Star?*

Savannah: *Star?*

Savannah: *Goddammit, answer me.*

Savannah: *Star, you bitch, don't fucking do this.*

Savannah: *Damn you. Why do you always fucking leave?*

One week later

Savannah: *Star?*

Four weeks later

Savannah: *Please answer.*

Six weeks later

Savannah: *Stay safe. I love you.*

Eight weeks later

Savannah: *I need you.*

Lodestar: *What's wrong?*

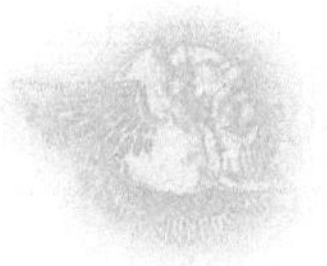

LET IT BEGIN WHERE IT ENDS...
THIRTY YEARS LATER

My hair whipped in the wind and a hoot escaped me. It set off a chain of events that had a rusty laugh coming from my Old Man.

Behind me, as if we'd organized it—the Posse was capable of many things but this wasn't one of them—a chorus of hoots worthy of a choir shot off around me.

It was an impressive feat considering the roar from the hogs' engines, but we were on our way.

At long goddamn last.

Rex's appointment at the doctor's a month ago had shuffled things up a gear. He had angina—totally under control—but it had made me question what we were waiting for.

The big road trip he'd been dreaming of since he'd hit fifty, the one he kept putting off because of business, was like a beacon for him. A dream.

Well, I was tired of that. I wanted the dream to become reality.

I knew he wanted it too, and because I wasn't as stubborn as him, I'd made it happen.

I might have retired a couple years ago, but I was still terrifying. Enough that Nyx had stopped griping about not being able to leave West Orange because his granddaughter might take her first steps without him. Maverick had finally stopped bitching about leaving his computers behind, and Link and Steel had let bygones be bygones—they'd been arguing ever since their kids had gotten together.

Sin had said he'd go only if Tiff agreed, and that had taken some of my greatest wrangling because they'd gotten into a crash a decade or so ago and she'd refused to get on the back of a bike since.

I'd twisted Cruz's arm via Indy, because he didn't like leaving the tristate area now that his youngest was in graduate school in the city.

Storm had been the easiest to convince, mostly because my SIL and he loved long road trips. Last year, they'd ridden the Cabot Trail up in Canada but it was easier for them because their kid was now Prez of the Coshocton chapter. Keira'd argue that that made nothing easier, but I disagreed.

Digger and MaryCat had ridden up too—we'd gotten close when her son, Gray, and Sommer had been diagnosed on the spectrum. It was good to see her cut loose behind Digger.

Sweet Lips was shouting something back at his Old Lady that had her head tipping back in a laugh that made me smile.

Hell, even Hawk, Quin, and Amara were here, which had been another rough argument too, seeing as none of them liked leaving their animal sanctuary behind. Hawk and North were hollering something at each other before I turned back to the road ahead.

I'd begged, stolen, and borrowed to make this ride happen.

We were going through the upper states of the US first, visiting the Montana chapter before we headed down to Route 66—the classic route—and then, when we made it down to Vegas, we were going to stay there for a month so I could catch up with Hunter and his family there before we returned home the long way—through Texas and along the East Coast back to the city.

All in all, it'd take twelve months minimum because I'd sketched out the itinerary to within an inch of its life so that, at one point or another, Rex would get to visit each state in the continental US.

And hell, maybe next year, I'd treat him to a trip to Alaska and Hawaii, but that could be for us.

This was for family.

I turned my head to stare back at the motorcade and I grinned as I wondered what Bear and Rene would think—I knew she'd be thrilled at the bright pink leather Posse cuts the Old Ladies wore, while I knew he'd be happy Rex was fulfilling a dream. Both of them, I knew, would be happier still that all their kids were together.

Sisters who'd bled for us; brothers who'd killed for us.

We were wrinkled and some of us were sick, we had arthritis that'd make this trip hard on our bones, and some of us probably rattled with Viagra—Link—but fuck, we were still kicking.

Still riding.

Still dark and dirty, and we would be until the day we died.

I had no means of knowing when that'd be, but until that day when Rex and I and the rest of our generation toddled off this mortal coil, when we passed that baton on to our kids for the final time, we were going to live it up the only way Satan's Sinners knew how—*on the back of a Harley.*

LODESTAR'S STORY IS COMING... IN
FILTHY FECK!

www.books2read.com/FilthyFeck

AUTHOR NOTE

I know.

Trust me, I know.

And breathe.

And then breathe some more.

Thank you for trusting me, thank you for reaching this point, thank you for falling for this band of brothers who are Sinners 'til they die.

I think we all know where I'm going with this series...

Before I go, I wanted to let you know a couple things. My stats, re. America not being safe for women, come from RAINN. I watched Grease every day, twice some days, for a WHOLE summer so you know where I got that inspo from lol, and these words:

But fuck, we were still kicking.

Still riding.

Still dark and dirty, and we would be until the day we died.

They made me cry every single goddamn time I read them.

And breathe some more.

Okay, so if you need more from the Sinners, lovelies, be sure to check out MaryCat & Digger's story - **FILTHY SINNER** - www.books2read.com/FilthySinnerSerenaAkeroyd

BUT before then, don't forget FILTHY KING is dropping in JUNE!!

And it's important because you **WILL** meet Rachel again in that book and you'll also meet **RORY & HUNTER** in their book in August!

You've met some people along the journey that is Rex and Rachel's story, and yes, they do have books, be they published or on their way.

Published stories outside of the Sinners' series include:

Luciu & Jen - **THE DON** - www.books2read.com/ValentiniOne

Declan & Aela - **FILTHY DARK** - www.books2read.com/FilthyDark

Savannah & Aidan Jr. - **FILTHY HOT** - www.books2read.com/FilthyHot

To-be-published stories:

Conor & Lodestar - **FILTHY FECK** - www.books2read.com/FilthyFeck

Hunter & Rory - **The Revelation Duet (Title TBA)** - www.books2read.com/ValentiniThree

Savannah & Aidan Jr. - **FILTHY KING** - www.books2read.com/FilthyKing

AND!!

You met The Disciples!!

I'm so pleased to announce that I'll be co-authoring a project with

Cassandra Robbins!! A character from her Disciples will be falling for a Fecker!!

You can preorder here: www.books2read.com/FilthyDisciple

:O

I hope you're as excited about that as I am!

For all the lowdown, feel free to join my newsletter: www.serenaakeroyd.com/newsletter

But more importantly, be sure to join my Diva reader group. There'll be massive giveaways going on during release week AND it's where I drop news and updates that aren't really revealed elsewhere! www.facebook.com/groups/SerenaAkeroydsDivas There'll also be a bonus scene dropping in my groups when Rachel hits 500 reviews!! <3

Much love to you all, and hope you're excited for the next book in the universe: **FILTHY KING!**

Serena

xoxo

PS. Flick over a page for the reading order for the universe. <3

THE CROSSOVER READING ORDER WITH THE SINNERS & VALENTINIS

FILTHY
FILTHY SINNER
NYX
LINK
FILTHY RICH
SIN
STEEL
FILTHY DARK
CRUZ
MAVERICK
FILTHY SEX
HAWK
FILTHY HOT
STORM
THE DON
THE LADY
FILTHY SECRET
REX
RACHEL

<u>FILTHY KING</u>
<u>FILTHY DISCIPLE</u>
<u>THE CONSIGLIERE</u>
<u>THE ORACLE</u>
<u>LODESTAR</u>
<u>SILENCED</u>
<u>END GAME</u>
<u>FILTHY RICHER</u>

FREE BOOK!

Don't forget to grab your free e-Book!
Secrets & Lies is now free!

Meg's love life was missing a spark until she discovered her need to be dominated. When her fiancé shared the same kink, she thought all her birthdays had come at once, and then she came to learn their relationship was one big fat lie.

Gabe has loved Meg for years, watching her from afar, and always wishing he'd been the one to date her first and not his brother. When he has the chance to have Meg in his bed—even better, tied to it—it's an opportunity he can't refuse.

With disastrous consequences.

Can Gabe make Meg realize she's the one woman he's always wanted? But once secrets and lies have wormed their way into a relationship, is it impossible to establish the firm base of trust needed between lovers, and more importantly, between sub and Sir…?

This story features orgasm control in a BDSM setting.
Secrets & Lies is now free!

CONNECT WITH SERENA

For the latest updates, be sure to check out my website!
But if you'd like to hang out with me and get to know me better, then
I'd love to see you in my Diva reader's group where you can find out
all the gossip on new releases as and when they happen. You can join
here: www.facebook.com/groups/SerenaAkeroydsDivas. Or you can
always PM or email me. I love to hear from you guys:
serenaakeroyd@gmail.com.

ABOUT THE AUTHOR

I'm a romance novelaholic and I won't touch a book unless I know there's a happy ending. This addiction is what made me craft stories that suit my voracious need for raunchy romance. I love twists and unexpected turns, and my novels all contain sexy guys, dark humor, and hot AF love scenes.

I write MF, menage, and reverse harem (also known as why choose romance,) in both contemporary and paranormal. Some of my stories are darker than others, but I can promise you one thing, you will always get the happy ending your heart needs!